The Wellspring

Book One of the Crystal Key Trilogy

Gregory E. Shemeld

MY MUSE

Sing my muse,
Of birth and life
Of music unsung
Of battles yet to be won
Of death and time's decay

Sing my muse
Brightly into this wordless void
To me, sing.

CONTENTS

ONE: TOM

The start of another day that's going to suck the life right out of me.

Tom set off for work in the golden time of an August morning. The air was hot, heavy and already sticky. The grass that lined the sidewalk was baked and brown, and his hard-soled dress shoes struck the concrete with crisp, steady clicks that echoed in the hushed spaces between the apartment buildings. The humid breeze caught the bottom of his red power tie and tugged it sideways until he caught it with one hand and brushed it back down against his white dress shirt. His other arm, cocked at the elbow, cradled his grey suit jacket while his hand jangled the keys and coins in the pocket of his grey dress slacks. The sound was an absent-minded accompaniment to the brief but utterly routine trip to his car to begin another utterly routine day stuck in the cubicle at the plain box office building where he worked.

But this day, there was a word that was rattling around his head like a fly that he could not swat away. Abstinence. Like a pop song that he could not stop humming. Abstinence. It was such an odd word to be stuck repeating to himself over and over. Was it an unsubtle comment from his subconscious about his ongoing lack of sex? There had certainly been a long drought in that department, but the word implied it was part a voluntary plan of clean living, an honest attempt at living a noble, virtuous life. It certainly was not. He had just reached the point as an overweight, fifty year old single with male pattern baldness (and with his remaining, greying hair an unruly, occasional vertical mop). The opposite sex looked at him as an "ew", rather than as a "maybe." At least, that was how it seemed to him in his enforced (self-imposed?) loneliness.

Abstinence. And, he thought soberly, even if he found a woman to take mercy on him, he was no longer sure if the equipment down there would even work. Masturbation was also a concept that was fading into a barely remembered past. But again, that was not voluntary either. Life had simply decided for him that abstinence was his present and future. He was a sexless worker drone. That was how it was, and how it was going to be.

He reached his car, already warming in the early morning summer sun, and stopped jangling the coins in his pocket long enough to push the button in the fob to unlock the doors. After lobbing his briefcase into the back seat, he settled into the driver's seat, latched the belt, fired the motor, and backed the car out of his space and headed out of the lot. All of this was on mental autopilot, except for that damn word. Abstinence.

As he wound his way through his familiar morning route out of his densely packed residential neighborhood, with his car joining more and more other cars as he approached the city's downtown, he began to feel an uncomfortable tightness in his chest. Perspiration began beading on his forehead, despite the cooling air flowing from the air ducts. Abstinence. The jangly, laugh-happy morning show playing overly loudly from the car radio could not even drown it out.

It was not until he was well into his commute, when his car joined the thousands of others on the main concrete arteries of the city heading into downtown that his awareness of the new and unfamiliar pressure on his chest finally crowded out the word looping in his mind. The tightness increased on his chest to the point where his breathing began to pick up as he tried to gather himself. But he could not catch his breath, even as he kept sucking air in and out of his lungs attempting to catch up with his need for air. The sensation grew worse.

He grew lightheaded, and he began to worry about his ability to drive. His car was still on the expressway, so he pulled it over to the side and put it in park with the emergency blinkers on. Thinking it was an asthma attack, he reached into the glove box and pulled out his inhaler. After taking a couple of puffs, he sat in the seat and concentrated on pulling air in and out of his lungs despite the tightness in his chest. Abstinence. The word was still there, rattling around, but it had retreated to the back of his consciousness. The stress of the moment was becoming too great.

With cars whizzing by in a blurred stream to his left, the drivers unaware and untroubled by his crisis, Tom knew he needed help, right away. He realized that his cell phone was in the briefcase in the back seat. He had to get to it. Tom unbuckled the seat belt and twisted around in the seat to reach between the front seats. Reaching around with his left arm, he extended his fingers toward the handle.

Then, suddenly, there was pain, a sudden, sharp jolt in his chest that made him withdraw his arm. His breathing was now raspy and more desperate. He clutched at his chest, panicking, unable to do anything about the frightening sensations.

Tom wondered whether he should take it out of park and keep driving down the side of the highway until he reached an off-ramp of the expressway. He shook his head at the thought. Between his raspy breathing, lightheadedness, and gradually increasing panic, he did not trust himself to drive any farther. For better or worse, he was stuck where he was.

What else could he do? Should he get out and try to wave someone down? He turned and looked out the side window. Other cars were still whizzing by, without a trace of slowing near the immobilized vehicle in the right margin. With each vehicle that went by him in the adjacent lane, his car rocked slightly on its tires from the rush of compressed air. It looked dangerous to even open the door, much less get out.

Even so, Tom knew he had to do something. He put his hand on the door handle and looked into the side mirror, waiting for enough of a gap between the oncoming vehicles to open his door. After a few seconds, he saw his chance. With one big intake of breath, he quickly pushed the door open, and swung his legs out onto the pavement.

And as he lifted his shoes over the doorsill, one heel caught as he slid sideways out of the seat. He tumbled out of the door, landing on his hands and knees on the asphalt and the white lane line underneath his chest. He heard a short tire squeak to his left as a driver jumped on the brakes to avoid him.

He turned his head to see a small hatchback with faded, sunburnt grey paint barreling towards him. Underneath the glare of the windshield in the morning sun, he could see a woman with a rounded hairdo and wide rimmed glasses, and a very surprised expression on her face, working the steering wheel to avoid him.

Tom raised his left hand towards her. "Stop, please stop," he gasped between his raspy breaths.

But instead of coming to a complete stop, she maneuvered her car and crowded into the next lane to swing around him. Once her car was clear of his open car door, he heard her motor rev as she punched the accelerator to return to highway speed and go on her way.

By now, the cars behind had seen the commotion and slowed, bunching up as they repeated the detour of the car in front of them. By the time he struggled to his feet, rising up on one leg and then the other, four or five cars had already completed their avoidance of him as they bypassed him and went on to the rest of their day and the rest of their lives, otherwise undisturbed.

By then, the pain and the pressure in his chest was becoming unbearable. His breathing had become hurried gasps for air, and he pressed his right hand over his pounding heart as if that would somehow calm the unendurable stress that was building inside of him. His face was twisted into an expression of fear and panic.

Tom closed his door and managed to stagger a few steps next to his car until he reached the clear pavement behind the rear of the car. He raised his left hand and waved toward the oncoming drivers in the closest lane to stop. But now that his body and his door were no longer hazards in the driving lane, they whizzed by, one after the other. One driver even gave him an irritated short toot of the horn for being too close to traffic as his car rushed past.

Finally, his knees buckled and he went down, gasping for air. His hands caught his fall, but his body continued downward until he rolled over and laid on his back on the warming asphalt. The bright summer sun in the eastern sky overhead blinded him until he could shield his eyes from it with one hand. But being flat on his back seemed to help, a little. "If I could just lay here for a few minutes," he thought, "I'll pull myself together."

But even as he thought that, Tom could feel his consciousness slipping away. His awareness of the cars moving past him lost their precision, blurring together into a formless mass of motion. His mind barely registered the police cruiser that was slowly moving towards him in the side lane with its emergency lights flashing.

Tom knew that he was about to pass out. Grimly, he thought to himself, "Well, I guess today did suck the life right out of me." His last conscious thought in this world was, "It was a pretty nice day, though."

TWO: ABBY

There was an empty, cold darkness, vast and silent. Tom existed as a formless presence in the void, incapable of thought or action. Frozen in time, he felt nothing, no up or down, no fear or joy, no sense of motion or stasis.

Yet, instead of dispersing into the nothingness and vanishing forever into the totality of the universe, Tom's spirit held together, his soul still carrying his memories and thoughts and his sense of self. In a dimension without time, light or form, he still existed as the sum of all that he had been, recognizable and unique.

Then, from nowhere and everywhere at once, there was an intense flash of white light. Reality and time and all of Tom's senses returned all at once. His eyes were closed, and his mind was still rousing itself slowly from whatever journey his soul had made.

There was a huge bang, the sound of thick slabs of wood being shattered against hard stone, the sound of rushing water, and the rush of cold, thin air against exposed human skin. And in the background, a woman cried out in pain and fear, "Leanna!"

For an instant, Tom thought that none of this had anything to do with him. He opened his eyes, just in time to see himself falling into the frothing, blue-grey waters of a churning river.

The icy cold water smacked against his body and swallowed him, shocking his body with a ferocious, instant chill. Instinctively, he reacted by using his arms and legs to fight against the current and his descent toward the bottom, trying to pull himself toward the surface. He felt the loose shoes that had been on his feet fall away, but the movement of his arms and legs as he tried to swim were hampered by a loose, woolen robe that clung to his body. The bone-chilling water was quickly draining the heat from him, and he had difficulty fighting the current, tumbling as the water rushed downstream and carried Tom with it.

But spurred on by an instinct for self-preservation and desperate to catch a breath, Tom fought against all that. He stroked as much as his numb limbs could muster, eventually righting himself and struggling toward the grey light of the surface.

Just before his lungs were about to burst,

he managed to get his head above the water enough to clear his nose and mouth. He held his head back and gasped for air as he bobbed in the swirling current.

He was surrounded at the surface by broken timbers and debris. He grabbed a flat panel that floated next to him, both to get his head further out of the water, and to steady himself in the current.

For the first time, Tom looked around. He was in the center of a churning river, sliding past a wall of trees on either bank. Although the river was not too wide, in the desperation of that moment, neither riverbank appeared to be easy to reach. He began to kick his numbed legs to generate forward motion, but the robe and the icy water held him back.

To his side, he heard the sound of water tumbling into a pool. He turned and faced the direction that the water was flowing. To his horror, the river fell away a short distance ahead into a waterfall, with spray and mist rising in the air from below.

Panicking, he let go of the wood and struggled with his arms and legs to swim to the nearest side. But the river was moving too quickly, and there was no obstacle in the river to latch onto to stop him from going downstream. He could see ahead of him in the water that the edge of the riverbed approached. Helpless, he and the debris around him were carried out into the air at the edge of the falls, tumbling as he fell.

Tom looked down in that instant. To his

horror, he was headed toward a group of rocks poking up from the surface of the water at the base of the falls. He cried out in terror, a strange, thin high-pitched shout that echoed in the basin. He held out his hands as if they would somehow stop his fall.

But instead of a hard impact on the rocks, there was an explosion of white light and heat in the air beneath him that temporarily blinded him. As his body continued downward, he seemed to fall into a huge, heated cushion of air that slowed his descent and deflected him off to the side. After a few more half-seconds of sideways motion in and through the sudden, unnatural warmth, his body fell back into the icy water, shocking his senses again.

But instead of a flowing river, he was now in a calm pool at the base of the falls. It was still extremely cold, and it was all he could do to keep swimming. Yet, he was able to finally right himself as his bare feet contacted the soft, yielding mud of the riverbed. With the additional support beneath him, he managed to propel himself slowly to the shore. He staggered out of the water, dragging himself through the wet sand at the riverbank until he reached more solid ground a short distance in.

Although all of this had only taken place over a few minutes, Tom was completely exhausted and gasping for air. Shivering in the cold thin air, he collapsed and rolled onto his back. Thin tendrils of long, soaked hair covered his face, until without thinking he reached up with one hand and pulled them off to the side of his head.

He was still focused on his breathing, gasping and spitting out water and pulling in short, deep breaths to calm his beating heart. Unlike his episode in the car, the intense pain and pressure in his chest was gone. He had a fast, but otherwise normal heartbeat that reflected his exertions to save himself, but not a heart attack.

Soon, his breathing had steadied enough and his heartbeat had slowed to the point that he was finally able to focus on his surroundings. Tom opened his eyes.

Above him, there was a low, grey sky of dense clouds, with only the light of the day showing the sun was present. The clouds seemed unnaturally close, and he could see the tendrils of mist on the undersides of the clouds gliding only a relatively short distance above his eyes. Each breath in the damp, heavy chill air produced a puff of mist from his lips.

The oppressive chill and the cold water soaked into his clothes seemed to catch up to him all at once. His body shook with one intense shiver and convulsion after another before settling into a lesser, but still continuous tremor. He wrapped his arms over his chest, trying to hold in whatever warmth his body could muster.

For the first time, his mind registered the differences between how Tom had left for work that morning, and what was happening at that moment. He was no longer wearing his standard issue grey business suit. The robe that hampered his movement in the water was a body length, grey woolen cloak. There was no sign of his shirt, pants, belt, socks, and tie. There was no watch on his left wrist. Just one continuous piece of loose, itchy wool, tied with a cord at his waist.

The arms that now cradled his chest seemed much lighter and thinner than normal, with much less muscle mass than the "guns" that he worked on at the gym to preserve his aging and fading masculinity. His shoulders and chest were much thinner. And when he pressed his arms over his heart, something else was different there as well. He was not sure quite what. His entire body had much less weight, as if he was barely making an impression on the sand beneath him.

But those thoughts were pushed to the side as he heard a rustling in the nearby bushes. He turned his head in that direction, to see two figures pushing their way out of the underbrush towards him. They were tall and thin, wearing outer hooded blue-grey cloaks and inner clothes tightened with a leather belt. Their faces were long and boney, with high cheeks and thin lips held together in an expression of earnest seriousness. Shorts swords in leather sheaths hung off the belts, and each had a quiver of arrows strapped to their backs and a long, thin wooden bow slung over one shoulder. They wore tight brown leather boots, covered in flecks of mud. Both of them had the silhouette and the stride of women.

Their piercing blue eyes were locked on

him, taking his measure as they strode into the open and approached him. Realizing that he was alive and conscious, one asked, "Are you alright?" The way she spoke the word "alright" caught in his ears, as he detected a foreign accent.

Tom considered her question. For all the intensity of the past few minutes, it struck him that he was not feeling any intense pain, just a general soreness and exhaustion from the experience and the intense chill of his surroundings. He thought there were no broken bones or sprained joints, at least. Perhaps the pervasive cold was numbing his sensation of any injuries. But he had the sense that he had escaped any serious damage despite the trauma of the experience.

He looked up at her and shook his head. "No, I don't think so," he said. Even as the words left his mouth and echoed in the air around them, his own voice startled him. It was a high, thin voice, like it belonged to a child or a woman. It was definitely not the manly baritone that he was used to. He caught himself before going on to avoid hearing his voice again.

The hooded women reached him. The woman that had spoken to him dropped to a knee to look him over, her expression serious and genuinely concerned. "You don't appear too worse for wear," she said, again betraying an accent that to him seemed vaguely British. Definitely foreign. She continued, "You are white as a sheet, though. You must be freezing."

Almost as if his body agreed with her, an intense body-length shiver passed through him. Not wanting to speak again if he could help it, he nodded his agreement.

She stood again and began removing the bow on her shoulder and the quiver on her back. When she began unbuckling her outer coat, she lowered the hood over her head.

Tom was shocked to see two pointed ears on either side of her head, like she was something out of a science fiction movie or renaissance cosplay, with small white jeweled earrings in each lobe. Her face was taught and serious, with thin, brown arched eyebrows and high cheekbones. Her hair, a mix of brown and light brown, was obviously much longer but at the moment was gathered tightly around the sides of her head and twisted into a bun behind her head. As she breathed, short bursts of mist exited through her thin lips into the chill air.

As she removed the outer grey cloak, he saw a tight tan leather tunic with a loose white tunic beneath. Her pants were the same tan leather, held in place by an ornately decorated belt and silver buckle. Her belt held many loops with items wedged within, and little pouches, like some comic book hero's utility belt.

If he was not so confused and cold and shivering in the soft sand at the edge of a riverbank, he might have laughed at the two refugees from a renaissance fair. They looked like two full-blown nerds. But they seemed earnest and genuinely concerned for him, and after the morning he had just had, he was not in joking mood. At that moment, Tom's physical distress was all too real.

After she had taken off the cloak, she reached down and offered him a hand to help him stand. He nodded and raised his right arm to take it. As he did, the sleeve of his robe pulled back, revealing a small hand with thin fingers, a thin wrist and narrow hairless forearm. They looked like they belonged to someone else, but his mind was controlling their movements. The sight of his own right arm and hand shocked Tom, but he went ahead and grabbed the woman's hand. She began to pull him up.

His robe, still soaked, clung and weighed him down as she lifted him to a standing position. As Tom stood shivering in the thin air, the woman wrapped her cloak around him and drew the hood over his head.

To his surprise, even standing straight up, he was still several inches shorter than either woman. Although he had seen tall women before, to have two of them now right next to him was another small little jarring off-pitch note in what he was experiencing. Even so, he pulled the cloak tightly around him, grateful for the newfound dry warmth it provided. He managed to croak quietly, "Thank you."

The woman asked, "What is your name, my dear?"

"Tom," he answered. He cleared his throat. Something was still wrong with his voice. Too high and small, it sounded like a squeak against the background of the waterfall a short distance away from them.

The woman furrowed her brow, confused. She began to mouth a question, when she was cut off by a male voice, hidden behind the screen of underbrush, who called out to her, "Raenah, cum nobis! Illic 'a carro illo Confracta navis in vertice lapsos. Et humanum corpus mulieris!"

Tom had absolutely no idea what he had just said. These people were definitely foreign.

She turned her head and shouted back, "Minuto adero! Nos invenit puellam ibi vivit."

Looking back down at Tom, she said, "We found the wreckage of a wagon a short distance from the top of the falls, and a human woman, apparently deceased. Were the two of you together?"

He had no idea what she was talking about. He shook his head, and spoke in his new, unfamiliar voice, "No, I was by myself. I was driving to work this morning, but I think I had a heart attack. I got out of my car and passed out. But the next thing I know, I was in this river, heading over the falls. I managed to wade onto the shore, but I have no idea of how I got here. This all seems very strange to me."

She frowned and answered, "Are you unharmed, then?" She seemed to have ignored intentionally the part about the heart attack.

Tom did a mental evaluation of his pain level. There was some minor, vague pains, probably a few bruises and some small cuts.

He was still quite cold, and his body shook with involuntary shivers. The hooded overcoat was helping, despite the soaked robe underneath. Drips of chilled water fell onto his bare feet as he stood between the two women. "No," he said, his voice quivering, "not hurt. Just cold as hell."

She nodded. "Then, we must get you somewhere sheltered. There is a vacant hunting cabin near hear that we can use." She reached her arm around his shoulders to guide him away from the river. "My name is Reanah, by the way. In case you do not speak the Old Tongue."

He did not understand what she meant by that, but the idea of getting some place warmer, and indoors with something wrapped around his numb feet, appealed to him at that moment.

Tom paused a moment before venturing, "Reanah, you and your friend seem very strange to me, too, to be honest. The ears, the clothes and all. Where are you guys from?"

Both Reanah and the other woman snapped their heads around. Reanah answered, a little curtly, "Why, this is our homeland, little one. You, human, are the stranger here."

Tom looked up, wondering if he had offended her. He certainly did not mean to do so. He decided to wait on any further questions, at least for the moment. Even though he had many, many questions. But all he wanted to do at that moment was to get out of the chill air. Instead, he said, "O.K. Lead the way."

Reanah nodded and turned and began to walk away from the river. Tom fell in line between the two women. They reached the edge of the river and slid between the outer branches of two prickly bushes, picking up a dirt deer track that wound through the thick pine and ash trees.

Tom, barefoot, focused his eyes on the trail before him as he walked gingerly forward, trying to avoid pine cones, loose debris, tree branches and any other sharp edges. The high tree canopy overhead hid the dim sunlight, making the air seem even more cool and damp. Tom thought to himself that he could not remember such a quick change in the weather, from the hot, humid, sunny August morning to this.

Only a short distance in, they approached an open clearing. A tidy wooden cabin stood in the center, illuminated by the sunlight passing through a gap in the overhead tree canopy. It looked like something out of a Swiss holiday postcard, with ornate window shudders, a short porch with rough carved, weatherworn trim, and a mortared fieldstone chimney. It was surrounded by an uncut patch of green, dewy grass and yellow and blue wildflowers.

Four horses with pommeled leather saddles, with packs of gear still tied behind, stood idly unattended, eating the grass. As Tom walked past, they looked up briefly with big brown eyes and swiveling their ears in his direction, before returning to their grazing. Small birds chirped untroubled in the trees.

The cabin seemed completely isolated from civilization. Tom was surprised that there were no four wheel drive vehicles there, or even twin tire tracks worn into the grass leading to it. He did not notice any sort of electrical or other line to the cabin, no satellite dish facing the heavens. He supposed that the people who found him were on some sort of camping excursion, making do without any modern conveniences. The whole scene had a very quiet, way-out-in-the-woods feel.

But it made no sense to Tom. As far as he knew, almost no time had passed from lying down behind his car on the downtown highway, from when he was plunged into the river. Surely, Tom thought, he couldn't be very far from where he had left his car.

Or could he? Was he out much longer than he thought? How far away was he, really, from home? The where and when of that moment seemed far removed from where he had come from. Tom wondered for the first time how long it would take to get back to his apartment. He wanted nothing more than to get back there and get out of his wet clothes and into a warm cup of cappuccino, even if he had to call in sick to do it. He had a few personal days coming to him. His boss would understand. Today, that would come in handy.

Despite the seeming isolation of the cabin's location, he was hoping either it or one of these people would have a phone he could use. But then a quick, light breeze sent another sudden shiver through his body, reminding him as to how far up he was in the mountains. Grimly, he realized there was probably no good cell service here. He wrapped the cloak even tighter around his body, preoccupied with his physical needs of the moment. Just get to someplace warm and dry, he thought. The rest could wait.

He followed Reanah up the steps to the cabin, his bare, numb feet slapping quietly against the planks of the porch compared to the sharp clatter of the boots of the two women accompanying him. Looking around at both of them, he was again struck by how much taller they were than him.

As they approached the door, in the distance behind them the same male voice echoed in the clearing, calling out to them, "Reanah legatum, ubi es? Veni cum qua potes fide restituis?"

Irritated, Reanah turned to the other woman and said, "Tell him I will come as soon as I can, and that I found one survivor. Secure the accident scene and I'll be along shortly."

The other woman replied, "That was no accident, Reanah. Surely, that human woman who drowned was chased into the river by robbers. But she could not ford the stream there, and her cart was shredded on the rocks. She would not have risked that of her own accord."

Tom took in the conversation, shivering in place but otherwise feeling detached from whatever it was they were talking about. Even so, Reanah gave the woman a look which was basically a non-verbal "shut the hell up."

The woman's face turned red. She darted a quick look of pity at Tom before nodding at Reanah and turning away. Her boots clattered down the steps as she headed out of the clearing in a different direction from the group's route in.

Reanah sighed and gave Tom a quick smile of encouragement. "Just a moment. This is a private cabin and the door is more than likely locked. But I carry a master key for situations such as this." Tom was surprised. He had just assumed that the group was staying there. Was their cabin somewhere else, or were they really just roughing it, camping out in the open? He supposed he'd find that out later. Just like everything else he'd wanted to know.

Reanah turned her attention to the solid-looking, weathered hardwood door that barred their entry. There was an old style brass doorknob above a keyhole in an old, outdated lock face. It seemed flimsy to Tom, instead of a generic hardware store deadbolt. Again, though, it was not Tom's problem.

Reanah reached into a small pouch that dangled off a strap hung on the left side of her utility belt, and pulled out a very ancient looking iron key flecked with bits of rust. She inserted it into the lock, and tried turning it. At first, it would not give, her key not being as much of a master key as she had represented. But after straining on it enough that her hand began to quiver with the effort, it finally gave way with a grating, solid clank. Reanah exhaled with relief, turned the doorknob and swung the door open.

The cabin's interior was dark, still and dusty as the two walked into the room. The layout appeared to be one large, relatively open space. The only light that illuminated the interior came through the opened doorway, other than some small thin shafts of light that managed to penetrate the closed window shudders on each side.

But there was enough visibility for Reanah to pick out a dresser off to the side. She opened each of the drawers, quickly scanning the interior of each but quickly closed them again. Finally, after going through each one, she sighed in frustration. "Nothing," she said. "No clothes. I'll have to check my pack to see if I have some you can borrow, even if they'll be a little large. Better than what you've got on, that's for certain. But first, I'll go around the house and open the shutters. Be back in a few minutes. In the meantime, take off those wet clothes and see if there is some kind of blanket in here to cover yourself until I return."

Tom nodded as Reanah strode back out the door. He breathed a sigh of relief, grateful to rid himself of the clothes that still were clinging to him and sucking the warmth from his body. He unwrapped the outer cloak Reanah had given him and tossed it over the back of a nearby chair.

As Tom undressed, Reanah made her way around the outside of the cabin, opening each of the shudders over the windows.

More and more light began to enter the room as Tom worked. For the first time, he looked down at the still wet clothes covering his body, the same ones that were apparently on him when he fell into the river. There was no collared shirt, or tie, or grey dress pants and leather belt. Instead, there was a very simple dress-like woolen robe with an added hand-sewn floral design on the top, extending below his knees. The material was thicker than he would have expected for something that looked like a dress, more handmade than something bought at a chain department store.

But why he had it on in the first place was a complete mystery to him. He would have never bought, much less voluntarily put on, anything like it. He had no memory of how he had come to wear it.

There was no zipper or row of buttons down the front or back. He realized that to get it off, he would have to pull it up and over his head. He gathered the material on each side in his hands and worked it up the length of his body and across his face until it came loose over his head. Finally, he pulled his arms free and wriggled out from beneath it. The dress dropped into a pile at his feet.

As it came free, a big mop of long, wet light brown hair was pulled up and then fell forward in front of his face. Which was strange, he realized, because he had just been to the barber the weekend before. Also, he had never let his hair get that long in the first place. In his entire life, did he ever have hair that

24

long?

Tom used his hands to gather the hair and pull it back behind him, until the cold, wet tips brushed the back of his shoulders below his neck. Strange, he thought.

He froze for a moment. The small facts that had been accumulating around him—his high, thin voice, his unusually long hair, his small stature, the different clothes—were beginning to add up to a greater whole. Tension and dread were coursing through him as he slowly looked down toward his naked body.

Tom did not see the normal sight looking downward at himself—a muscular male chest covered in a mat of dark and greying hair, and a protruding stomach that reflected a soft, middle-aged dad bod and hid everything below the waist from view.

Instead, he saw hair-free, youthful skin and a view from above of two, not large but definitely female breasts with protruding nipples. And instead of a fat belly that obscured the view of his lower body, his stomach was flat though undefined, and his waist was much narrower than he had seen for decades. Now there was a straight view down to his hips, which widened out to either side before curving back to the thin, spindly legs and small, delicate feet beneath.

More distressing, though, was the lack of any sign of a penis or testicles, just a flat front between his hips and the hint of a light mat of pubic hair that extended downward between his legs and below his sight. He even leaned his head forward a little to make sure. Nope. Nothing a man would expect to see there.

An involuntary, shocked gasp was all that Tom could manage. With his new and unfamiliar vocal cords, it came out as a girlish squeal, "Eep!" Stunned, he could feel his face and the tips of his ears flushing as he staggered toward a small oval mirror mounted on the wall over the dresser. He had to look.

Peering into the aging, distorted glass, the reflection of the face of a scared, wide-eyed, mid-teens girl with a long mop of unruly hair was staring back at him.

This time, the involuntary reaction from his lungs was more violent, a sudden, uncontrolled burst of air that engaged his vocal cords, releasing a much louder yelp, almost a scream that echoed around the interior of the cabin. In shock, he backed away from the mirror, almost falling over as his feet stumbled onto the dress on the floor.

Hurried boot steps sounded on the porch outside the door. Reanah called to Tom as she strode through the open doorway, "What? What's the matter?"

He involuntarily crossed his arms in front of him, hiding the soft, yielding flesh of his breasts underneath. Tom turned and faced her, managing to finally form words in between panicked breaths. He shook his head and gasped hurriedly, "Nothing. Nothing at all."

Reanah frowned at Tom's obvious distress, thinking that he was just another overly shy girl.

"Good," she said as she tossed a bundle of dry clothes toward his head. "Get dressed."

Tom tried to grab the fabric in his hands without removing his arms from his chest. He manage to grab one corner of a pant leg. The other clothes fell to the floor.

Reanah waved her hand at him dismissively. "Do not be embarrassed. It is just the two of us. I ordered the others to wait at the horses. Put those on and we will be on our way."

But his head began throbbing and he could feel himself growing lightheaded. "If it's all the same with you," he said. "I'd like to sit for a few minutes to collect myself." Without waiting for her permission, he slid over to the edge of the nearby bed before he could faint, and buried his face in the ball of clothes in his hand.

As he forced himself to take steady, calming breaths, Tom closed his eyes and tried to make sense of the craziness of the situation. But nothing came to him. The physical sensations that he felt in this new world were too immediate and real to be a dream. He had experienced the swirling water and pain and cold like nothing in any nightmare he had ever had, as real as anything in his previous, boring suburban life. And now, sitting in a remote cabin in the high mountains, wherever the hell it was, he had someone who appeared to be an elf looking at him. His mind swirled and swirled without stumbling on any reasonable explanation. Tears began to swell in his eyes.

Seeing his distress, Reanah softened her tone. "Here, let me look at you," she said as she sat on the bed next to him. "I must say, for all that you've been through, you are remarkably uninjured." She slowly pulled the clothes from his hands. "If you are not in any intense physical pain or discomfort, please dress so we can get to headquarters. Someone can assess you there."

He nodded but kept his eyes shut as she coaxed him back to a standing position. One limb at a time, she helped him put on trousers, then raised his arms and slipped a course-fabric tunic over his head. Finally, when he was again completely covered, he returned his arms to his sides and opened his eyes.

On him, Reanah's clothes were loose and baggy. Even with his belt tightened to the last belt hole that the buckle could use, he would have to use his hands to keep the trousers from falling down around his ankles. To discourage that, he sat back down on the bed. Reanah handed him a pair of ankle-high soft leather boots. Tom had to curl his toes inside of them to keep the boots from falling off as he moved.

Tom felt ridiculous, like a child trying on a parent's clothes and not pulling it off. He could not believe how physically small he was. He estimated he was five feet tall, at most, and probably one hundred pounds.

As himself, getting ready for work in the morning in his apartment, he had stepped on his bathroom scale and weighed north of two hundred fifty pounds. Then, he was an honest

six feet tall. His shirt and pants fit tightly,
especially around the collar, reflecting the fact
that he had purchased them when he was ten to
fifteen pounds lighter. He had looked like a
middle-aged stuffed sausage. Other than the
occasional guilt-inspired trip to a gym, he had
not bothered to do much about it.

Tom sighed and used his hands to try to
wipe the tears and stress from his face. Almost
to himself, he said quietly, "Well, I guess there's
not much point in asking if I can use your cell
phone."

Reanah frowned, "Excuse me?"

"Never mind," Tom answered quickly.
"Just thinking out loud."

"Good," Reanah said. "Then let's depart."
She went over and picked up the wet woolen
dress where Tom had left it on the floor. "I'll
carry this for you. You'll want it back once it
dries out."

Tom was not so sure about that. He had
never worn anything resembling a dress in his
life. Its only virtue was that it would fit him
better than anything belonging to Reanah.

To complete his outfit, Reanah handed
him the outer cloak she had given him at the
riverbank. The difference with dry, rather than
wet, clothes was immediately noticeable. Tom
felt as if he could finally handle the chill
mountain air. He pulled the hood over his
head and nodded that he was ready to go.

For the present, Tom was absolutely
determined to keep his new body covered up.
Before seeing again whatever was underneath

those layers of borrowed clothes, he needed to get somewhere by himself, to process mentally what was going on.

Reanah returned the nod and gently guided him back out the door. As he walked, Tom used his hands to gather the material around his waist to take up the slack. Once out on the porch, Reanah relocked the door and left Tom standing there as she quickly circled the house to close and latch the shutters.

In the clearing, the others waited, standing patiently by the horses. The female elf that had also found Tom was now joined by two male elves that he had not seen before. They also had pointed ears and lean, angular faces. If anything, these men were even taller than the women, and whereas the women were lithe and athletic, the men had the broader shoulders and the builds of fit, toughened boxers. Physically, the three of them and Reanah were an imposing group.

The men's dress was identical to that of the women, tunics and trousers and hooded overcoats.

Seeing them as a group, the elves' similar wardrobe gave the appearance of a common, militaristic uniform. Between their tall statures and their clothes, in Tom's reality they might have been all members of the same coed basketball team, dressed in elfish cosplay. But they were clearly not playing around. The group oozed a seriousness and purposefulness that was slightly intimidating to Tom.

Reanah and Tom went down the steps to

approach the group. But before they left the shadow of the cabin's porch, Reanah stopped Tom and faced him. She bent over and whispered to him, "Please, young one. Tell me your real name. I cannot call you 'Tom' in front of the others."

He jerked his head, confused. Why not call him by his actual name? He wondered whether Reanah believed him when he told her his name was Tom. Obviously, she did not. Reanah could not match his real name to the person she saw standing before her. That was why she wanted a different answer from him.

But Tom felt that if Reanah was not going to accept the truth of his identity, he was not going to make it easy on her, either. So, he blurted out the word that had been echoing unbidden in his head since before his heart attack.

"Abstinence," Tom said. "My name is Abstinence."

Reanah absorbed that word with an obvious jolt. "Abstinence?" she asked, as if that was also another obvious lie.

But, for reasons even he could not articulate at that moment, Tom insisted, "Yes, Abstinence. But you can call me Abby for short."

This time, the new nickname seemed to satisfy Reanah. She resumed guiding him toward the others. "Abby it is, then."

THREE: HADREA

She was a fire that burned white-hot, that consumed. Hadrea was tortured by a unique and terrible vision, acquired long ago. It was an extreme certitude, an absolute Truth which exposed for her the hypocrisy of society, the benevolent fiction of human religion, and, most of all, the lie that there was such a thing as a happy and loving family. There was no doubt in her mind of her creed, of her personal view of the order of the universe. As a result, there was no law but her law.

As a member of the Sisterhood, her vows should have prevented what she did. But her crimes against those who shared the Known World with her were real enough—murder, mutilation, experimentation in black magic. In a reflective moment, Hadrea might have conceded the justice of her confinement.

But there were no more quiet moments for her now. Hadrea's Truth held her in a frightening, final embrace, sucking the remnants of her humanity and leaving a desolate, angry soul.

So, a frightened civilization made her suffer. Deep within an underground dungeon in the western human outpost known as Pearl City, she was a frail, old woman wrapped in a fetid blanket, shivering as cold, hard stone sapped the warmth from her limbs. Hadrea detested her physical body--so transient, so in need of care. Her Truth considered such limitations as incurable weakness, a sign of human fragility before the timeless power of Nature.

Hadrea's defense was to retreat within her own mind, into a dark void hiding her inner self. There, she swore her own, new oaths, declaring revenge on those who had resisted her. Ideas danced through the haze of her consciousness like dry leaves in a swirling winter wind. "They cannot withstand me. They are insignificant before me. Soon I will be ready, and death my ally. They will deliver themselves into my hands. Then, they will face my Judgment." Her Truth listened, and smiled.

Beyond the limits of her cell, black night passed. Moonlight glimmered vaguely through the fog. Ghostly mists rose from the mirrored surface of the river which surrounded the brooding central keep, twisting as they floated in the breathless air. A chill dew clung to all that the hand of man had built in Pearl City-- hundreds of stone and brick buildings topped by bound thatch, narrow, twisting cobblestone streets laid over centuries, the tall, proud outer wall which overlooked the cultivated fields rich with the promise of spring. The sole evidence of life was the muted beat of a lone sentry's footsteps as he paced the inner wall. Restful, weighty silence blanketed the sleeping city.

But deep within the dungeon, sleep was irrelevant to Hadrea. Her inner fire burned on, restless and hungry.

Hours later, a cold, biting dawn came, announced by the feeble light which brightened the fog into a shadowy grey. For Hadrea, events in reality happened only at the fringes of her consciousness. She barely perceived the rough hands of prison guards which lifted her up and dragged her from the cell. Long flights of spiraling stone steps passed before her glazed eyes as if in a dream, as they moved from the chill dungeon levels toward the warmer rooms above.

Through passageways and down corridors, the people who saw Hadrea pass all wore the same silent mask of shock and derision. To them, despite her appearance as a stooped, frail elderly woman, she was still as dangerous as a coiled snake.

Weeks ago, there was a sudden burst of dark magic around her hideaway on the outer border of the Queendom, magic that had all the hallmarks of occult. Together with her assistant Sidra, Hadrea was pushing the limits of what was possible with magic to a dark, forbidden place. Then, almost as strange, there was a sudden absence of magic around her formerly impenetrable cabin, as if the magic, once used, had suddenly drained her of her ability to defend herself. She had gone from a formidable, if aged, witch, to a non-magical mortal.

In some ways, this change was even more frightening than before. For years, Hadrea seemed content to declare the area around her home as off-limits to all the other races, even the orcs and goblins that would have been attracted to the types of magic that she practiced. Beyond that, she seemed to have no care about the rest of the world. While she stood charged in the human courts with many crimes, the law knew better than to chase her into her den. Thus, Hadrea never had to answer for her crimes, and her victims received no justice.

In the obvious absence of her defenses, the authorities of Pearl City did not wait for the Sisterhood, headquartered far away in the capital of Crystal City, to discipline one of their own. Instead, the local constabulary used the opportunity to finally arrest her. And, when a group of soldiers arrived at her home to take her, she offered no resistance. Her assistant was gone, missing without a trace, but Hadrea herself was there. Indeed, it seemed as if she had been waiting for them to arrest her.

So, the authorities returned her to human society, to be judged by those for whom she had such contempt. Yet, even as the legal process moved forward and she finally received the trial for which many of her victims had for so long waited, there was a troubling nag at the back of many peoples' minds. Did she intend to be arrested? Was this all part of whatever sick plans that she had concocted at the end of her natural life? Those skilled in the magical arts and who spent time monitoring the flow of magic in and out of the Continuum, like members of the Sisterhood, said that what Hadrea was doing in her last days of freedom was highly unusual. She had first accumulated a large influx of magic, then spent it in one spectacular burst that seemed, at least to them, to have caused no obvious harm whatever. It was as if a tidal wave was seen in the distance, then mysteriously never reached the shore.

And she gave no reason or explanation for what had happened, even if it was only to taunt them as to what she had done. She only said vaguely that they would "find out." It was in keeping with her contempt for all other people, and for the justice that was now bearing down on her. Hadrea seemed resigned to her ultimate and certain fate, content with what they were going to do to her.

So, finally, came the day of her sentencing. Guards arrived at her cell and took her several levels above. After winding through the stairs and corridors of the keep, Hadrea's escorts paused before a set of massive wooden doors. They rapped a heavy iron knocker, sending loud reverberations down the hallway, startling Hadrea from her disconnected reverie. In reply, the doors parted with a weighty slowness.

A ceremonial guard in a gleaming red robe faced them. With a self-important sneer, he addressed the prisoner. "The Lords of the High Court summon Hadrea!" To Hadrea, the words were distant and meaningless, the man insignificant.

The guard turned and struck his long wooden staff on the stone floor, then began a stately march through a large court room. Willing her limbs into motion, Hadrea and her escorts followed, shuffling through the courtroom toward the five solemn judges eyeing her from a raised platform. A select, well-connected few who were allowed to witness the secret proceedings, made up the sparse audience. They looked at Hadrea with dread, disbelieving that she had actually been caught or that her powers were gone.

The guard halted in front of the platform, struck his staff again, then stepped aside. Reaching a docket which stood below the higher platform on which the five judges sat, the escorts stopped Hadrea and gradually loosened their grip on her shoulders. Almost involuntarily, Hadrea's legs stiffened, supporting herself in a wobbly, arthritic stance.

Gradually, Hadrea sensed that her fate was before her. Her bleary, unblinking eyes stared on the indistinct faces staring down at her, gradually bringing the faces of the five women into focus. The prisoner stood weakly before the High Court.

The Chief Judge glared down at her. Hadrea recognized her by the large black and yellow hat perched precariously on her fat, oversized head. To Hadrea, she was another insignificant human who had no right to judge her. Hadrea thought to herself, "Just like these petty locals. You can guess the rank by the size of the hat!" A wicked smile crossed her face.

The scowl rippling across the jowly face of the Chief Judge revealed her intense contempt for this defendant. An expectant silence settled around her as she fingered the stiff, ink-stained parchment in her hands. "Hadrea," she bellowed, breaking the tension, "are you prepared to hear your sentence?" The Judge waited for Hadrea to acknowledge the presence of the court.

The prisoner seemed not to notice, staring blankly in return. Yet, the angry darkness within her begged for release, and she longed to cry out the words echoing in her mind, "Fool! Yes, this is your moment. You may indulge your naive sense of justice. If you only knew what is in store for you and all of the Known World, you would look on me and despair!"

But to the others in the courtroom, there was no outward sign of Hadrea's thoughts, only a vague glimmer in her eyes. Irritated, the Judge could wait no longer. She dropped her eyes to the paper before her and read aloud, her thick, self-important voice intoning Hadrea's sentence. "This Court finds Hadrea, originally of Pearl City and lately of parts unknown, guilty of sedition, high treason, and of practicing the Dark Arts. Your misdeeds must not be tolerated. The judgment against you will serve to remind others of their duty."

The Chief Judge paused, glancing at the prisoner to gauge any reaction. Finding none, she returned to the parchment before her. "Hadrea, the High Court sentences you to be burned at the stake. At noon tomorrow, this sentence will be executed in the Central Square of Pearl City. May God have Mercy on your mortal soul!" The Chief Judge tossed the verdict aside and glared down from the bench, waiting for Hadrea's reply.

Hadrea hid her burning eyes, focusing on the cracks on the grey marble floor before her, and shifted her frail limbs only slightly. But her voice, when it came boomed through the room. "I am no criminal. Yes, I sought to overthrow a long line of idiot queens. This is not treason, but patriotism of the highest order." Clenching her fists, she gathered herself, feeding from her hate and letting her anger flow through her. She lifted her head toward the tribunal and thrust a bony finger toward the Chief Judge. "I defy you and your law! It is nothing to me. For I have seen Perfection, and I am its instrument within the world of mortals."

Hadrea held her gnarled hands before her eyes, and giggled as though her fingers amused herself. "Do you not see? Our souls are trapped within these bodies of flesh and blood. Mortality makes us insignificant. Our lives come and go, but the Earth takes little note."

Scanning the judges' faces with wide, bulging eyes, Hadrea said, "But you are going to set me free, aren't you? I am grateful, my children. For once I am free of this mortal shell, I will bring order to humanity. My Truth will become your truth. I will become your God!"

In unison, the judges rose in fury. "Blasphemer!" one cried. "Unholy monster!" shouted another.

But the old woman only smiled as the guards grabbed her and dragged her toward the exit. Just before reaching the doors, Hadrea called out, "Who was on trial here? I find your precious Queendom guilty--of stupidity, arrogance, and a vain sense of morality. Yet when I execute my sentence, your God will not lift a finger to save you!" The guards succeeded in dragging her out of the room, and the doors to the courtroom slammed shut behind her, cutting off Hadrea's cackling laughter which faded away down the outer corridor.

The next day, dawn broke with dark skies hovering low over the Queendom of Distan. Thunder rumbled through the streets and lightning flashed among the clouds. The citizens moved through their daily routines with a vague sense of distress, uncertain why this day should seem different from any other. But they knew instinctively that it was, without understanding precisely why.

In the depths of the Keep's dungeon, Hadrea stood at the door of her cell, waiting eagerly. The dim torchlight that flickered in the musty corridor made no distinction between night and day, but Hadrea knew her time was coming.

Shortly before noon, two guards and a solemn black-robed priestess approached. As the executors of the Queen's law, this was a role they had played before, part of the preamble which led ultimately to death in the name of justice for those who had transgressed. Yet, though they were the keepers, though they were in control, they felt fear of this scrawny little elderly woman with the wild eyes and the devil's own heart. A key twisted open the rusty lock, and the group entered the condemned prisoner's cell.

Hadrea's face broke into a wide smile, and she began pacing excitedly. "It is time! It is time!" She wrapped her arms around her chest, shouting her joy toward the ceiling. "I knew I was worthy! I knew I could make myself ready! Oh, Perfection, I will soon be one with thee!"0

Terror sliced through the hearts of the others in the room. Despite her apparent physical frailty, Hadrea's magical powers were legendary. She could bend others to her will, and used the forces of nature to serve her ends. Those who opposed her either disappeared or died at her whim. Was she now really bereft of those powers? It did not seem possible.

The Sisterhood, and by extension the Queen, tolerated her methods as long as Hadrea helped to maintain the established order's iron rule over the people. For years, the Queen and those that ruled in her name ignored the gossip about Hadrea's methods, grateful for a ruthlessly effective servant who got things done.

It was only when Hadrea began going off into the wider world on her own initiative, pursuing her own secretive research with her assistant Sidra, that the rulers of Distan began to worry about her as a potential threat. It was said that Hadrea and Sidra had even been to the far north, to a place with a powerful wellspring of red magic called the Source. That area was ruled by a group of female vampires called the Coven, and it was forbidden for any Sister to go there. Not that anyone in their right mind would want to, which was why Hadrea's venture there raised such concern.

Once rumors of her travels there had been received in the capital of Crystal City, an arrest warrant was issued for her and Sidra. They were charged with suspicion of the use of rogue magic, and unauthorized travel to hostile territory. Other charges would be added later, stemming from Hadrea's many previous misdeeds that had been conveniently forgotten while she had been one of the main enforcers of the Sisterhood's will. But the point of it all was that they were done with Hadrea. Once caught, even a fair trial would result in a certain execution.

The story of her capture had also raised concerns. The guard that found her reported that she had been hiding in the shadows of her cramped, derelict cabin, mumbling a strange incantation. Hadrea's hands glowed with a strange red fire, and as the guard approached

Hadrea, the guard found herself gripped by an immobilizing terror.

At the last instant, the guard freed herself from the oncoming spell and threw her body at Hadrea. They tumbled to the pavement, and a large, heavy golden key with an imbedded blood-red ruby fell out from beneath Hadrea's robes. The magic which sustained Hadrea vanished, and the guard subdued the old woman. Hadrea was arrested and the key confiscated.

Without her precious golden key and the magic-storing gem imbedded within it, rumored to be the legendary Crystal Key itself, Hadrea was nothing. Stripped of her talisman, she lacked the power of its dark red magic. Hadrea could not avoid her fate.

Now, within the hour, the sentence of the Queen's Court would be carried out. The group sent to retrieve Hadrea from her cell were standing there, ready to do their part. Still, Hadrea's joy at the prospect was unsettling. The priestess and the two guards stood frozen for a moment before the priestess forced herself to speak, "Um...er...Do you wish to make a confession, my daughter?"

Hadrea laughed. "Yes," she said with a broad grin and a nasty growl in her voice, "I wish to confess my years of service to an inbred line of rulers, my years of self-satisfied ignorance, and for all the petty concerns which marked my life before I found the One True Way."

The priestess stared in shock, then stammered, "You...do not wish to make a confession?"

Hadrea's harsh chuckle in reply echoed around the cell. She put her arm around the priestess's shoulders. "Mother Abigail, you have always been very amusing, in an uncomprehending way. But let me assure you, I will give you special attention once I am no longer limited by my mortality. You will enjoy a privileged place in my New Order."

The priestess jerked herself from under Hadrea's arm and raised her ancient, leather-bound bible toward the prisoner. "Repent, sinner!" she shouted. "Save your soul while you still can! Pray for Her forgiveness or you will suffer eternal torment in the depths of Hell!"

Sudden, intense hate filled Hadrea's face. She raised her bony fist toward the priestess. "Fool! I will soon show you what immortality means. Then, you will beg me for forgiveness."

The priestess angrily motioned to the guards. They grabbed Hadrea and roughly dragged her out of the cell and up the stairs.

In the large, paved square in the center of Pearl City, a small, hushed crowd gathered. Elsewhere, people went on with their lives, but an uneasy, unnatural silence pervaded the normally bustling city. The peasants paused at the market stalls, interrupting an otherwise steady stream of commerce. Within the city's wall, thousands of lives slowed to a crawl as noon approached.

There was no overt reason why this should be so. Most citizens had forgotten about the withered old woman in the Keep's dungeon. Those that were aware of the death sentence to be executed that day had considered Hadrea as a problem solved. She would meet her end soon enough and be forgotten forever.

Yet beneath the surface lingered a doubt, an unnamed restlessness which seemed to slow time itself. As the sun rose in the eastern sky, burning off the morning dew, a wooden pyre rose in the center of the square. Those gathered for the event, which had happened often enough to engender a routine by the participants and the audience, were not their usual festive selves. Quiet, anxious faces appeared in the windows of the stone buildings surrounding the plaza.

Then just before noon, from the west, tall black storm clouds glided quickly toward them, first dimming, then blotting out the sun entirely. Distant thunder echoed through the streets, the sound tugging at the unnamed fear in every soul.

Then, at one end of the square, the crowd parted, and an excited murmur moved like a wave through the spectators. A flat wagon pulled by a pair of draft horses clattered toward the pyre. Mother Abigail stood like a figurehead on the front, mumbling words from her torn bible that no one could hear. Behind her, Hadrea stood as erect as her infirmities allowed, casting a wide-eyed, defiant expression toward the pensive faces staring back up at her.

45

As the bells for the fateful hour struck in the nearby church tower, the winds grew from a light breeze to the swirling, humid winds of an approaching storm. Thunder boomed closer, and lightning flashed among the clouds.

Hadrea and her executioners reached the pyre. Anxious citizens crowded in as waiting soldiers lifted Hadrea from the wagon. Holding their prisoner between them like a limp rag doll, two men dragged Hadrea over the loose timbers of the pyre toward a thick, central pole.

At the top of the pile, Hadrea snarled angrily as the solders bent her arms behind her and tied her securely to the stake. One guard tried to cover Hadrea's head with a black hood, but Hadrea jerked her head away. The guard smirked and tossed the hood at Hadrea's feet.

It was noon, and the executioners were ready. The intensity of the storm increased, and the dark clouds overhead began to boil. One of the soldiers took a flaming torch and lit the base of the pyre. After a moment's hesitation, the fire caught and began to spread quickly, spurred on by the winds whipping around the square. Soon, tongues of flame groped toward Hadrea's feet. The spectators, far from being elated at the coming death of a black-hearted killer, looked on in silence, praying for the end to come soon.

Lightning flashed across the sky, and the concussion from the thunder cowered those in the square. A dry wind whipped furiously through the crowd. The bonfire grew until flames soon wrapped themselves eagerly around Hadrea's body.

Hadrea's filthy prison robes started to burn. Her face twisted with agony. Her arrogance faded in the face of oncoming death, as she struggled vainly against the bindings around her wrists. Hadrea screamed, lifting her face toward the black, roiling sky.

Suddenly, a lightning bolt exploded from the clouds and struck the burning pyre. The concussion threw the surrounding crowd to the ground, leaving a pile of jumbled limbs and twisting bodies.

Above them on the pyre, a deep black void appeared around Hadrea, growing until the dying prisoner was lost from view. The darkness spread, opening like a chasm from reality into some dark, nameless place. As the storm pulsed with its own wicked energy, the void grew and grew, rising above the buildings around the square and soon blocking out the roiling sky. The citizens of Pearl City cowered helplessly on the ground, pinned by a roaring wind.

Then, the darkness surrounding Hadrea separated from the ground and rose toward the sky, a huge ball of terrifying blackness. Beneath it on the ground, the entire pyre—the wood, the fire, Hadrea—was all gone. The clean, dry pavement stones left behind bore no clue of the conflagration that blazed there only seconds before.

The hushed, terrified crowd looked up. The darkness continued to rise and expand, reaching the flashing, roiling grey and black clouds. It disappeared into the storm, and seemed to draw energy from the contact. The wind blasted into them, howling in a full force gale, but no rain fell.

Straining to see, searching the sky for any sign of what had become of the darkness, the crowd began to make out a leering, ghostly face, etched like an engraving into the clouds. It was Hadrea. Her apparition stared back down at them in satisfaction, her expression bright with glee.

Hadrea's voice thundered over the city. "People of the Queendom of Distan! Welcome to the New Order!"

As if Hadrea's words had commanded an angry Nature, a total, enveloping darkness exploded outward from the storm overhead, eclipsing the sun and plunging all of Pearl City into sudden, terrifying night.

Now, the people of Pearl City would discover the ghosts within their own souls, and despair.

FOUR: JADE CITY

For the better part of two days, Reanah led her party by horseback toward an elven outpost known as Jade City. Located in the rugged, mountainous border region between the lands of the elves and those of the human race, it straddled a high border road known as the Jade Pass that connected the two Queendoms.

For Abby, formerly Tom, it was either the strangest two days of his fifty-plus years of adult life, or of the first two days of experiencing someone else's teenage life. The group rode with Abby riding on the saddle behind Reanah, alternately hugging her waist or holding onto the rear of the saddle.

He spent his time in their journey in a confused funk, trying to puzzle it out. Reanah would occasionally turn and ask, "Are you alright? How are you doing?" Abby would either say "Fine" or just nod in reply, but his mind was constantly churning, trying to make sense of it all.

Abby never had a moment alone, which was something that he desperately wanted. During the years from birth to heart attack in his own reality, Tom accepted everything in the modern, science and technology-based world around him as normal. He lived in houses and apartments, not camping out in the woods. He drove cars, not horses. He had a cell phone, computer, stereo, television and modern appliances.

In this new reality, as far as he could tell, none of those were present. Food came from either as breads or dried meat or fruit from their packs, or from small game they opportunistically hunted or fish caught in the local streams as they moved along the mountain trail. Tom was never an outdoors person. On the other hand, Abby's world was definitely a do-it-yourself world.

But, as Abby came to realize, camping is always easier when you have other people with you who know what they are doing. Reanah and the other three in her group handled the food, fire and camp setup, while Abby stood idly by. All he had to do was sit down when all was ready, even though that meant for him a lot of time standing to the side, feeling useless.

Even so, on their little trip through the pine forests of the high mountains, the most difficult part for Abby was the lack of indoor plumbing. The party drank water from canteens refilled in whatever stream they crossed. Which was fine, Abby supposed, but how could he be sure?

And if they needed to go to the bathroom, that meant going off away from the others a short distance, and relieving themselves on the pine needles which covered the ground. No toilet, much less showers or a bathtub. Not so far. Abby realized that later, thinking about the cabin that they had broken into. There was nothing resembling a bathroom in the interior. That meant there was probably an outhouse there that he hadn't seen. He could only hope that was not typical.

This came up the first time Abby needed to urinate. Sitting on the back of Reanah's horse, swaying from side to side over the horse's hips, the pressure had built within Abby's bladder to the point of being uncomfortable. He knew he had to do something.

At a rest stop, Abby asked to go off to the side alone, trying to be casual about it. He knew it was going to be unsettling enough to do that with this new body, but to have someone watch while he did it was going to be even worse.

Reanah, though, had no intention of letting him from her sight. Abby's heart sank when she answered his request by stating she would accompany him for his "own safety." The two walked away from the others until finding some small shrubs in the undergrowth beneath the tall trees. Pointing to a spot, Reanah said, "This is fine. Go ahead." She continued to watch him carefully, her arms folded in front of her chest.

Abby could feel his face redden. As a man, this would have been so much easier, just to turn his back, point his penis in the right direction and let it loose. Not that whipping it out in front of a woman was easy, but when you have to go, you go. Even that option, though, was at that moment not available.

Abby did check to make sure. Trying not to be too conspicuous about it, but he did feel around in his crotch area, hoping to find something resembling his manhood. Nope. Unfortunately, the parts that he had taken for granted for over fifty years were not there. Finally, he gave up.

"Oh well," Abby thought as the pressure on his bladder was at its height. "Here goes nothing." He dropped his trousers, leaned his back against the trunk of a tree, and squatted. Urine spattered out beneath him, but Abby was grateful for the relief.

After emptying his bladder, he could feel a few lingering droplets of moisture down there. Abby awkwardly shook his hips to set them free.

Once this bit of unpleasantness was over, Abby stood, pulled up his trousers and tightened his belt. His face was beet red, and his mind was swimming with the shock of the experience. Reanah sensed his discomfort, but not the reasons for it. "Don't be such a prude," she said. "I'm in the military. That's nothing I have not seen before."

For Abby, though, that only deepened his confusion and his embarrassment. The fact that she seemed to take it all in as normal was, for him, not normal. All of this, this strange, unfamiliar place with this new body and new identity, was outside of his experience. He did not know how to process it in his mind. It was a crisis only he seemed to be aware of.

Nevertheless, the group moved along on their journey, not hurriedly but purposefully. Reanah was trying to get them to where they were going. Somewhere safe, she said, but toward a destination that she did not share with Abby.

And Abby never had a clear understanding of what he meant to Reanah and the others. Was Abby someone that they were helping, a survivor of some tragic accident, or was he a prisoner? Certainly, he did not think he could just thank them and leave. He may not have been tied up, but Abby was going with them whether he wanted to or not.

Reanah's demeanor and her serious military bearing did not clear that up. She was kind but serious, concerned but distant, depending on the moment. She asked Abby to let her know if he needed anything, but never let Abby out of her sight. When the party slept, Reanah was always within arm's length of Abby, and someone else was always keeping watch through the night even as Reanah slept. Were they in danger? Were there bandits or wild animals or anything else that could harm them? The others were wary and alert all the time, but otherwise as they traveled, Abby could not tell what the hazards were.

The others, one female and two male elves, automatically deferred to Reanah as the leader. They kept addressing Reanah as "Legatus", which was a mystery to Abby until he finally asked Reanah what they meant. "Lieutenant, in the Old Tongue," she answered gruffly, tapping at a small decorative broach in the shape of two elm leaves on her tunic which represented her rank.

The other woman in the group had a broach with one elm leaf, while the men in the group did not wear any obvious form of rank at all. From their behavior and the way they addressed each other, though, Abby guessed the woman, called Naida and sometimes just referred to as "Alterum", to be the second in command. The two male elves were the grunts, and Abby never got their names or titles.

Abby eventually gathered that they had been some sort of military unit on patrol when they found him. But Abby could not get much more from them, unless he had the courage to ask. Even then, answers were given reluctantly, as if he was not entitled to them.

While they spoke English (which they referred to as "Common") some of the time, they often chatted away among themselves in a language that Abby thought was vaguely familiar, but one he could not understand. Reanah called it the "Old Tongue". To Abby, it sounded like an altered version of the Latin he learned decades before in high school, but he could not remember enough to pick up more than one or two words in a sentence or paragraph. Certainly, he did not understand enough to know what they were saying, gathering the meaning from their gestures or what they were doing at the time, rather than from the words themselves.

The group realized fairly quickly that Abby could not understand their language, so they spent most of the time speaking it among themselves when they did not want Abby to know what they were saying. They would only break out of it when they addressed Abby directly, and it was mostly Reanah that did the talking, in her vaguely British accent.

Abby spent the bulk of the trip alone with his thoughts among these strangers, waiting to find out their destination and what they planned for him. As confused as he was on an ongoing basis by his new reality, he tried as best he could to relax and enjoy the views in the forested mountains, breathing in the crisp, clean air that was a far cry from the ozone-laden, heavy air of modern civilization.

Then, finally, late in the second day that they traveled, they left the narrow trail through the forest when it reached a larger one, still dirt but more of a road. This allowed the riders to start widening out side-to-side in pairs instead of having to ride single file. After a couple of hours, that led to an even wider, graveled road that could accommodate horse-drawn carts and wagons.

At this point, Abby saw other elves for the first time, moving in either direction on the road. They were more of the same tall, thin people with pointed ears and medieval dress. They rode horses, behind horses towing simple carts or wagons, carrying crates or barrels or cut wood or stacks of hay. They looked like ordinary, simple people going on about their business, not forest creatures swinging through the tree tops that he might have expected from the fictional stories of Tom's world.

As they passed each other, Reanah's group might nod, smile or wave depending on the receptivity of the others on the road to a greeting, but no one stopped and Reanah kept their own party moving along. At one point, the uniformity of appearance of those traveling on the road caused Abby to smirk to himself, "Everyone's from the same 'ye olden times' festival. I hope when we get to where we're going, there's a taffy stand." Reanah noticed Abby's wry smile enough to ask if anything was the matter. "Nothing," Abby answered quickly.

As they passed, those around Reanah's group seemed to take particular notice of Abby, looking at him in a steady, measured way which made him uncomfortable. If Abby accidentally met their gazes, he looked away quickly, focusing on the road or the back of Reanah as they traveled. It just reinforced Abby's feeling that he was the stranger here.

The road dropped into a shallow valley as it moved eastward, widening out into cleared land and farms. The houses looked like postcards from an idealized version of old Europe, sturdy mortared stone and hand-hewn wood, surrounded by pens with wooden rails that housed chickens, ducks and goats, with individual properties set off from the road with stacked fieldstone walls. Traffic grew more noticeable and dense as they approached their destination.

Finally, around one wide bend, in an open area in a ravine wedged between two vertical mountainsides, Jade City was before them. The most noticeable feature from the outside was the large wooden wall topped with ramparts and watch towers, with massive square-beamed gates that faced the party as they approached. The gates were open, pushed to either side and latched in place. Through the opening, Abby could see in the interior larger, sturdier versions of the mortared stone and thick beamed buildings that had lined the valley on their approach.

A good number of Jade City's residents, with their own horses or handcarts, were milling around either at the gate or just beyond, giving a hint of the commerce going on inside. The guards on duty at the gate and on the walls had a casualness to them, belying any sense that the area outside was a dangerous place.

For Abby, it was a bit of a letdown. "This is it?" Abby asked aloud to no one in particular. "This is the 'city' that you were talking about?" Abby was used to skyscrapers and massive buildings built of concrete, paned glass and steel, and a commute to work that took a half hour or more depending on the stops and starts of the commute. "If you want to see a real city, you should see where I'm from."

Reanah answered coolly, "We'll get to that, I promise," before adding, a bit defensively, "It is not size that makes a City. Whatever you are used to, a place earns the term if it contains a wellspring. You are young, but you should already know that. Unless you were raised to be ignorant."

Abby's face reddened. It was the first harsh comment from Reanah since she had found him at the base of the falls in the mountains. His first instinct was to give her a snappy comment back in return, that all of this was brand fucking new to him and that she should cut him some slack.

But he caught himself. Reanah looked at him and saw and heard a teenage girl. She could not see the fifty year old man from a modern city within his new body. Until he could figure out what was going on, Abby knew he needed to be smart and keep his mouth shut, at least for the moment.

The group rode on in an awkward silence until they were through the gate. No one stopped them or asked what their business were, only drawing hopeful glances from the merchants hoping for a sale. They wove their horses between the people in the narrow streets, moving toward the town center as the sun was going down in the western sky behind them. The air cooled as evening descended, and Abby could feel the chill breezes off the mountain slopes that surrounded the town.

Abby noticed that while most of the residents were the same tall, thin, pointed ear race that he had seen since arriving in this new world, there were also some people who were more human, more normal to him. They were smaller but bulkier than the natives with normal human ears and plump faces, mixed in the crowds they passed. They were all dressed in the same renaissance fair clothes that everyone around them wore, wandering freely and transacting the same types of business as the natives, but there were clearly two distinct groups of people in the crowds.

Noticing this raised a bigger question for Abby. He had been thinking of Reanah and her group as elves, because that was the only word he knew that could summarize their uniqueness. While he had only one fleeting glimpse of his new face in a mirror, his body and face was definitely different from those of his escorts. Did this world really have multiple races? Was Abby human, and all those that looked like Reanah, really elves? It did not seem possible in any reality that he trusted. But seeing the two types of races mingled together in one place, it seemed the only likely conclusion. Elves were real, and he was a traveler in their lands. The realization reinforced the silence that Abby imposed on himself as Reanah led the way toward their ultimate destination.

As night fell, they arrived in the center of Jade City. There, off a square plaza, sat a larger, thicker and more impressive two story stone building in the same general style as the rest of the surrounding houses. Two long horizontal hitching posts on either side of the doorway and long wooden water troughs serviced the horses tethered in front. Elves wearing the same style of clothes as Reanah and her group milled around in front. Illumination came from lampposts spaced in the area at regular intervals, and their glass-enclosed bulbs glowed with a strange, green-tinted light.

Reanah directed their horses to an open section of a hitching post, then dismounted. She made no announcement, but with a great sense of relief, Abby knew it was the end of the ride. He lifted a leg over the saddle and slid down the horse's flank to the ground, and immediately began rubbing the soreness out of his backside and thighs. The trip had been Abby's first introduction to an extended horse ride, and he hoped it would be his last.

Reanah, for her part, was also noticeably relieved. "Come, young one," she said, "Let's get some help for you." She put her arm over Abby's shoulders and led him inside. Their boots clattered on the hardwood planks as they made their way up the steps and through the opened doorway. Reanah offered nods of recognition to one or two other elves as they passed in the hallway.

Finally, they entered a large room with long tables parallel to each of the other three sides of the room. On the far end, seated behind the table, sat an overweight female elf, the first heavyset one Abby had seen. She had extended epaulets on the shoulders of her uniform, her hair wound tightly behind her head. She exuded an officious bearing.

Eying Reanah's group as they approached, the elf finished berating the red faced elf male soldier before her. "I'll send a report to your superior, and let her deal with you. Men are not paid to think. They are paid to do as they are told and no more. Dismissed." With a curt wave of her hand, she sent the soldier away.

Reanah approached the table and snapped to attention. "Lieutenant Reanah reporting, Colonel," she said. "I have a human girl that needs some clothes and some food." Then, continuing in the Old Tongue, but also dropping her voice as if that would help hide what she was saying from Abby, "Ego vis ad liberare a secretis fama plena. Puella opus interpellari."

She needn't have worried, as Abby did not understand what she said. He assumed, though, as he stared wide-eyed at the two of them, that Reanah was saying something about him.

But the part of the conversation in Common encouraged him. The idea of real food was a promising start, not the dry survival fare and scraps of cooked rabbit and squirrel he had eaten for the last couple of days. And, even more, he was looked forward to being alone, finally, with his new and unfamiliar body.

The elf behind the table quickly eyed Abby up and down, before replying, "Very well. I'll have some things brought to her. Take her to Room C in the next wing, then come back here to be debriefed. That is all."

Reanah stiffened and clicked her heels to acknowledge the dismissal. She turned and put her arms over Abby's shoulders and said gently, but with a little condescension, "Now, that sounds good. Doesn't it Abby? Get you out of my oversize rags and into real human girl clothes? Plus some real food to boot."

The idea of having to put on "human girl clothes" actually did not sound promising to Abby at all. But at that moment, he felt like he could devour two supersize fast food meals, something he had probably done too many times in his life. That is, Tom's life. Which, he thought dryly, is why he had a heart attack and wound up here in this crazy reality to begin with.

So, Abby dutifully trotted beside Reanah as she led the two of them out of the room and down the hall. After taking a couple of corners, they found the correct room and Reanah unlatched the door.

They entered a small room dominated by a decent-sized bed with a fluffy looking, almost domestic white comforter. Cream-colored linen sheets were folded neatly at one end. On the side, there was a small utilitarian wooden dresser and frame chair. The space on the floor between them and the bed was covered by an oval rug with woven flower patterns. Small framed paintings of flowers adorned the walls. For a room in a military headquarters, it was surprisingly homey.

The strangest part of the room were the four small square boxes mounted in wrought iron holders at each the top corners of the room. Each glowed with a soft light, basically white but tinged with a greenish hue. They provided the illumination in the windowless room.

Reanah gave Abby a little push into the room, and quickly said, "Someone will be along." She ducked back out.

As the door shut behind Reanah, Abby noticed a full length oval mirror which hung from a nail on the back of the door. It clattered as it came to rest again in its place as the door latch closed. Then, Abby heard a second, weightier click as Reanah locked the door behind her.

Abby would realize later that he had been locked in. But at that moment, he was transfixed by the reflection of his image in the mirror, by the stranger staring back at him.

Days before, when he had first caught a glimpse of his new body in the small mirror in the cabin in the woods, he had only seen himself for a quick instant before he had pulled away in shock. Now alone for at least the next few minutes and steeling himself to study what he was seeing, Abby could not take his eyes off from the image.

He saw a girl of maybe sixteen or so, with a slender build and not very tall, only five feet in height at best. Reanah's baggy clothes hid the form of the body beneath, but the build was noticeably thinner and much, much lighter than when Tom used to disappoint himself with a side glance in his own apartment's mirror. The girl's face was round with the plump cheeks of a teenager, with a nose that was smaller than the one he used to see when Tom had shaved his face in the morning. The lips were plumper and more girlish, even pouty, to an unsettling degree.

But the eyes were what he focused on the most. As a man, his brown eyes were sort of small compared to the rest of his face, semi-hidden by his fat cheeks. But as Abby, the grey-green eyes were the most prominent feature of the face, large and almost bug-eyed, with a sudden intensity as he stared in amazement. They were topped by eyebrows that had been tweezed and clipped by someone into thin elegant lines that set off the eyes below. Abby stared into those eyes, transfixed, and the image stared right back at him.

After several moments of self-absorbed silence, what finally distracted Tom away from Abby's eyes was the state of his hair. It was a sandy-brown, frazzled, tangled mess. He sort of tugged at it with his fingers for a few moments, and shook his head so that the tips of the hair brushed the tops of his shoulders.

Even in his youth, when his hair actually grew on his entire head, Tom never had long hair. To be a real man, his grandfather always said when Tom was a teenager, you had to have short, trimmed hair. That became easier once male-pattern baldness began to set it. Keeping the rest closely trimmed just looked better.

From his first moments as Abby, after he had pulled himself out of the river, and during their journey to Jade City, Tom had been aware of his new hair's unruliness. But each time a lock would go in front of his eyes or accidentally into his mouth, he would quickly brush it away and back behind his head, as if it belonged to someone else. Now, seeing it in total, he realized it would be his responsibility to manage it. He gave a quick glance over to the dresser. There was no comb or brush to try to fix it. Later, he thought, he would take care of it.

To Tom, all of this was quietly horrific. There was such a dissonance between the person he knew he was, the Tom who had lived a full, if boring, life in a modern, tech-filled world, and the young girl who looked back at him in that mirror. He had no idea of the world that she had been born, and grew up in. Who was she, really? Where did she come from? From what he had seen already, her reality was completely foreign to the way he had lived his life for over fifty years. It was some sort of medieval, fantasy world come to life.

"Please," he thought, addressing the sentiment to whatever deity that must have done this to him, "Get me out of this. I want to go home." Given what Tom had experienced right before coming to this reality, he was not sure what he would be returning to.

Or, if it were even possible to go back. But he did offer a quick prayer, wishing himself to be out of this girl's reality. Tom could not imagine having to continue on like this.

A sudden, harsh knock from the other side of the door startled him out of his quiet self-torment. Abby answered weakly, almost croaking, "Yes?"

He heard the mechanism of the door lock snap back open, and the knob turned and door swung inwards. A large, muscular male elf dressed in the same uniform but unadorned with any rank, stepped quickly through the opening. Abby backed up a couple of steps to allow him entry.

"Some clothes for you, miss." He offered a stack of carefully folded clothes topped by a pair of soft leather shoes. Abby gestured that he should put them on the top of the dresser. As he did, he continued, "The food is being prepared in the kitchen and will be along shortly."

Abby nodded. "Can I also get a brush, or comb? Something?" He tugged a little at the wild strands of hair around his head, as if the need were obvious.

The elf gave a quick upwards glance at the mop on Abby's head. He nodded quickly, then turned and ducked back out of the room. The door closed behind him, and Abby heard the latch again lock into place.

This time, Abby ignored the reflection in the mirror and reached forward. He grabbed the doorknob. It turned freely in his hand but the door would not open. Locked. Again, he wondered, was he a prisoner? What was going on?

Still stunned and overwhelmed, Abby turned and shuffled back toward the bed, stopping to grab the new clothes and shoes. He sat on the edge of the bed, head down, cradling the new clothes on his lap.

The prospect of changing was daunting. As smelly and oversized as Reanah's loaned clothes were, getting naked to do so was another level that he would have to get used to. When he first saw this girl's body in the mountain cabin, Tom had been properly shocked. And ever since, he had been waiting for a quiet moment alone to see it again, to study the person he had become in a suitable privacy.

But the thought of stripping off at that moment held him back. It seemed wrong to do it, as if it violated whomever this girl had been to do so. The result was that even though he had the time and privacy to do so, Tom sat still where he was, occasionally turning his head to see himself, now Abby, in the mirror. He could only look for a few seconds at a time before, discouraged, he turned his head away again. So, Abby spent the bulk of his first time alone, his mind swimming in confusion, staring at the floor in front of his feet.

Finally, it was not the soldier that returned first, but Reanah who knocked and quickly entered without first waiting for Abby's permission. She took a quick look at Abby, still dressed in her clothes, and made an annoyed face. She whispered in low, tense voice, "Are you not yet changed? My superiors will be along in a few minutes." Somehow, Abby's hesitation to change clothes was a reflection on her.

Abruptly and without asking, Reanah began to pull off Abby's shirt, tugging at the arms and pulling it roughly up and over his head. Strands of hair got stuck in the fabric, and Abby issued a brief gasp of pain and protest. But otherwise, he did not fight Reanah's efforts.

Once the shirt was free, Abby crossing his arms defensively over his breasts, hiding them more from the reflection in the mirror than from Reanah. But Reanah said, "You and your modesty. Do not be such a prude."

Reanah urged Abby to a standing position. He cooperated but kept his back turned to the mirror. Reanah returned to her efforts and kept at it until she successfully removed Abby's pants and boots.

For a few moments, Abby was naked. This time, the lure of the mirror was too much. As Reanah unfolded and shook out the new clothes, Abby confirmed his worst fears. There was no part of his manhood left. He was now this scrawny, still developing teenage girl with pert breasts and an inward curving waist and outward curving hips, and a little tuft of pubic hair between her legs. No black mass of chest hair, no wide shoulders or muscular arms and legs, or even the pot-belly that caused him embarrassment, but not enough to actually do something about. And definitely no penis or scrotum. And his head was topped by a mass of long, tangled hair. His heart sank into despair.

Reanah readied a loose, white chemise. "Hold up your arms," she said curtly. At first, Abby shook his head and refused. Reanah insisted, "Come on. Do not be a baby." Finally, Abby gave up and lifted his arms, keeping his eyes focused on the side wall rather than the mirror.

Reanah slipped the chemise over his body. It covered the length of his torso to just above his ankles, with loose sleeves and a squared collar which exposed his neck and a section of his upper chest. On his own, Abby quickly tied the strings below the collar to cover the exposed part of the chest.

Then, Reanah slipped the outer dark green dress over Abby's shoulders, which extended all the way to just above the floor. The dress was tied together over the center of Abby's chest with matching eyeholes and leather laces tying the folds of the fabric together. Reanah started slipping the laces through the top holes, then handed the ends to Abby. Speaking as if to a recalcitrant teenager, Reanah said, "Here. You can manage to finish this, can't you?"

Abby reluctantly took the laces in his hands. Then, he looked up at Reanah's face, and much to his own surprise, he started crying. It was not a full-on crying jag, but some light sobbing with real tears suddenly streaming from the corners of his eyes. Embarrassed by the sudden outpouring of emotion, Abby took one hand and covered his face, hiding it from Reanah. "Sorry," he said between hiccupped breaths. "This is all just too much."

Reanah's expression and tone softened. She said, "It's all right. I know this has all very stressful for the past few days." Gently, Reanah took back the laces and finished tying the front of the dress, ending in a bowtie over Abby's neck.

Abby nodded. Trying to collect himself, he whispered, "You have no idea."

Just then, there was a knock at the door. Irritated at the interruption, Reanah turned and snapped at the door, "What?"

The door unlocked and the male elf soldier stuck his head in the opening. "I have the meal."

Reanah waved him in. The soldier slid in through the opening, carefully holding a tray in his arms. Mist steamed from the bowl of soup in the middle, surrounded by an apple, a smooth rounded wooden cup filled with water and a couple of small slices of bread. He carefully set the tray on the dresser, and reached into his rear pocket and withdrew a brush. Holding it out to Reanah, he said, "The girl asked for this."

Taking it from his hand, Reanah nodded. "Dismissed, soldier." He snapped to attention before turning and retreating out the door. The door closed and the lock clicked back into place. Every time that Abby heard the door lock when someone left, he wondered sarcastically to himself, "Am I really that dangerous?"

Reanah grabbed the chair from next to the dresser and faced it toward the side of the bed. In a soft tone, she said, "Sit here and eat. It will help you to feel better."

Abby nodded, stifling his sobbing and trying to gather himself as best he could. He stood and sat in the chair. Reanah transferred the tray from the dresser to the top of the bed. Abby took a wide flat spoon from the tray and carefully sampled the still-steaming soup. "Smells good," he said, stirring through the vegetables and potato slices. He had forgotten how hungry he was. Between sips of water from the cup, he carefully blew the heat away from each spoonful before putting the soup in his mouth. He never knew vegetable soup could be so tasty.

Reanah stood behind him and began to brush out the knots and tangles in Abby's hair. They continued that way for several minutes in silence, Abby eating and Reanah brushing out his hair into a semblance of normal. Gradually, Abby began to calm down.

Finally, Abby finished the meal, using the bread to dab up the last moisture from the soup.

"Better?" Reanah asked gently, flattening out the hair over the top part of Abby's back.

"A little, yeah. Thanks," he answered. He stole another glance at himself, the little girl, in the mirror. Why was he here, in this place?

And, he wondered again, what had happened to the girl who used to be in this body? Those questions would continue to dog him every time he had a contemplative moment. He shook his head and turned away. He had no idea.

With a grim expression on his face, he took the green leather flat shoes and put them on his feet. He placed small thin leather straps over the tops of his ankles, attaching them to small buckles on the outside of each foot. Abby stood, testing the fit by taking several small steps around the end of the bed. He had never seen shoes like that before, but they fit his feet much better than Reanah's oversize trail boots. It was a relief to finally have comfortable shoes in which to walk around.

Abby took a deep breath and nodded at Reanah. He was as ready as he was going to be for whatever was next. Reanah nodded back at him and smiled.

Moments later, in the hallway outside the door, Abby heard the approach of several sets of hard soled boots. After a quick knock on the door, the latch clicked open and the door swung inwards. An older female elf entered, with her uniform and epaulets adorned with the most obvious set of medals and decorations that Abby had seen yet. She was quickly followed, then flanked by two larger male guards who carried serious, stern expressions and an air of protective menace. She was older and less physically fit than Reanah, though still in good shape. Abby's eyes were drawn to the broach she wore on her chest, a golden metal leaf with an ornate design, not just leaves but with a strange, grape-like fruit and a connecting branch that cut diagonally across the design.

Reanah looked surprised to see her, and gave her an extra crisp snap to attention. "General," she said.

"Lieutenant," the elf answered, as if Reanah's deference was expected. She turned toward Abby and walked forward a couple of steps. Sticking out her right hand, she said in a more casual tone, "I'm General Tavi, commander of the garrison here. You must be the human girl the lieutenant discovered near the scene of the fatal accident. Possible robbery by human bandits, I understand. Nasty business." She caught herself and raised her finger to her lips. "I mean to say, of course, the robbers were allegedly humans. Mustn't presume another example of human-on-human violence." She chuckled as if that was funny. "The races must all get along now. Mustn't we?" She ended the thought with broad smile and the completion of a delicate handshake with Abby, only lightly grabbing the tips of his fingers in her greeting.

Abby thought to himself, "Bit of a pompous ass, this one." He smiled and kept his expression otherwise blank. "Yes, ma'am," he answered quietly.

As Abby spoke, another person slipped quietly into the room and slid past the guards into Abby's view. This time, finally, it was a human woman, probably in her mid-fifties. She had a cheeky, round and a well-aged friendly face, and wore a better but similar version of the clothes Abby was given, with an off white muslin undergarment and a green overdress of a thicker, better material and brass eyelets in the open front, tied with leather laces over a plump bodice and ample belly. Abby saw laced leather boots beneath the hem that clicked on the floor as she moved in the room. A soft leather bag with a tasseled cover hung loosely over one shoulder.

She seemed harmless enough, but the others, once she entered, deferred to her immediately. Even the general stepped aside quickly to allow her approach to Abby. The woman spoke to Abby in a soft, friendly tone, "I'm Sister Dana, the Sisterhood's representative here in Jade City. What's your name, dear?"

Although this was the first human that Abby had spoken to, she spoke in the same vaguely British accent as the others.

"Abby," he answered, clearing his throat as he spoke.

Sister Dana nodded, "Abby. Very well. Nice to make your acquaintance." She turned to the general. "I'll have a pleasant conversation with our Abby here and speak to you later."

General Tavi's head twitched as if she had not expected to be dismissed so quickly. After a heartbeat, she answered coolly, "Very well, then. Abby, it was very nice to meet you. Sister Dana will debrief you and I'll attend to

you as I can. Let me know if you need
anything. Good day, ladies." She again gave
Abby a light handshake, then turned and left
the room. The two guards quickly trailed her
out the door.

Reanah exchanged glances with Sister
Dana as if hoping for permission to stay. But
she did not get what she was looking for.
Instead, Sister Dana said with a friendly, though
firm, tone, "You too, Lieutenant. If you do not
want to wait out in the hall, go to the mess and
I'll let you know when I am finished."

Reanah dropped her head to acknowledge
the command. "Ma'am," she said. She stole
one last glance at Abby before heading out the
door. Abby was befuddled by how Reanah had
looked at him as she left. Was it concern? Was
it a warning? But without a chance to say
anything more, Reanah was gone and the latch
clicked shut on the other side.

Once they were alone, Sister Dana turned
and faced Abby, gently grabbing his hands in
her own. "Now then, young lady. Let's have a
look at you."

Sister Dana set her bag on the bed and
opened the top flap. She withdrew a small,
square wooden box, with ornately carved
corners and small hole drilled into the center of
one side. She closed her eyes and whispered
some words that Abby could not make out.
After several seconds, to Abby's surprise, he
could see a faint white glow coming from its
interior through the side hole. As Sister Dana
continued to chant quietly, the brightness

within the box gradually increased until it came out of the box as a faint, focused beam out of the hole.

Finally, Sister Dana opened her eyes stopped her incantation. She turned the box so that its beam pointed at Abby. She began using it to examine Abby, waving the beam over parts of Abby's body and working down from head to toe. Sister Dana's eyes were not actually looking at any part of the box as she moved it about, but she seemed to be getting information from it just the same. Abby stood stiffly, waiting for Sister Dana to finish whatever it was she was doing.

Sister Dana said, as much to herself as to Abby, "Some superficial bruising on your arms and thighs. But nothing seems broken or badly damaged. You'll recover soon enough from your injuries on your own." Sister Dana looked into Abby's eyes for confirmation.

"Yes," Abby replied, nodding. "I'm not in any real pain. Just some soreness."

The beam from the box stopped and Sister Dana seemed satisfied as she returned it to her bag. "Indeed. Nothing physical."

Sister Dana gestured for Abby to sit on the edge of the bed, and positioned the chair to face him. Sister Dana sat close enough for their knees to almost touch.

She reached into her bag and withdrew a strange looking, carved cylindrical wooden tube, closed on one end and open on the other, with a hand grip underneath. At the closed end of the cylinder, a white gem, looking very much like a cut diamond, was embedded in the center. It looked like it had been carved from a single piece of wood with a high amount of skill, covered with careful and elaborate engravings similar to the one on the box.

Sister Dana held it up so that the open end pointed at Abby's face. For the moment, it was inert. Sister Dana seemed to be holding it up more as a threat of what was to come, as if Abby should already have an idea as to what it was and be fearful of it.

In a calm, practiced tone with a trace of aggression, Sister Dana asked, "Why don't we start with your name, your full name? Abby is your nickname, is it? Short for Abigail?"

"Abstinence," Abby corrected. "And I don't have a last name." At least, he thought, not yet anyway.

Sister Dana chuckled. "Now, what sort of mother would name her child 'Abstinence', I ask? Seems like a strange choice. And even if you do not use a last name, surely your family must have had one."

"I gave myself the first name," Abby answered. "I haven't come up with a last name, yet."

Sister Dana furrowed her brow in confusion. "So, you are a runaway, then? The elves say they found you downstream from a terrible accident—a robbery that ended badly for a human woman, apparently—that occurred near their patrol. What do you know about that? Do you know who the woman was?"

Abby shrugged and said, "I don't know anything about that. I woke up in the river and I heard someone, a woman, calling out. No idea who it was. She yelled, 'Leanna!" Mostly, I was just trying not to drown. I went over some falls before I could manage to swim out. That's when Reanah found me. Lieutenant Reanah, I should say."

"Well," Sister Dana countered, "what about prior to that? Where did you come from? How does a human girl come to be in the elven highlands in the first place?"

Abby paused a moment. Should he tell her the truth—that he was a fifty year old man from a place with an apartment and cars and concrete highways and a job that literally sucks the life out of you? That he was stuck here in her reality in a teenage girl's body? At that moment, telling the actual truth seemed the wrong thing to do. It would not seem believable to this woman.

Sister Dana grew impatient. "Nothing else to add, then?"

Abby pursed his lips and shook his head. "Not right now," he answered. "It's too soon."

Sister Dana sighed. "Well, dear, I am sorry but I cannot wait." Gesturing toward the device in her hand, she asked, "Do you know what this is?"

Abby shook his head. "No idea."

Sister Dana turned it around end to end in front of Abby's eyes. "It is what the elves call a 'loquitur veritatem' in the Old Tongue, or what we Sisters refer to as a 'truth teller'. This particular one was constructed for human use. There is a white diamond at this end, to allow me to channel the white spectrum magic that humans are attuned to. It derives its power from the magic flowing upwards from the wellspring beneath this place. If it were for use by the elves, it would have a green gem, to match their race's spectrum color."

Abby furrowed his eyes in confusion. "Wellspring?"

Sister Dana, still smiling gently, could not help a derisive chuckle. "My gracious, dear. Who raised such an ignorant girl? Yes, a 'wellspring'. Prosaically, of course, the basic meaning refers to a water well that accesses a layer of groundwater, so that the water just flows naturally to the surface. In the context of magic, as I mean it, it refers to a place where a fount of magic flows up from deep beneath the earth. From a dimension called the Continuum, the source for all magic of every type. Because of the dimensional filters that such magic passes through on its way to the surface, it can have different colors: white, green, blue, red, yellow and so on.

"Any place that is called a 'city' in the Known World will have such a magical wellspring beneath it. That is why this place, really just a frontier outpost, is called Jade City. It earns the designation from the wellspring of green-tinged magic from the Continuum that reaches the surface here.

"Elves, specifically the magically attuned ones of their race, have a natural affinity for such green magic. Each of the races has a natural talent for magic of a certain color. Dwarves work best with yellow magic. Orcs, goblins, vampires and other nasty creatures of darkness use red magic. Blue magic was the preference of the now-extinct fairy race, and now it is more neutral and can be used by all the races, though its power is diminished compared to the others."

Pointing to herself, Sister Dana continued, "Humans, though only the women of our race, have an affinity for white magic. Those women who have a natural skill for it are recruited at an early age to become members of the Sisterhood. We are the custodians of the knowledge and lore of the white magic on behalf of all the human race, to use it for the benefit of all."

To Abby, this seemed like a bunch of nonsensical gobbledygook. Magic? That seemed crazy. He shook his head in confusion and said, "There's no magic where I'm from. All of this is new to me."

That actually surprised Sister Dana. "No magic! Really? Wellsprings as I describe them are scattered throughout the known world. Wherever you were born, surely there had to be one near you? And, surely, a Sister would have tested you for your affinity for white magic at a much younger age? That is the way of things wherever there are humans. It is the law."

She seemed genuinely taken aback. "What did you do for heat, light, and power? What happened when someone was sick or injured?

You could not have been so removed from the modern conveniences that magic from wellsprings provide. Your family could not have lived as savages to that extent."

Abby laughed at Sister Dana's incredulity, drawing a sour face from the Sister in reply. But Abby hesitated before replying. If Sister Dana could not imagine a world without magic, Abby could not imagine a world with magic. His world, Tom's reality, was a world in which science and technology was the backbone of society, and electricity and fossil fuels provided the power for his 'modern' conveniences.

For a second, he considered blurting it all out—who he really was, where he was from. But there was something in Sister Dana's manner, despite her outward warmth and friendliness, which prevented him from just telling her. He did not trust her.

Instead, looking for more information, Abby asked, "What's with the box and that thing? Why do you need objects to help you? If you can use magic, can't you just cast a spell?"

Sister Dana chuckled, "It's not like the fairy stories, dear. There are no wands, and no incantations that will cause something to happen. If one is close to a magical wellspring as a source of magic, the devices allow trained, attuned persons such as myself to invoke its power. But to actually use magic, a tool for the specific purpose is required. To turn it on, as it were.

"The first device you saw is for healing. It's called a 'medicus', and has a rare bit of metal, earthenium, a catalyst that conducts magic imbedded in the center. It can both detect and repair physical injury, even serious ones."

Sister Dana waved the cylindrical tube with the embedded diamond before Abby's eyes. She continued, "This, on the other hand, is the truth teller. As the name suggests, its magic requires the person on whom its power is trained to speak only the truth. In my hands, it will help me to draw whatever I wish to know from you."

She leaned forward and continued, more intently and with a trace of menace in her voice, "So do not attempt to hide information from me, or lie to me my dear. One of the effects of it is that a lie or deception will result in physical pain for you. The more that you resist me, the more it will hurt you."

To Abby, Sister Dana seemed to enjoy explaining that to him just a little too much. He quickly glanced around the room, suddenly feeling trapped by the windowless, small space and the locked door that would prevent him from fleeing.

Abby countered, "And if I refuse? Perhaps that will not work as well as you think." His tone was brave, but he was actually trying to stall until he could think of something he could do to defend himself.

Sister Dana waved her hand, dismissing the idea. "You have no choice, dear. If I have to call the guards in to pin you down, I will. But that will only make the process more difficult, for both of us but for you especially. No, this will go much more easily if you simply submit and answer my questions fully and truthfully. Then, we can both proceed through the rest of your time here on good terms."

Abby's mind raced, but he could not think of anything he could do. He even considered punching Sister Dana square in the face. But there were guards right outside the door, and he had no idea what this magic user could do to him if he assaulted her. For the moment, he had no options, other than to bear whatever was about to come.

Sister Dana's took his silence as refusal. She raised the cylinder and pointed its open end toward Abby's face. At first, he was staring down an empty wooden tube. But Sister Dana furrowed her eyebrows in concentration, and a white glow tinged with green began to build within the device.

As the glow shone in his face, Abby started to panic. Although he was not bound physically to the chair, he began to feel pinned in place, unable to move. He could only stare straight ahead as the magic began to build.

"Now, then," Sister Dana began calmly, "tell me your real name."

Abby began to feel a pressure emanating from the beam. His full name—first, middle and last—the one from Tom's birth certificate, began echo in his mind. The pressure continued to build, until reciting his name was almost the only thing he wanted to do at that point. Fighting and struggling against the urge, Abby closed his eyes and protested loudly, "No!"

There was a sudden flash of pure, white light, like a camera strobe going off. A sharp, almost deafening crack echoed through the room. Sister Dana yelped in pain and her hand recoiled. Her truth teller went dark and fell to the floor. The white diamond embedded in the closed end of the device broke free and rattled separately away, ending up under the bed.

The pressure on Abby vanished as if it were never there, and his mind returned to its own, private thoughts. In the seconds after, as Abby's eyes recovered from the sudden burst of light, Abby stared wide eyed in confusion at Sister Dana. What happened? Did she mean to do that? He waited for her to explain.

Sister Dana, though, seemed even more surprised than Abby, returning his stare with obvious shock and confusion. There was even the first glint of fear. Of Abby. She opened her mouth to speak, before giving up and reverting back to a stunned silence. She obviously had no idea as to what had just happened.

Finally, after several seconds, Sister Dana recovered herself enough to remember to retrieve the pieces of her device. She dropped down to her hands and knees on the floor, grabbing the wooden portion of the truth teller in one hand and reaching under the bed to locate the diamond with the other. Once they were collected, she sighed and returned to the chair, facing Abby once again.

This time, though, there was more of an air of Sister Dana facing an equal, rather than another mere victim of her manipulations. Abby, for his part though, still had no idea what the hell was going on.

"Well, my heavens," Sister Dana gasped finally, "that's quite something. I felt a pushback from you, quite a large one. Do you have the ability? Are you attuned to magic, I mean?"

Abby shook his head. "No, I don't think so." That was a truthful statement that she did not have to force from him.

Sister Dana said, "Are you sure you've never been tested? As I stated before, members of the Sisterhood will attempt to test young girls within the Queendom between six and eight years old to gauge their aptitude. The ones that show a positive result are sent to Crystal City to study with our order. Surely, you were examined when you were at that age."

Abby had no idea whether the girl whose body he now inhabited had been tested or not. Presumably, she had been checked and failed the test. Otherwise, Abby supposed, she too would have wound up as a Sister.

"No idea," Abby answered, and gave a follow up that was true enough, for him. "I've never been tested for magical aptitude in my life. Remember, I already told you that I've no prior experience with this magic stuff."

As truthfully spoken as Abby's words were, Sister Dana did not appear to believe them. Finally recovered from her shock, she said, "Well, perhaps. Or perhaps not. For all I know, you are a rogue magic user that has been caught for the first time. We will see." Rising to her feet, she continued, "I do not have my instrument to test your aptitude with me. My guess is that what has happened here is a good preliminary positive result." Almost to herself, wresting with the ideas swirling in her mind, she concluded quietly, "Perhaps we'll try again tomorrow. Rest up. The Mother of Sisters says 'the truth will reveal itself to those who seek it.' I am sure that will be the case for you and me as well."

Even that sounded to Abby like a bit of a threat. He remained silent as Sister Dana turned to leave.

She eyed Abby warily. "I'll return tomorrow afternoon and we'll continue this. Perhaps in the meantime you'll consider the benefits of being more cooperative. It could assist your case if you are found to be a rogue witch."

Abby remained seated. He did not like the sound of that. "Fine," he said quietly.

Sister Dana turned and went to the door and knocked twice. The door unlocked from the other side, and a guard pushed it open. Without another word or farewell, Sister Dana left.

Almost immediately and before the door closed again, Reanah entered with a worried expression on her face. As the door closed and locked behind her, she slid quickly to the chair facing Abby. In a low, confidential tone, she asked, "What happened? I heard a loud report, like a muffled thunderclap. Everyone out in the hallway all started at the sound of it. When the guard opened the door, I half expected to see both of you unconscious in here."

"Nothing," Abby growled, still angry with the thought that Sister Dana was going to extract information out of him, painfully if necessary. "I mean, I don't know what it was. For a second, I assumed she did it. Or her truth thingy broke." His voice rose as his frustration poured out, "Then, she acted as if I did it. She even called me a 'rogue witch', whatever the hell that is."

Reanah frowned. "Those are grave words to use against you. A rogue witch is an unauthorized magic user. All human women with the aptitude must by law be members of the Sisterhood. Other races have similar rules as well. Those that will not join can be imprisoned. Those that use magic to commit criminal acts can be put to death. Even summarily, if the threat is dire enough." She sighed before finishing, "The fact that she confronts you with that charge is quite serious."

Abby grew angry. "That's ridiculous! I just find out that there is such a thing as magic, for real, and now I'm accused of using it? I don't know what gave Sister Dana that impression, but she's wrong, Reanah. I swear it as much as I can swear that anything is true."

Reanah seemed to want to give Abby the benefit of the doubt, but she said, "I want to believe you, Abby. Truly. You must tell me one thing, though, and I will judge you harshly if I find you have lied to me."

"Sure, Reanah," Abby answered. "Just ask."

Reanah replied, "After we found you at the base of the falls, one of my party went back with one of our detectors, one that can sense the use of magic after the fact. He found traces of it in the air, like the glowing embers of a spent campfire. Someone had used magic there quite recently before our arrival." She met Abby's eyes to burn the question into him, "Tell me true, was that you?"

Abby returned her gaze and said with as much sincerity as he could project, "That wasn't me, Reanah. Promise. I can't tell you if someone else was there. I didn't see anyone except you and the other female elf. But I had nothing to do with that. I was too busy trying not to drown."

Reanah nodded, "Well, in your favor, there were certainly no devices on your person, or any we could locate in the area. The accident site upstream seemed absent of any trace of magic whatsoever. Also, we were many miles from any wellspring. The fact that any magical imprint was present there at all was an oddity, to be sure." She seemed to make up her mind as she concluded, "I do take your words to heart, Abby. Unless you demonstrate something that I have not yet seen to disprove your innocence, I believe you. If I can help you with Sister Dana, to keep her from coming at you too aggressively, I will." Reanah seemed quite sincere about it.

Abby was relieved that he at least had one person on his side. He said, "What is it with her, anyway? We had only talked for a couple of minutes before she whipped out her truth teller. She didn't even give me a chance to lie to her."

Reanah shrugged. "She is not malicious. Not really. It is just that she is like a wolf once she senses her prey. She will not stop until she catches what she is after, whether she shreds it or not."

"And what does she want to get out of me, then?" Abby countered. "Whatever she, or even you, thinks, I am no threat to anyone." And, to repeat the point to Reanah, he concluded emphatically, "And I have no magical ability whatever. None. Period."

Reanah visibly sighed with relief. "Very well, then. You and I have an understanding."

Abby said with a quiet grimness, "That still leaves tomorrow, though. Sister Dana said she is coming back with her own magic detector. After what just happened, I don't like the idea that she's going use one of her little toys on me again."

Reanah leaned close to Abby and whispered, "Don't fear. I'll speak to my commander to see if she'll have a word with her. Jade City is a military outpost, administered by our Queen's government.

Ours is the law here. I'm sure the General can convince Sister Dana to moderate her approach to you. There's no need for such tactics."

Despite Reanah's assurances, Abby felt sick to his stomach. What had he done to deserve this? Suddenly, he felt very much like a prisoner, and this room with the nice fluffy bed and clean sheets was his cell. Fatigue came over him, finally catching up to him after the long day.

Abby reached up and began to rub his temple. "If it's all the same, Reanah, I need some rest. Right now, all I want to do is sleep."

Reanah straightened up and nodded. "Of course. This is quite a lot for a young girl to deal with. Relax. Rest up. You'll feel much better after a good rest. I'll attend to you in the morning."

Reanah made her way to the door. Before knocking to exit, though, she pointed up at one of the wall sconces that were illuminating the room in each corner. "Do you want me to turn these off? It will make it easier to rest."

Abby looked around. He had noticed them on the way in. The four little ornately carved wooden boxes provided the room with a soft white light tinged with green. Having listened to Sister Dana's explanation of magic and wellsprings and the elves' affinity for the green types of both, Abby guessed that was the reason for their greenish hue.

Given that he had no idea of how to operate the magical devices, Abby nodded. "Please. That would be better."

Reanah went to each one and reached up with one hand while mumbling an incantation. After a few seconds, the light coming from the top of each box dimmed, then went out. Before turning off the last one, Reanah said gently, "Good night. Rest easy."

She knocked on the back of the door. The door unlatched and swung open, and the light of the hallway spilled into the now-darkened room. Reanah reached up and turned off the last light box, then quietly slipped out the door. It locked behind her.

The room was now completely dark, except for a small sliver of light coming from beneath the door. Abby was finally alone, and exhausted. He used his hands to position himself on the center of the bed to lay down. The sheets were still folded in a pile at the end of the bed, so he stretched out on top. Even so, it was still a big improvement from a blanket on the forest floor, which were the accommodations of the last two plus days.

Abby shook his head and whispered into the darkness, "What a crazy world." Within moments, he was asleep.

***

Abby woke sometime in the middle of the night. He was not exactly sure what time it was. There was still a thin sliver of light coming from the bottom of the doorway, but there was a complete lack of background noise coming from the hallway. It was utterly still.

No one was talking, no one was moving. If he had to guess, it was in the early hours of the morning.

Abby blinked and tried to focus on what he could see in the room. The little light that was present was barely enough for Abby to see his own hand as he waved it in front of his eyes. He cursed himself for not asking Reanah to leave just one of the light boxes on.

Abby slid to the side of the bed and sat up in the darkness. He wanted to use this quiet time to be able to finally reflect and consider what to do to help himself. And, he wanted to see himself in the mirror once again, to see the person he had become.

To do that, he would first need one of the light boxes to be turned on. For a moment, he thought about knocking on the back of the door and calling to someone in the hallway to do it for him. But he was not sure if anyone was actually out there. Besides, he wondered, would anyone actually help him, or just tell him to shut up and wait until the morning?

Abby did not even know what they were called, or how they worked, exactly. He did not remember seeing any sort of an on/off switch on the light boxes, or wires connecting them to the wall. Each box just sat in its metal sconce, glowing until someone turned it off.

Reanah had spoken to each one, as if there were some spell required. She had repeated the words four separate times. Abby wondered if he could remember them. If so, perhaps he could figure out how to turn one on himself.

Surely, a non-magical person could operate a light switch. It couldn't be that hard, he thought. In the few days he had known Reanah, he did not ever see any sign that she had magical powers or magical devices in the same way as Sister Dana. There had to be a trick to it, if he could puzzle it out.

Although he was still quite tired, Abby decided to attempt to turn on one light box before he went back to sleep. Besides, he reasoned, a little light would allow him to make the bed properly. Worst case, if he failed, he would ask Reanah in the morning how to do it. It would be his first acquired knowledge in this new reality, to help him control his own situation at least a little bit.

Turning to the task, Abby realized he would need to stand on something to even reach one. Reanah was tall enough to just extend her hand over her head and touch them. With his diminished stature, Abby was not going to be able to manage it without a chair.

He remembered that the chair was on the other side of the bed from the one he was currently facing. He quietly slid off the bed and found his shoes. He slipped them on and tightened the laces, then slowly felt his way around the foot of the bed. He kept one hand touching the bed, and waved the other arm in the darkness until he made contact with the top of the chair.

Once he had a hand on it, there was just enough light from the doorway for Abby to take a couple of steps toward a corner of the room. He positioned the chair against a side wall underneath one of the sconces.

Once in place, Abby stepped onto the chair and rose up until he had both feet safely beneath him. He reached up. His fingertips slid up the bottom of the metal of the sconce, until he touched the light box with the fingers of both hands. He gently lifted it out of its mount, then carefully backed down until he was back standing on the floor.

In the almost total darkness, Abby turned the light box over for a few seconds in his hands, examining it by touch. There was no obvious switch or button, even though he kept pressing his fingers on various parts of it, looking for something to trigger it into operating. Besides the carvings, which seemed strictly ornamental, he could only detect the hole drilled into one side that allowed the light out of the interior.

Finally, he decided to test his memory of Reanah's incantations. He closed his eyes and tried to repeat the words as best he could. But he mispronounced even the words he could remember, and he never got close to repeating each of the phrases, in the proper order.

He grew discouraged. It seemed such a simple thing, but he could not make it work.

At the end of his efforts, Abby tried to command it by force of will. "Turn on!" he said, his frustration making his voice louder than he intended. He froze, wondering if anyone outside the door had heard him. After several seconds, though, the silence of the night was undisturbed.

Abby exhaled in relief. He returned his attention to the light box. He would try one last time before giving up and going back to bed.

In thinking later about what happened next, Abby would wonder what inspired him to try what he did. In his frustration, he decided to see if he did, indeed, have some magic in him.

Abby closed his eyes and focused his concentration on the light box. This time, instead of reciting some memorized incantation, the command to the lightbox was from within his mind, transmitted via his fingertips. "Turn on," he thought over and over, without speaking the words out loud.

Nothing happened at first, and he almost gave up. But he continued to focus, repeating the words in his mind, trying to connect with whatever in the box was receptive to receive his command.

Suddenly, his mind found the connection he was looking for. Instead of the outer wooden material of the box, his mental focus shifted to the small bit of metal lodged within it. Earthenium, Sister Dana had called it.

Once Abby's thought had touched it, the metal flared into life as magic flowed outwards from Abby into the box. Abby opened his eyes.

White light, pure in its whiteness and much brighter and much more intense by several factors than the soft green-tinted glow that had illuminated the room during the day, poured from the small opening at the top of the box. The room was now fully illuminated from the one light box in clear, stark brightness, causing Abby to blink for a few seconds until his eyes adjusted to the sudden, unexpected onslaught of light.

Thinking the sudden illumination was visible under the door in the hallway, Abby tried using one hand to cover the opening. He did succeed in cutting the amount of light in the room, but he noticed something else. His hand, his smallish girl's hand, was glowing with white magic as well, as if his own skin was infused with it. He quickly looked at his other hand, then with his free hand drew the sleeve back on his chemise and examined his forearm. All of the exposed skin glowed. Looking down the length of his body, he could see the glow even through the clothes. He glanced at the mirror. Even his head and face shone like some oversized light bulb. He did not feel any pain at all, but the effect was unnerving.

Abby began to panic. Had he done something to himself? What was happening?

For an instant, his grip loosened on the light box and he fumbled it, almost dropping it. As it flipped around in his fingers, the beam of white light coming from the top of the box flashed around the room as the box spun.

Abby noticed suddenly that the beam seemed to penetrate the walls and ceiling of the room as it spun around, the light penetrating and illuminating what was on the other side of the formerly solid surface. The beam even revealed the innards of the wall—a mortared stone center covered by plaster and a thin outer layer of paint—and penetrating into the space beyond. Startled by this, he gathered the box back into his right hand, and put his left hand over the opening to prevent the beam from coming out. His hand, though still giving off its own glow, was unaffected by the beam, cutting it off and keeping it within the light box.

Abby paused for a moment to think about this distinction. The beam could go through a solid wall but not his own hand, which itself was infused with its own magic. He could not think of why that might be, but resolved to experiment with it for a few moments.

He again listened for any sign that anyone in the hallway had noticed. The only sounds were Abby's own tense breathing and beating heart, which he tried to calm as best he could. Even though the beam was hidden, there was now enough ambient lighting in the room, mostly coming from him, that Abby could see everything illuminated with a ghostly white light.

After a few seconds of gathering himself, Abby thought about the way the beam penetrated through to the outside of the room. Could he use it to look around? He walked hesitantly toward the door.

When he was ready, Abby rotated the light box until it faced the back of the door, and slowly withdrew the hand blocking the beam.

A bright, wide circular beam shone outward, making the door transparent on the area it contacted. Abby could see out into the hallway beyond. He moved it around, up toward the ceiling then down the wall on the far side. He could see a wall sconce with a light box, giving off the normal, soft, green-hued light. As he moved the beam down, toward the floor, he caught a glimpse of the back of an elf solder, apparently sitting on the floor, sleeping. Abby gasped and quickly covered the beam up with his free hand. Once gone, the door and the walls of the room returned to their normal, solid state.

Abby stood for several seconds, both confused and fascinated. The light beam had passed through solid wood and stone, as if it was not even there. But with the beam covered, the door and the wall returned to normal. Although he did not understand what was happening, Abby realized this was something he could use to his advantage.

He decided to try to do more than just look around. Abby closed his eyes, trying again to make a mental connection with the bit of earthenium in the light box. It reacted in reply. This time, instead of pulling back, Abby continued to pour his concentration into the connection.

The beam from the light box and the hand he was using to cover the beam seemed to interact with each other, and the intensity of the beam and the glow emanating from his skin began to get slowly brighter and brighter.

There was still no pain or any other physical sensation accompanying this effect.

Once the magic had grown to a high intensity, Abby carefully set the light box on the top of the bed, facing a side wall, and pulled both his hands away.

Now, the light emanating from the box covered a much wider area. It exposed a circular opening from just above the floor to almost the ceiling. Abby could now see through the wall and into the darkness of the room beyond.

Fascinated, Abby moved slowly toward the illuminated area, and extended a hand. He expected at some point to touch the wall, even if it were transparent. But instead, his fingertips and then the rest of his hand met no resistance as they passed through where the wall should have been. Abby was dumbfounded. The wall was not just transparent. It was as if the wall was not even there!

In disbelief, Abby ducked his head and stepped through the opening. His entire body passed through without resistance.

As the light continued to shine from the room behind him, he looked around. This room was slightly different. Instead of a bed and dresser, there was a square meeting table with simple wooden chairs on each side. Off to the side, there was a writing desk and chair, with papers strewn loosely on the top and an ink well and blotter and quill pen in one corner.

Abby surveyed the scene for several quiet seconds before realizing this room had one other thing that his room did not—a window. Moonlight from a clear spring night shone in through it. He moved carefully towards it, avoiding contact with the furniture. Reaching it, he gently unlatched the two panes and pushed them outwards. Cool, damp air poured in, sending a chill through him. But he gratefully breathed in the freshness of the air. It tasted of freedom.

He leaned out of the window and looked out into the street. There was enough light from the sky to see the outlines of the surrounding buildings, and the cobblestone street below. A light fog was barely present, obscuring the details of more far away objects.

He was on the ground floor. Abby estimated the distance to the pavement below to be about ten feet. It would only be a short drop out of the window to the street.

If, that is, he wanted to leave. It would almost be easy. But getting out of the building would only be the start of it. What made him hesitate was the thought of being alone, fending for himself in this strange, new place. For all Reanah's soldierly gruffness, Abby could tell she was basically kind, and she was looking out for him in her own way. If he left, it would be a violation of the trust Reanah had put in him.

Sister Dana, though, was another matter. Abby took it as a threat when Sister Dana declared she would be back to question him again. This time, with some new magic toy to try on him, who knew what she would do? Even though Reanah said that Sister Dana was not that malicious, Abby did not like the idea of her using her magic to mess around with his mind. His past as Tom was his secret, and Sister Dana did not deserve to know about it. Unless he felt like telling her, or Reanah, or anyone else.

Abby glanced back at the opening in the wall. The light box in the previous room was still shining its bright, white light, but it seemed to be losing a little of its intensity. Abby walked over to the opening in the wall. The lessening of the beam had caused the opening to recede. If he went back now, he would actually have to both duck his head, and step over the base of the circle. Abby realized that if he wanted to return, he would have to do it soon.

At that point, though, Abby had basically decided to leave. He had no idea where he would go or what he would do. But he knew he had to go.

Briefly, he thought about going back to the place in the mountains where he had come into this strange, new world. Perhaps, whatever opening in reality had passed him through to that place was still there, and he could go back to his own world. He could be Tom again.

But, instinctively, that did not seem to be the correct answer. In his gut, he felt there was somewhere else he had to go, something else he had to do. Then, and only then, would he be released from this place.

By that point, the light from the other room was noticeably dimmer, and the opening in the wall had shrunk to a circle about two feet across in the middle of the room. He looked at his own hands. They, too, had lost much of their luminescence. Abby realized he did not have much time left with the illumination in the room, before he would be left in darkness again.

Quickly, he scanned the top of the room, looking for more light boxes. There were a couple in their mounts on wall sconces, one right over the writing desk. Abby quickly spun the desk chair around and climbed onto the top of the desk. He gently removed the light box and climbed back down, being careful not to trigger it in any way. He did not want this one to get out of control in the way the other one did. He resolved to himself that sometime later, away from this place, he would play with it and figure out how to make it work properly. He wedged the light box into an opening between two pieces of fabric in his outer dress.

At that moment, though, Abby's goal was to leave. But he did feel genuinely sorry about leaving Reanah without a final goodbye. To assuage his guilt, he decided to leave a quick note for her. He picked up the quill from the desk and uncapped the ink well. Tom, in his youth, had played around with fountain pens, but he had never tried an actual quill pen.

In the last of the dying light coming from the neighboring room, he dipped the quill into the well and withdrew it with a large drop of ink dangling from the end. He gently applied the pen to a sheet of thick, handmade paper—

and promptly made a large, unformed blotch. "Crap," he muttered. He tried to drag the pen out of the still wet ink to form a 't', but he only managed to make a vertical line before the ink dried too much to trace anything more.

Abby exhaled his frustration, but decided to try again with a little more finesse. He dipped his quill again into the well, but this time rubbed the end on the lip of the bottle to remove any excess ink. This time, he managed to cross the 't' and started on an 'h'. With a little patience, he kept at it and managed to write out, "Thanks, Rena, sorry Abby" in rough letters across the width of the paper.

By now, the opening to the other room was almost closed, and the last of the light from the other room was dying out. He put the quill down and looked at his thin, delicate fingers. The glow was almost gone from them as well. Instead, the two fingertips that had touched the pen, plus the thumb, were now covered in ink. For a moment, he almost wiped them off on his clothes, but thought better of it. He rubbed the stained fingers back and forth on another sheet of paper until the ink was at least dry on his fingers.

As he turned to returned to the window, the side wall had returned to its solid form, and his former room was lost to his view. The only light in the room came from the night sky shining through the opened window, illuminating the room in grey relief. There was no going back now.

Abby went to the window and climbed onto the sill. As he went through the opening, he realized that one good thing about being much smaller, younger, and lighter was that he was able to fit easily through the frame. He spun around and gently lowered himself over the ledge, hanging from it for a few seconds until he was sure he had a good idea of the distance to the cobblestones below.

Finally, he let go and dropped quietly to the street. The soles of his shoes made a subdued slap as they contacted with the pavement, but someone would have had to been standing within a few feet to hear it. Abby sensed that no one had any idea that he was there.

His first instinct was just to start running. He did run for several strides, with the light sound of his shoes echoing between the buildings in the deserted street. What slowed him down was not the noise he was making, or the effort of running while wearing a long dress that reached down to his ankles, but the new and uncomfortable sensation of his breasts as they bounced and jangled under his chemise. This was something he was most definitely not used to, and he quickly slowed to a normal walking pace.

Surely, Abby thought, girls can run without a bra on, can't they? Perhaps if he was more used to them, he could manage it. But not right at that moment. He rationalized that a normal walking pace would attract less attention anyway, and it would be some time before the elves realized he was gone and sound the alarm.

He wondered in passing whether this reality even had bras. Abby shrugged and chuckled that perhaps his destiny was to bring bras into this world. Invent the bra and then go home. The thought made him laugh out loud.

The sound reverberated between the buildings and Abby realized that he would have to be more careful. Until he was out of Jade City, he would not be safe. Just get out of this place, he thought to himself. Figure the rest out later.

He drew the crisp, cool air freely in and out of his lungs, enjoying the sensation. At least in this body, he did not have asthma anymore. That was one good thing.

FIVE: SIDRA

Under the same starry sky, many miles to the east in the grassy plains east of the same mountain range, night was hiding the exodus from Pearl City. Hadrea's magic had worked its powers of the former citizens of the town, transforming them and placing them under her control. Now, there was a long line of roughly two thousand newly created ghouls winding its way south, bound to Hadrea's service.

The ghouls were the former human residents of Pearl City, left behind after Hadrea's storm of dark magic had finished its work on them. Their bodies had been burnt and bruised and, for some, bones had been broken and limbs ripped from torsos. Yet there was no death for these creatures. The human souls trapped within each ghoul providing the living life force sustaining the creature they became. But they lost all control over their own bodies, which Hadrea's magic took over into a kind of collective, shared intelligence. They could see and hear and feel pain. But there would be no relief for them, no healing or reprieve from the pain that coursed through their bodies. They were slaves to the spirit and magic that now trapped and held their shattered minds and drove them on as they shuffled on the road south.

Any living creature, whether animal or human that now crossed their path, were quickly dispatched in a frenzy of chasing, then killing, then ripping of flesh. Coordinated by their collective hive mind of the undead, they moved in packs at a time before returning to the rest of the brood to return to their steady march. While anyone who had known them in life might have still been able to recognize the faces, their individuality had been scrubbed from them, and their frightened souls were trapped and helpless. Their cell was their own body, and they had as much control over their destiny as a prisoner has over a jail.

The price for Hadrea was the death of her mortal body. Her mind and her consciousness still existed as a vague swirl of dark mist, barely perceptible even if one looked directly at it. To exist, she needed a source of magic to sustain herself. At that moment, she had one, barely. If she wished to grow and become corporeal once again, far more power than was currently available was required. But she already had a plan to obtain a new source of magic for her needs. She just needed to be taken there.

Leading the parade, though, was a very different creature from all the others. A solitary figure that did not need sleep or food, she walked with an imperious dignity that belied the fact that she, too, was a servant. Dressed in a white flowing gown that would have seemed inadequate to the chill air and the open road, her pale skin glowed in the moonlight as a constant reminder of the power that coursed through her.

Her eyes were a fierce green and her lips were blood red, prominent features in contrast to the rest of her pale face, framed by the long, straight black hair that framed her head and rested halfway down her back. Her hard expression bore the serious, determined mien of a true believer, certain in her beliefs and power. As distasteful as it was to have this horde of ravenous mindless rabble behind her, she would see this through, in return for what was promised.

Sidra had come to her present state by choice. She had been an apprentice to Hadrea when both were members of the Sisterhood. The two had been assigned by the Mother of Sisters to study dark magic and lore, though both had a natural aptitude for it. Hadrea was the teacher and mentor, older and more knowledgeable on the subject than any other Sister. Sidra was the enthusiastic student, sponging up what Hadrea could teach and yearning for more. They traveled extensively in search of books and lore about dark magic, with the intention to learn the means to defend the Sisterhood against such magic.

But more and more, as the months and years went by, their obsessive work became about enhancing their own power, as they began to grasp what was possible with dark magic. They became estranged from the Sisterhood, and refused to be bound by its rules and vows. Once they were confident in their power and skill in the dark arts, once their goals were in place, it was time for them to strike out on their own.

To begin, they traveled to the northernmost mountains in the Known World, a place even more northerly than the Iron Kingdom, the lands of the dwarves. They managed with effort and determination to locate a place known in legends simply as The Source, a powerful wellspring of red magic. To those versed in the lore of magic, red magic and dark magic were synonymous, and any wellspring of red magic acted as a magnet for demons, ghouls, and other creatures that derived their power from, and used, dark magic.

The Source was controlled and guarded by a coven of vampires. Like ghouls, vampires began first in this reality as other humanoids, born and raised into the world as a human, elf or dwarf. A new vampire was created by the fatal bite from another vampire. After some period of time, usually after the funeral, the newly created vampire rose from the grave, empowered by dark magic, and eventually migrate to the northern regions of the Known

World, drawn both by the power of The Source, and by the protection of the other vampires.

Although Hadrea and Sidra had traveled to that place as companions, and had known each other for years, it was only on their arrival that Hadrea made her true intentions known. The vampires had, of course, caught them fairly quickly on their approach, but Hadrea had offered no resistance, despite her considerable skills and defenses. And she had also cautioned Sidra to not resist their capture.

Thus, the two humans had been brought into the heart of the Coven by its rulers to learn their fate. The Coven resented the intrusion of the humans, and detested them as Sisters of the Sisterhood, a group which hunted them and was their only real rivals in terms of magical power and knowledge of magical lore. Even in that faraway place, the Coven knew that the humans, in the presence of the Source and thus able to draw power from it, were to be feared.

Under normal circumstances, the humans would have endured a violent, tortured death, and, if they had begged for mercy, the Coven could have decided whether to grant them the privilege of becoming vampires themselves. Yet, apparently, the humans had come of their own free will, and had not defended themselves when they were captured. Why?

When the humans were standing before the Coven and faced with that question, Hadrea's answer was to withdraw from a hidden pouch near her heart, a large ornamental golden key with a large red ruby inset into the large end. It was the same key that had dropped to the floor on Hadrea's arrest, and the same key that Sidra would later steal back from Pearl City in the place where the Sisters had attempted to secure it. It was the same key that Sidra now cradled in her hands on her journey south, at the head of Hadrea's new army of ghouls.

It was the Crystal Key of Amadine. Made centuries before in a lost time and for an unknown purpose, the Crystal Key had been designed with one sole purpose, as a storage device for a gigantic amount of magic. Etched into its sides were words from an ancient language, an incantation that allowed the user to both open it as a means to store magical power, and to release the magic, guided by the will of its user.

In the hands of a skilled magic caster, such a device, once fully charged, would give the user access to almost unimaginable amounts of power, without the need to be close to any wellspring. It was as if Hadrea held her own private wellspring in her hands.

Hadrea had found it almost by accident, years before, in a basement room in the Sisterhood's Keep, its magic long spent and the crystal dark and dead. It had been locked away for decades, logged on an archivist's inventory, then forgotten. Once Hadrea came upon it, the red color of its gem gave away the intent of its maker, as a vessel of dark magic. She immediately recognized its potential. And, over time, Hadrea had deciphered the incantations, and learned it basic functions. She, and she alone, knew how to use it.

So, Sidra had been more than a little shocked when Hadrea presented the Crystal Key to the Coven, revealing it to her and them for the first time. To Sidra, it was a kind of betrayal. In all the time that the two knew and worked with each other, Hadrea had never mentioned the Key, not once. When Hadrea announced her plans for the two of them to travel north and find the Source, she did not reveal her possession of the Key and her desire to show it to the Coven.

Sidra, then, had assumed it was just another trip to locate more of Hadrea's bobbles and dark lore to add to their collection. It was only after their meek capture and only after the two had been brought irrevocably into the heart of the Coven, that Hadrea revealed her true plan.

In hindsight, Sidra might have guessed that Hadrea's true intent was gain access to the Source for her own purposes, it being the largest wellspring of red magic in the Known World, and closest to Hadrea's home outside of Pearl City. The others were much, much farther away to the east, in the Lands of the Dead. And in those dark places, it was unlikely that the two of them would be able to reason and bargain with the creatures that might come upon them there.

The Source, then, was the only place in which the Crystal Key could be fully charged and still allow Hadrea to return to her home to enact the remainder of her plans. All she would need was the cooperation and assistance of the Coven, the custodians of the Source. That assistance was what Hadrea had come to the Coven to bargain for.

In order for the Key to be fully charged, it would take the entire Coven several days of chanting and invocations, to draw magic from the Source into the Key's gem. And, once charged, the holder of that Key would be formidable, even compared to the combined power of the Coven at the heart of their power. Yet, Hadrea was asking that the vampires simply charge the Key with their magic and hand it back over to her, to do with it as she willed. Hadrea expected, then, the price extracted by the Coven to be a high one.

In that crucial moment, the Hadrea's need for Sidra's presence became clear. She was the pawn in Hadrea's plan, the offering Hadrea would make to the Coven. Sidra would have to give up her humanity and become a vampire herself. Once Sidra had become thus transformed, she would no longer be a Sister but a member of the Coven, bound by its rules and subject to its will. Going forward, Sidra would be as much their instrument as Hadrea's, as Hadrea enacted her vengeance on the rest of humanity.

That would mean her death as a human, there in that dark and frightful place. In order to become a vampire, the bite from a vampire would have to drain her blood so completely that she would die. Then, she would rise again, still possessed of her mind and memories, but no longer human. She would be an undead creature of the night, subject to their limitations and cravings, an enemy of the living.

Sidra, though, had few options at that point. That was the beauty of Hadrea's plan. Sidra could try to run, defend herself as best she could before she was cut down. The only way she could insure that she would not become a vampire against her will would be inflict the final, fatal blow herself, guaranteeing that it was not a bite from one of the creatures that caused her death. That meant committing a form of suicide, resisting but dying in a manner and at a moment that Sidra would have to control herself.

But Hadrea had picked her well for this role. Sidra held herself too high in esteem to destroy all that she was by suicide. And, more importantly, Hadrea knew there was something Sidra wanted more than anything, a price that would make her personal sacrifice worth it to obtain.

Sidra wanted to be the head of the Sisterhood, the Mother of Sisters. In Sidra's generation of Sisters, she was not the best, most favored of them. From her induction at the age of eight, through her education and training, Sidra had excelled. But she was never considered among the best and brightest of her group. When it came time for awards or special favors, Sidra was always in the running, but never the winner.

Even more damning was her chosen field. Studying the dark arts and black magic was necessary but controversial within the Sisterhood. Those who specialized in them were viewed with suspicion, as if there was something basically flawed in their character. Sidra's assignment, then, was really a sign of disrespect of her abilities, and of her personally. As a result, Sidra would never be on the track toward leadership in the Sisterhood, seen as a talented academic but as an odd duck who dabbled in dangerous work.

When the fateful moment came, when Sidra had to decide whether to flee and fight, or give in to Hadrea's machinations, she stated her demand. Once Hadra had taken over the Known World, she would be the Mother of Sisters. Those Sisters that distrusted her or would not associate with her, or even laughed at her, all of them would serve her. Their fate would be in Sidra's hands.

Much later, Hadrea had been almost casual about it when Sidra questioned her to explain herself about the predicament that Hadrea placed Sidra into. Of course, Hadrea said, she was going to tell her. Why, she added, the fact that she had brought Sidra to that place and revealed the secret in her presence, surely that was a sign of Hadrea's trust and respect. Sidra was always integral to her plan, she claimed.

In the end, Sidra agreed to make her sacrifice. She would give up her humanity, and her vows to the Sisterhood, to secure the Coven's cooperation. Hadrea, for her part, agreed to give the Coven a prominent place in what she called her New World Order, once she had exacted her revenge on the rest of humanity. Thus, the bargain was struck and Hadrea's plan moved inexorably forward.

Yet, as one of the leaders of the Coven stepped forward to drain the lifeblood from Sidra, there was a fleeting moment of horror and regret. As Sidra died as a human being, the last thought in her mind was, "What have I done?"

When Sidra rose again, an undead vampire, her mind and her memories were intact, but her soul and her will belonged to others. She completed the transformation by disavowing her oaths as a Sister, and swearing new ones as a member of the Coven.

And the Coven completed their side of the bargain. Over several days, a group of seven vampires used their spells and incantations, and the power of the Source, to infuse the red gem in the Crystal Key with a gigantic amount of stored red magic. When the Coven handed the Crystal Key back to Hadrea, she in that moment became the most powerful sorceress in the Known World.

Hadrea and Sidra then left with their prized possession. First on foot in the still-thawing and dangerous narrow mountain passes, and then by a stolen horse and carriage, they traveled west then south, skirting the edge of the mountains that divided the realm of elves and humans.

For Hadrea, the travel was difficult. As a woman in her late seventies, she suffered fatigue and hunger and the vagaries of the weather. Getting to the Source had been difficult enough. Going home again simply added to her misery. At least, she told Sidra, all of her human frailties would be ended soon enough.

Sidra, on the other hand, found herself liberated from such petty human concerns. She felt no cold, and had no need for sleep, only the constant need for blood to satisfy her hunger. She did have to cover herself in the daytime, hiding herself from the sun's rays, but it was not like the stories she had heard in her youth of vampires being turned to ash by any direct sunlight. The sun's rays did pain her, to the point of making her cry out in agony, but were not fatal. She managed to keep traveling in the daytime by covering herself under a blanket in the back of the carriage, while Hadrea guided the horse. Sidra then drove at night, while Hadrea slept.

Finally, they reached Hadrea's goal—Pearl City, the place where Hadrea had grown up and where she still kept a home. Sidra hid on the outskirts, waiting for Hadrea to execute her plan.

The citizens of Pearl City viewed Hadrea with deep suspicion and even fear, even with her roots in the area. Her status as a Sister insulated her to a certain degree, but her neighbors whispered tales of her work in the dark arts, stories both real and imagined. There were insinuations of corruption during her previous time as a high counselor in the Queen's government. It would not take much for them to believe the worst in her.

So, when an incriminating document suddenly and mysteriously appeared, the local authorities had the information they needed to charge her with all her crimes, both real and imagined. And the Sisterhood's ruling Council of Elders simply looked the other way as Hadrea was tried and sentenced to death.

And it was all part of Hadrea's plan. To Sidra, the only flaw in it was Hadrea's unwillingness to entrust the Crystal Key to her before Hadrea's arrest. Hadrea insisted on keeping it, right up to the moment she was taken into custody.

During their trip, and in her short time in Pearl City, Hadrea had bound herself to the magic stored in the Crystal Key. Even though the Key was taken from her and locked away after Hadrea's arrest, by then the Key and Hadrea had become linked, part of each other. On Hadrea's death by fire, almost all of the magic stored within the Key was released in one massive burst, transforming the human residents of Pearl City into the ghouls that now marched behind Sidra.

Sidra's task, then, was to go into the town and recover the Crystal Key once Hadrea had secured her revenge over her former neighbors. With no one there to stop her, Sidra found the safe in which it was stored in the town hall, broke in and recovered it.

Then, and only then, Sidra could contact Hadrea's spirit. Hadrea had finally achieved her own form of immortality, free from physical needs and the natural decay of old age. The Crystal Key and its red magic sustained her, but she was bound to it and thus dependent on its connection with her. And she needed Sidra to carry it, and her, to the next stage of her plan.

So, under the cover of night, Sidra marched south with the beginnings of Hadrea's new army trailing behind her. She held the Crystal Key in her hands, bearing it and Hadrea's spirit.

Sidra had an idea as to where they were going. The magic in the Crystal Key, put there by the Coven, was almost spent. Hadrea had used a gigantic burst of it in her attack on Pearl City and the enslavement of its residents. Now, far away from the Coven and any assistance they might provide, Hadrea needed her own source of magic to recharge it.

And she could not stay in Pearl City to do that. While it, as any City did, had its own wellspring, this one of the white magic favored by the human race, Hadrea knew she could not stay there. She and her new army, as formidable as they were, would not have been able to resist a full-on effort of the united races and the combined power of the Sisterhood to retake Pearl City. It was only a matter of time before they roused their defenses to defeat her.

No, Hadrea needed her own private domain, one not shown on most maps of the Known World, in which to hide and gather her strength. That was where Sidra, and her tireless legs, were leading Hadrea's ghouls south, ever south.

For Sidra, fatigue was not an issue. The benefit of being a vampire was that she had an almost unlimited endurance, and could walk constantly. Although she could sleep, she found that she did not need to do so. Her needs were her newfound appetite for blood to sustain her, and protection from the sun during the daylight hours. Sidra had two or three ghouls surround her, holding a sheet above her to protect her white skin from the rays.

It always surprised Sidra that they kept encountering humans as they went along. She assumed that if they were rational creatures, they would have fled upon the approach of Hadrea's army. It was one thing to be caught off guard in the early stages of their march. But in the later stages of their journey, she assumed that people would have been warned of their coming. Yet, there were always stragglers and stubborn people who refused to leave their homes, or disbelieved the tales of the horde army coming at them. They learned the truth soon enough, and it was the last bit of knowledge gained in their mortal lives.

For them, their fate was the same as the citizens of Pearl City. Upon being caught and brought before Sidra, Hadrea's spirit would call forth the magic remaining in the Crystal Key and they would also be consumed by dark magic. It transformed the young and old, male and female. In doing this, Hadrea gradually increased her army's numbers as they continued on their way.

Finally, after three weeks of nonstop travel, they reached their destination—the abandoned remains of Sapphire City. They arrived in the late stages of a dark day, with grey clouds hovering low and threateningly overhead. Sidra, still bearing the Crystal Key and the spirit of Hadrea in her hands, led the way for the forefront of Hadrea's ragtag army through the open and broken city gate.

It was a former human city that had been derelict for so long that most maps failed to show it. It used to be the southernmost city in the Queendom, but gradually became abandoned through lack of steady trade and the exhaustion of its natural resources.

The most important factor in its decline, however, was the diminution of the power of the blue wellspring of magic beneath that inspired its name. The blue tint to its power made it less usable to the races than the other types of wellsprings. Elves favored green wellsprings, dwarves yellow ones, humans white or clear ones, and red for the undead and other creatures of darkness. Blue wellsprings could be used by all, but their magic was weak, and could only power the most basic of magic-powered devices. It could provide heat and light and power basic necessities such as water pumps, heaters and small light sources, but that was about all.

It was exactly as Sidra had guessed. Hadrea intended to use the wellspring, as weak as it was, to repower the Crystal Key. But how such a weak magic source could aid their cause was a mystery that escaped Sidra, at least for the moment.

There was not much for Sidra to see. She picked her way through the rough cobblestone streets, which had stones missing or sections heaved and grass growing in the gaps. Most of the buildings were open shells, their thatched roofs either in a bad state or completely collapsed into the center of the structure. Windows were missing, broken or so dirty that it was impossible to see through them.

As far as she could tell, any humans that might have lived here had fled before their approach. Even animals and birds seemed absent. There was a stark, empty silence, other than the scattered sounds of stray droplets of water falling randomly from the sky, striking surfaces around her as the skies hinted of a coming rain.

Sidra was nonplussed by what she saw. She sighed in exasperation and muttered out loud, "What a shit hole!"

Within the Key, Hadrea's spirit heard her and replied, "Patience, my dear, it is necessary to our plans. Do not question me. You will see the wisdom of this soon enough."

Chastened into silence, Sidra continued unimpeded to the center of the town. As she did, she gradually began to sense, more than see, the presence of the blue wellspring that was beneath her. It was a faint, yet pervasive sensation, the hint of a once vibrant source of magical power that was now a shadow of itself.

Finally, she reached a structure that was more substantial and in better condition than she had yet seen. It was Sapphire City's municipal hall, a large rectangular stone structure with the ends of large beams showing around the edges of the tall, well-constructed wooden shingled roof. Amazingly, it seemed intact enough to provide shelter.

It was a relief to Sidra, as the rain was beginning to gather itself into an actual spring shower. Even though her conversion to a vampire had eliminated many of her human frailties, she still hated getting wet. As she had found out often during her travels with Hadrea, it was hard to maintain her normal bearing of superiority when she was soaked. In that sense, as Hadrea liked to tell her, she was like a cat. Rain brought out the sour Sidra.

Sidra walked slowly up the steps. The large heavy doors were intact and unlocked, but debris scattered at their base indicated the doors had not been opened in some time. Sidra, still holding the Crystal Key in her hands, slipped it into a leather pouch tied to her waist. That was where Sidra would have preferred keeping the Key as she traveled, but Hadrea complained when Sidra tried to do that, claiming she could not see what was around them as they moved. So, Sidra was forced to bear the Key and Hadrea's spirit like a waiter holding a dinner tray for most of their journey. Now, though, Sidra put the Key in a place more comfortable for her, for once, and Hadrea would have to just shut up about it.

Sidra grasped the large brass doorknob and, pressing her shoulder into the weight of one of the doors. The hinges creaked in protest but gave way. She pushed her way into the interior.

The interior was musty but, thankfully for Sidra, dry. Scattered garbage and debris was everywhere, evidence of vagrants that had previously sheltered there. The wide hallway before her was bordered by several open rooms. In one, there was a large stone and mortar fireplace, full of ashes which had spilled out onto the wooden plank floor. In another room, scraps of paper, scrolls and forgotten ledgers were piled in one corner, with a large table but no chairs dominating the center of the room. The other rooms on the first floor were empty but for the layer of dust and scattered spider webs that were everywhere.

At the end of the hallway, stairs rose to a landing then turn toward the second floor. Sidra stood on the landing and looked around. She could see hints of the various open and closed doorways of the second floor, but did not walk the rest of the way up. Sidra assumed this would probably be her home for some time, a thought which depressed her.

Suddenly, there was a commotion below her. Two ghouls were dragging a crying human boy, probably ten years old with a round, chubby face, through the main entrance. Sidra came down from the landing to meet them, gliding regally down the stairs. The ghouls pulled the yowling boy between them until they reached Sidra, then knelt before her.

For a moment, the boy, terrified and gasping his breaths, paused in his sobs as he beheld the tall, beautiful woman with long, straight black hair and unnaturally white skin before him. He looked up at her with eyes and an expression that hoped that she would save him from his predicament.

"Finally," Sidra exclaimed, "I'm famished!"

To her, he was not a human being, but dinner. This was what it had come to for her. During her early days as a vampire, she might have felt sorry for him, and attempted to console her victim by asking his or her name and where they were from or some other personal detail. And while their fate was still sealed (Sidra never let a victim go), she would assure them that she had no intention of extracting their blood until they died, thereby creating a new vampire.

After all, in the lands south of the northern reaches, Sidra was a unique creature, and she did not want to go around cluttering up the lands with more vampires. That would only be competition for her.

But, once her thirst was slated with the blood of her victims, in the end they all died, whether by her knife driven through their heart, or, once she was on the move with Hadrea's army, simply returning them to the ghouls to dispose of.

By this point, though, Sidra was hardened to the routine. She eyed the boy for a second before she said firmly, "Hold him down."

The boy let out a frightened yelp as the ghouls kicked the boy's feet out from under him. He flopped with a thud to the floor. The boy cried out, thrashing as he tried to escape the grip of his captors. The ghouls leaned onto his arms and chest, pinning him in place.

The boy protested, "No! What are you doing?" He looked up at the woman looking calmly down at him. Between sobs, he begged, "Help me, please!"

Instead of answering, Sidra knelt down and tossed her hair back over her shoulder, out of the way. It was only when she opened her mouth, exposing the extended canine teeth that had become more and more prominent in her time as a vampire, that the boy finally realized what she was.

Terrified, he screamed and struggled against the weight of his captors. Sidra leaned back for a moment, silently waiting for him to exhaust himself before continuing. Finally, she grew impatient and said, "Relax, dear boy. Do not fight so much. I have no intention of killing you."

The boy, exhausted, did not answer. Instinctively, he did not trust her. He heard the lie in her gentle words. But he was spent physically, and could no longer resist.

Satisfied that he would lie still, Sidra leaned in toward the boy's neck, a small smirk of anticipation on her face. She opened her mouth to begin her feast.

The boy, sensing his fate, whispered to her, "What have I done?"

Sidra, at first, was not going to respond. But in that moment, she could not help herself. She breathed into his ear, "Nothing. Nothing at all."

Sidra plunged her fangs into his neck, drinking deeply. The boy screamed at first, writhing in the grip of the ghouls, but weakened as Sidra had her fill.

Then, almost too late, Sidra stopped herself and pulled away. He was weak and barely alive, his eyes closed and his breathing coming in quick, shallow wheezing gasps. Sidra wanted him to be like all the others. He needed to die by some other means.

She leaned back and stood up. Snatching a dusty piece of fabric from a nearby counter, she wiped her face clean, then checked to make sure she had not sullied her dress.

Satisfied, she waved dismissively at the ghouls still holding her victim between them. "Dispose of it," she said. The two nodded eagerly, then lifted the limp boy and carried him out the front door.

Sidra heard through the open doorway the shriek of the group of ghouls milling around outside the front of the building. They grew suddenly agitated with the promise of their own meal. With one last startled cry, the boy perished in the sudden frenzy as the ghouls ripped his body to shreds.

"As I promised. I did not kill you," Sidra whispered to herself. Now satiated, any thoughts of the boy vanished from her mind.

Sidra returned to the task at hand. Recovering the Crystal Key from her hip pouch, Sidra asked, "Well now, Hadrea. What next?"

Hadrea's spirit did not reply for a moment, and Sidra wondered what Hadrea had turned her attention to. "Hadrea?"

Finally, after several more moments, Hadrea's presence returned as a black mist swirling above the storage gem embedded into the Key. "It's perfect! It's exactly as I had hoped."

Sidra snickered in reply. If Hadrea was referring to the blue wellspring beneath the derelict city, Sidra did not understand how that was possible. She scoffed, "What do you mean? This is the weakest wellspring I've ever encountered. No wonder it was abandoned. I would be surprised if it could light an illuminer."

Hadrea answered dryly, "Do not mock me if you lack the understanding to see its potential. Its weakness is only a temporary condition. Come dear, find the stairs to the basement. I will show you."

Sidra, carrying the Crystal Key before her, spent several minutes going through the rooms of the first floor, looking for the passage downward. Unlike Hadrea, she could not simply transpose herself into the basement. Finally, in a rear corner of the building, in the kitchen area, she found the door leading to the basement.

She opened it and peered downward into the pitch blackness. Even with her enhanced night sight, the darkness of the lower level seemed absolute. Sidra was not anxious to go down and stumble around. Returning to the kitchen, she searched a few moments more until she found the stub of a candle and some loose matches in a drawer.

After lighting the candle, Sidra cradled the Crystal Key with her left arm, and raised the candle before her with her right arm as she slowly descended down the stairs. Cobwebs crisscrossed the space before her. Grimacing, she tried to avoid them by ducking and weaving her way forward. Sidra may have become a vampire, and a being of formidable power, but spiders still creeped her out.

Reaching the basement, Sidra lifted the candle and looked around. It was a windowless space, smaller than she expected. She assumed the basement went the length and width of the entire building, but it only matched the space of the kitchen above. Below the low, thick-beamed ceiling, empty wooden shelves lined the walls, and a small table and chair stood near the stairs. On the side which was the foundation of the back of the building, there was a small fireplace with a pile of ashes and remnants of burnt firewood. It was not much to look at, just another storage room stripped of supplies in a deserted city.

Hadrea's voice, though, was full of excitement. "Perfect, indeed! Just as I had hoped."

Sidra furrowed her brow. "How?"

Hadrea insisted. "Patience, my dear."

Sidra growled, finally letting her frustration out, "Enough! It is always 'patience' with you, Hadrea. I have come too far to be toyed with anymore. Tell me, at last, why we are in this wretched place."

In reply, Hadrea's laughter cackled in her ears. "Very well, my dear. We have done well enough to reach this point. But the true beginning of my ascent begins here and now. All before has been leading to this. Come, put the candle down where it can provide some light for us. We will begin, here and now."

Sidra did as she was bidden, returning to the table near the stairs. She steadied the candle on one end until melted wax pooled around its base and it could stand on its own. As she waited, Sidra could feel below her the blue magic of the wellspring pulsing quietly, dormant and resting like someone at the edge of sleep. Sidra thought to herself, "This had better be good."

Once Sidra returned to the center of the room, Hadrea's voice was calm and certain as it echoed in the space around her. "You see, dear, this place is positioned directly over the center of the wellspring. As faint as it is, I came here, not because of what this place is, but of what it can become.

"Buried within the libraries of the Sister's Keep, I found the ancient histories that go much further back than the events taught as rote in the Academy. Thousands of years ago, when humans had just begun to populate their race and settle the Known World, this place belonged to exotic creatures of magic that no longer even exist.

"Specifically, this area belonged to the fairies, and what we refer to now as Sapphire City was the center of their kingdom. Blue was their preferred magic. They found their strength in the wellspring here, and maintained it by their presence and use of it. As a result, the wellspring here was much more powerful centuries ago than it is now."

Sidra was skeptical. She had always viewed the legends concerning fairies as myth, not fact. "Really? They actually existed? You believe that?" Sidra was genuinely surprised that Hadrea took the notion of fairies seriously. Her training at the Sisterhood's Academy had taught her that fairies were only creatures of myth and lore. She never supposed that, at one time, they could have been real. "Why would their true history have been forgotten? If they were real, why did they disappear?"

Hadrea continued, confident in her belief, "Perhaps it was inevitable that they became extinct. Fairies were immortal but fragile. Their numbers were never significant, and they did not repopulate freely. It is not even known how fairies were born. Some histories say that fairies were never infants or children in the same way as other races. Whatever natural process created them produced fairies in their full, adult form. But that happened only sporadically. Only if fairies were undisturbed, could they survive.

"Thus, when humans began to invade and settle in the same lands as their homeland, the fairy race was never going to survive their contact with humans. In fact, the human women of magic at the time, who prior to the formation of the Sisterhood were simply called witches, used the power of the fairies' own wellspring to defeat them. The race of fairies were wiped out, and not one has been seen in many hundreds of years.

"This wellspring, though, remained, and humans claimed it as their own. They named and built Sapphire City as their first capital here. But something unexpected happened. Without the natural interaction of the fairies to keep the blue magic flowing freely from the Continuum through this wellspring, its power began to fade.

"Humans continued to propagate and explore and expand their settlements gradually northwards. Finally, once the locations of white wellsprings were discovered, humans were able to tap into their own natural magic affinities, and settlements grew up around them instead. When the massive white wellspring under present-day Crystal City was discovered, the human rulers of the time moved from this place, and established their capital and founded the Sisterhood there. Humans were able to settle permanently there, thriving in the presence of such a potent and free flowing source of magic.

"This place, then, with its diminished blue wellspring, was left as a mere outpost at the edge of the Queendom. Its legacy was as a dying remnant of the first foothold of humans in the Known World, and even that distinction faded away eventually as the wellspring weakened to the point of irrelevance. Humans stopped living in this area, preferring the aids and conveniences of the places that we know today, tied to the wellsprings that remain active and vibrant.

"So, you and I are left with what remains. A barely-present blue wellspring, beneath an abandoned, derelict city. Something that, as you said, could not even light an illuminer."

Hadrea's voice grew in its intensity and certainty as she concluded, "But today, now, we will change that. We will attempt something that, to my knowledge, has never been done before. We will use the power that remains in the Crystal Key to cleanse and reopen the portal beneath us to the Continuum. Instead of the pitifully weak blue wellspring of the present, there will instead be a full-throated, vibrant one. And it will belong to me! To use as I will."

Sidra furrowed her brow. "You mean us. It will belong to you and me. You forget who has been carting your soul around in the gem in the Key since Pearl City."

Hadrea cackled, "Yes, my dear. Of course, when I say 'I' that means 'us.' Certainly, you are present in my plans as well."

Sidra let that pass. It sometimes did feel as if Hadrea only thought of her as a cog in the machine of Hadrea's ambitions. But they had come too far, and Sidra had already given up too much of herself, to doubt those plans now. And she would demand that Hadrea satisfy her price in the bargain, when the time came.

Sidra shook her shoulders as if to shake physically the doubts from her mind. "Fine, then," she answered tersely. "Let's get on with it."

Sidra lifted the Crystal Key in her hands until she could see it before her eyes, the candlelight flickering off its golden surface and the facets of the red ruby imbedded in the large end. "Ready," she said, the anticipation building within her.

She closed her eyes and opened her mind, and began to chant the incantations that Hadrea had taught her. Hadrea's disembodied voice joined with hers, echoing in the surrounding darkness. Soon, Sidra could feel the magic within the Crystal Key answer their call. Red magic flared in the gem, suddenly illuminating the room around them in stark, crimson relief. Sidra could sense the depth of its power. The noise of it filled the room as a vague rumble of an approaching storm.

Hadrea broke off her chanting and called out, "Direct it into the wellspring! Drive what magic remains in the Key against the flow until it contacts the Continuum!"

To Sidra, that did not seem possible. In her days as a schoolgirl at the Academy, she had been taught that magic only flowed one way, from the Continuum through the wellsprings— outwards always outwards, to the mortal world.

Nevertheless, she obeyed. Sidra used her mind to grapple with the energy being released from the key, and she could feel Hadrea's spirit join in her efforts.

With one massive imposition of their will, Sidra and Hadrea gathered the remaining magic in the Crystal Key and drove it downwards, into the wellspring below them. At first, the wellspring gave way easily in its weakness, and Sidra could feel the blue magic retreat in reaction to the red magic, which bulled forward in a wave of power, rushing towards the Continuum in a dimension far below.

Sidra could feel the red magic clearing the way as it moved forward, widening the path as it went. Hadrea, too, could feel the effect. "Yes, yes!" she gasped in excitement. "It is working!"

Sidra, though, maintained her concentration and kept repeating the incantations. Hadrea rejoined her, and together they directed the downward rush of red magic.

After several moments, though, the momentum began to slow. Despite the effort of the two women driving the flow of red magic, the blue magic in opposition began to resist and push back. The red magic slowed its momentum until finally it reached an equilibrium with the blue magic and stopped, well away from the Continuum.

"No, keep driving it," Hadrea commanded, her voice suddenly tinged with anxiety. "It must reach the other side."

Sidra did not reply. She was trying her best, but it did not seem as if there was enough of the red magic left in the Crystal Key to overcome the resistance of the blue magic. They had used too much of the Key's reserves in reaching this point.

For several tense moments, the two women chanted in desperation, trying to find the necessary force of will and magic to push through. Sidra had never experienced this kind of sustained effort before, and for the first time, she began to wonder about the consequences of failure. There was so much magic in play, so much force building in the conduit within the wellspring. She suddenly realized that if they could not sustain their efforts, this could end badly for her.

Then, in her fullest concentration and at the farthest reach of her perceptions, Sidra sensed a small breach by the blue magic in the gathered force of red magic, like a tiny leak in a dam. Sidra could sense Hadrea's presence as she tried to repair the opening.

But it was too late. The blue magic had gathered itself in resistance, without any consciousness to guide it, but as a reaction of the physics of its basic nature. The natural flow was outward, ever outward. And now, the blue magic reacted to the forces that were pushing it in the wrong direction by resisting and pushing back.

And unfortunately for Hadrea and Sidra, the Key had nothing left to give them. Their side had run dry. In the space of a few heartbeats, Sidra could feel the blue magic gathering itself from the limitless supply of the Continuum.

Once the breach occurred, the wall of red magic that the women had built began to fall back, retreating in the face of the push of the resisting blue magic. It was slow at first, but the speed of the red magic began to pick up speed as it headed back towards the two casters. Sidra and Hadrea kept chanting desperately, trying to control it. But the magic that they had sent into the wellspring was lost to their control, and was rushing back toward them.

Sidra broke off her chanting, and yelled, "What now? What do we do?"

Hadrea, though, did not answer. Her spirit seemed lost and confused, frozen in the moment. She had clearly not anticipated what was happening.

In horror, Sidra realized that Hadrea's plan had failed. And she knew that once the magic returned to them, it would be a wild and sudden burst—potentially life threatening.

So, in a frantic split second act of self-preservation, Sidra abandoned her efforts to control the magic speeding back toward them, and instead gathered the remaining fragments of red magic around her as a shield. Time seemed to slow as she weaved and strengthened the shield, positioning it beneath her in the opening of the wellspring. She managed to progress further in those few heartbeats than she would have expected, but there was never going to be enough time for her to complete the task.

In a sudden concussive blast, a torrential mix of red and blue magic reached the outlet of the wellspring. Sidra's improvised shield saved her life, and was enough to deflect the energy around and away from her and the town hall above her head. But the force of the magic that reached her was enough to lift her off her feet, and sear her with a wild energy that did not physically burn her or her clothes, but ripped at her nerves and consciousness with a pain that felt as if she had been suddenly dropped into a vat of boiling oil.

Sidra screamed in agony, and she was tossed on the floor in a helpless heap. The Key tumbled away from her. Hadrea's spirit vanished.

All around the town hall, for several hundred feet outside the zone of protection of Sidra's shield, anything on the surface, whether stone or wood or soil or grass or ghoul, was lifted up and out in a giant detonation. The blast threw it all up into a giant ball of dirt and smoke, and debris rained down over the rest of Sapphire City. The concussive sound, louder than any thunder, boomed out for miles. A tall column of dust rose in the otherwise still air.

Fortunately for her, the structure of the town hall above Sidra shook but did not fall, leaving it and a few of the closest buildings as an island in the devastation. The shock of the explosion rendered Sidra unconscious for several moments. Dust and the smell of singed wood lingered in the air over her.

When Sidra awoke, pain lingered as an afterglow from the magic that had coursed through her body. She groaned, straightened out her body and rolled onto her back, covering her face with her hands. After breathing in and out full lungfuls of air to recover, she called out weakly, "Hadrea?" Seconds passed. She tried again, "Hadrea?"

The spirit did not answer for several moments more. Sidra wondered in the silence if Hadrea's essence had been broken and dissipated by the shock of the magic. Was she gone?

Yet Hadrea, too, had managed to preserve herself in the explosion. Her soul stubbornly survived, but barely. Hadrea had no mortal body to be injured. But her mind and emotions and memories, the essence of her soul that had been preserved after her execution in Pearl City, was still bound together by magic.

In the last moments before the wave of magic struck, her soul had retreated into the red gem of the Crystal Key. It had protected her, but the red magic that had been stored there was completely spent. Hadrea had hidden herself in an empty vessel. Her spirit silently remerged from the gem into the room, wondering herself why she still existed.

Her answer was the blue magic that was flowing out from the wellspring. No longer just a trickle, the magic flowed upwards toward them in a clear, strong stream, though not nearly as much as Hadrea would have hoped. Hadrea sensed now that the wellspring's power was roughly equivalent to, or slightly less than, the wellsprings of some of the outlying cities, such as Pearl City or Jade City. But it was nowhere close to that of those in the major cities, and was dwarfed by the Source or the one in Crystal City, or the one that belonged to the elves in their capital.

Hadrea had hoped their gambit would renew the wellspring into the one that had been here, the one that had preserved the fairies from the dawn of time until their extinction. She hoped it might even be the strongest of all of them. That was what she required for her plans, and she did not have it, still.

After quietly gauging the strength of the flow for a few moments, Hadrea's incorporeal voice broke the silence, "I am here." She had survived only to know that she had failed.

Hearing Hadrea's return, Sidra's concern gave way to anger. Still trembling from the aftereffects of the detonation, she gasped, "Is this it? Is this all that we receive for our efforts?"

Hadrea replied wearily, "My plan worked, but not nearly well enough. The theory was correct. But we had used too much of the stored energy of the Key in my destruction of Pearl City and the journey here. The remaining magic was not enough to clear the path all the way to the Continuum."

Sidra yelled her frustration in reply, "Your miscalculation almost killed the both of us! And all you have done is announce our presence to all the others. They will know we are here and will guess as to what we have done!" Had Sidra still been mortal, she would have begun crying. Instead, as a vampire, there was no relief from the tension and anger swirling inside of her. Her porcelain face was contorted in an expression of despair, but no tears streamed down her cheeks.

Hadrea, though, was not ready to give up. Sidra's despair instead flared her own anger, and she replied harshly, "Get hold of yourself! There was nothing wrong with my plan. Only that we needed more magic, much more, to accomplish our goal. The Crystal Key could only do so much for us in the initial try."

Sidra countered angrily, "The initial try? Madness! Then what are we supposed to do?" She would hold her tongue no longer. "There is no other device that could have brought as much power to bear as the Key did, however much we had used it to get here."

Hadrea answered calmly, "Then we must have more, mustn't we? As you can sense yourself, our efforts were not in vain. Not at all. We have made a good beginning."

Sidra snorted her disgust in reply, but Hadrea continued, her voice regaining her strength and authority. "Perhaps fully charged, the Key may yet be enough. So, we will simply have to charge it again."

Sidra countered, "Go back to the Source? Are you insane? The Coven will never give of themselves that much again." Her anger and frustration caused her to forget any lingering pain. She rose to her feet, and this time her trembling was in anger and frustration. She continued, "And to stay here and charge the Key with what we have would take a generation to accomplish. Others will come to stop us and claim this wellspring as their own once again. We simply do not have that much time. The Sisters will never let this stand!"

By that point, Hadrea had recovered her full composure. She answered in a commanding tone, attempting to regain the upper hand over her apprentice. "No, there is enough power here that I can maintain my presence and consolidate my power over this area. And I already had another option, ready to pursue if necessary. There is another way."

This was almost too much for Sidra. Another way? To her, it did not seem possible. She replied weakly, "And what of me? What am I to do? Hadrea, I am at my limit."

Hadrea said simply, "You will take the Key and find him. The one with the power to recharge the Key."

Sidra was astounded. In disbelief, she blurted out a laugh and said, "Him? That's insane. What do you mean, him?"

To Sidra, it was impossible. By all the known physics, men simply did not have the power of magic. That applied to all the known humanoid races, whether elves or dwarves or humans. Hadrea could have announced that Sidra was to find a talking horse or to find a dog that walked on two legs and took tea in the mornings, and it would have made more sense.

But Hadrea answered confidently and smoothly, "Yes, my dear. Him."

Still in shock, Sidra fumbled for a reply, "And what of you? If I leave and take the Key, how will you maintain control over the ghouls? They might as well be a mob of rabid animals. How will you maintain order here?"

Hadrea laughed in a disparaging tone which offended Sidra's pride. "My dear Sidra. You forget who I am. With the power of the renewed wellspring at my disposal, I will have all the control I need."

Sidra knew it was pointless to argue with her. She tried to change the topic. "Then, let's go upstairs, Hadrea. This all has been too much for me. Let's get out of this dark shithole. Please."

Wearily, Sidra bent down and retrieved the Key. Exhausted, it was almost too much to walk up the stairs into the kitchen, but Sidra forced one foot forward, then the other, until she crossed into the open central area of the ground floor. She turned and looked outside through the open main entrance. Dust was still settling in the surrounding area. The ghouls that had survived were thrashing about, directionless. Sidra wondered what sort of devastation she would see once she went outside.

But as Sidra stood there, Hadrea's spirit was almost chirpy, renewed by its faith in its own invincibility. "You will do as I say, Sidra," the spirit said into the silence. "This is victory delayed, not denied."

Sidra's spirit sank. However much she wanted her reward—to be the Mother of Sisters—she did wonder for a moment how much easier things would be for her if Hadrea had been blinked out of existence by the forces they had unleashed. It would have been a merciful failure, because Sidra would at last have been her own person.

Hadrea, though, continued as if her plans were already set into motion, "If you are concerned I will have no one to talk to, Sidra, you forget our special guest. My own personal souvenir from our victory at Pearl City." Her spirit called out to the ghouls in the immediate vicinity, "Bring her in!"

Sidra turned to see. Carried by the shoulders between two hulking male ghouls, a frail old human woman dangled limply, with strands of greasy grey hair covering her face. Sidra had almost forgotten. It was Mother Abigail, the local priestess who had attempted to take Hadrea's confession before her execution. Sidra wondered how the priest had managed to survive this long. Being Hadrea's plaything usually did not end well.

Sidra said with obvious disdain, "Well, Hadrea, if you've someone to replace me, I suppose I'll get on with it. Off on your fool's errand."

There was a flash of anger in Hadrea's reply. "Do not question me, child. Take the Key and go. I will commune with you through the Continuum at points on your travel, and provide you with guidance as to your target as I continue to glimpse him in my thoughts.

"For now, go back to Pearl City. All signs point to his presence there, either now or in the near future."

Sidra sighed. There was no point in arguing. "Very well, mistress," she replied, once again adopting the tone of someone used to taking orders. "I look forward to hearing from you."

Sidra returned the Crystal Key to its pouch. At least, with Hadrea now able to exist without it, she could just leave the Key stored until she needed it.

Sidra strode toward the exit, glancing at the unfortunate former Mother Abigail as she passed. The woman managed to turn her head and look up at Sidra. Her eyes silently begged Sidra for release. For a brief instant, her desperate expression caught Sidra off guard, and tugged at the remnants of humanity still within Sidra's heart.

But Sidra steeled herself at the sight, and turned away as she walked by. Humans were in her past. Now, they were just food to her, objects to satisfy her own needs. Mother Abigail was Hadrea's toy now.

The thought left her mind by the time she had exited the building and went down the steps. Sidra could feel the weight of the Crystal Key in the pouch next to her hip as she passed through the throngs of ghouls clustered in the courtyard.

Order seemed to be returning to their movements as Hadrea began to reassert control over the area. The ghouls parted before Sidra as she strode forward regally, her head held high and proudly.

Sidra felt the power and potential within her. She turned her thoughts to her goal. The man who could use magic. She was confident. There could be no one that could resist her, even this nameless man who Hadrea had sent her to find.

Sidra chuckled and shook her head at the notion. A man, with magic. What a ridiculous idea.

SIX: DACY

After his escape from Jade City, Tom, now Abby, had not done much to hide himself. He had simply walked through the open eastern gate in the early morning hours, the quiet sound of his shoes echoing in the empty, foggy stillness as they scraped the gravel with each step forward. The sentries on duty had paid him almost no notice as he headed out. The authorities at the headquarters had no idea yet that Abby was missing.

The guards should have noticed. It was unusual to see a lone human girl, dressed in a simple green peasant's dress but otherwise carrying no supplies or pack. They did see in her hands, they reported later, the inert illuminer that she turned over and over as a sign of the tension within. She seemed nervous, but was otherwise not suspicious. Nothing obviously amiss, they thought, so they did not stop her. As gatekeepers to Jade City, they were concerned more with incoming traffic, rather than outgoing. So, they had not stirred from their posts as she left, heading out alone onto the open road as the first red glimmers of dawn shone in the eastern sky.

Not bothering to hide himself, Abby walked eastward on the twisting road leading through the mountains. He was finally left to his own thoughts, and had the time to ponder what a strange, confusing experience it was.

As he breathed the thin, mountain air, it did not seem like a dream. He could feel the chill air being pulled in and out of his lungs. He could feel the cool dampness on his shoulders that caused him to shudder occasionally, until the sun rose in the sky and finally warmed the air around him. He could smell the scents of the patches of yellow and blue mountain flowers around him. All of it seemed as if he was in a real, physical place. And he was experiencing it in someone else's body.

Then, there were the other travelers on that road. For someone used to cars, trucks and concrete highways, the sight of horses and wagons and carriages and carts was unfamiliar and strange. But seeing them close up and hearing the various voices and the grunt of the horses and the grinding of wooden wheels on the dirt and gravel, he marveled at it all. Even when he had to step around the occasional smelly pile of horse dung, buzzing with black flies, it simply reinforced the fact that he was in this world, whether he wanted to be or not.

Even more amazingly, he had almost gotten used to the sight of elves. On the eastern side of Jade City, there were fewer of them and more humans going about their business. At first, Abby found himself staring wide-eyed at them as they passed, until he told himself to be more discreet about it. When they caught his eye, some offered a quick smile or wave, while others ignored him entirely. Everyone seemed to have a place to go and something to do. Except for himself, Abby realized.

He kept up a steady pace, made easier by the youthful legs that had no trace of the arthritis that Tom suffered with in his middle age. Then, there was the hair, the big, unruly pile that covered his head. As it was gently moved around on top of his head by the occasional breeze, he found himself taking the loose strands of long sandy hair that would fall in front of his face and pulling them back over his shoulders. He was self-conscious about it at first, but over the hours it gradually became a reflex. It was something else new that he had to deal with. He did wonder whether he could locate a pair of scissors to lop most of it off.

But that was one of the lesser concerns on the list of things Abby needed to worry about. His most immediate concern was the lack of food. He was fine during the first few hours of his journey. But gradually, hunger began to gnaw it him more and more, an emptiness in his stomach that needed to be addressed.

The night before, his last meal was soup and bread, not very substantial. But even that was an improvement over the dry trail rations that Reanah had fed him in their journey out of the mountains. That was filling and adequate for his needs at the time, but not any sort of real food. He kept wishing that there was a drive-through fast food place in this reality, where he could step up to a counter and just order a big, fat greasy burger and a pile of overly salted fries.

He tried to manage the hunger by filling his stomach with water. At least in this section of the road, finding water was not a problem. Every so often, there were tiny streams washing off the surrounding hillsides. Abby would gingerly step up the side slopes until he found a good foothold, hold the tendrils of dangling hair back out of the way, and bend over and drink his fill. It seemed clean enough, but it was a far cry from the ubiquitous bottled water of his own world, which in retrospect seemed almost too easy to get.

The presence of easy water was reassuring. But it did have one consequence. Every so often, Abby's bladder demanded to be emptied. So he would look for an opening in the undergrowth, and head off a short distance into the woods.

The most humiliating part was how he had to pee. As Tom, if he was caught out away from a bathroom in the outdoors, he simply found a secluded tree or bush, unzipped his pants, pulled out his penis and empty his bladder. Now, as Abby, he had to gather the bottom fabric of his dress, and squat down to do it, irrespective of the cold air and the mud and crawling creatures below him. Even as necessary as this was, Tom did not think he would ever get used to this. Every time, he felt his face flush, likening himself to a newly castrated man. Then after finishing, since there was no roll of toilet paper handy, he found himself shaking his body to free himself of the last few droplets of urine. The whole experience was almost too much.

Almost immediately, one of the top items on his list of things he wished for in his new reality was a fully functioning bathroom. One with a toilet and toilet paper and hot and cold running water and towels and soap and a door that he could shut and lock. Did this world even have those? He had yet to see one. If not, he thought, perhaps he could invent indoor plumbing, too.

Despite such practicalities, Abby kept moving eastward down the road. By late in the afternoon of the first day of his journey, he began to notice in the distance ahead of him the back of a lone figure, walking in the same direction. The person appeared to be weighted down with a heavy backpack, with other items loosely attached and flopping at the sides.

Gradually, Abby closed the distance between them. From behind, Abby could not tell if it was a man or woman, though the person seemed to be about as tall as he was.

He or she appeared to take no notice of Abby's approach.

Finally, when Abby was within a few yards and the sound of their footfalls was audible to each other, the figure spun around suddenly and faced him. It was a young human girl, about the same age as Abby's physical age. Dressed in a simple brown tunic and trousers, she had dark brown hair knotted behind her head, with big brown eyes and a round face. She wore sturdy leather boots covered in flecks of mud and dust. The backpack she bore was heavy enough that it almost made her lose her balance when she turned to face Abby, but after a few uncertain steps, she regained her balance.

She barked at Abby, "Oy! Watcha doin' sneakin' up on someone like that?"

Abby was a little taken back, but replied calmly, "I was just walking. I thought you could hear me behind you."

"Well call out next time, girl," she answered, the words coming out quickly. "Don't give someone the frights! You never know who's out here, ya know?" After her initial burst, the girl moderated her tone, "I could have popped you, that's all." Before Abby could answer, she stuck out a hand. "Name's Dacy. Means 'glowing.' When I was born my parents thought I'd be their little ball of sunshine. You can tell how that turned out."

Abby returned the handshake. "Abby. Stands for 'abstinence.' Nice to meet you."

Dacy eyed Abby up and down. "Well, ain't you a little princess. Nice dress." Her quick eyes noticed the illuminer in Abby's hands. "Did ya nick that from the elves? You might have thought to bring a little more than that with you though, love." Rather than answer, Abby let the questions wash over her, interpreting them as rhetorical.

Then, unable to keep herself from wobbling as she tried to stand still, the girl wearily pulled her shoulders out of the straps of the backpack and let it drop heavily to the ground. She groaned and begin to rub her shoulders with her hands. "That's a load there! I just brings what I need, but even that is about the limit of me."

Thinking about what might be in that backpack, Abby's gnawing hunger made him blurt out a little sooner in the conversation than he would have hoped, "Do you have any food? Please? I'm really hungry."

Dacy laughed. "Well, that's a how do you do! I like that. Get right to the point." Her voice took on a harder edge, even as she continued to smile, "Do ya have any money, love? I'm a businesswoman, after all. Nothin's free out here."

Abby shook his head and held out the illuminer. "This is all I have."

Dacy chuckled her disdain. "Oh, dear. Even if we were near a wellspring—which we ain't—I've never been able to use them things. It's no use to me, love."

Abby could not hide the disappointment in his face. For a moment, he could feel moisture welling up in the corners of his eyes. The sensation surprised him. He wiped his cheeks to collect himself so that he would not start to cry.

Noticing the gesture, Dacy said, "And sobbin' ain't gonna get you anywhere, neither. Trust me. I know all the tricks." After a moment's pause, she continued, "So, anyway. Where you headed?"

Abby shrugged and answered with a trace of resignation, "I don't know. Somewhere else."

Dacy laughed. "Ha! Story of my life. Someplace else gots to be better than where you is. Ain't that right?"

"I suppose so," Abby answered. "I'm not from around here. I just don't know my way around, that's all."

Dacy said with a broad smile, "You's not from around here. I got that right away. You do talk funny, let me tell you."

Abby thought to himself, "If you only knew." Trying to seem less helpless, Abby countered, "So, Dacy, where are you headed?"

Dacy gestured forward down the road. "Pearl City, the west border town of Distan and the end of the Jade Pass. People's been sayin' that everyone up and left. Gone without a trace. Not sayin' I believe it. Gonna see for myself. If it is, should be ripe for me to pick up a few things there. If it ain't already been cleaned out by the time I get there, that is."

The story did not make any sense to Abby, but he let that pass. It was just something else about this world that he did not understand.

"Can I at least walk along with you, then? I could use the company. Plus, I could help carry some of your stuff. Your backpack looks like quite a load."

Dacy did not seem hostile to the idea, but she eyed Abby suspiciously. "No thanks, love. I mean, you can walk along with me. Beats you walkin' in front of me like we's strangers, right? At least we'd have each other to talk to." She gestured toward her backpack. "I just don't want to unpack. You understand. It's my stuff, and I've managed this far. Don't worry about me. I can make it the rest of the way."

Abby nodded. "That's sounds fine. I could use someone to talk to."

"Me, too," Dacy said. "I'm not used to company, though. Don't take me the wrong way. I'm actually nice once you gets to know me." She turned and picked up her backpack. Despite her assurances, Abby could see the pain in Dacy's face as she return the load to her back. She hopped a little to center the load and settle the straps into position on her shoulders.

Dacy continued, "When we get to the next place, we'll ask for food together."

"Ask for food?" Abby asked. "So, you don't actually have any?"

Dacy grimaced as if she was reluctant to admit it. "Not really, but I ain't no beggar, neither. I'm just sayin' it's easier to get something for free than payin' for it. Right? Sometimes, they just give it to you. Other times you have to do a little work to earn it.

But that'll put some food in your belly and your coin stays in your purse."

Abby nodded. "Sounds good. Thanks."

"Good then," Dacy answered. "Let's get movin." With that, Dacy nodded and swung around and resumed her march forward, and Abby walked beside her.

Over the coming hours, Dacy filled the air between them with her history, how she ran away from home at fourteen and had been on the road alone for almost four years. She was from a place called Moonstone City, a border town that straddled the northern lands between the humans and dwarves.

She seemed to measure her travels by her gradual accumulation of the contents of her backpack, most of it obtained by simply taking them. Dacy had no embarrassment about it, quite the opposite. The tales were full of her cleverness in the acquisition, and usually ended with, "And I ain't been pinched yet for it, neither."

Abby even began to wonder just how much food, if any, Dacy actually kept in her backpack. As she talked about getting this or that token or bauble from various places, Dacy kept saying how she was never hungry for long, and always clever enough or with just enough money to keep herself moving to the next place. Perhaps, Abby wondered, if that was why Dacy did not share any food with him. She had no food to give.

Abby mostly listened, with only a few words at various points tossed in to keep the conversation moving. Fortunately for him, Dacy seemed less interested in Abby's past than regaling Abby with stories of her own cleverness and resourcefulness. When the subject of Abby's history came up, the conversation almost always looped back around to Dacy and her exploits.

It was a one-sided conversation, but a relief for Abby to have some company. The miles through the Jade Pass went by much more quickly, and Abby appreciated Dacy's easy storytelling. He found himself smiling often as Dacy's tales poured forth. And for her part, Dacy seemed to appreciate finally having an audience.

They kept going the rest of the day, resting only a few minutes at a time, until it was too dark to see. They camped a short distance from the road in an open area in the forest, with Dacy lighting a fire that made the night much more tolerable for Abby. Neither ate any food. Tomorrow, Dacy kept saying, tomorrow they would both get a meal. She did at least share water from a canteen with Abby, rather than make him fend for himself, which Abby appreciated as an act of kindness.

After dawn broke the next morning, announced as a vague lightening of the dewy morning fog, the two travelers arose and headed east. Abby offered again to share Dacy's load, feeling it unfair to be carrying the stolen luminer as his sole possession, while Dacy wobbled as she tried to manage the weight of her backpack.

But Dacy replied, indignantly, that she could carry her own fucking stuff, thank you very much. To Abby, it was a little harsh given their otherwise pleasant time together, but he let it pass. If Dacy could get food for the both of them, he was willing to let her be in charge.

As the sun burned off the fog, the air warmed to a comfortable pleasantness. Finally, the road, with every bend or straight, began to incline consistently downwards. Through the screen of trees, Abby began to glimpse a vast plain before them, with cultivated fields dividing and cutting into the dominance of a vast, mature tree-filled forest that filled in the space east of the mountains.

Over the next few hours, as the road wound downwards between the foothills, it began to flatten out, and Abby had the feeling that the mountains were finally behind them. Unlike the approach to Jade City, the fields and crops were not continuous, but interspersed between long stretches of forest. The trees were tall and, judging by their thickness very old, with their branches covering most of the space over the road as an airy canopy of leaves. Even in the early afternoon, there was no truly open space and the sun never had a chance to bear down on the pair as they trudged forward. There was the occasional passerby, but they were few and far between compared to the traffic on the western end of the Jade Pass. And, at least to Abby's eyes, there were no homes by the side of the road, only the occasional dirt trail with rutty wagon tracks that wound off into the interior of the forest.

Finally, in the late afternoon, Abby could see an opening in the trees ahead of them. As they crossed the threshold at the edge of the forest, sunlight gleamed into the eyes of the weary travelers. They passed into truly open, warm air, as the cool of the forest gave way to sunbaked green and growing fields at various stages of cultivation on either side.

Abby could see small groups of people, all humans, working the soil. It took Abby a few moments to realize that the groups consisted mostly men with rakes or shovels or bags of seed, being directed by a lone woman who stood off to the side without any tools in hand but who carried, even at a distance, an air of authority over what was going on around her.

The sight reinforced a suspicion that that been growing in Abby for some time. As Dacy continued to chatter away beside him, Abby realized that during his time in this new world, he had only ever seen women in charge. Reanah was in charge of her group of scouts. The headquarters in Jade City was run by women. The only men he had seen were always subordinate to, and doing the bidding of, a woman.

Abby was still turning this over in his mind when he and Dacy came upon a large gate to their right. On the southern edge of the road, the gate was an impressive display. Its base was cut, mortared stone, and wrought iron rose from pillars on either side, arching over a wide, graveled road that exited the main highway. The road that ran underneath led straight towards a collection of houses in the distance, with continuous cultivated fields on either side.

Abby looked up at the design in the arch overhead. There were individual symbols worked into the wrought iron, but Abby could not understand them. It was not any language or alphabet that Abby recognized.

Dacy had walked over to a plaque on the right side of the gate. After reading for a moment, she gestured at it, chuckled and said, "Look at this. Can you believe them people?"

Abby walked over to the plaque. The writing was the same style of lettering as on the gate overhead. He had no idea what it said. After studying it for a moment, Abby looked back at Dacy and shook his head.

Dacy looked surprised. "What d'ya mean? It's in Common. You mean you can't read this?" There was a little distain in her tone that made Abby blush with embarrassment.

Dacy pointed at the symbols. "It says, 'Rivertree Crossing. Property of the Harris Family. Vagrants banned and solicitations not welcome.' The nerve!"

Abby looked back at the plaque. As much as he understood the verbal language called Common in this new world, he apparently could not understand the written word. The thought chilled Abby. His future looked suddenly much more daunting, if he could not read.

Dacy picked up on Abby's discomfort. After a moment, her voice took on a softer tone when she spoke, "Come on, luv. Nothing to be ashamed of. Not everyone goes to school. Me, I only went a couple of years. Picked up the rest along the way. All I needed, really. I'm in the school of hard knocks, now. You and me both."

Abby nodded and exhaled in frustration. "All right," he thought grimly. "If that's how it's going to be."

To Dacy, he tried to sound more confident, "Well, are we going in or not? I'm still damn hungry."

Dacy answered, "Sure we are. Let's find out what it is about these people that makes their shit not smell."

Abby smiled at that. "O.K. Let's go."

The two walked through the gate and headed down the driveway toward the settlement before them. Abby spent his time studying the collection of buildings as they approached. The style of the buildings was similar to those in the elf kingdom, sturdy stone and mortar with white plaster with thick beams and sturdy wooden windows and doors. Four of the buildings, topped by tightly wound thatch, were smaller and off to the side. There were two large barns in the background, surrounded by wooden rail fencing and gates. Abby could see brown and black quarter horses, and cows mottled in black and white, scattered in the fields around and beyond the center complex. The whole place had an air of organization and competence.

The centerpiece was a large, three story structure that dominated the others. Although in the same style as the smaller homes, the scale of the mansion belied the simplicity of its design. Two wings on either side anchored the house, with a recessed center section with a working water fountain in the courtyard. Rows of evenly spaced windows with wooden shutters, some open and some closed, hinted at the large number of rooms within. All around the various buildings, people engaged in their designated tasks moved purposefully, paying the two weary travelers almost no notice, other than a hurried glance before looking away. If Abby and Dacy were not supposed to be there, the staff were not going to call them on it.

But the sight that struck Abby the most as they approached was the structure on the top of the center section. Whereas each wing had a sturdy conventional peaked roof with wooden hand carved shingles, the central portion had a flat roof with a strange metal construction incongruously standing on the top. It was a giant metallic funnel resting on an iron framed scaffold, its open end facing horizontally in an easterly direction. The contraption had to be at least thirty feet tall, and looked like a weird out-of-place addition to a simple farming scene.

As they moved toward the front entrance, Abby gestured toward the device and asked, "What the hell is that thing?"

Dacy answered, "A magic collector. Built by dwarves and has some dwarvish name that I can't even pronounce. It collects the magic from some far off wellspring, and they use it to power the whole place. Even though we's a long way still from Pearl City, it helps them run all the pumps and lights and heaters and everything."

Abby could see more of the detail of it as they approached. The base of the funnel was mounted on a circular frame that allowed it to be adjusted up or down, or side to side. Thick wires protruded out of the narrow end, winding down until the bottom end was attached to the frame of the structure as it headed out of sight into the house. Abby thought, "What a weird steampunk contraption it is."

Dacy laughed. "That's how you know these assholes got money. Sort of announces it, don't it? They could have put the damn thing on top of one of the barns. But no, they gots to put it right on the top of the damn palace, as if that weren't enough by itself. What's the use of buyin' one from the dwarves and payin' to haul it all the way here and set it up, if no one sees it, eh? Makes me sick."

As they neared the front entrance, there were large central double doors beneath a sheltering roof that extended outwards, over the carriage driveway that passed in front of the house. On the doors, there were two large brass letters of the same indecipherable alphabet as at the gate, surrounded by elegant carvings. Abby assumed the letters were the first letter of the family name, probably an "H", for "Harris." He grimly realized he would have to start noting and remembering such little details if he was going to learn to read.

Seeing the grandiose nature of the entrance, Dacy pulled Abby up short and said, "With that sign at the gate, ain't no way we can just knock and introduce ourselves." The two looked around for an alternate entrance.

To the side, on the far right corner of the central section, they could see stairs leading down to the basement. "That's our ticket, luv," Dacy said. "Let's give that a try."

They walked over to the stairs, then down to the lower level. The door was open, and warm air blew out and met them as they entered. They could hear muted voices and the commotion of activity in the rooms off the central hallway. Dacy led the way, and seemed to pick one of the rooms at random into which to stick her head. "Eh, miss. Who's in charge here?"

Abby followed in time for him to hear a young woman dressed in black with a white cap answer, "That'd be Mistress Paulina. She's in charge of the staff. End of the hall on the right."

Dacy smiled quickly and nodded. "Much obliged, luv." She turned and led the way down the hallway, reaching a black painted door with a little rectangular tag that Abby again could not read. He assumed the word designated Mistress Paulina's title, whatever it was.

Before knocking on the closed door, Dacy unstrapped her backpack and laid it on the floor, then surprised Abby by pulling out a brush from one of the side pockets. She quickly brushed her own short hair until there was a noticeable part down the middle of her head. Then, without a word, roughly grabbed Abby by the shoulders and spun him around. Dacy gave Abby a quick brushing, ordering and straightening his shoulder length hair into something more presentable.

Dacy returned the brush to its pocket, and used her hands to brush herself off and lessening at least some of the wrinkles in her clothing. Then, she did the same to Abby, while muttering quietly under her breath, "These types don't like messes." She sighed, "But there's only so much you can do after bein' out on the road. You've got a nice dress, but it ain't clean, that's for sure. Stand up straight and try to look as best you can." Abby nodded, though he wondered why Dacy was being so fussy.

Dacy turned and knocked. "Come in," replied a muted woman's voice from the interior. Dacy pushed the door open and entered, with Abby trailing.

A woman in her mid-fifties was seated behind a desk. Her black hair was suffused with grey streaks, and tied purposefully behind her head. She wore a black dress, but it was noticeable more frilled and detailed than the first girl's simple dress, and there was a thin silver necklace, doubled into two loops, around her neck. She was writing on a parchment with a quill pen, and there were neat stacks of papers on either side of her. The room was lighted by simple light boxes in each corner, giving off a low yellow glow.

Her face soured as the two visitors entered, and she put the quill into a holder as she sighed in exasperation, "Didn't you girls see the sign at the gate? No vagrants or solicitations. That means the likes of you."

Dacy replied indignantly, "No ma'am, we ain't neither one of them kind. We just looking for food, but we ain't beggars neither. Just a little something before we's back on the road."

Mistress Paulina shot back, "And if I've a bed for you, that wouldn't hurt either, would it? Or a bath. For one night, or two, or ten? That's it with the likes of you, isn't it? Ask for a little and take a lot. If Lady Harris had to give away shelter and food to any imprudent traveler who couldn't manage their own needs, there wouldn't be anything left for those that work for it, would there?"

Dacy shot back, "No, ma'am! We ain't lookin' for no charity. We can do some chores for it, if you can't part with it easy. I've got a little money, too, if what you charge ain't too dear."

Mistress Paulina snorted in reply, eyeing them as if they were just like any of the others that had come knocking at her door before. She turned toward Abby and said sternly, "And what about you, girl? What do you have to say?"

"Nothing, ma'am," Abby answered. "I mean, I haven't eaten anything in three days. If you can spare anything, we'd be very grateful."

A puzzled look passed across Mistress Paulina's face. Abby wondered if it had to do with his accent. Without addressing it, though, Mistress Paulina continued, "And what do you have to offer in return, then? If you had to pay, I mean. You girls have to learn that nothing in life comes free."

Abby could feel hunger urgently gnawing at him. It was one thing to push aside the sensation when there was nothing to eat, but he felt at that moment so close to getting actual, cooked food. He would have traded anything he had to eat. But, besides his clothes, Abby had only one earthly possession.

Almost without thinking, Abby withdrew the elf illuminer from its hiding place within his dress. He extended it toward Mistress Paulina and said, "This is all I have in this world, ma'am. If you could help us out, this is yours."

The sight of the illuminer piqued Mistress Paulina's interest, and she reached out and accepted it from Abby. Turning it over in her hands, she said, "This is a nice one." She let the tips of her fingers pass over the engravings on each side. "I like the carvings. First class work. Must be elvish." Looking back up at Abby, she said, "I suppose you nicked this, eh? A little souvenir of your time with the elves?"

Abby felt his face redden. He did steal it, but he would never admit that to her. "No, not at all," he said defensively. "That's mine. I assure you."

Watching the back and forth, Dacy seemed to think a deal was done. "Well, there you are," she said. "What's that going to get us? Seems like that's worth a meal and a bed for each of us tonight, at least. Plus a bath, too."

Mistress Paulina shook her head. "No, it's a start but not nearly enough." Facing Dacy, she said with a trace of anticipation, "You said you had a little money. How much?"

Dacy stammered, "Well, just that. A little."

"How little?" Mistress Paulina said, "Ten marks, at least, for all you're asking."

Dacy seemed dumbfounded. "Ten marks? For what? That's like a full week at a respectable inn." She tried to turn the negotiation back on Mistress Paulina. "Look here. I'd rather walk back out and sleep underneath your stupid gate. Let all the passersby see us dirty vagrants sullying up your precious place. How's that sound?"

Mistress Paulina chuckled. "Then I'd have the sheriff after you, dear. Let you both get your accommodations at the jail. Granted, it's room and board, but not nearly as nice as what I have for guests here. Though I warn you, you'd spend almost as much getting out of there as you would paying us here."

Mistress Paulina tried to sound as if she were being generous. "There's no need for that. I was outside a little while ago and it felt like rain was coming. If you want a roof over your heads tonight, you have to deal with me."

She eyed them as if she knew she had them where she wanted them. "The illuminer plus five marks. That's a meal tonight and a room for the two of you. You best take my offer while you can."

Dacy seemed deflated. For all her outward confidence, Abby could tell Dacy felt as if she was the one getting played. But Dacy reached into her trouser pocket and withdrew some coins. After counting them out, she extended her hand toward Mistress Paulina. But before she handed the money over, Dacy made one last attempt at a better deal. "And a bath, too. And you clean the clothes we got on. Any good inn does that anyway, right? Same price. All of that and you got a deal."

Mistress Paulina laughed. "Of course, dear. I should have said those were included as well." Abby doubted that, but stayed silent.

Satisfied, Dacy nodded and handed over the money. She said with a trace of disgust in her voice, "Told ya. We ain't no charity cases."

Mistress Paulina laughed the laugh of a victor. "Thank you. Just business, right?" She slipped the coins into a pocket on the front of her dress.

Abby wondered grimly if any of that money was destined for the owners of the house, or just Mistress Paulina herself. At that point, it did not really matter. After sleeping out in the open air for most of the nights spent in this reality, he was relieved to have even one night of comfortable accommodations.

Mistress Paulina stood and put her arms on Dacy and Abby's shoulders, guiding them toward the door. "Come, girls. Get whatever you brought and follow me. I'll show you to your room."

She led them out the door, and waited while Dacy retrieved her backpack. Her eyes seemed to notice Abby's lack of possessions, but she made no comment. The three then turned in the hallway and went past two large openings on their left for a room which contained a large kitchen. Two men and a woman were moving purposefully about, working between a large stove with an overhead metal hood, a large metal box which to Abby seemed like it might be a refrigerator, and a large block table on which there were several individual trays being prepared. The aroma of cooked food in the air, with traces of meat and spices and baking bread, set off the hunger alarms in his belly. If Abby was hungry before, he was starving now.

Mistress Paulina continued on until she reached a simple wooden door and withdrew an assortment of keys from a side pocket. They jangled as she flipped through them until she found the correct one, and unlocked the door. The door groaned on its hinges as it swung open.

Inside, there was a windowless room with two small beds against the far wall, with white cotton sheets folded neatly on the end of each. There was no dresser, or nightstands, and the only other furniture was a simple rectangular table with one chair on each of the long sides. The walls were bare of decorations, and the room lacked any flowers or frills. The room was lighted by four illuminers in simple metal mounts in each corner near the ceiling, already on and giving off a dim yellow glow.

Mistress Paulina gave them a gentle but firm push into the interior of the room. "Now, don't be wandering around," she warned. "You're guests of the household but the rest of us don't like being interrupted while we're working. I suppose you'll be wanting your food first."

Abby and Dacy nodded vigorously, like two little kids promised ice cream. It was really all either of them wanted at that point.

Mistress Paulina continued, "Well then, someone will be along in a few minutes. Once you've eaten, I'll be wanting you to use the lavatory right away. It's empty while the staff is working, but it gets busy once our day is done. If you leave out the clothes you're wearing, I'll have them laundered as well. As promised." She fingered the edges of Abby's green dress and smirked, "Shame to see something this quality get all dirt and dusty. As someone in charge of cleanliness, it offends me."

Breaking out of his silence, Abby managed to croak, "Thank you, ma'am." In his mind, the words were, "Fuck you, bitch."

Satisfied that all was in order, Mistress Paulina started to back out the door. "Any questions, ladies? No? Good. See you in the morning." She slipped out and closed the door quietly behind herself.

Remembering his experience in Jade City, Abby listened carefully to hear whether the lock was turned, but there was only silence. After a moment, he sighed in relief. They were not locked in.

Dacy, though, was fuming. "Five marks," she groaned. "For one night! Should have held out for at least three or four nights for that price. That lady's a hawk and we's the rats. The food better be the Queen's own, at least. Somethin' to make it worth it."

Abby nodded. He was appreciative of Dacy including him in the bargain, even if he had no idea how much five marks was actually worth. "Thanks, though. I really needed this."

"Me, too," Dacy admitted. "Just sticks in my craw, that's all."

Fortunately, it took only a few more minutes for the food to arrive, and Dacy and Abby were already seated at the table in anticipation of it. A late teenaged male with facial acne and dressed in head-to-toe black knocked and quickly entered with two simple wooden trays stacked on top of each other. He placed a tray before each of them, then quickly removed a covering white cloth to reveal the meal. Before either could ask his name or even thank him, he ducked back out again, gently shutting the door behind him.

At that moment, though, Abby could care less about manners. The same smells that had ignited his hunger as they walked past the kitchen were the same odors steaming up from the dishes before him. There was a thick cream broth soup with green herbs and tiny round onions and pieces of chicken, and a plate of salad with fresh lettuce and carrots and tomatoes with a thin oil dressing. On the central plate, there was a round piece of juicy beef brazed with grill marks on the central plate. Next to the beef was a still warm, thick portion of brownish bread and a small pat of soft white butter. Finally, in the corner was a small mug filled with water. It smelled and looked so good! Abby thought to himself that even the elves had not put out a spread like this.

So, Abby and Dacy wordlessly picked up their utensils and fairly attacked the food. The only sounds were the metallic clacks of knife and spoon and fork contacting the plates and the lip smacking of open-mouthed chewing (from Dacy), as the two quickly erased the food from each tray. After days on the road with nothing but water consumed from mountainside runoff, it was the most satisfying meal Abby had ever had, in either lifetime. He even concluded the meal with an unembarrassed, contented belch that drew a chuckle from Dacy.

They leaned back in their chairs, finally relaxed. "Compliments to the cook, whoever it is," Dacy said as she picked gristle from her teeth with her fingernails.

"Yes, indeed," Abby answered quietly.

They absorbed the contented silence for several minutes. Before too long, there was a quick knock at the door and the same servant stuck his head in the door. "Ladies, if you will," he said, "I'll show you the way to the lavatory."

Dacy said, "And you are?"

"Kevin, miss," he answered, as if that did not matter. He gestured for them to go with him.

Abby and Dacy rose and followed him out the door and down the hall. Abby tried to make conversation. "So, Kevin, how long have you worked here?"

Kevin frowned. He did not seem to resent the question as much as he considered it unnecessary. "I dunno," he answered quietly, "maybe two or three. My mum works here as a field supervisor and got me this gig. Beats working outdoors in the mud and the weather."

He sighed. "But Mistress Paulina is threatening the house men with that. Workin' in the fields. Says we're all going to be farm hands, cause we're short since what happened to Pearl City. Ain't no temporary workers to fill the need."

That peaked Dacy's interest. "Yeah? Pearl City? What do you know about it? That's where we's headed. Heard some crazy shit's gone down there."

Keith shrugged. "Don't know too much about it. One day there was this big storm that moved in, and the next thing you knew, everyone in Pearl City's gone. Just up and left without a trace. Supposedly they all headed south somewhere, but I do not know. That's as much as I know happened. Some people's saying even weirder stuff than that. There's talk of dark magic and the undead, but I can't really believe any of that sort of stuff is real. Didn't see any of it myself, and I've not been there since."

Dacy offered brightly, "Me and Abby's headin' there. Sounds like easy pickings. We can do alright for ourselves if the place ain't been cleaned out first."

Keith reached the lavatory and pushed the door open for them. "Like I said. Don't know much about it other than what people's been sayin'. Just rumors really. But I'm gonna be mad if I have to go out into the fields, ya know? It's crap for me."

The three entered a large room with a tiled floor and a large metal bathtub perched on a raised platform in the center. The far wall had two large windows filled with an opaque glass that let in light but otherwise kept the privacy of the room. Two white dressers were stacked with towels and small glass bottles that Abby presumed contained various lotions and soaps. On the other wall, two shower heads jutted out from the tiled wall, separated into stalls by half-wall dividers, with drains centered in each small metal trays mounted on the wall holding roughly cut bars of white soap. Two enclosed lavatory stalls with swinging doors were in the far corner.

It all had the look of a purposeful, simple communal lavatory, but Abby thrilled at the sight. He walked quickly to the enclosed stalls and swung open a door. In it, there was a recognizable toilet, a round bowl with a fixed seat, and an inlet tube sticking out of the back leading up to a water tank mounted on the wall. Thin sheets of paper were stacked neatly on a shelf in the back of the stall. A chain hung from a lever mounted on the water tank, and Abby reached up and tugged it. There was the familiar swoosh of water as it swirled through the toilet bowl and down the drain.

Abby thought he'd never been so excited to see a toilet. He tipped his head back and gasped toward the ceiling, more to himself than the others, "Oh, thank God!" In his mind, he thought, "Looks like I won't have to invent a toilet after all." It was Abby's first sight of indoor plumbing since he had been in this new world, and it was the best, most encouraging thing he had seen so far. He was getting more than a little tired of doing his business next to a bush.

Keith looked a little indignant. "Even the servants have all the modern conveniences, miss. Lady Harris insists on it. This place has had power and indoor plumbing for twenty years, soon as the collector got installed on the roof. Even the servants' houses gots bathrooms as well. The Harris's is good people, ya know?"

Even Dacy looked thrilled by the prospect of using the facilities. She went to the large central bathtub and opened the taps, testing the water flowing out of the faucet. "Yep. They's hot water, too." She smiled as she shut off the water. "If you sees Lady Harris, give her my compliments, luv. Much appreciated."

Keith shook his head. "No, Mistress Paulina wouldn't take kindly to that. As far as she's concerned, Lady Harris ain't to know nothin' about you two. The family shouldn't even be aware of you being here. Didn't you see the sign out at the gate?"

Dacy had a flash of indignation. "What is it with you people?" She gestured toward Abby and herself. "We's no charity cases. We pay our own way in this world. Don't we Abby?"

Abby, still basking in the discovery of working indoor plumbing, nodded in agreement but let Dacy take the lead on expressing outrage.

Keith raised his hands to ward off Dacy's anger, and answered, "Don't take no offense. What I mean is, I don't think the Harris's know when we take in travelers like yourselves. This is just something that Mistress Paulina does on the side, I think. Her own little business. I just do what I'm told. Just please keep to yourselves. It makes it easier on the rest of us."

Still piqued, Dacy gave Keith a dismissive wave. "Fine. So, we're going to get to it, if you don't mind."

Keith nodded and began to leave. "You've got a half hour. Then once the farmhands start coming in for dinner, the staff gets to use this on a schedule."

Dacy broke into a wide grin. "Yeah, I saw some of them sweaty fellas out there on the way in. You send one or two of the beefier ones in here and me and Abby will take good care of them. Won't we, Abby?" She gave a knowing flick of her eyebrows at Abby. In reply, Abby could feel himself flush in self-conscious embarrassment.

Keith ignored the sentiment. Just before exiting, he said, "Just bundle up your clothes and leave them in that hamper in the corner. There's a couple of robes in the drawers. We'll launder your clothes and return 'em to you clean in the morning." Without waiting for a reply or a goodbye, he turned and quickly exited, closing the door gently behind him.

"Tremendous, thanks," replied Dacy brightly to the closed door. Then, to Abby's surprise and with no preamble, she slipped off her boots and quickly pulled off her clothes. Abby stood still and stared, dumbfounded, as Dacy unselfconsciously removed one article of clothing then another. Soon, female body parts that Tom thought he would never see again were right in front of him. And, unbidden, the word that haunted him in his last moments as Tom was back, echoing in his mind. Abstinence.

Once completely naked, Dacy moved over to one of the dressers and perused the small bottles lining the top. "Lord, look at this crap," she said, somehow mixing wonderment and contempt. "Oils, lotions, perfumes, three different kinds of soap. Ooh! Bubble bath?

Are you kidding me? For the staff? They's some pretty pampered servants, if you ask me."

Dacy picked up the bottle of bubble bath and, after flashing Abby a big, wide grin, moved to the tub. She turned on the taps, and poured a long, slow stream of the gooey substance into the water. As the tub filled, she playfully used her fingertips to pop the bubbles accumulating beneath the flowing faucet.

Abby watched, frozen in place, amazed at Dacy's lack of self-consciousness. If Dacy had turned around, she would have seen Abby staring slack-jawed at her, eyeing every move and detail of her body—the curve of her neck, the smooth youthful skin untanned where it had been sheltered from the sun by her clothing, the way her skin folded then smoothed around her waist as she subtly moved on her feet, the feminine curve of her hips and legs, and the way gravity and body movement emphasized the presence of her breasts. And for Tom, the most jarring part was seeing Dacy's very feminine body covered in unapologetic body hair—hair in the armpits and fuzz on her legs and forearms; in his world, women plucked and shaved and waxed, and idyllic photo shopped images of the result were the norm in photographs and videos. The sight of Dacy in her natural state was both sexual and non-sexual at the same time, the reality of a teenage girl without clothes, being herself.

It took a few moments to sink in that Dacy expected Abby, too, to disrobe and share the bath with her. After all, he had to do it to reap the benefit of being in a fully functioning lavatory. For a split second, he considered telling Dacy that he would wait outside until she finished her bath before taking his turn. But that would only draw attention to his discomfort, and they only had a short time to use the facilities. Then, Tom realized that Abby was his costume, his cover against being an old man pervert sharing a bath with a teenage girl. Even though that was what he was. He muttered to himself, "Just be cool, Tom. She'll never know the difference."

Hearing Abby's voice, Dacy turned. "What was that?" The tub was almost ready.

"Nothing," Abby chirped, the high, nervous tone in his voice almost giving it away. A little self-consciously, Abby turned his back on Dacy and set to removing his own clothes. He kicked off his shoes and slowly untied the laces on the front of his dress. Then, he awkwardly pulled the bottom hem of the outer green dress up from the floor, up the full length of his body and over his head—the final removal delayed by having to take a few moments to extract his unruly mat of hair from the folds of the cloth before it was free. He similarly pulled the inner chemise up and over his head, piling the thin white cotton material on top of the dress on the floor.

Once again, Tom was fully naked with this new and unfamiliar body. He chanced a glance at his arms and legs, trying not to appear as if he had never seen them before. Like Dacy, there was no evidence of any effort at hair removal, light, sandy hair that was just a sort of unpoliced fuzz, a pale imitation of what he was used to as a fifty year old man—a full-on mat of thick black curly hair flecked with grey. And in the foreground as he looked down were his very female breasts, otherwise normal and not remarkable in their size or shape, but weird to Tom in their unfamiliarity and newness. The sight made him uncomfortable enough that he crossed his arms in front of his chest, hiding the protruding nipples and pinning the soft flesh against his body, not for Dacy's benefit, but his own. On top of everything else Tom had to deal with in this strange new world, they were just too much.

From behind him, Dacy called out, "Come on, Abby. The water's perfect. Let's stay in until they kick us out."

At that moment, which was the moment of truth, Tom could not do it. As much as he wanted a warm bath to soothe the aches and pains in his sore limbs, it would just be wrong, he thought, for a fifty year old man to share a tub with a naked teenage girl—whether the girl knew what was really happening or not. He knew.

"Naw," Abby replied softly, "I'll just take a shower. You enjoy yourself."

Dacy shot back, "Oh, don't be such a priss. Ain't never shared a bath before? Didn't ya have any brothers or sisters? Didn't you all share a tub? Come on!"

Abby answered, "Sure, when I was three. Besides, I'm more used to showers." That actually was true enough for Tom. He never took baths, and it lent an authenticity to his refusal. "Not today, thanks."

Dacy laughed. "Fine. Suit yourself. Just realize there ain't no other place like this for miles and miles. Don't whine to me later about how much you miss a good bubble bath."

"Fair enough," Abby said as he breathed a sigh of relief. Keeping his back to Dacy as she entered the tub, he crossed the room to one of the shower stalls, his bare feet slapping the floor as he moved. Once he stood near a shower heads, he removed one of his arms from his chest just long enough to adjust the taps to get the water flowing through the shower head.

After a few moments of testing with his fingers, the temperature of the outflow was to his satisfaction. Abby grabbed a bar of soap and slid underneath the shower head. He let the streams soak into the pile of hair on his head, using his hands to gather and straighten the lengthy individual strands into one thick one that rested in the center of his shoulders, extending part way down his back.

As he did, Tom's mind was still holding the image of Dacy before she had entered the tub. A woman's naked body. It had been so long since he had seen one. He could feel his cheeks begin to flush.

Abby lathered the bar of soap until his hands were covered in soapy foam. Closing his eyes, he started with his face, rubbing it clean of days of sweat and dirt. Keeping the bar lathered up, he moved down his neck and shoulders. He opened his eyes as he cleaned his arms and hands, and he was struck by both their awkward-seeming thinness and yet intriguing femininity. Next, and a little more self-consciously, he moved onto his chest and stomach, trying to not make too much of a show as he cradled his breasts and explored his nipples. They were more sensitive than he imagined, yet as he proceeded he found that the self-examination was less sexual and more curious than he thought it would be.

He bent over and rinsed the accumulated sweat and dirt off his hips and legs and feet. Like Dacy, there was an accumulated peach fuzz hair covering his legs that he did not expect. Would he have to shave them at some point? He was used to shaving his face, not his legs. Was that a thing here or not? He wondered about that as he proceeded.

Finally, and with some trepidation, he used the soap bar to fully cover both hands in lather. Giving a quick glance over his shoulder to make sure Dacy was not watching, he quickly put both hands into the hairy pubic area, cleaning everything his fingers came in contact with as quickly as he could. He did not know much about women, but he knew that he had to keep "down there" as clean as possible.

But it was jarring to not have a penis and scrotum as exterior evidence of his manhood, something he simply had as Tom for over fifty years. They were not present anymore, no longer a natural part of him. Grimly, he noted that with this new body, with parts he learned about in eighth grade health class so many, many years ago, there was a lot he did not know. This was the new normal, and it was going to take some time to get used to.

Within his mind, he felt like the same Tom that he always was, with all the accumulated experiences and memories and life lessons that made him who he was. But now, as Abby or whoever this girl really was, his soul was being carted around within a new vessel. It was strange that taking a shower would make him have to confront that fact. When Abby was covered up by clothes, he was aware of the differences, but they were not in the forefront of his thinking. He spoke and viewed the world as Tom did, and dealt with the world as Tom would.

Now, Tom was Abby, a new person in a new world, possessing nothing other than the dusty, smelly clothes that were piled loosely behind him. It created a dissonance within him that was jarring and uncomfortable. Thinking about it sent a cold shiver down his back. No longer slightly aroused from thinking about Dacy, he began to get upset. As the water continued to pour steadily down on him, he could feel his eyes begin to tear up. He quickly stuck his face up toward the shower head to clean the tears away, before Dacy could see him start to cry.

Gathering himself, he took a quick glance over his shoulder. Dacy was not having any sort of existential crisis, just enjoying herself as she lounged in the tub and swished the bath bubbles floating on top of the water. Her face, flushed from the heat of the bath water, was a picture of contented bliss.

Abby, though, had enough of his existential crisis and self-pity. Taking a deep breath to calm himself, he turned off the taps and walked quickly to a dresser to retrieve a towel, his feet slapping the tiles as he moved. He quickly dabbed himself dry, then wrapped his torso with the towel in the way he had seen women do it. He gathered the wet, still soaked pile of hair behind his head, straining it with his fingers before letting it rest behind his back.

As he tried to regain control over his emotions, Abby turned toward Dacy and said in a low tone, "Come on Dacy. Time's up."

Dacy groaned as she reluctantly raised herself up out of the water. Abby grabbed a fresh towel and quickly handed it to her, both as a courtesy and also with the unstated hope that Dacy would cover herself up sooner rather than later. It was all very innocent, but Abby was very uncomfortable with all the nakedness that was going on at that moment.

For her part, though, Dacy was still basking in the moment. "Oh my Lord," she said with a contented purr, "that was just what I needed right now." She was in no hurry as she toweled herself dry.

Abby tried to make it not obvious as he turned away to avoid staring at the various nude body parts in front of him. "Me too," he answered blandly. "Just what I needed."

His attempt to be casual, though, did not fool Dacy. She laughed at Abby's obvious discomfort. "Relax, silly. Don't bother me to be seen in the buff. Never has. If you want to keep your modesty, fine for you. But if we's going to be stickin' together, you're going to have to get used to it. This is just as God made me, and I ain't that shy about it."

Abby nodded, but he did not imagine ever being completely relaxed about it. Whether it was Dacy's nudity, or his own.

Then, there was a sharp rap at the door. It was jarring enough that Abby started at the sound. Suddenly feeling more modest, Dacy quickly wrapped the towel around her body and called out, "Come on in, my good man." She giggled at having to hurry before a man could see her.

Abby frowned. For all her lecturing, Dacy apparently did have some boundaries.

Kevin quickly entered, trying to avoid making eye contact. "I'll take your clothes to be laundered," he said. He quickly retrieved the two piles of dirty clothes on the floor and left, making a point to leave the door all the way open. "Now, if you'll follow me back to your room."

Abby and Dacy, wrapped in their towels and suddenly feeling self-conscious in the working area of the basement, quietly followed him down the hall until they reached their room. They ducked in the opening and Kevin quickly closed the door behind them, leaving the two alone. Someone had cleaned out the dinner trays and made the beds in their absence, leaving the room neat and tidy.

Dacy, wearing a wide smile and clearly delighted with how it was going, hopped onto one of the beds. Abby, a bit more deliberately so that the towel would not expose his torso, drew back the covers of the other bed and slid in between the sheets. Stretching his legs out, he propped himself up in a sitting position against the headboard, drawing the sheets back up so that his lower body was covered.

By the time Abby finished adjusting himself, Dacy had loosened her towel, sitting cross-legged on the top of her bed with her back and the side of her legs covered, but without enough material to keep her chest covered. Abby could see Dacy's breasts through the opening in the fabric as she spoke. He tried not to stare.

"Well, enjoy this luv, and rest up," Dacy said contentedly. "We gets one spa day before its back on the open road. It's not too far from here. Should be able to get to Pearl City in one full day of walking."

Trying to pull his mind away from the sight of Dacy's chest, Abby made a point to look her in the eyes as he asked, "Then what? What's your plan?"

"Ain't no plan," Dacy said idly as she gingerly picked dirt out from beneath her fingernails. "Just takin' one day at a time. Like always. But if what everyone's been sayin' about Pearl City is true, should still be a lot left for us once we get there."

Abby said, "That's it? Don't you ever worry about not having a roof over your head, or knowing where your next meal's coming from? Or just grabbing whatever you can when you can get it? That's not what I'm used to. You can't plan on that." Abby quietly slapped his hands together for emphasis as he continued, "I need a home. And regular meals. I need a job. I need a routine. That's my life, and it always has been." He did not like admitting that, but a safe, stable and routine life was something he took for granted, until he no longer had one.

Dacy chuckled, "Aw, luv, don't be such a stick in the mud. You're young yet. Live a little. Get out and see the world. That's me. I've been doin' this for three years now, and I ain't never been really hungry or really cold. I've always had just enough of what I need to make it to the next place and keep going. Trust me. If you stick with me, you'll be all right."

Abby was unconvinced. He still had the last three days of near constant hunger, and sleeping out in the open air, fresh in his mind. To him, it was camping out, and he did not like camping. It was the most hungry he had been in over fifty years of two different lifetimes.

So, Abby was not happy with the idea of making it up as they went along. But Dacy seemed very sure of herself, and Abby had no other options at that point. Even as he argued with Dacy, Abby knew that accompanying her was all he could do, until he could figure out something else.

The two bantered on or a little while after that, until Abby began to feel the accumulated fatigue of the last few days. He may have been occupying a much more youthful body, but he still appreciated a good sleep as any middle aged man.

Finally, Abby cut off the conversation with Dacy abruptly. "Well, that's it for me, if you don't mind. I'm done."

Dacy seemed surprised, as if she wanted to keep talking for some time. "Really? It's early yet. Suit yourself, I guess. Though if you fall asleep I probably won't be far behind."

Abby did a quick survey of the room to see if there was any sort of switch to turn off the four illuminers providing the light to the room. Not finding one, he said good night to Dacy and slid his body fully under the covers, pulling the sheets up to his neck. He quickly slid off the damp towel and dropped on the floor beside the bed. Abby rested his head on the pillow and exhaled a deep breath filled with his exhaustion. Within moments, he was asleep.

After several hours of the best sleep he had yet experienced in this new world, Abby woke up. The illuminers were still on, which made him wonder whether Dacy even knew how they worked. Or whether she just preferred to sleep with the lights on.

Either way, Abby had no idea what time it actually was. He sat up and glanced around the room. There was a deep, blanketing silence which suggested it was the middle of the night. The only detectable sound was the light, contented breathing of Dacy as she continued to sleep in the neighboring bed.

His eyes drifted up toward the four illuminers in their simple iron mounts in each corner of the room, which bathed the windowless room in a soft yellow glow. They fascinated him as a tangible evidence of magic, yet they were treated by those in this reality as completely ordinary. Again, Abby noticed there was no obvious switch or control for the lights. It frustrated him that he had no idea how they actually worked.

He decided to try again to turn one off, only this time, he hoped, with a little more discretion than his last effort in Jade City. That had caused an illuminer to flare out of his control, though the side benefit of that was that it allowed him to escape the headquarters. But he remained completely clueless as to how and why any of that had happened.

Abby was determined to understand at least one new thing in this new world, to give him a little control over his own situation. Turning a light on or off seemed basic enough. Others seemed to do it effortlessly. It was now his chance to take the time to work it out for himself.

As he opened up the sheets and slid out of the bed, completely nude, the chill that hit his warm skin almost made him reconsider the effort. Moving in the coolness of the room made his skin break out with goosebumps all over his body. But he was focused on the task, and reasoned that it would only take a few moments to try.

Abby grabbed a chair and positioned it with its back against the side wall nearest his bed. He climbed onto the seat and stood up, extending his hands to examine the illuminer over his head.

From the outside, it was just a plain wooden box with an open hole on one side, out of which came a soft yellow light. This illuminer was less ornate that the one in Jade City, and was also different in that there was a small copper wire that extended out from one side and passed into a tiny hole in the wall. Quickly glancing around the room, Abby realized that all of them were similarly wired.

The ones in Jade City had no such connections. Did the elvish versions not need any such wiring? If so, Abby realized, that meant each elvish illuminer also probably needed to be handled individually in order to be controlled. With the four in this room all wired, he thought that perhaps they could all be turned on or off as a unit.

Abby looked around the walls of the room, trying to identify any sort of a light switch. Was it somewhere outside, perhaps right next to the door? He did not remember seeing something like that either time he had entered the room. For a moment, Abby looked at the back of the door, trying to decide whether to take a quick peek out. His continued nudity discouraged him, and he did not feel like retrieving the still damp towel from the floor to cover himself.

No, Abby thought, he would just study this for a few moments more, then go right back to the welcoming warmth of the bed.

Returning his focus to the illuminer, he recalled again how Reanah had spoken softly to one in Jade City to turn it off, as if it had required some sort of spell or trigger to operate. Was it just a matter of knowing the right words to say? That did not seem appropriate for this wired, human version of an illuminer. Surely, he thought, there had to be some way to turn the damn thing off. Otherwise, how would anyone within this room be able to control them?

Abby reached up and gently lifted the illuminer from its mount. He turned it until he could look directly into the opening on top. Through the yellow glow, he thought he could see a tiny little speck of metal floating in the center of the source of the light. Earthenium, Sister Dana had called it, the catalyst that interacted with magic and made a device operate.

Abby rotated the illuminer in his hands, looking for any sort of switch. Nothing. But as he focused his sight and his mind on it, he began to feel another sensation. The magic that powered it seemed to trigger something within Abby, a sensation that felt disturbingly similar to what had happened in Jade City. It was if some dormant force within Abby suddenly awoke, surging into life.

This time, though, instead of letting it simply pour out of him, Abby recognized what was happening, and used his will to try to rein it in. He partially succeeded. Instead of magic exploding out from his hands, as it had in Jade City, this surge was much lower in intensity. Even so, a substantial pulse of white magic poured into the illuminer as a bright wave. Abby's magic reacted with the magic already within the device and pushed it backwards, into the wire which fed the illuminer. For an instant, the other three illuminers in the room flared with Abby's magic, suddenly lighting the features in the room in an intense, clear relief, as if the whole room was illuminated by a photographer's strobe light.

Suddenly, there was an audible pop that came from elsewhere in the house, somewhere in the floors over Abby's head. The room's illuminers went out completely.

But instead of the room being plunged into absolute darkness, there was a soft glow that filled the room. To Abby's shock and dismay, Abby's own body shone with white light, a residue of his magic. In Jade City, the effect had not been as striking because most of his body had been covered with clothing, and he had only noticed it on his hands and forearms. Now, there were no clothes on Abby's body to hide the effect. From head to toe, Abby's body shone with a disconcerting, eerie light.

In a panic, Abby hopped off the chair. His first instinct was to dive under the covers of his bed and hide until the glow faded away. But as he took his first steps in that direction to do exactly that, he glanced over at the other bed.

In the ghostly light, a pair of wide, frightened eyes was staring back. Dacy was awake, her face frozen in an expression of slack-jawed shock. For the moment, Dacy seemed to have lost the capacity to speak. Abby froze in mid-step, and the two looked at each other for several seconds.

Then, there was a commotion outside the room. The sounds of hurried footsteps passed in both directions in the hallway, and a woman's voice called out, "Candles! We've lost power. Get some candles from the cupboard and take them upstairs into the residence."

That jolted Abby and Dacy out of their immobility. They both turned their faces toward the back of the door, holding their breaths in case someone was going to enter. There were several seconds of continued hubbub outside of the room, but without a knock on their door or a turn of their doorknob. It became clear that the guests were not the focus of the house staff at that moment. Abby breathed a sigh of relief. They had at least a little time to themselves.

Abby was the first to move. He turned and took a couple of steps to the nearby dresser, and began opening the drawers, searching. Abby said to Dacy in a hurried whisper, "Look for a candle and matches. They can't see me like this."

Dacy, though was slow to respond. She eyed Abby with silent, uncomprehending wonder as Abby continued to search.

To Abby, Dacy's continued silence was almost as surprising as the effect of the magic. He was used to her talking, all the time, and her sudden muteness was unnerving. Finally, in frustration, he turned toward her and said, "Dammit, Dacy. Help me."

That finally stirred Dacy, and she slowly opened up the covers and stepped out of the bed. Like Abby, she was not wearing any clothes, but their mutual nudity was the least relevant fact of that moment. In a daze, Dacy moved to a desk on the other side of the room, slowly opening and closing individual drawers in her search, but never really took her eyes off of Abby. Abby wondered, "Is she afraid of me?"

As that thought crossed his mind, Abby pulled open the last bottom drawer in the dresser and found a stubby candle in a holder and a couple of matches. Abby quickly turned and hurriedly whispered to Dacy, "Got it! Just a second." Dacy, barely moving and still mute, had not made much progress in her search. She was staring at Abby in a way that was making Abby increasingly uncomfortable.

Abby searched the surface of the dresser for a few moments, looking for something to strike the match on. Then, he glanced back at the candle holder, and saw a rough strip of papered grit glued on its side. He rubbed the tip of the match on it, and it flared to life. He then lit the candle's wick, creating a low flame that flickered before finally settling into a steady, slow burn. Grateful that there was now at least a little light in the room independent from himself, Abby gently set the candle holder on the dresser and turned back to Dacy.

Even with the candle's low light illuminating the room, the glow from Abby's body still seemed to captivate Dacy. The gentle white light was already starting to fade as Abby crossed the room toward her. That motion seemed to startle Dacy out of her trance, but Dacy flinched at Abby's approached. Still wide-eyed, she held up a hand to keep Abby from coming too close and said in an urgent whisper, "Stay away from me! What are you? Some sort of freak?"

Abby thought to himself, "If you only knew." To Dacy, though, he tried to be reassuring. He whispered back in a soothing tone, "No, no. This is only the second time it's happened. The first was in Jade City. I had some sort of reaction to an illuminer, and the same thing happened. There was some sort of reaction. But this time, the only thing I was trying to do was to turn off the lights. I'm as surprised as you are, believe me."

Dacy was not frightened, but seemed wary. "So, you've got the magic, then?"

"I don't know," Abby replied. "I guess so."

Dacy frowned. "But we're so far from a wellspring. I mean, I'm no expert, but unless you've tied into the collector on the top of the house, that shouldn't have happened."

Abby shrugged. "I was touching an illuminer that was wired into it. Maybe that's how it happened."

Dacy sighed, "Maybe. Well, if it's true then, that you've got the talent, that's a problem for us."

That sent a shot of fear through Abby. "Because I'm a rogue witch?"

"Yup," Dacy nodded. "And they's illegal."

The two paused for a moment as a set of feet quickly shuffled past their door. They could hear undistinguishable voices move down the hallway.

Once they passed, Abby whispered, "Keep your voice down. If something's happened, we don't want anyone to think we had anything to do with it."

"Why? What d'ya mean?" Dacy countered, a little too loudly for Abby's tastes. "What have you done?"

"Nothing. I mean, I don't know what happened. I heard a loud sound when I tried to light the illuminer. It flashed for a second and then went out." He gestured toward the other illuminers. "They did the same thing. Then, everything went dark. Except for me."

Abby looked down at himself. The glow was still present, but had faded significantly. The color of his skin was coming back, from a washed out white when the magic was at its strongest, to a more normal tone. "See," he said, holding up an arm to Dacy, "it's going away. Whatever is going on, it's almost finished."

Dacy lapsed back into silence, studying Abby from head to toe. Her frown showed she was mulling this new development in her mind. Her stare made Abby self-conscious of his nudity.

Abby quietly returned to the safety of his bed and slid into the sheets, covering himself with the blankets so that he was completely hidden. He took a quick peek down the length of his body. Even as he had tried to reassure Dacy, Abby thought to himself, "This isn't real. This is not happening." He drew the sheets up over the top of his head and shut his eyes.

Both Dacy and Abby remained silent for some time, each pondering the situation. There was continued movement outside the room, though it seemed calmer and less hurried than it was initially. Abby had the sense that the staff were working on solving the power outage. He hoped that he had not broken anything too badly.

It was several minutes before Abby heard Dacy settle back into bed. He wondered whether Dacy would give him away to the others. Was there some sort of reward for turning in a rogue witch? He hoped not. Or, at least, that Dacy did not need the money enough to betray him.

Resolving to talk it through with Dacy in the morning, Abby lay inside the sheets for a while longer, eyes shut. Eventually, his breathing calmed and his heart slowed down. He was able to fall asleep again.

Sometime later, Abby woke. There was a shuffling in the room around Abby's bed. He pulled the covers back and sleepily looked toward the sounds. Dacy was fully dressed, going through her backpack on top of her bed. Abby glanced over in the corner, and saw his dress and chemise, freshly laundered and folded, on top of a chair, with his shoes positioned carefully on the floor beneath.

Abby realized to his relief that the illuminers were back on. Whatever the problem was that he caused, someone was able to fix it. The candle had long since burned out on its own, leaving a pile of melted wax in its holder. The only light came from the four illuminers, glowing with their normal soft yellow light.

Abby withdrew an arm from beneath the covers and turned it over in the air. The glow was gone. It looked otherwise completely normal, that is, normal for a teenage girl. The lack of muscle mass and smooth, youthful skin was still disconcerting to him. Even so, Abby breathed a sigh of relief. No one would be able to tell that he had magical ability, at least visually. That was good enough for now, he thought.

Abby turned his attention back to Dacy. He needed reassurance from her. "You O.K.?" he said quietly. "I mean, are we O.K.?"

Without turning, Dacy nodded. "Fine, I guess. You and me's going to have a talk later, though. Once we get out of here, that is."

As confidently as he could, Abby said, "That's right. We'll talk this through. Get the truth out between us. You deserve it." Even as he said that, though, he knew he could never bring himself to tell her the full truth about himself, who he really was and the place he had come from.

But that was a problem for later. At that moment, Abby just wanted to know that Dacy was not going to rat him out. Dacy did not seem inclined to do that, at least for the immediate future.

Taking that as encouragement, Abby exited the bed and quickly dressed, sliding on the newly cleaned chemise and dress, and tying the laces which bound the front of the dress. He realized he was getting better at dressing as a girl.

The hair, though, was another matter. It was still a wild, unkempt mess. After slipping on his shoes, Abby asked Dacy for a brush. Dacy withdrew one from her backpack and handed it silently to Abby with a wary expression. As Abby brushed the knots from his hair, he realized that a suddenly quiet Dacy was more disconcerting than the normally talkative one. Dacy was clearly spooked by the events of the night before. The silence between them continued as Abby brushed the knots and stray strands out of his hair, into something more presentable.

When they were ready, Abby handed the brush back to Dacy, and Dacy returned it to its place before slipping on her backpack. She winced at the obvious soreness in her limbs as she lifted the weight onto her back and settled it into place. Abby, with nothing to carry and feeling awkwardly unencumbered, opened the door and led the way out of the room.

They passed the kitchen and retraced their way down the hallway toward Mistress Paulina's office. As they went by the other rooms in the basement, Abby could see the house servants moving through their morning, taking little notice of them.

Reaching the black door of Mistress Paulina's office, Abby knocked. Without waiting for a reply, he stuck his head in without fully entering. As Dacy waiting in the hallway behind, still lost in her thoughts, Abby spoke for both of them. "Thank you, ma'am. Your hospitality was much appreciated."

Mistress Paulina was seated at her desk, preoccupied and a little annoyed with the interruption. Looking up, she said, "Yes, yes, girls. You're welcome. Fair accommodations for a fair price. Don't be spreading that sentiment around, though, this is not a hotel."

Abby nodded in reply. He just wanted to get out of there with as little fanfare as possible.

Mistress Paulina continued in a warning tone, "When you leave, please go directly out to the gate. Don't speak to anyone. And try not to be seen. Lady Harris doesn't take kindly to seeing strangers wandering about on her front lawn first thing in the morning."

Despite his own desire for a quick, painless exit, Abby could not resist a smart-ass answer.

"Really? I thought we were here because of the hospitality of Lady Harris. Give her our thanks and compliments, will you? Tell her she has a lovely house."

Mistress Paulina shot an irritated glance at Abby and said dryly, "Of course. I'll give her your warmest regards. Now go, please."

Abby grinned an impish smile and began to back his head out of the door opening. But, remembering the events of the night before, he could not leave before asking one final question. As innocently as possible, Abby leaned again into the room and said, "So, tell me, Mistress. What happened last night? It seemed like there was some sort of commotion."

Mistress Paulina gave a dismissive wave of her hand, "The power went out. It does that sometimes. But that is none of your concern. We have very good head technician here, and she was able to get the system working again after only a short delay. I'm sorry if it caused you any inconvenience."

Despite her obvious desire that Abby and Dacy be on their way, Abby persisted. "Good, I'm glad," he said smoothly. "But do you know what happened, exactly?"

Mistress Paulina paused in her paperwork at the question. She seemed unsure herself. "Strange, really. That has only happened rarely before—when the roof collector had been struck by lightning. Only a couple of times in the twenty years I've been here." She waved the thought, and Abby, away with the same dismissive hand gesture. "No matter. Off you go. I've got more to do than banter with the likes of you." She returned to shuffling papers on her desk.

With a knowing smirk that Mistress Paulina missed, Abby replied, "Thanks again." He quietly backed out and gently closed the door. Abby sighed with relief. At least Mistress Paulina did not blame her two guests for what had happened. Good, he thought. Only Dacy really knew it was Abby's fault.

Abby looked at Dacy's face, trying to assess her current state of mind. She had heard the entire conversation, but had not interjected herself into it once. Still standing meekly in the hallway, wobbling gently under the weight of her backpack, Dacy looked back at Abby with a blank expression. Abby wondered what was going through her mind, but was too afraid to ask at that moment. There would be time for that later. But Dacy's continued silence was unnatural and unsettling.

Abby frowned with concern as he turned and led the way out of the basement. They trudged up the steps into the front courtyard area. There was a light, chilling fog hanging in the still air and a heavy dew on the grass. They continued on in silence, heading out on the road leading to the main gate. To the east, there was a featureless brightness coming from the still-hidden morning sun, though dawn was only moments away.

Abby risked a glance back at the house. A few of the windows in the face of the building showed light coming from within, either glowing through the curtains or in narrow gaps between the fabric. Abby could only imagine what those elegant rooms must look like, or the elegant people that lived upstairs in the main floors of the house. It was a little jarring to think that those people might take offense at the sight of him or Dacy.

The sight made Abby realize just how far he was from having the basic necessities—food, shelter, clothing—that the inhabitants of that grand house took for granted. As Tom, he had all of those things and the job that supported them. Now, as Abby, all he possessed was the clothes on his back. And Dacy, using the last of her money, was the only reason that he was able to have one blissful night of comfort. Abby knew harder times lay ahead.

They continued on in silence toward the main gate. Groups of farmhands were also heading out, passing into the fields as clusters of vague dark forms in the fog. Abby stared straight ahead as he walked, monitoring Dacy only by the sound of her boots scraping the gravel of the road behind him. He did not want to say anything to her until they were safely off the premises.

At last, Abby and Dacy passed beneath the metal arch and walked into the middle of the road. Once there, Abby turned and faced Dacy with a scowling expression. "O.K., Dacy," he said with anger in his voice. "You're freaking me out. Let's have it out right now."

Dacy recoiled at the suddenness of Abby's confrontation. Her eyes widened in reply as she steadied herself against the weight on her back and brought herself to a complete stop. For several seconds, she stared back at Abby, trying to find the right words to begin. Finally, she said weakly, "I dunno. Magic's something I'll never understand, and it scares me, to be honest. I don't get why some people have it and the rest of us have to make do without it."

She looked away and sighed. "When I was the age to be tested, two Sisters came to our village and checked all us over. Two of the girls ended up goin' off to the Academy in Crystal City, to the Sisterhood. To a better life. Gettin' an education. Seein' and doin' things, ya know? And I was stuck behind, with my crappy family in my crappy town."

She turned back and looked directly into Abby's eyes. "So you're one of them with the magic. That's fine. I don't care as long as you don't put some sort of hex on me. But tell me true. Why ain't you with the Sisterhood? Why is you a rogue witch, just wandering around on your own? That's the part what frightens me. Makes me think you're one of the bad ones."

Abby shrugged. "I don't know. You've got to believe me when I tell you that this magic stuff is brand new to me. What happened last night only happened once before, in Jade City. The same thing happened when I touched an illuminer—a big explosion of magic. Both times, I had no idea why or how it happened. Or, how to control it. That's it. I'm as clueless about all of this as you are. I couldn't hex you even if I wanted to. I swear to you that's the truth."

Dacy seemed to believe Abby, but countered, "Don'cha see, though? Even if it just happened the two times, that makes you a rogue witch. You're illegal if you have magic, unless you're one of the Sisterhood and you've sworn their oaths. And I'd be your accomplice. Both of us would get pinched if the law found out."

Abby held his hands up in a gesture of helplessness. "Fine, Dacy. What do you want me to do?" Unable to help himself, Abby started to get emotional. Tears welled up in his eyes, and his voice quavered as he spoke, "I'm out here by myself, not knowing what the hell I'm doing or where I'm going." He started to cry. He could not stop himself. "I need your help. Please. Get me someplace where I can take care of myself. A job. A roof over my head and regular meals on the table. Something besides being out here in the open, waiting for the first bad storm to kick my ass." Abby turned and tried to collect himself, wiping the tears from his eyes. To himself, he thought, "Damn. That came on real fast."

Dacy's tone was sympathetic, but still wary. "Abby, I don't think you'd hurt me, on purpose. That's not it. When we met, I thought right away that we'd be fast friends, once we got to know each other. You and me. We's good company, ya know? But last night scared the shit out of me. You've got to understand that. If you really don't know how to control it. Once the magic in you gets cranked up, who knows what'll happen to me."

Abby regained a little of his composure, but his eyes were still full of tears when he turned back to answer. "I absolutely guarantee I won't hurt you. I mean, it's true that I don't know how it works. Not yet. But I'll never use the magic against you. I swear it." He raised his right hand. "My most solemn oath. I promise."

Dacy seemed reassured, at least a little. "All I know is, once them Sisters learn how to use that shit, it's like they's not real people anymore. They's way better than the rest of us, just cause they were born with it and we weren't. Don't let that happen to you, if they ever get their hands on you."

"I know what you mean," Abby replied. "When I was in Jade City, this one Sister was going to question me, and make me answer if I didn't do it voluntarily. It scared the crap out of me. What she was going to do to me was wrong. I'll never be like that. I promise."

Abby moved closer to Dacy, and extended his arms out to invite a hug. For a moment, Dacy seemed as if she was going to pull back, but instead stood still as Abby approached. With the backpack in the way, Abby could not reach around Dacy for a full embrace. Instead, he settled for a slightly awkward hug of Dacy's shoulders.

Still, the gesture reassured Dacy. "O.K., fine," she said. "Just some warning next time."

"No problem," Abby answered, his face relaxing and finally breaking into a smile. "No more touching illuminers unless I tell you first."

Dacy nodded in reply. She, too, seemed relieved, even though she could not bring herself to smile. "Come on. Let's go. I want to get to Pearl City before the whole place had been picked clean. Maybe then, you'll have your own stuff to carry."

The two travelers turned east, into the rising sun that had finally broken through the early morning fog. The rays warmed their faces as they headed down the road, into the new day.

SEVEN: REANAH

Reanah was grateful for the rest, but not the hassle. It was a little over a week since Reanah had brought in the odd little human girl to Jade City, and the discovery had brought a welcome relief from the grinding routine of her patrols. But her commanding officer had held her back for more and more debriefings, after the girl's subsequent escape. Sister Dana was furious, and Reanah knew she was trying to find a way to blame Reanah for the screw-up.

Reanah had done nothing wrong, and answered the same questions firmly and without flinching, but with a growing impatience. Reanah told how her team had come upon the wreckage of a wagon. In it, they had discovered a deceased human female. Signs pointed to a robbery, with the human having apparently driven into the river in a failed attempt to escape. The human had been struck with three arrows, one fatally through the chest. The signs and tracks appeared to show that she had been chased by three riders on horses, and the woman had apparently panicked and driven her horse and wagon off the established road and into the water. But rocks in the stream had broken off one of the wheels, and she was killed in the attack.

A subsequent search revealed the teenage girl a distance downstream, at the base of a water fall. The girl, confused and in some distress, had denied any knowledge of the accident. Reanah found her at the time to be credible. The girl, during the subsequent travel to Jade City, had not volunteered more information about her past. And no, she had not seen any evidence of magical ability from the girl. Reanah had not pressed her to give more details. As she told her inquisitors more than once, including Sister Dana, "That was your job."

Reanah's interrogators had filled in some of the missing pieces, based on the evidence collected at the scene and brought in by Reanah's patrol. The robbers had taken the woman's valuables, but had left her identity papers behind. The woman's name was Teresa, aged thirty-five, and her daughter was Leanna, aged sixteen. They claimed to be from Quartz City, a minor human city in the northeast corner of the Queendom of Distan.

In order to make the passage, they had been issued travel papers at the border. Records showed she and a human girl had passed through Jade City on their way to Emerald City, the capital of the elves. Their listed reason for travel was "business", and their wagon was filled with high priced fashionable dresses favored by the rich. Had she completed it, the journey would have been very lucrative for the woman, but part of the lure and justification for the high prices was due to the risky travel required to bring them from the east into Emerald City.

As a much more down-to-earth elf, Reanah never understood the appeal of such fineries, but Reanah appreciated the audacity of the two humans' attempt to make the crossing. It was a shame, really.

The identity papers and the subsequent research on their movements only deepened the mystery of the surviving girl. Instead of identifying herself as Leanna, as stated in the identity papers, she had strangely claimed to Reanah that her name was "Abstinence", or "Abby" for short. And she spoke with a strange accent that definitely did not come from the area around Quartz City. Was she in fact this Leanna, or indeed someone else?

When Reanah discovered her, she was standing by the side of a pool underneath a waterfall with several prominent boulders jutting from the water. It did not seem possible that she could have gone over the falls without being seriously injured. So, all in all, when the girl said she knew nothing about the robbery upstream, there was a truth in it that Reanah believed. But if she was not connected to the robbery, and was not the missing girl Leanah, who was she, really? How did she get there?

As far as Reanah was concerned, that mystery was not her problem. Let Investigations take the lead on that. She was just a Scout, after all.

Furthermore, Reanah did not see how they could blame her for the girl's escape. It was true that Reanah was the first one to find her missing the next morning. True, the guard outside the door was asleep at his post. But the door to the room had been locked when she had entered. She was sure of it. The only item out of place was a functioning illuminer, lying on its side on the bed instead of its mount on the wall. Nothing else was amiss.

It was obvious that the girl had escaped through the open window of the adjacent room. The girl had clearly been in there. One of the illuminers of that room was missing, and there was some indecipherable message scratched in ink on a piece of paper. Clearly, some sort of taunt for her captors.

But Reanah had no idea how the girl had managed to do it. And as far as she was concerned, if it was magic that allowed the girl to escape, it was Sister Dana's duty to figure that out. Magic was outside of Reanah's realm of expertise, and the girl was not her problem. Reanah had repeated that last part often during questioning.

It was politics, she knew. That's all. Mustn't embarrass a Sister. And her superiors needed someone more senior than the unfortunate male grunt that had fallen asleep outside of the room while on guard duty. No, they needed at least a junior officer to pin this on. And Reanah was worried that it would wind up being her. The thought made her more and more angry as the days passed. Reanah was convinced that they were going to make her the scapegoat. Fuck that, she thought.

Still though, it was a nice change to have a few extra days of rest before going out again on patrol. The routine had gotten old. Out for two weeks at a time, then back for a couple of days or so, then going out again with another group. Their standing orders were to roam the mountains between the realms of the elves and humans, looking for any bandits (almost always human), and any stray undead that had wandered into the area. That was Reanah's job, and she and her team were good at it.

Still, she was looking for new challenges, and she had been mulling over requesting a new assignment. But the girl's disappearance would not look good on her record, if it was stuck on her. She could be looking at a negative lateral reassignment, or an actual demotion. She was determined to fight against that, as best she could.

So, when Reanah received word that she was to report to General Tavi and to do it double-time, she had a sinking feeling that bad news was about to land on her head. She just knew that she would be stuck with the consequences of the girl's escape. The thought infuriated her.

As Reanah strolled quickly through headquarters, her frowning expression serving as a warning for others not to bother her. Her mind roiled with the possible outcomes, most certainly negative. The other shoe was about to drop, and she was sure she was not going to like it. Her facial expression tightened into a sour grimace.

Reaching the door to General Tavi's office, she paused to gather herself for a moment. Losing her temper in front of the general would only make it worse for her. She took a deep breath and exhaled away some of the tension, then knocked quietly. "Enter", came the muffled reply from within. Reanah pushed open the door.

The General was an older elf with a hard, tight face and a stiff military bearing. Her green uniform was crisp and pressed, with epaulets on her shoulders and medals arranged neatly in rows on her chest. Her hair, brown flecked with grey streaks, was gathered in a purposeful tight bundle behind her head. Reanah was sure that the General was much older than she appeared to be, and any actual battles were well in her past.

Still, Reanah respected her. She did not really know the General that well. The difference in rank was enough to keep them separated most of the time. Reanah dealt the most with her supervising colonel. And when they did speak, their relationship was all business.

Now in General Tavi's presence, Reanah snapped to attention. The sight of her desk had always made an impression on Reanah. Its surface was strewn with parchments, letters and maps. Nearby shelves were stocked with books, with more papers and scrolls wedged into the available empty spaces. Reanah had never seen so many documents in such a relatively small space, and there was more expensive, handmade paper in here than in many libraries. As much as Reanah hoped to advance up the chain of command in her career, the thought of dealing with so much of it gave her pause. Higher rank always meant more paperwork. And Reanah hated paperwork.

But General Tavi was in a unique position. Jade City was more a military outpost than a residential town, straddling the border between the lands of the elves and humans. Her office was the command center of both the local military and the civil administration. The orders that flowed from General Tavi's ink-stained fingers affected every aspect of life in this region. So, the fact that she had called Reanah to personally attend her in her office, was probably not a good sign.

Reanah held her correct military posture for several seconds, waiting for the General to acknowledge her presence. Finally, at the risk of impertinence, she said, "Reporting as ordered, General."

General Tavi took a few seconds more to finish the missive in front of her, the feather quill dancing in her fingers. Finally, she pushed the paper aside and laid the quill in its holder, then wiped the ink from her hands with a cloth as she begin to speak. "Lieutenant. I'll get right to the point. This concerns the missing human girl."

Reanah's heart sank. She knew it. "General, ma'am," she began to protest, the words spilling from her quickly. "You know that I had nothing to do with the girl's escape. The door was locked when I exited that night."

General Tavi held up a hand to stop her. "Relax, Lieutenant. No one thinks that you let the girl go. The guard that fell asleep at his post will be subject to court martial, but I don't see any need for any further discipline than that."

Reanah was so relieved that she almost bent over as she exhaled the tension from her lungs. But, remembering where she was, she quickly caught herself and straightened back up into a proper posture.

The General continued, "Nevertheless, there are some unresolved questions. The morning after the escape, Sister Dana had used her dowsing rod to detect signs of magic in the girl's room. It revealed the residue of a concentrated magic that was used in the vicinity, either by the girl or someone else who aided in her escape."

General Tavi eyed Reanah sternly, coming to her real point. She continued, "Perhaps, however, you can help us with one puzzling detail." She reached to her side and grabbed a piece of parchment with a noticeable ink blotch in one corner. Reanah knew it was the paper found in the neighboring room, but she had never actually seen it. "Does this mean anything to you?"

Reanah took the parchment and quietly examined it for a moment. The blotch appeared to be the attempt of a novice to use a quill pen, taking too much ink on the tip so that when the user applied it to the paper, it quickly spilled out in one large blot. Simple enough. Next to that, though, someone had obviously tried to write…something. The symbols were not anything that Reanah recognized in either the Old Tongue or Common. Was it some sort of code? Reanah could not decipher it.

After a few moments of study, Reanah handed the paper back to the general. "Sorry, ma'am. I cannot make any sense of it."

The general said, "I was with Sister Dana when this was brought to us. It came from the room next to the missing girl's room. She obviously tried to leave some sort of message behind before her escape." She chuckled. "I swear to you that the Sister turned white when she saw those letters."

Reanah furrowed her eyebrows in confusion. "Really? Why?"

General Tavi replied, "Well, according to the Sister, these letters are some form of ancient language that has been seen in some caverns and crypts. Sister Dana had apparently participated in a study of this language in her youth. It is analogous to our alphabet, and may have even been a predecessor of the Old Tongue. Thousands of years old, apparently. No one knows what sort of race used this alphabet, where they came from, or what may have happened to them. They were here briefly, then gone without a trace."

General Tavi shook her head in disbelief. "In any event," she continued, pointing to a word in the middle of the message, "Sister Dana said she believes that this is your name, misspelled. The last word could be the girl's nickname. It was obviously from her, and Sister Dana believes it was some sort of message to you."

Was there a tone of accusation in the General's voice? Reanah was not sure. Surely, no one could think that she understood some long dead language. She replied, somewhat defensively, "General, I have no idea what it says. Truly."

General Tavi studied Reanah carefully for several seconds. Then, she relaxed her features and said, "Of course not. How could you? I suppose if you were an expert in some lost language, we would already know that by now. Still, it does not make much sense that the girl would leave you a message if you could not decipher it yourself."

Reanah's face flushed, and she shook her head in protest. "No, General. I do not know why Sister Dana would think that I might understand this writing. I am certainly no expert on such things, and I had known the girl for only a few days. I have no idea what this is about."

General Tavi nodded as if she were satisfied. "Yes, of course. You have been a loyal and competent officer in the Queen's Army. I have never known you to do anything other than your duty." She reached to the side and picked up another piece of paper. She handed it to Reanah and watched her read it for several seconds, then continued, "Here are your new orders. You can do your duty, and prove your continued loyalty, by finding and returning the girl back here."

Reanah felt as she had been slapped in the face. Continued loyalty? What was she implying? She stammered, "Is that why I was not immediately sent after the girl after her escape? Because I was under suspicion?"

"I did not suspect you," the general replied smoothly. "Others had raised questions. That's all."

It was all Reanah could do to keep from yelling back at her. With all the self-control that Reanah could muster, she answered with her voice grating in her throat, "Then perhaps Sister Dana should get off her fat ass and go retrieve the girl herself. Musn't have any co-conspirators in on the effort, after all."

General Tavi cut her off. "Enough, Lieutenant! You forget yourself."

Reanah had to bite her lower lip to keep from responding. The two elves stared at each other for a few seconds, General Tavi daring her to say anything more. But this time, Reanah did catch herself. She knew that with another burst of anger, a few more ill-chosen words, and she might wind up in the stockade and subject to court martial herself.

Finally, having made her point, General Tavi relaxed her expression and waved Reanah away. "That's enough for now, Lieutenant. You have your orders."

Once again in control of her emotions, Reanah answered smoothly, "Yes, General. But the girl is most likely long gone by now. She could be anywhere."

The general nodded. "I agree. And if this was a more pressing issue, we would be doing more." She stood and walked around the desk until she faced Reanah. She looked Reanah directly in the eyes with a stern expression. "Look, Lieutenant. I personally do not believe the twaddle that you let the girl escape, even accidentally. But there have been questions raised. Because this involves the Sisterhood, this is a sensitive political matter. Something must be done, and you are the one to do it. You understand."

No, Reanah thought, she did not understand at all. She was a soldier, and a good one at that. Not a politician. She never played those games.

General Tavi put a hand on Reanah's shoulder and said, "Give yourself some credit, Lieutenant Reanah. I know your loyalty to the Queen is absolute. Years of commendable service are not tainted by one incident." She dismissively waved her hand. "As far as I am concerned, the door was unlocked and the guard was asleep. Nothing more. The simplest explanation is usually the best."

"If that is what you believe, then why me?" Reanah replied. "Is this some sort of punishment?"

"No," the General answered smoothly, "but you do know what the girl looks like. You interacted with her the most during her time in our custody. Perhaps the girl even would trust you enough to not run if she were to see you approach her. I would have wanted to send you in any event."

As if she had made her point, General Tavi began to walk back around her desk towards her chair, talking as she moved. "Frankly, I do not care if you actually locate the little bitch. Just make a good faith effort. Take a few days. Ride out, go to the closest human settlements. If anyone has seen her, pursue those leads. With luck, you may even locate her. If you do, bring her back here. Otherwise, at your discretion, come back and report that she is no longer in the area. I will back you at the expense of any objections that Sister Dana may have." She reached her chair and sat down, leaning back with an expression that suggested their conversation was over.

Reanah knew that she was risking further aggravating the general, but in desperation asked, "Make a good faith effort? So, you do not actually care if I find the girl or not?"

General Tavi gestured at the stacks of parchments on top of her desk. "As you can see, I have many more issues that I am concerned with at this moment. I do not have the resources to mount a full search, and I do not see the need to do so. Yes, to answer you frankly, I am trying to get Sister Dana off my back." She pointed a finger toward Reanah to emphasize her point. "And you are the one to do it. Use your best judgment. I trust you. Dismissed, Lieutenant."

Reanah opened her mouth to argue, but the general was already returning her focus to her papers. As frustrated as she was with her new orders, she knew that any further objections would be useless. After a couple of seconds of silent anger, she snapped to attention, clicking her heels together. Then, she turned and left the room, closing the door behind her.

After several quick strides down the corridor, at a distance unlikely to be heard by the general, Reanah finally blurted out in frustration, "Fuck this!" Faces turned toward her outburst, but she ignored them. Her hard expression warned off anyone who may have been tempted to ask her what the matter was. Anyone who had worked at headquarters for any length of time knew better than that. Lieutenant Reanah, they knew, could sometimes be a very prickly pear.

She was still fuming through the entire time that it took to gather her possessions and pack her horse. She did not even bother to get word to the other members of her scouting party that she was going off on a solo mission. They would find out soon enough, probably from her replacement.

And she was still wearing a 'do not bother me' expression as she rode through the eastern gate, heading out on the road through the Jade Pass toward the Queendom of Distan. She assumed that the girl was headed back to the lands of the humans. That would be what Reanah would do if she were her.

If General Tavi did not actually care if the girl was found or not and she only doing this to satisfy Sister Dana, Reanah was determined to get this over with as soon as possible. How long was this going to take? Two or three days at most, she thought to herself. Just enough to make it seem as if she had made a real effort. Even if all she actually did was ride around and talk to a few people. She could not imagine actually finding the girl at this point.

As she rode into the cool evening spring air, with the light of the sunset warming her back, Reanah tried to make herself feel better with that thought. This would not be too difficult. She would be back before her colleagues even knew she was gone. Two or three days at most. The thought cheered her up, at least a little bit.

EIGHT: PEARL CITY

For Abby, the day-long trudge into Pearl City was monotonous and wearing. He was already sick of walking for hours and hours on end. When he was Tom, he was always baffled by joggers or walkers or treadmill owners. They always seemed to him like hamsters on a wheel. He could never dedicate himself to a routine in which the point was to make yourself tired and sweaty. To the smug exercisers and gym rats, Tom always said he was happy with himself, doughy and beer-bellied as he was. Of course, if he had been dedicated to fitness, Tom probably would not have had his heart attack and would not be Abby now. He wondered grimly if that was the point of all this. One way or the other, the universe was going to make him exercise.

For Dacy, the only distress occurred on the few occasions that they passed any wagon or cart heading in the opposite direction, loaded down with items pilfered from the abandoned town—furniture, clothes, garden implements, tools, pots, pans and dishes. Each sighting was a reminder of what she was missing. Dacy could not get there fast enough for her share, and would offer a jealous appraisal of each load they passed. "Ooh, that's nice…Look at that one…Can't wait to get me hands on one of those." And so on.

At least, the prospect of free stuff brightened Dacy's spirits enough to change the subject from those that Abby did not want to talk about: magic and Abby's past. Abby was happy to let these topics drop. He did not understand the why or how of magic, and he did not want to make up some bullshit story about who Abby was. Because, he vowed to himself, one thing he would never do would be to tell Dacy about Tom, his real past. She would never believe, or understand, the very different world that he had come from.

As much as he could, he stoked Dacy's anticipation of what they might expect to find in Pearl City on their arrival, and the two chattered away about it for hours. Was there money, jewels? Well, they agreed, probably not. People had probably already picked through the homes of the richest ones, and the stores and any bank in town. Looters were never good at sharing, which they agreed was so unfair. Dacy kept making a point of saying that she only took what she needed and could carry, and they should do the same. She was an ethical thief.

So, the two resolved, at Dacy's insistence, that Dacy would choose what to keep or leave behind. Dacy had some definite opinions about value versus weight, and could decide accordingly. Of course, Dacy promised that Abby would finally have her own load of clothes and tools and baubles to haul around, as much as Abby could carry. One good haul in Pearl City, Dacy explained, and they would be able to barter and pay their way around the rest of the Queendom of Distan for some time.

Or even better, Dacy wondered aloud, maybe they could get their hands on a couple of horses and their own wagon. Yeah! They would not have to walk anymore. They should each get one of those and a good load of stuff besides, maybe enough to start their own trading business. Right? That was only fair.

Abby thought that contradicted Dacy's earlier representation that she only took what she needed, but he let it pass. He had the feeling Dacy thought she deserved nothing less. As Dacy kept saying, for all the crap she had gone through in her life, from running away from home at fourteen through years of wandering around, up to and including her recent eighteenth birthday, she deserved a little good fortune. And if everyone in Pearl City had been crazy enough to up and leave, Dacy was going to get hers. She was entitled to it.

Dacy was reluctant to talk about her past, but Abby did get more information as Dacy sprinkled it in to their conversations during the day. Dacy was the youngest of four children.

Her mother was a trader in Moonstone City, on the border between the realms of the dwarves and humans. Although the family was relatively prosperous, her parents were constantly bickering and fighting, and Dacy, a born troublemaker, was often a source of the tension.

At fourteen, she was ready to leave a place she regarded as a dead-end backwater. So when an uncle tried to molest her (a detail she just threw in as an aside), she packed up what little she had and left. And she had been on her own ever since, proudly so. As she kept repeating, "I ain't never been really hungry. Ain't never really needed for anything, but what I gots on my back."

Abby took Dacy's willingness to share her past as a sign that she was becoming more comfortable with him. But, Abby did not reciprocate. He had not yet constructed the story of who Abby was, because he did not know enough about this new world to build a plausible lie. And he could not bring himself to talk about his real past, as Tom, and the world that he really came from. As long as he was stuck in this body, he did not know how he would ever be ready to do that. So, Abby did not volunteer anything about his past, and Dacy did not seem inclined to ask.

By the time the sun was setting behind them, the two travelers were moving toward the outer edge of the town. From a distance, Pearl City looked like a larger, flatter version of Jade City, spread out on a low river plain instead of being forced to wedge itself within a mountain pass. There did not seem to be an outer defensive wall, just a line where the houses ended and the surrounding fields began. From a distance, the yellowing rays of the setting sun illuminated the sides of white washed square little homes that defined the roughly oval edge of town. The surrounding fields were devoid of people, left in a state of suspended spring cultivation.

Abby and Dacy kept moving forward, with Dacy suddenly lapsing into an unnatural silence as they approached. There was no gate or outer checkpoint to Pearl City to bar their way. The road that they were walking on passed between some outer buildings and disappeared into the dark mass of the rest of the town.

They reached the edge of town just after the sun set. Now, Abby and Dacy were alone. There was no one else going in or out of the town, and Abby could not sense the presence of anyone in their immediate vicinity.

To further dampen their spirits, there was no lighting of the road. Abby noticed what appeared to be lampposts, spaced evenly along the side of their route, but none of them were working. They were heading right into a dark, eerily silent place.

The only thing Abby did notice, quite strongly, was the smell of rotting, decaying flesh. There were no human bodies, but they occasionally passed the corpse of a horse or cat or dog or fowl or vermin, all in a similar stage of bloated, stiff, putrid decomposition. The people had vanished without a trace, but the bodies of the animals of Pearl City were still there. Abby guessed that they had all died suddenly in the same event.

Suddenly, Abby began to feel a little trepidation. What had happened here? For all of Dacy's chatter about coming to this place, she had never offered a reason for why Pearl City was this way. She probably did not know, and perhaps did not care. To Dacy, this was simply a golden opportunity to enrich herself.

Yet, here the two of them were, heading into this empty, dark, foreboding place. Abby could tell that this had once been a bustling, living place, but now it seemed desolate. And if all the normal inhabitants were gone, who did that leave behind? Thieves and robbers, or worse? The people who, like Dacy, viewed this as a once in a lifetime opportunity to remedy their poverty? What was Dacy getting him into?

It made Abby wonder about their physical safety. Abby had never seen any hint of a weapon on Dacy, and when Abby brought it up, Dacy would only say, "Don't worry 'bout it. I can take care of myself, thank you very much."

Fine, Abby thought as they continued on in silence, but what about me? In this new reality, he could not just pick up the phone and dial '911'. As a man, Tom had not thought very much about his own personal safety. He was not a fitness freak or weightlifter, just a regular guy about six feet tall, with a slightly doughy dad bod. He had never given a second thought to walking down a street alone at night. And if someone had approached him and asked for the time or directions, or just to strike up a conversation, it was never his first thought that he was in danger. Of course, it would have only taken one bad experience, a mugging or an assault, to pierce his sense of invulnerability. But, fortunately, something like that had never happened to him, as Tom.

As Abby, though, he had a lingering sense of dread as they made their way into the intimidating darkness that was Pearl City at night. How concerned should he be about his personal safety?

For her part, Dacy did not seem put off by their surroundings. She was quiet, but seemed resolved to follow through on her plans. Her main concern was not that she would be taking property that did not belong to her, but that others had already beaten her to the best loot. She seemed to regard herself as more of a scavenger than a thief.

It was low level criminal activity, to be sure, but what about anyone else in this place? Would they also be capable of assault, or rape or murder? Even in a world in which women appeared to be in charge, surely, Abby thought, the worst of human nature had to exist here too.

Some distance into Pearl City, the darkness around them was close to being total. Abby could barely see Dacy right next to him, much less what they were heading. He almost thought of asking Dacy to call a halt, right where they were, despite her determination to keep going no matter what.

Suddenly though, and remarkably, the street lamps began to flicker on. At the top of each of the posts that Abby had noticed on the way in, there was a large square box, resting within a metal frame with a design worked into each. Each appeared to be an oversize version of an interior illuminer, but with exit holes in each of the four sides. The frames depicted animals or flowers or some abstract design, but all were fanciful and seemed designed to show off the craft of the maker.

Grateful for the unexpected illumination, a curious Abby walked beneath one of the lights. Through the light emanating from one of the outlet holes, Abby could detect the same small bit of metal which he had previously seen in interior illuminers, which seemed to float in the center as magic coalesced around it and came out as a low yellow light. The light was less intense than a typical working streetlight in Tom's world, but it was enough to provide some basic illumination to their immediate surroundings.

As grateful as Abby was for the lights to be operating, this development raised more questions. Why were the streetlamps working in this otherwise dead and empty place? Was anyone operating these, or did they just turn on by themselves? Abby posed those questions to Dacy and only received a silent shrug in reply.

For Abby, it only deepened the mystery of this place.

Night settled in over them. As they walked alone into the interior of the hushed town, Abby noticed that the side streets immediately around them remained dark. Farther away, through gaps in the buildings, Abby could see other streets with lights, apparently the other main thoroughfares heading into Pearl City's center.

The houses they passed remained dark, and eerily silent. Some had open doorways, and various items lay in the streets—dishes or clothes or tools or cans or any other household items. Abby took them as evidence of a hurried departure, either by the original residents or by scavengers.

Occasionally, Dacy paused to examine whether a particular item was worthy enough for her, holding them up to a nearby streetlamp to appraise them. But in each instance, she dropped whatever she had picked up back onto the pavement. "Garbage. Crap," Dacy would say before moving on. Everything they were seeing had already been picked over at least once, and similarly discarded. Abby registered Dacy's increasing frustration as they moved along, but kept silent.

Taking advantage of the lighting, they continued on until they approached Pearl City's center. Abby and Dacy lapsed into a watchful silence. There was no wind to make random noises to cover the sounds their footfalls on the pavement. Each of their steps made an uncomfortable clack or scrape which echoed between the buildings in their immediate vicinity.

As Abby passed beneath the light of each individual streetlamp, he felt exposed. He listened as carefully as he could for any sound which would give away the approach of anyone else. Several times, he thought he could hear a knock or clunk or some other random sound. But when he turned to look, Abby's eyes could not penetrate the blackness beyond their illuminated street.

Abby grew nervous and fearful, and looked to Dacy for some reassurance. She too, seemed tense and wary, but beneath it all was a quiet confidence. Abby had the sense that Dacy thought she could handle almost anything that might come their way.

Finally, Dacy slowed as they neared a collection of streetlights that defined the town's center and main square. As Abby waited by her side, she stood and quietly appraised the dark buildings on either side of the thoroughfare. They were larger and of better construction than the buildings at the edge of town, evidence of the relative affluence of the former owners who lived in this neighborhood.

Picking one at random, Dacy walked up to the front door and tried the knob. Locked. She moved to the next home, one with the door slightly ajar. The door was damaged, having already been forced open. Dacy cautiously pushed the door inwards, cocking her head as she listened for any sounds in the interior. After a few tense seconds, she seemed satisfied.

Dacy waved Abby over. Slipping her arms out from the straps over her shoulders, she dropped her backpack on the ground. She rifled through one of its pockets until she located a beeswax candle and matches. She struck the match on the stone stoop, and carefully lit the candle wick until it sputtered into a steady flame. Neither Dacy or Abby spoke as this was happening. In the almost total silence, all but the quietest whisper would seem out of place.

The sight of a lighted candle, though, was a little jarring to Abby. He did not remember Dacy having a candle before their overnight stay in Rivertree Crossing. Before then, they had relied on a campfire, which Dacy had started with flint sparked into dry leaves. Abby decided that Dacy must have taken them sometime the night before, though Abby had not seen her do it. It was theft, but Abby was nevertheless grateful that Dacy had them.

Dacy motioned for Abby to grab her backpack and follow her into the interior. Abby was surprised that Dacy let him touch her stuff. That was progress, Abby thought to himself.

Dacy pushed the door fully open and lifted the candle up to light the way as she moved into the front foyer of the elegant home. Abby followed, almost dragging the bulky backpack as he carried it inside. Abby thought to himself, "Good God, this is heavy!" Abby could not believe that Dacy had carried this much weight around on her journeys. Dacy was a tough little nut. But it was also a sobering reminder to Abby of his own physical weakness.

As Abby pulled the backpack to a spot at the bottom of a staircase that curved around to the upstairs, Dacy moved behind Abby and tried to close the door. Dacy attempted a few times to make the door latch click into place, but the damage done to the door prevented it from fully closing. After a couple of tries to make it latch, Dacy gave up and took a nearby chair and propped its back against the doorknob to try to keep the door closed. But there was little friction on the marble floor that would prevent any determined intruder from shoving the door open. It looked to Abby as if a good, stiff breeze would push it back open.

Even though they were now in the interior of a building, Abby did not feel any safer. Dacy frowned, apparently with the same concern, but she seemed determined to stay in this particular building. They were both tired and ready to rest. It would have to do.

They turned and looked around the interior. There was enough light coming through the front windows from the exterior streetlamps that they could see the full height of the open foyer in ghostly relief. A chandelier hung from an ornate mount on the ceiling high above them. Next to Abby, a staircase with a thick dark wood railing and covered in red carpeting wound around the wall up to a second floor landing. As Abby spun around with his neck craned upwards, his shoes made crunching sounds from bits of broken glass on the floor. Abby looked down and saw the remains of a couple of wine glasses, apparently dropped by someone exiting the building.

On each side of the foyer, there were openings that led into other rooms on the first floor. From the light shining in through the windows, the room to the left looked to be a high-ceilinged reception room with plush chairs and a long padded couch. Facing them, the hallway that led into the interior of the house was pitch black dark. For a moment, Dacy lifted her candle and tried to see down the hallway, but other than seeing that there were more rooms on either side, it was difficult to see much with only the dim light of the candle's flickering flame. The darkness seemed to discourage Dacy from going farther into the first floor.

Neither had spoken since entering the house. They spent several moments standing quietly still, their senses trying to detect any sounds or signs of movement elsewhere in the house. But there was only a complete, dead silence. While that was reassuring, Abby's throat had gone dry with the tension of the moment. His nerves were still on edge.

Dacy, though, seemed satisfied. She gestured that she wanted to go up to the second floor. Abby nodded. Each grabbed one end of her backpack, and Dacy led the way up the stairs. The stairs were covered in a plush red carpet that muted the sounds of their steps as they ascended. But it was slow going. Both travelers were exhausted, and the candle's flame almost flickered out every few steps. Each time, Dacy paused to let the flame regain its strength before continuing on.

Their pace only added to Abby's deep unease and tension as they ascended. It felt wrong to be in this place. The overpowering silence seemed to suggest that they were alone, but they were intruding into someone else's private home.

Dacy's expression showed her stress, but she seemed determined to press on. Now that she was in Pearl City, Dacy was not going to be deterred now.

They reached the second floor landing and moved into the hallway beyond. As with the first floor, the rooms on the street side of the building were illuminated by the exterior light coming in through the windows, but the rooms away from the street were pitch black. The two rooms on the left seemed to be children's bedrooms, at least from the frilly curtains and bed coverings. The dressers in each room had been ransacked, with the drawers pulled out and clothes scattered on the floor.

Turning to the dark rooms on the other side of the hall, Dacy paused for a moment and lifted up the candle to illuminate their interiors. But they could not see much in the dim light.

Rather than explore those rooms, they bypassed them and pressed on to the room at the end of the hallway. The large, ornate painted door was closed, but when Dacy tried the brass knob it was unlocked. She pushed the heavy door open and they entered.

The room was large with a high ceiling, partially lighted by the light coming in from the left side of the room. Stretching across both sides of the second floor, it was obviously the master bedroom. Beneath an ornate glass chandelier, the center of the room was dominated by a four post canopy bed. The delicate white fabric that had covered the top of the bed had been pulled off three of the corners, but was torn and dangling on the remaining post, as if a thief had attempted to pull off the material but gave up before completing the task. Any sheets or pillows that might have covered the bed were gone, leaving only the mattress behind. There were two large dressers against the wall. Both had been ransacked in the same manner as in the other rooms, with drawers scattered around on the floor and only a couple random pieces of clothing left behind. On the other side of the room, there was a dressing table, also with its drawers left on the floor, with an oval mirror.

There was certainly no treasure for Dacy in this room. For the moment, though, she seemed satisfied. "This will be fine," she said, her soft voice a sudden, startling intrusion into the total silence around them. "We'll stay here tonight." Abby nodded in reply, still hesitant to interrupt the blanketing quiet around them.

They dropped the backpack where they stood, and Dacy gently closed the door behind them. Dacy slid a chair over to it, pinning the back of the chair against the knob in an attempt to bar entry. It did not seem like much, but Abby thought that if any intruders were going to try to enter, they would encounter at least some resistance coming into the room.

Abby and Dacy looked at each other and jointly breathed a sigh of relief. Finally, it felt as if they had achieved some semblance of safety. The intense stress of their entry into Pearl City and this particular house dissipated, replaced almost immediately in Abby by exhaustion. He turned and looked at the bed. Even without sheets and pillows, it looked very welcoming at that moment. Abby busied himself by freeing the canopy material and spreading it out on the top of the bed as an impromptu sheet.

Dacy, though, was still investigating. Lifting her candle as she went, she moved around the sides of the room, looking at the framed paintings on the wall. They were mostly portraits, presumably of the family that had resided there, with a couple of larger landscapes as decoration. Abby sat on the edge of the bed with his arms crossed in front of him, watching. He was too tired to do anything else at that moment.

It took only a few minutes for Dacy to satisfy her curiosity. But finally, she too was ready to rest. She returned to her backpack and pulled a simple round candle holder from it and wedged the lighted candle into it. She walked to the opposite side of the bed from Abby and placed the candle holder on the small nightstand next to it.

The two weary would-be burglars kicked off their shoes and stretched out on the bed. Taking the extra fabric on either side, they pulled the bed cover over themselves as a sort of blanket. Abby realized that this was the first time that the two shared a bed together, but his overwhelming fatigue pushed that thought away quickly. Instead, he simply rolled onto his side with his back to Dacy, and fell asleep quickly.

Morning announced itself early, with the eastern sun beaming through the curtain-less windows. Abby woke to the sound of Dacy rummaging through the walk-in closet off to his left. He sleepily rubbed his eyes and gathered his hair loosely behind his shoulders. After several moments of silently debating whether to get up or not, he took a deep breath, flipped off the bed cover, and swung his legs over the edge of the bed. As he stood up, his bare feet contacted the cold, hardwood floor, sending a chill upwards through this limbs.

The material of his green outer dress had bunched up around his waist, revealing the white chemise beneath. The thought passed through his mind that he would want to find a shirt and pants (with a belt and pockets) that fit him, somewhere in Pearl City. He was getting tired of wearing a dress.

As he rubbed the sleep from his face, Abby's eyes scanned the room, taking in its elegance. The walls were painted a light emerald with white trim, hung with the painted portraits and landscapes that they had seen the night before. The carpet was a plush floral design that spoke of the wealth of its former owners, but was now covered in the debris of a ransacking—papers, items of clothing and broken personal possessions. Dust was noticeable on the standing objects in the room.

Through the open closet doors, Dacy turned and met Abby's gaze. "You're awake," she said with a slight undercurrent of impatience in her voice. "Good, come in here. There's actually stuff left." Abby knew that now that daylight was here, Dacy was impatient to get on with her search for valuables.

Abby nodded. He grabbed the bunched up dress fabric around his waist, and was about to straighten it out and slip it down to its normal position. As he did, though, he looked down and noticed something.

There was blood on the white chemise undergarment, deep crimson stains spotting the fabric. The sight was enough to shock Abby into being suddenly, fully awake. He blurted out, "What the hell?" He quickly reached down and grabbed the edge of the chemise and pulled it up to expose his legs. His thighs were covered in the same deep crimson blood. He exclaimed in a loud, breathy burst, "Oh my fucking God!"

Abby's sudden distress drew Dacy out from the closet. "What? What's the matter?" She quickly looked around the room and fumbled for a knife at her side, as if expecting that some intruder had discovered them.

Instead, Abby was pointing down at his legs, and almost shouted in reply, "Look at this. Look! What the fuck?"

Dacy took a quick look at the blood on Abby's legs, but seemed unimpressed. She exhaled in relief and chided, "Don't shout like that! You scared me to death!"

Abby, though, was still in distress. "I'm bleeding! What the hell?"

Dacy rolled her eyes. "It's your period, dummy," she said. "Why is it bothering you? When was your last one? Didn't ya know this was coming? Was it early or late or something?"

Abby shook his head and replied, "No! I mean, I guess I don't know." His period? He thought to himself, "Oh, my fucking God!" He took a few deep breaths, trying to calm himself.

Dacy asked casually, "Did you have any aches? Were your boobs sore?" Almost in disbelief, she repeated the question, "Didn't ya know this was coming?"

The questions horrified Abby, but he answered as calmly as he could, "Yeah, I guess. But so was the rest of me from all this damn walking. I thought it was just part of everything else, and it never crossed my mind. Not once, I promise you. This has never happened to me before."

That surprised Dacy. "What d'ya mean? Are you saying this is your first one? That's impossible. You're what, sixteen or seventeen? You're only a little younger than me. I can't believe you're just starting now."

Abby raised his hand and nodded. "Hand to God. I have never had a period before in my life."

Dacy laughed at Abby's earnestness. "Fine, princess. Take off your dress and we'll get you cleaned up." She began to tug at the laces of Abby's outer dress to untie and loosen them. "You're in luck. They's some cloth undies in the closet that got left behind. Plus some nice frilly blouses like this one. As long as this frock's still clean, we can just swap out your chemise with another one."

Abby could feel his face flush. On top of everything else, this was almost too much. As he stood still and let Dacy help him undress, he thought to himself, "I've got to deal with this now, too? Fuck!"

Within moments, Dacy helped Abby pull off the outer dress and the blood-stained chemise. Once the undergarment was off, Dacy began to tear its fabric, ripping the cotton cloth into smaller strips. Dacy pulled off a canteen from the side of her backpack and wet a handful of fabric. As if she were a patient mother cleaning a child, she began to clean the menstrual fluid from Abby's legs.

Abby stood awkwardly while Dacy worked, shifting uncomfortably on his feet. He kept his eyes up, not wanting to see his nude form or the consequence of having a female body.

But Dacy's patience apparently had some limits. After a few moments of working on Abby's legs, Dacy took a clean swatch of cloth, wet it, and handed it to Abby. "Here," she said, "clean your privates yourself. We ain't that kind of friends. Not yet, anyway." She flashed a wicked smile that made Abby uncomfortable, but he let the remark pass.

Even though it was long past time for modesty, Abby turned slightly away from Dacy and cleaned his pubic region as best he could. Yet, even after he had finished, he still felt dirty and sticky. 'Unclean' was the word that popped into his head. He wondered out loud, "Maybe there's a working bathroom, somewhere close. We should try to find one. I'll feel better if I can get to some running water. I need a bath or shower. A bucket of clean water. Something."

"Yeah," Dacy replied in a reassuring tone. "If them streetlights work, there might be one with the taps working someplace. We'll look in a little bit." She took another clean patch of fabric and folded it into a thick square. "Here," she said, holding it up before Abby's face. "Take this and wedge it down there inside some panties. Change it out with new ones as ya need to until the bleeding stops. Hopefully in a day or two, maybe longer. You'll just have to see."

Abby nodded, despairing of this new development in his new reality. He could feel the tears welling in his eyes, and he fought to keep from weeping.

Dacy noticed the effort. "Naw, luv," she said. "Don't get fussed up. Happens to all of us. You'll get used to it." She motioned toward the closet. "Come on. Let's find something for you and get your clothes back on. You'll feel better once you do."

"Thanks," Abby replied, choking back tears. "I mean, it's just on top of everything else. You know."

Dacy answered, "Like they say, 'Life sucks, then you die.' But unless you plans to give up now, might as well keep going, eh?" She began moving toward the closet. "Come on. They's stuff in here."

Abby nodded and shuffled uncomfortably behind her as the chill air in the room dried the moisture on his newly cleaned skin. They entered a large walk-in closet, with dresses of various fabrics and colors folded neatly on shelves, and shoes of varying styles and length of heels lining the floor. Given the ransacked state of the bedroom, Abby was surprised there was this much left. He wryly thought to himself that the previous robbers must not have appreciated the former owner's style.

Dacy bypassed the more formal wear and headed toward a trunk on the far side of the room. The latches were already open, so she flung open the top and began to rummage through the contents. It was full of underwear of various sizes and types. Dacy grabbed one of the larger ones and tossed it at Abby, hitting him in the face. It was a torso length piece with frilly lace borders. "See, mate?" Dacy giggled, "That'll suit you. Maybe you won't even need anything else over it. Just wear it around by itself. You'll get plenty of male attention then."

Actually, to Abby, it seemed rather tame. As Tom, he had seen much racier underwear online—barely there thongs and bras and panties with holes in strategic places. Other than the material itself being very thin and revealing, this one looked positively dowdy in comparison. He tossed that one to the side.

Dacy kept searching until she found a pair of simple cotton panties. She tossed it over her shoulder and Abby snagged it out of the air. Grateful to finally having something covering up his bare, chilled bottom, Abby slipped it on. Then, taking the folded up bit of fabric that Dacy had given him, he gingerly wedged it into the front as a sort of loose bandage over his private parts. Abby knew without actually looking in a mirror that it looked a little ridiculous, but he breathed a sigh of relief. Everything happening below his waist at that moment was making him very uncomfortable.

Dacy continued her search until she found a longer, full length undergarment that more closely matched what Abby had worn before. "Here. This'll do. It's more of a nighty, but it'll work fine under something else."

Abby nodded and said as he slipped it over his head. "Thanks. But if we could find some trousers and shirts—I mean blouses—that would be better. I'm tired of dresses."

"You won't find those here," Dacy answered. "Not in this room, anyway. The lady of this house probably wouldn't be caught dead in a pair of trousers. And look at these shoes!" She held up a pair of high heeled, black dress shoes. "Can you imagine walking more than twenty feet in these? Oh, my gawd!" She laughed as if the very idea of high heels was ridiculous.

Abby shrugged. As a man, he always did appreciate how women looked sexy in high heels, the way they emphasized a woman's legs and butt. On the other hand, he never had to wear them. And as Dacy dangled the black heels in front of his eyes at that moment, he studied them as if they were some sort of curiosity. But Abby was never tempted to take them and try them on. For the time being, he knew the comfortable low leather shoes he had gotten from the elves would do.

Now that he again had at least something on, Abby was growing impatient. "Come on, Dacy," he said. "Let's get going. Unless you want to put on a fashion show, let's see what else is out there. There's got to be something more practical out there, for both of us."

Dacy nodded, though she seemed a little disappointed. She apparently did want to go through the rest of the stuff in the closet, if only to laugh at it. "Yeah, lets," she answered with a twinge of disappointment. "But that's why we's here, right? To get the real goods. Stuff we can sell and trade later?" As if her own comment decided the matter, Dacy nodded at Abby and led the way out of the closet.

Abby crossed the room to the side of the bed. He finished dressing by pulling the outer green dress on over the nightie and lacing up the front. He put on his shoes, then moved over to the dresser topped with an oval mirror in the corner. He intended to just take a quick look at himself to make sure he looked somewhat normal.

But Abby paused at the reflection in the mirror, again taking in the full view of his new female self. Abby was amazed. Even after the length of time he had spent in this new body, it was still jarring to see the teenage girl with a slightly sour expression and straggly unkempt long hair staring back at him. "Damn," he thought to himself. "This is going to take some time to get used to."

But even as Tom thought that, he doubted that he would ever get used to it. To him, the girl's body was a costume that he was wearing (and that he could not take off), and Abby was a character he was playing.

It was how he had to move through this unfamiliar and strange world, which seemed to contain pieces of the reality he knew, but also stark differences as well. The lack of technology made everything around him seem quaint and innocent. But the presence of magic, including his own ability to use it, was startling and beyond anything he understood. And underneath it all, Tom sensed desperation, evil and ill intent. After all, he and Dacy were in a city unnaturally empty of its rightful residents, devoid of all but those who would clean it out if they could for their own selfish needs.

In the end, though, Tom knew that he had no choice in the matter. He also lacked any real personal possessions, or control over his well-being. Even more than Dacy, he needed to come out of Pearl City with the stuff he needed to begin a life in this world.

As far as the why of it, though, Tom knew he might never find out how or why this happened. He wondered whether perhaps this was God's punishment for whatever he had done wrong in his previous life. Was this what the afterlife looked like, for someone like him? A nothing and a nobody, someone who had died without leaving anything of consequence behind?

Yet, for all that Tom had been through, even up until that morning, it did not seem like a hell. The flames of Perdition were not roasting his flesh, and he was not being tortured. He was just calmly breathing and taking in the sight of himself as a new person in a new reality. Instead, it seemed more like an exchange, one reality for another. A new start, even. And in his heart, he knew he was expected to make it work, as best he could. If this was his lot now, Tom was determined to press on to see where his fate led.

As Tom turned these thoughts over in his mind, Dacy had been glancing over, wondering what was going on. Abby had locked on to the image in the mirror, and had stood still for several moments. It was time enough for Dacy to gather her things and repack her backpack.

Finally Dacy grew impatient. She announced, almost as a command, "O.K. princess, let's go."

The jolt of it finally snapped Abby out of his reverie. He turned and nodded, then moved across the room and grabbed one end of Dacy's backpack. Together, they lifted it up and headed toward the door. With one last glance back at their overnight accommodations, Dacy led the way out of the room, down the hallway, and back down the stairs.

In the light of a new day, the house seemed much more normal and welcoming. The sun shining through the largely curtain-less windows illuminated the interior clearly as they moved through it.

As they passed through to the downstairs, Dacy and Abby glanced into each passing room, looking for something worthwhile to grab. But it was obvious that the place had already been picked clean by previous fortune seekers. Other than broken and discarded bits of a wealthy family's possessions, the rooms were largely empty. Abby did catch sight of a large couch in the front room, which he surmised was left, just like the bed upstairs, because it was too big and bulky to escape with easily.

The first floor was covered in more loose debris than the upstairs. Not bothering to do any sort of real search, the two picked their way carefully through the garbage and headed toward the front door. Without having to discuss it, they knew there had to be better opportunities for them, elsewhere. They were done with this place.

The front door was open several inches, with a chair still propped up behind it. Abby surmised that a stiff breeze had probably shoved it farther open during the night. Dacy, with one free hand, removed the chair and swung the door fully open. Carrying the backpack between them, Dacy and Abby headed out into the street.

The full brightness of the morning sun made Abby wince. His eyes took several seconds to adjust, but Dacy never stopped moving. She turned right to continue their journey down the main thoroughfare into the town center. All was quiet, and there was no one else in their immediate vicinity.

But as Abby looked around, scanning the passing windows, doors and alleyways for signs of anyone else, he had the feeling that they were not alone. There was a vague presence on the outer edges of his perception, an impression of malice that brought his senses to full alert. Even more strange to him, it seemed that the presence, however far away and undefined, was aware of him in return. It unnerved and frightened him.

His perception of it was real and tangible enough to cause Abby to whisper to Dacy, "Someone's out there, Dacy. Watching. Someone bad. Be careful."

Dacy turned and stared at him with a puzzled expression. It was clear she had no idea what Abby was talking about. But after a couple of seconds of the two staring at each other, with Dacy waiting for more and Abby with nothing else to offer, Dacy shook her head dismissively and turned again in the direction they were traveling. Dacy, though, was wary, and neither attempted to break the silence around them.

After several more minutes of walking, the thoroughfare ended into an open square at the heart of Pearl City. Abby and Dacy paused to take in the sight. On the one edge to their left, there was a series of residences, a row of buildings with a common facade, even more opulent than the ones on the approach to the town's center. They formed almost a continuous three story wall that took up the entire side of the square, with rows of large square paned windows and doors to mark the entrance to each. To the right, it appeared to be the central municipal building, a large, squat, unimaginative structure with separate smaller buildings of stores and offices to either side. On the far end, there was a large church with a round stained glass window and old style flying stone buttresses holding up the sides.

But it was what they saw in the center of the square that drew a surprised gasp from Dacy. As if drawn toward it, Dacy began to walk quickly in that direction, pulling the backpack and Abby along with her. Abby craned his neck, trying to see around Dacy as she moved forward.

They came to the edge of a large circular crater, gouged through the square's pavement and into the earth to a depth of several feet. It was perhaps fifty feet in diameter. To Abby's eyes, it looked as if it would have required a large excavator to dig such a hole, but there were no shovel marks in the sides, and no sign of the removed dirt or stones in the immediate area. It was as if a hole had suddenly appeared where there had not been one before.

Dacy was obviously startled by the sight. Without warning, she dropped her edge of the backpack and exclaimed, "Gawd, would you look at this!"

Recovering his balance from the sudden load on his hands, Abby gently set down his side of the backpack. "What? What is it?"

Dacy made a face to express her impatience. "You can see it, can't you? Right in front of your face?" She gestured toward the hole in the ground.

"Well, yeah, I see it," Abby answered. "So what?"

"There should be a pedestal here," Dacy answered. "A large square pedestal which is the marking point of the center of the city. Every town's got one. It's where they do announcements and speeches, and sometimes a band plays. If someone gets executed, that always happens here, too." She turned back toward it to marvel at the sight. "I wonder if this has anything to do with why all the people are gone."

As she talked, Abby walked forward to stand at her side and inspect the hole. Again, though, a sudden feeling of unease and malice came over him. As before, Abby detected someone or something focusing on him, but it was not specific enough for Abby to identify its source, or whether the presence was near or far away. Nevertheless, it induced a growing physical feeling of nausea that Abby was having trouble ignoring. He clutched at his belly, trying to calm the sensation.

Finally, after Dacy had said something to Abby about the hole and not received an answer, she noticed Abby's discomfort. "What? What's wrong?"

But it was not Abby that replied first. As if in answer to Dacy, from the far end of the square, a male voice called out to them, "Hey! You two! Hallo!" The words echoed harshly between the buildings of the square.

Dacy and Abby swiveled their heads to identify the source of the voice. In front of the large church at that end of the square, a man with a thickly grown beard in his early twenties was standing outside the church doors, waving at them. Once he saw them looking back at him, he motioned for them to come over.

In reply, Dacy simply waved back, but made no move to head in that direction. She smiled at him, but whispered under her breath, "Fuck you, asshole."

But the man persisted, calling out, "They's good stuff in here, but we need some help. More than enough to share! Come on, you two. I'll make it worth your while."

Dacy sighed heavily, obviously undecided. She turned and asked Abby, "What d'ya think? We ain't even started looking ourselves."

Abby shrugged. Still bothered by nausea, he did not feel up to assessing the dangers of their situation. He would have to rely on Dacy and her street smarts. "I don't know. It's up to you."

Dacy continued, musing out loud, "First person we find in Pearl City, and he wants to help us? Don't trust it." Then, she sighed, reconsidering. "The only thing is, though, he might have found something he couldn't handle himself. Like a safe or a barred door. You wouldn't think so, but churches is always full of good loot. For the poor, of course. And we's poor, right?"

Abby replied blandly, "Yeah, I guess." It was true enough that they had no money, after their overnight stay in Rivertree Crossing. Abby knew that even in a different reality, money meant survival. On the other hand, it seemed wrong to take money, if it was there, from a church.

Dacy, though, seemed ready to approach the stranger. Even if she had her own doubts, whether about taking money from a church, or any possible danger, they were not enough to stop her. She raised her voice and yelled back, waving, "O.K. We'll be there in a minute!"

The man nodded, turned around and headed through the church's double doors. Dacy turned to locate the backpack on the ground. Almost more to herself than Abby, she growled, "Come on. Let's see what this fool's got for us."

Dacy and Abby retrieved the backpack and made a slow march across the square to the spot where the man had stood. Dacy paused for a moment, gazing up at the impressive stone face and stained windows of the church, before continuing on through the heavy double doors. She led the way into the chill, darkened interior.

For his part, Abby was still troubled by the nausea and unease from some unknown, unstated threat. For the moment, though, he felt that the danger was some distance from them. He chewed his lips nervously, but kept silent.

The quality of the air changed almost as soon as they entered, from the relative warmth of a sunlit spring morning into the chill of a large, cavernous stone building. Light streamed in through the stained glass windows on the eastern side of the church, illuminating the interior with a mix of colors, infused with an ever-present dust that hung in the air.

Dacy and Abby looked around. Once their eyes had adjusted, they saw the stranger who had called out to them, waiting for them with a broad grin. He stood in an opening of a side hallway, leading to the rooms adjacent to the main space of the church.

Once their eyes met, he broadened his smile into a wide, toothy grin. "Thanks ladies. If you can help us, it'll be more than worth your while. Promise you."

That did not reassure Abby, but he remained silent as he and Dacy dropped the backpack where they stood and walked over to the stranger. Dacy did not return any smile to the stranger, instead carrying a stern expression on her face which showed she was ready to transact business.

As they approached, the man stuck out a hand and said, "Name's Tulio. My brother Brendan and me been here for a couple of days now."

Dacy returned his handshake with a quick perfunctory motion. "I'm Dacy," she said, then gestured behind herself without looking. "This here's Abby. What'cha got for us?"

Tulio chuckled quickly at Dacy's earnestness before continuing. "This place is pretty much cleaned out, but we found a room in here that's been sealed. If we can get in there, there good stuff to be had. I'm sure of it."

Abby stood quietly, looking up at Tulio as he spoke. His size intimidated Abby. He stood several inches taller than Abby or Dacy, with broad shoulders and hard facial features. Tulio's oily long brown hair and a rough full beard were accompanied by a whiff of pungent body odor that made Abby involuntarily wriggle his nose. This man was obviously a stranger to soap and water.

Dacy, for her part, seemed not to notice or care about any discomfort she had in his presence. She was there to transact business.

With her arms folded in front of her, she asked, "What's the problem?"

Tulio said, "Come on and I'll show you." He gestured toward the end of the hallway, where a set of wooden stairs rose toward the second floor, then led the way. Abby and Dacy followed him up.

As they reached the landing at the top of the stairs, they saw Tulio's brother Brendan sitting cross legged on the floor in the corridor ahead of them. He had a similar build and features as Tulio and his clothes and hygiene seemed in a similar state. He was intently focused on the door knob in front of him, jabbing at the lock with a thin steel pick. The multiple footfalls of the approach of three people finally pulled his concentration away from his task.

Brendan looked up at Tulio, then his eyes flitted between the two strangers behind him. He nodded toward Abby and Dacy, and said in a low voice which was full of caution, "Hi. What's up?"

Abby repressed an involuntary smile, and thought to himself, "An actual 'what's up' dude in this place. Who'd have thunk it?" He nodded back at Brendan when their eyes met.

Tulio approached the door that was the subject of Brendan's attempt at lock picking. It had a small, rectangular nameplate on the front which read, "Mother Abigail". Tulio gestured at it with a frustrated wave of his hand. "This is the room. Can't pick the lock. Can't get in. Something's up with it."

Dacy seemed unconvinced that these two relatively large men could be having trouble with a simple looking door. "So, break it down," she said. "What's stopping you?"

Brendan seemed annoyed. "Course we tried that," he said defensively. "It's like it's sealed with magic or something. You think it's so easy? You try it."

As if challenged to prove her mettle as a thief, Dacy stepped forward. "Sure thing. Ain't no door ever stopped me," she said. She gestured for Brendan to hand her the lock pick. "Here. Let me have a go at it."

Dacy bent over and worked the pick in the lock for several seconds, with Brendan looking over her shoulder as if assessing her technique. Tulio, on the other hand, ignored them and focused his attention on Abby, looking Abby up and down as if he was assessing a prime cut of beef. Abby tried to ignore his stare, but Tulio's gaze was making Abby increasingly uncomfortable.

After trying for several seconds, Dacy emitted a low growl of frustration. She stood up and nodded at the two men. "Yup. Thought so. It's sealed with magic. Gotta be. I can't even get the pick to move anything inside the lock."

Tulio finally shifted his gaze from Abby. To Dacy, he said, "That's what I thought, too. The priest must have sealed it up the morning everyone disappeared. Must be some pretty good stuff in there to be protected like that."

Dacy answered, "Yup. More than likely the best stuff that was in the whole church is in that room." She grinned. The thought that she might get her hands on something truly valuable seemed to tantalize her.

But for Abby, another thought popped into his head. He interjected, "So, wait. Magic? Are you saying the priest here did that? I thought only the Sisterhood could do magic."

The others looked at Abby as if he was hopelessly ignorant. "No, Abby," Dacy corrected, "All priest's is sisters, but not all sisters is priests. All women with magic are part of the Sisterhood. But if one of the Sisterhood feels the calling, they can go into the church, instead of just bein' another workaday Sister. The priest here would have been a Sister first."

Abby nodded mutely in reply, but thought to himself, "How the hell was I supposed to know that?"

Tulio said to Dacy, "So, anyway, I was thinkin' that maybe one of you gots one of those little elvish knickknacks that can break a magic seal. Least, that's what I was hopin' when I called out to you outside."

Dacy shook her head. "Nope. Sorry."

"Fuck!" exclaimed Brendan.

Tulio, though, maintained his composure. "So then, girls, any other ideas about how to get in there? Does either of you have enough of the talent that you see the seal?"

Dacy immediately shook her head in the negative and made a face as if that was a ridiculous question.

Abby, though, was intrigued. Could he see the magic binding the lock? He stared at the door, trying to discern anything think unusual about it. At first, he saw nothing. Finally, after several seconds, he began to pick up a faint glow emanating from the door frame, almost lost in the light streaming in through the open doors on the other side of the hallway. "Yes," he said quietly. "I can see it. The seal I mean."

Dacy's head snapped around, and she shot Abby a quick, disapproving frown. From Dacy's reaction, Abby knew immediately that he had said too much. He could feel his face and the tips of his ears flush with embarrassment.

Tulio clapped his hands together and chuckled. "Well, then. Now we're getting someplace!" He seemed to enjoy the interaction between Dacy and Abby, as if he had tricked Abby into revealing a secret. He continued, pointing at Abby, "See'n you got someone right here with the magic, we got all we need. Am I right?"

Abby bit his lower lip to keep from snapping back from him. He lowered his eyes to the floor to shield himself from Dacy's continuing stare of disapproval.

Tulio pressed the matter. He flashed a wicked smile at Abby and said smoothly, "It's okay, honey. We's all friends here." But Abby did not take it as friendly. Tulio seemed to enjoy calling Abby out for slipping up. He had something over Dacy and Abby now.

Dacy, though, answered as if she and Abby had the upper hand. "O.K. Like you say, we's all friends here and all. What if we do get you in there? What's in it for us? It's got to be divided fair, whatever's in there. The two of us ain't gonna end up with your scraps, once you decide what you want."

Tulio protested, "No. Fair and square. Just remember that me and Brendan found it. First dibs, and all. We wouldn't even be talking about this if I didn't wave you girls over here."

Dacy nodded. "True enough. But once we get in there it got's to be fair. How about we take turns choosing? First you then me. Like a pick up team of lawn ball." She stuck out her hand at Tulio to seal the agreement. "Come on. Shake on it."

Tulio seemed to enjoy Dacy's brashness. He reached out and returned Dacy's handshake. "Done. It's a deal," he said. "Show us what you've got."

Dacy nodded to confirm the agreement. "Good," she said.

She turned toward Abby and roughly shoved him by the shoulders toward the door. "O.K., Abby," she growled. "Open it." Dacy stood with her arms folded, waiting for Abby to do something.

Dacy's flare of anger surprised Abby. He stared at Dacy as if she had lost her mind. "You're kidding, right? What the hell am I

supposed to do?" But Dacy only stared back
with a scowl on her face.

Abby felt trapped. He realized, too late,
that Dacy wanted Abby to keep quiet about
whether he could see the seal on the door.
They could have come back later, after the men
had given up trying to enter the room. Then,
they would have had whatever was inside all to
themselves.

Abby stood frozen for a moment, unsure
of what to do. His inaction drew a quick
chuckle of contempt from the two men. Tulio
blurted out, "I knew it. All talk." Abby felt his
face flush with embarrassment.

Finally, Dacy relented. In a more gentle
tone, she said, "It's O.K., Abby. Just try it. See
if you can get us in there."

Abby tried to gain some measure of
control over the situation. He turned to Tulio
and said, "We're all friends here, right? If I get
us in, you guys have to keep your mouths shut
about it."

Tulio grinned and shrugged. It was
obvious he was not making any promise about
keeping Abby's ability secret. But it was too
late to worry about that now. Abby could only
hope that the two men would not betray him,
that there really was honor among thieves.
That would have to do, for the moment.

With nothing left but to try, Abby turned
back to the door to focus on the task at hand.
He faced it for several seconds, trying to think
of a way to access his magic. The others stood
by quietly, waiting for something to happen.

For Abby, the question was how to trigger the magic. As Abby stood there in the hallway, he had no illuminer with its tiny bit of earthenium to help him. There was no catalyst to help him access his magic. How could he summon it without something to help him?

This was something that he had pondered during the hours of their journey from Rivertree Crossing into Pearl City. If he indeed had magical abilities, how could he access its power when he wanted, on his terms? If he could learn how to trigger its release without an outside stimulus, Abby knew he could learn to use his magic. He would not be as helpless in this new world.

Surely, he thought, the women of the Sisterhood knew how to call upon the magic without such a trigger. This had to work, if only he could figure it out.

Abby closed his eyes and used his mind to look for the magic within himself. He tried to recreate the sensations he felt when the magic had come to him before. For several moments, his mind searched, trying to sense something, anything. But without earthenium to coax it out of him, there seemed to be nothing there to find.

The others started to shuffle uncomfortably on their feet. Abby could feel their impatience, and it was distracting him. But he did not give up. If he really had magic, he was determined to figure out some way to use it.

Then, suddenly, Abby remembered the magic of the seal around the door. Could that help him? He moved closer to the door and spread out his hands until they touched each side of the doorframe. Once he was sure his fingertips was inside the area affected by the magic, he closed his eyes and focused on the seal itself. His fingers tingled as they touched the magic surrounding the door.

Then, thankfully, there was a reaction. From deep within himself, from a source that was still too distant for him to appreciate clearly where it was coming from, white magic sprang forth. A sudden, blinding glow illuminated Abby's body, shining through even his clothes until he was a solid ball of light. The others in the hallway gasped in shock and backed away, covering their eyes against the intensity of the glare.

Abby reveled in the sensation of the magic flowing through his body and soul. He felt alive and powerful, even if he did not understand why or how or what was happening. If only he could feel like this, he thought, all the time. Then, everything would be all right.

With his power in full force, Abby returned his attention to the magic surrounding the door. Compared to the magic that was now at his disposal, the seal suddenly seemed like a flimsy, pitiful defense. Obeying his will in a way that it had not done before, Abby used his power to grab the fabric of the magic that opposed him and shred it. Within only a couple of seconds, and with a flick of his mind, the seal was gone.

But Abby was not yet done. Even though his task was complete, he allowed the stream of magic to flow through an out of him, expanding out from his body in waves. He could feel the substance of the building over and around him fading into transparency. It was an intoxicating rush that he did not want to let go. In the warmth of the moment, he wanted to see how far he could reach out into the world.

It was only when Dacy cried out in alarm that Abby caught himself. Although she was physically only a few feet away, Dacy's shout seemed far off, like a voice calling out to him from across a wide valley. But it was enough to reach him in that moment.

Abby opened his eyes. He saw Dacy's face in an expression of wide-eyed terror, yelling at him. "Stop! Please stop!" Strangely, the top of her head was illuminated by sunlight, even though they were still standing in the hallway before the closed door.

Puzzled, he looked up and only saw open sky above him. The hallway ceiling and the floor above him was completely transparent, as if it simply vanished from the rest of reality.

Abby then looked down and around him. To his shock, only a few feet away from him in either direction, the floor and walls had also vanished, leaving Dacy and Tulio and Brendan only a few feet of solid wood near Abby's feet on which to stand. Somehow, their proximity to Abby's bubble of power had preserved the few feet of available standing space. They were on the floor, terrified, huddling for protection around Abby's legs. All around them, the drop on either side disappeared into the blackness of the basement of the church.

In the haze of the moment, Abby realized that this was the reverse of what had happened the other times he had accessed his magic. Then, close-by walls and objects had disappeared, leaving the surrounding areas unaffected. This time, the closest physical objects remained, and intermediate ones had either vanished or been made transparent. And he had no idea why.

Abby suddenly realized the precariousness of their situation. He would have to shut his magic down, immediately, or he and the others would fall for a distance that was sure to injure them all. Instead of letting the magic simply fade away over a period of time, letting objects gradually become tangible again, he had to cut it off, abruptly, to let reality snap back to itself.

Using all the concentration and will that he could muster, Abby used his mind to interrupt the flow of the magic, cutting it off almost instantly. The fountain of magic ceased with an abruptness that surprised even himself. In one moment, magic was pouring out of him, and in the next, nothing.

As the white magic vanished, every solid object that had temporarily vanished in its glow, returned to its rightful place. The sky above and openness of the view within the church building around Abby disappeared, obscured first by the building's roof and then the ceiling immediately above them. The floors beneath and the walls around them reappeared as if they had never left. Suddenly, Abby and the others were back in the relative closeness of the hallway outside of the door, with only the natural light of a nearby window shining upon them.

But Abby was at that point the only one left standing. The three others, who were to all appearances tough, street-smart and world-wise, were on the floor quaking in terror at what they had just seen. They stared up at Abby as if he were some sort of wild creature let loose in their midst, unsure of what to do.

For his part, Abby was exultant. He exclaimed in a triumphant voice, "That was awesome!" Adrenaline was coursing through him, and a faint white afterglow emanated from his skin. He looked like a wild-eyed ghost, dressed in real life, solid clothes.

After a moment, Dacy finally managed to speak. "Oh my God, Abby! What the hell just happened?"

Abby shook his head. Breathless but in a calmer tone, he replied, "I don't know. That was one hell of a rush, I'll tell you that." He cackled a harsh laugh, savoring the lingering sensations.

The others lapsed into silence. They rose to their feet, testing the solidity of the floor beneath them and checking themselves to see if anything adverse had happened. Nothing seemed overtly amiss. But the men, who had earlier viewed Abby as secondary to Dacy's lead in their discussions, were suddenly very wary of this other, quieter girl.

For Abby, the final remnants of the magic faded away. As it did, Abby began to feel light-headed, and was suddenly wobbly on his feet. He took a few steps away from the others and sat against a wall, steadying his breathing to keep from passing out. The last of the magical glow on his skin faded completely away.

The whole experience had only taken a few minutes, and it was not the first time that he had used magic, but this instance felt very different to Abby. The difference was the scale and power of the magic he had unleashed. The other two times that he had experienced the magic, triggered by the earthenium within the illuminers he had touched, the magic was limited and only had small effects on the reality around him. It simply happened without any ability on his part to call forth, or control, the magic.

This time, his contact with actual, cast magic had unleashed a torrent of unfocused power from some source that he sensed but could not identify or understand. And Abby felt as if he caused it to happen, and that he was able to draw the magic back when he wanted to. More significantly, the seal that had bound the door was gone; Abby had broken it with magic under his will.

The realization gave him some hope. It meant that he was only just beginning to discover his potential for magic. If he could learn to use and control it, he would have power. Whenever Dacy or anyone else talked about a member of the Sisterhood, it was with a mixture of fear and respect. That could be him. He would be someone everyone else had to respect, even fear. He would worry later about whether the law considered him a rogue witch, as "illegal", or not. If magic was a part of this world, and he could use it, he was determined to learn how to do it.

Abby liked that idea. It was about time, he thought, that he had some power over his new reality. Until this point, he had felt like a tiny, wind-blown speck of dust in this unfamiliar world.

Not anymore, he thought. Not anymore.

***

The others watched warily as Abby recovered on the floor in the hallway. The two men slowly stood up, never taking their eyes off from Abby. Even though Abby looked once again like a normal human, a petit teenage girl wearing a green peasant dress seated against the hallway wall, they were not necessarily reassured. They had never seen that sort of magic before, even from the few members of the Sisterhood that they had come upon in their lives. Who was this monster in their midst, really? The only thing that reassured them was that Abby's magic had not been trained on them. But if it were, what sort of danger would they be in?

Dacy, while also shaken, was less fearful. She had enough experience with Abby to doubt any malicious intent. Even though she had no idea who Abby was or where this strange girl had come from, Abby did not seem like someone who would intentionally hurt anyone. Whether they could actually be friends and traveling companions, though, remained to be seen.

After staring in wonderment at Abby for several seconds, Dacy rose and returned to the business at hand. She tried the doorknob, to see if Abby actually accomplished the removal of the magical seal. It turned easily and Dacy pushed the door open. Dacy stood in the hallway and chuckled. After the drama of the previous few minutes, all to gain entry through this door, the ease of it in the end seemed rather anti-climactic.

Dacy strode through the doorway into the center of the first room. It was Mother Abigail's office. To the right, there was a desk covered in parchments, books and small bits of paper on the right. To the left, there was a mostly empty bookcase with books stacked horizontally on the shelves.

Facing her, there was an opening to a small, austere bedroom, with a smallish bed and nightstand, and an armoire in the far right corner. Light for both rooms came from a small rectangular window mounted high up on the far wall.

Dacy's first reaction was disappointment. There did not appear to be anything immediately noticeable as valuable. Dacy might not have expected a priest to have overt displays of wealth—a jewelry box or golden cups or high-end china in a bedroom—that had probably already been looted from the homes of the wealthy around the main square. But there should be something, somewhere in these rooms, worth taking. Dacy could not imagine that there was a seal on the door simply because a magic-user valued privacy.

After all, this building was the central church of Pearl City, a decent sized town in the Queendom of Distan. Mother Abigail would have to secure the parishioners' weekly tithes somewhere, before forwarding them on to the diocese in Crystal City. She would have been the conduit of funds from the worshipers to the church. In Dacy's mind, the magical seal was a dead giveaway. Money, and a good amount of it, had to be here, if only she could find it.

Dacy's musings were interrupted by the heavy clomping of the boots of the two men as they came into the room. Dacy turned around. Now fully recovered from the shock of Abby's burst of magic, and similarly anticipating what they might find, their expressions were now of opportunistic greed. They, too, knew that this was where the money was, and they were determined to locate it.

Tulio grinned and clapped his hands. "Alright," he said, "what do we get for all that?"

"Your fair share, right?" Dacy shot back. "We go evens with everything. That's the deal."

Tulio laughed. "Ain't been found yet by you, though, little miss. Can't divide up something we don't has yet."

With that, the three began to search the room, picking through the papers on the desk, opening drawers, and searching the corners. As they worked, a slightly dazed Abby wandered into the room behind them, standing still and watching the others scrounge through Mother Abigail's possessions. Dacy glanced at her with some concern as she searched. Abby still seemed a little out of it.

Their initial survey of the two rooms was disappointing. The papers and documents seemed ordinary, her clothes were plain, and the books, of poetry, religious theory and history, were of the dull variety favored by bookish nerds. The three thieves had no use for any of it.

Dacy, her back growing tired from the strain of bending over again and again, stood up and exhaled in frustration. "Fuck this," she whispered as she put her hands into the small of her back and stretched her spine to relax the tension. It was just their luck, she thought, that they had stumbled into the office of one of the few honest priests in the Queendom. Dacy's ongoing quest for quality, free stuff in Pearl City looked to be frustrated. Other than perhaps giving Abby some extra clothes in the form of some simple, basic robes and shoes, it seemed like they had come up empty.

But Tulio did not seemed deterred. Even after Dacy and Brendan had given up their searches, he continued to look. He began using the butt end of a hunting knife to tap on the walls and floors. "Got's to be here, somewhere," he said, almost to himself. "You watch. Ain't no way there's nothing here."

Taking Tulio's cue, Dacy started to inspect closely the floorboards of the office, looking for any hatches or loose pieces of wood. She lifted a small dusty rug near a bookcase. Nothing. But as she tossed the rug away into the corner, her eyes caught sight of a glint of metal, high on the side of the bookcase.

She quickly moved towards it, trying to relocate what she had seen. The bookcase was out from the wall a couple of inches, and Dacy reached up as high as she could with the tips of her fingers. She first searched from the top down on the back of the bookcase, then along wall behind.

Finally, Dacy located a metal clasp at around her shoulder height, on the wall centered directly behind the bookcase. Keeping her eyes focused on the spot, she stepped around some books on the floor so she could see it more clearly. With the dim light in the room, it was difficult to see in the blackness behind the bookcase. But there was clearly some sort of latch, and perhaps even the outline of a small door.

"Oy," Dacy called out to the others. "Found somethin'."

Tulio and Brendan crowded in behind her with eagerness in their eyes. Dacy turned her head and said, "They's some sort of a catch there. Help me get to it."

Dacy tested the side of the bookcase to see if it would move. Surprisingly, once she began to tug against its weight, it began to swing easily outwards from the wall as if the other side was pivoting on a hinge, until the front of the bookcase bumped up against a small stack of books on the floor. Dacy quickly bent down and moved them out of the way.

Encouraged, Dacy gave one good tug on the side of the bookcase. Despite its weight, the bookcase swung quickly on its pivot like an opening door, until it fully revealed the wall behind it.

The latch was located on one end of a small rectangular door built into the wall. Dacy tested it for any sort of lock, but it unclasped immediately. With a sigh of relief, Dacy realized that Mother Abigail had merely contented herself with applying a magical barrier to the room itself, and not anything within it. Almost in disbelief as to the ease of it, Dacy opened the door to the hidden compartment.

Within it, there was a small shelf and a small padlocked iron box and two rolled parchments to one side. They did not look like much, but Dacy's instincts were that they were valuable.

Tulio tried to reach over Dacy toward the iron box, but she blocked him with her shoulder. "Oy! Wait a second," Dacy protested. "I found it. I pick first!" She was determined that these idiots were not going to cheat her out of her fair share of the loot. And, Abby's too, of course.

Tulio backed off. With a dry growl, he said, "Ladies first, your highness." He had a grinning, wild expression that Dacy did not trust. She had no idea of what he would be capable of, now that a prize was within reach. Dacy reminded herself to keep one eye on him. Brendan, for his part, seemed less of a threat as he looked on from a few feet away.

Satisfied that the men would restrain themselves, at least for the moment, Dacy took the box and moved over to the desk, placing it on top of the loose papers. A cursory try at opening the lid showed that the lock was engaged. The box itself was heavy but not overly so, with just enough substance to its materials to pose an obstacle if they could not overcome the lock. But Dacy remained confident. As long as no magic was involved, she was usually pretty adept with locks.

Reaching into a side pocket, she recovered the pick that Brendan had used in his attempts on the outer door. She smiled to herself. The men probably did not realize until that moment that she had pocketed it when they were out in the hall. No matter, she thought. She was not concerned with their opinion of her at that point.

She worked the pick into the box's lock. After exploring the inner mechanisms for a few moments with the tip of the metal, she carefully pressed against a tumbler. In reply, Dacy heard the gratifying click of a lock unlocking. The box snapped open. "Ha!" Dacy cried in satisfaction.

This time, Tulio was not going to be denied. He crowded in on Dacy, pressing up against her back. Dacy responded with an elbow to Tulio's stomach, then turned and shoved him back. "Hey! Ease off!" she exclaimed, then added with a sly grin, "You did say ladies first."

Tulio rubbed the spot where Dacy's elbow had contacted his ribs. "I meant it as a joke," he said, wincing. "Calling you a lady, I mean."

Dacy ignored the verbal taunt and turned her attention back to the lockbox. With a sense of anticipation, she gently lifted the lid. Her initial appraisal was that it was a little disappointing. There was a small stack of paper money, and coins of assorted denominations covered the bottom of the box. And Dacy realized grimly, it had to be divided four ways.

But Tulio, catching a glimpse of the contents, was not to be denied any longer. He quickly reached over Dacy's shoulder and snatched the stack of paper bills out from in front of her. "Mine," he declared as he began to thumb through the bills to total them up.

"Hey, fucker!" Dacy protested. She reached up to try to snatch the bills back, but this time it was Tulio that blocked her with his shoulder.

"You said I got to choose first," he said. "I choose the bills. You can have the coins."

Dacy's face reddened as her anger ignited. "Not fair, asshole! We all agreed to share. You wouldn't even be in here if Abby hadn't gotten us in." She could see denominations of five and ten marks in the stack—which was not a lot, but more money than she had seen in a long time. The sight spurred her to try again to make a grab for them, but Tulio blocked her easily with his arm. To her despair, Dacy realized that the value of the coins would be nowhere near the amount of the bills Tulio was holding in his hand.

Tulio laughed and held his hands high over his head, taunting her with the bills. It was well over her head, but Dacy's growing frustration and desperation compelled her to continue to reach for the money. She waved her arms in vain, trying to latch onto Tulio's hands or forearms, but he was too strong and kept pulling away. As Dacy's face turned beet red with anger, Tulio enjoyed his little game.

As Tulio and Dacy jousted, and Brendan and Abby stood by watching, none of them heard the light footsteps approaching in the outside hallway. Abby, still in thrall and seemingly detached from the others' fight over the found money, was the first to turn and look to see the stranger's entrance.

A tall thin woman with a long face with sharp features entered. She had pale white skin and long black hair, dressed in a long white robe tightened with a belt with assorted implements hanging from it, and leather boots that rang on the wooden plank floor as she moved. The first sight of her was intimidating enough that Abby backed up a step as she glided into the room.

The stranger announced savagely, "Well now, what have we here?" Her forceful tone was enough that Tulio and Dacy stopped their struggle in mid-motion, and all four turned to face her.

She was not quite like anyone that any of them had ever seen. Her eyes were large and her expression was intense, like a hunter seeking prey. The redness of her lips and the black eyeliner that highlighted her eyes contrasted sharply against the whiteness of her pale skin. The stranger was gaunt, and did not look normal or healthy. She seemed like some sort of a ghost, but solid and real in the light of day. And she exuded a power and confidence that was immediately intimidating. Her eyes darted from one person to the next in the room, sizing them all up.

Dacy suddenly felt caught and chastened in her presence. She dropped her hands to her side and straightened her blouse.

The men, too, faced the woman as if they were caught out as thieves, with the evidence still in Tulio's hand. Despite the fact that the woman had already seen the money, Tulio hid the stack of bills behind his back.

But the woman did not seem interested in the money. She asked in a tone which demanded a truthful answer, "Who used the magic? Which one of you was it?"

The others, though, were stunned into silence. They exchanged glances among themselves, uncertain of what to do or say.

Several tense seconds passed. With no one volunteering an answer, the woman continued, "Cat got your tongue, eh? Well then, why don't I help loosen your lips?" She raised her arms with the fingers of her hands spread wide and declared, "Don't look now, but I've got you!" A sickening red magic poured from her fingers. The magic wrapped around and lifted them off their feet, pinning Tulio and Brendan against one wall, and Abby and Dacy against another.

Dacy struggled against it, but the suddenness and force of it was overwhelming. The pressure of it against her chest made it difficult for her to breathe, much less speak. Her claustrophobia started to kick in. For the next few moments, she focused simply on breathing in and out, trying to keep control of herself and not pass out.

With her prey safely trapped, the woman announced herself, "Well met, friends. My name is Sidra. A former Sister of some fame, if you've heard of me."

Dacy had never heard the name before, and, from the wide-eyed expressions of surprise and confusion in the others, she could tell they had not heard of her either. But no matter who she was, the way this woman wielded magic—

red magic no less—put an instant charge of fear into Dacy. Even in the first moments in this woman's presence, Dacy could tell that this Sidra was a sorceress of dark magic, and a powerful one at that. The thought passed through Dacy's mind that if they could not escape from her, they all were in great danger.

Sidra, for her part, assumed full control of the room. She put her hands on her waist and began to slowly walk by each of her victims, looking first into their faces, then up and down their bodies as if sizing up her catch. "Tell me what I wish to know," she demanded as she paced, "and it will go so much better for you in the end."

Once she had looked each one of them over, Sidra centered herself before them and said to the group, "Having only recently returned to Pearl City myself, I was drawn to this place within the past hour. By someone's use of magic. But which one of you was it? Come on, tell me!"

No one answered. Dacy tried not to look at Abby, fearing Sidra would notice the glance and focus on her friend. And although Dacy might have expected Tulio or Brendan to identify Abby as the culprit to save themselves, they too seemed to be resolved into silence, at least for the moment.

After a few more seconds waiting for a reply, Sidra nodded and said, "Well, then. I'll just have to puzzle it out. Won't I?"

Dacy expected her to turn toward the two women in the room. After all, if Sidra was looking for a magic wielder, who else could it be except for either Abby or Dacy? But strangely, Sidra turned to Tulio and Brendan, the two men.

Dacy was startled and confused. Men could not use magic, could they? The Sisterhood was an all-female institution for a reason. As far as Dacy knew, men simply were not capable of magic, not that she was any sort of expert.

Nevertheless, Sidra glided over to Tulio and Brendan to begin her interrogation. The two men stared back at her in confusion and fear. Her interest in them clearly did not make sense to them either. Held firmly in place by Sidra's red magic, Tulio seemed unable to speak, but his eyes shifted back and forth between Sidra and Abby, as if he hoped Sidra would make the connection.

Tulio's darting eyes only drew Sidra's attention to himself. "Let's start with you, young man," she said as she moved to face Tulio directly. "Was it you?"

Tulio began gasping for air, as if Sidra's concentration on him increased the pressure that he was feeling. His face was red and his eyes bulged in their sockets, and he looked to be in severe distress. Unable to speak, Tulio tried to shake his head, but only managed a couple of short twitches in either direction.

Sidra seemed unimpressed. "Come now," she said with irritation in her voice. "Do not let a little magic deter you from answering me." She held up her left hand, making a small gap between her thumb and index finger. "Imagine if this were the space I am allowing you within my magic. She then made the gap smaller. "How does this feel, instead?"

Tulio cried out in pain. Dacy thought she could hear either cartilage popping or even bones breaking in his chest. His head went down and Dacy thought he might have passed out.

Sidra reached up and cradled Tulio's chin in her right hand. Dacy could see that Tulio's eyes were still open, and he looked at Sidra with horror. He was completely at her mercy. Sidra continued, "Once again, was it you?"

Sidra released her grip and made a quick wave over him with her right hand. This time, Tulio reacted as if Sidra had let up the pressure on him. He managed to suck in a few desperate breaths before blurting out, "No! No! Not me!" He took in a few more breaths while Sidra waited, still making the gesture with the thumb and finger of her left hand in front of his eyes like an ever present threat. Finally, Tulio continued weakly, "It was the girl. One of them." With his arms still pinned, he could not point. But his eyes again shifted toward Abby.

Dacy turned her head toward Abby. She was also pinned against the wall, and winced visibly when Sidra's head swung to look at her. Abby exchanged a quick, frightened glance with Dacy. When their eyes met, Dacy tried to use her expression to communicate the thought going through her mind: "Come on, Abby.

Use your magic. Fight this!" But Abby either did not understand or could not do it. They were stuck where they were, unable to resist Sidra's power.

Sidra, though, seemed visibly disappointed as she left Tulio and moved over to size up Abby. "One of the girls, eh? How ordinary. And to think I had fulfilled my mission here with my first contact in Pearl City." Almost to herself, she continued with a tired disappointment in her voice, "Finding a magic-wielding man on my first attempt would have been too easy. Too bad."

Sidra shook her head to shake the thought away, then turned her attention back to the two men trapped against the wall. "Oh well. I suppose that a good meal will have to do."

Dacy did not at first have any idea what this mad, magic wielding woman was talking about. But Sidra's intent became clear as she leaned in toward Tulio's throat and opened her mouth wide to take a bite. Dacy suddenly saw what she had not noticed before—Sidra's pronounced canine teeth.

To her horror, Dacy suddenly realized they were not dealing with merely a former Sister or some sort of a rogue witch. Sidra was something that Dacy had only ever heard about in legends and wild tales, and never expected to actually encounter in her entire life. Sidra was a vampire, the stuff of nightmares.

Tulio came to this sudden horrifying realization at the same moment as well. He cried out in terror as Sidra's fangs plunged into the skin of his neck and she began to drink his blood. Tulio desperately tried to struggle against the red magic pinning him against the wall, but he only managed to twitch his limbs and wiggle his fingers as Sidra carried on feeding for several moments. The others in the room looked on in silent, terrified helplessness.

Finally, Sidra stopped and pulled back. Tulio's head dropped. He had finally passed out. For a moment, Dacy thought he was dead, but then she could see that his head was bobbing slightly with each tiny breath that he managed to take.

Sidra then turned toward Brendan. This time, there was no attempt to taunt or interrogate him. Sidra simply closed the space between them and plunged her fangs into his neck. Brendan screamed in terror. Blood began to trickle down Sidra's chin as she drank deeply.

Brendan's face went pale as he tried to resist. But he, too, did not succeed in making more than a few desperate twitching motions in his limbs as he struggled against Sidra's magic. Sidra fed until Brendan passed out. Then, she pulled away.

Sidra's meal seemed to please her. With the tone of someone who had just had a full course dinner at an inn, she burped and muttered, "Much better." Sidra reached into a pouch hanging from her waist and withdrew a blood stained handkerchief. Cleaning the blood from around her mouth and chin, she said to no one in particular, "I cannot tell you how difficult it is to show restraint as I travel around. Mustn't leave bodies around here or there. Mustn't make more vampires by mistake."

With those words still hanging in the air, Sidra reached to her side and withdrew a small sword with a jeweled hilt from a sheath hanging from the belt around her waist. Dacy's heart raced when she saw the gleam of the metal blade in the light in the room. The sight of it emphasized her helplessness. Whatever was about to happen, Dacy could not do anything about it.

The men seemed weakened and white-faced, but alive. Sidra moved first to Tulio. She calmly wound up and forcefully plunged the sword into his heart. It struck Tulio's chest with an audible thud, followed by a final pained, choking gasp from Tulio as he died.

Sidra then glided purposefully over to Brendan, repeating the same motion and driving the blade into his heart. After a couple of gurgling, bloody breaths, he too was dead. With a wave of her hand and a flicking gesture of her head, Sidra released the magic holding their bodies in place, and they crumpled to the floor.

Dacy began to panic. She had never seen someone as casually violent as Sidra, with such power at her disposal. But Sidra's magic held her in place, helpless, as Sidra moved to face Dacy and Abby.

Sidra made a show of wiping the blood from her sword blade with a cloth, turning the sword over in her hands so that it glinted before their eyes. "Now for the two of you," she purred. Dacy felt her heart skip a beat as a bolt of white-hot fear went through her.

But Sidra first directed her attention to Abby. "So, young one. According to our bearded friend, you were the one who touched the magic of this place. Tell me, then, was it you?"

Abby did not answer. Strangely, Abby eyes were not returning Sidra's gaze, as if her mind were focused somewhere else. Given what had just happened to the men, Dacy could not understand how that was possible. She could only hope that Abby was trying within herself to call forth her magic.

Sidra, for her part, seemed not to care whether Abby might put up a defense or not. She mused, "I don't recognize you as one of the Sisterhood. At least, your hairstyle of choice, if I can give that unruly mop of yours that much credit, does not reflect any sort of rank as I understand it. Surely, if you have the gift, you are rogue, aren't you?"

Abby remained silent and distant from the reality before her. Dacy, desperate and not caring whether Sidra heard her or not, yelled to Abby, "Do something, Abby! Anything! Break free of this!"

Sidra seemed to anticipate this. Ignoring Dacy, she growled at Abby, "I suppose that you think you can best me. Go on, call forth your powers, whatever they may be. Let me take your measure before I end your pitiful existence." Sidra paused, waiting for Abby's response.

In reply, Abby closed her eyes. There was a tense couple of seconds as Sidra braced herself for whatever Abby was going to try to do.

Suddenly, white light and magic bloomed from Abby, pulsing outward from her body. The magic that was holding Dacy in place was shredded and Dacy, suddenly unsupported, tumbled to the floor. Sidra held up her hands in a defensive gesture, calling forth her own magic and shielding herself against the power that was now pouring out of Abby. Red magic and white magic contacted with an audible boom as the power of their users struggled against the other.

As the intensity of the light grew in the room, the substance of the building itself began to fade around the combatants. The ceiling and walls and floor lost their solidity. Only the flooring directly beneath Abby and Sidra stayed solid, protected by the space that Sidra created around herself with her magic.

After a heartbeat in which Dacy was fascinated by the sight, she suddenly realized that there was about to be nothing holding her up. She tried to look for something that she could grab onto, reaching vainly for anything that could support her. But her hands flailed in the air, unable to grab anything solid. As the flooring beneath her disappeared entirely, she dropped helplessly into the darkness below.

The remaining contents of Mother Abigail's room tumbled down with her. Books, papers, the desk and chair, the bodies of Tulio and Brendan, all of it fell like a rain of heavy objects into the first basement level. Dacy fell flat on her back onto the solid wooden floor below, the air in her lungs punched out of her chest as she landed. Her right hand struck the back of a chair as she landed, sending a bolt of intense pain through her arm. There was a deafening crashing sound, and clouds of dust were thrown into the air.

Struggling to regain her breath and wincing from her pained hand, Dacy rolled up from her back until she was able to come to a sitting position. From the darkness in which she suddenly found herself, she looked upwards to where she had been only a moment before.

Red and white magic still bloomed and twirled and fought in the air above her. Abby and Sidra were locked in a battle of magic, perched on a tiny space of floor which remained solid beneath where they stood. Dacy could not tell if Abby knew what she was doing, or who was winning or losing. Even as waves of light and magic poured from Abby's body, it seemed extremely powerful, but unfocused and wild.

Sidra, on the other hand, wielded her magic with a purpose, preserving a shield that protected herself from Abby's magic. Her red magic danced and ducked and weaved, looking for an opening in Abby's onslaught of pure power. But however artful and practiced her magic was, it seemed that all Sidra could do at that moment was to defend herself.

The stalemate went on for several more seconds. Then, Sidra came up with a solution. With her right hand holding her magical shield in place, Sidra reached into an opening in her robe with her left hand, and withdrew a large golden object. At first, Dacy could not see what it was, but as Sidra twirled it over until she could grasp it on its long end, Dacy saw that the object was a large, oversize golden key, with a red crystal gleaming in the center. To Dacy, the sight was an absurd oddity at that moment, as if Sidra was about to present Abby with a ceremonial key to the city instead of trying to defeat her as an opponent in battle.

Once Sidra was ready, she held up the key so that the gem in the large end was in front of Abby, directly in the path of the waves of white magic pouring from her. For a moment, Dacy could not understand what Sidra was attempting to do, until she noticed that Abby's magic began to warp and bend. The red crystal at the center of the key was drawing Abby's magic into itself. The white magic stopped radiating outward, and instead began swirling like water running down into a bottomless, deep crimson drain. Soon, the bulk of Abby's magic was being pulled directly into the crystal of Sidra's key.

As that began to happen, the transparency effects of Abby's magic dissipated. The walls and floors around and over Dacy reappeared, gradually solidifying until the ceiling over Dacy cut Abby and Sidra off from Dacy's sight. In only a few seconds, Dacy went from viewing the brilliantly illuminated battle of magic above her, into being the only living survivor among the bodies and debris piled within a dark, lightless basement.

Desperate to get out of there, Dacy began fumbling around on the floor as her eyes tried without success to adjust to the sudden lack of light. On her hands and knees, she crawled forward, using her hands in the utter darkness to guide herself through and among the objects in her path, trying to locate a wall or door. The only sound that accompanied her efforts was a low, droning rumble as Dacy heard the continuing battle of magic in the room above.

Finally, she came to a solid wall at the edge of the room. Dacy stood up and held her arms out in either direction, seeking contact with something that could be a door or other opening. At that spot, though, her hands only felt bare wall. She took a couple of sliding steps to her right, hesitantly sticking out her foot to test how easily she could move. Each time that her boot contacted something, she was able to step over it and keep going.

Dacy kept sliding to her right against the wall, one tentative step at a time. As she did so, she tried to monitor the sound of the magic battle in the room above. It seemed to be continuing, but the sound was lessening, as if Abby's outpouring of magic was decreasing. Dacy had no idea what that meant, but she was determined to try to get back as best she could to help Abby.

After several minutes, Dacy worked her way sideways until she reached a corner of the room. Here, there were not as many obstructions on the floor, and she proceeded along the new wall a little more quickly.

Finally, and to her great relief, Dacy's fingertips found the frame of a door. She centered herself in the place she imagined the door to be, and reached to find the doorknob. Even with her right hand still stinging from her initial tumble into the room, Dacy grabbed the knob firmly and turned it.

It was not locked, and Dacy pulled the door open. Thankfully, the hallway beyond had a small amount of light in it, coming from small rectangular windows spaced at intervals at the top of the far wall. With a quick glance in either direction to make sure she was alone, Dacy slipped out of the room and closed the door behind her. For the briefest moment, Dacy wondered what anyone finding that room, with the bodies of Tulio and Brendan and the bulk of Mother Abigail's furniture and possessions all piled into it, would make of what they would discover. But that was not her concern, and Dacy let the thought go as she turned her mind toward getting back upstairs.

By then, the sound of the magic clashing above her had faded until Dacy could not hear it anymore. Not only had it grown ominously quiet, but there was no big concussion or other dramatic sound to indicate any resolution of the battle between Abby and Sidra. Dacy did not know what the lack of sound meant, but, in her last glimpse of the battle, Sidra seemed to be gaining the upper hand. Dacy was determined to get back upstairs to see what had happened.

To her left, Dacy spotted the stairs leading up to the level above. She jogged toward them, her boots clacking urgently against the floor as she ran. Once at the steps, she wound her way to the top into the interior of the church, then ran back down the hallway toward Mother Abigail's room. Dacy withdrew her dagger from the sheath at her side, then charged through the open doorway.

But neither Sidra or Abby were there. Instead, to Dacy's shock, there was a tall, lean figure in front of her in the now empty first room. Even as Dacy reflexively raised her dagger to strike, the sight of the stranger's uniform—the forest green of a scout in the Elven Defense Force—made her halt her attack in mid-motion. She skidded to a halt, right in front of a tall female elf with the lean, thin face and pointed ears typical of her race.

The elf had been focused on an object in her hands, and the commotion of Dacy's charge into the room startled her. She backed up a couple of steps as her eyes caught sight of Dacy's exposed dagger blade. She raised a hand and called out, "Hold, human! Stop!"

Dacy held her hands up to show she was not going to attack. But there was an urgency in her voice when she replied, "Where are they? Did you see them?"

"Who?" the elf asked as she defensively pulled her own dagger from its sheath.

Dacy answered quickly, "My friend and this crazy bitch that attacked us. She called herself Sidra. Not only could she use magic, but I swear…" She paused because she knew the strangeness of what she was about to say, "…that she is a vampire."

The elf furrowed her brow. "A vampire?" It was obvious she doubted Dacy. "If such things even exist," she said.

Without Tulio's and Brendan's bodies as evidence, Dacy knew it would be difficult to convince her. "You'll see," she replied. "She's around her someplace. Come on, you've gots to help me find me friend Abby."

The elf was still wary of Dacy, but her head twitched in recognition when she heard the name. "Abby, you say? You mean 'Abstinence', don't you?"

Dacy was surprised. "Yeah! Abby! You know her?"

"She's who I'm searching for," the elf replied. She raised a small circular device that was clenched in her left hand. "I managed to track her magic to this place before losing the signal."

That sounded a little ominous to Dacy. What did this elf want with Abby? But, Dacy decided that she would worry about that later. At that moment, she needed all the help she could get. "Well, come on then. Time's a wastin'. Let's find 'em both." She temporarily switched her dagger to her left and stuck out her right. "Name's Dacy. You are?"

The elf returned the handshake. "Reanah. Lieutenant Reanah of the Elven Defense Force."

"O.K., Reanah," Dacy replied curtly. "Introductions done. Let's go."

She waved Dacy forward. "Alright, then. Lead the way."

Dacy's mind raced. Where had they gone? Her first instinct was to go back into the hallway and follow it to wherever it led. But that did not make sense. If the elf had not already seen them, then Sidra and Abby were likely not still in the building. Were they already outside?

Dacy looked past Reanah into the room beyond, Mother Abigail's now-empty bedroom. The window in that room was open. Dacy raced to it and lifted herself onto the windowsill until the top part of her body was leaning out into the open air.

Looking down the street in either direction, Dacy saw no trace of Abby or Sidra. She steadied her quick breathing enough to listen carefully for any sounds that might betray their location. Nothing.

Dacy pulled herself back into the room and faced the elf. "Can't see or hear em'," she said with despair in her voice. "I don't know where they've gone."

Reanah sheathed her dagger and lifted her magic detector. After waving it in the air around her for a few moments, and occasionally checking the face of it for some sort of a reading, she settled on a direction that seemed vaguely southerly. "That way," she said. "There's traces of magic in that direction. It's faint, though. Might be them. Might not be."

Dacy nodded. That would be good enough for the moment. Dacy returned to the exterior window. She pulled herself through the opening, lowered herself until she was dangling from the windowsill, then dropped the remaining distance to the pavement below. After making sure the elf was following her, she turned south and broke into a light run.

The two ran for several hundred feet, turning a couple of corners but maintaining the same general direction. From behind Dacy, the elf rechecked her detector and called out, "That way!"

Dacy shifted her run in that direction, veering into an alleyway between a row of houses, before emerging on a parallel street. She turned and looked south.

A hundred yards in front of her, she saw two figures moving slowly in the street away from her. One was standing and walking. The other was lying flat, floating a few feet above the ground with nothing solid holding it up. At that distance, and from behind, Dacy was not sure that it was Abby and Sidra. If it was them, they had gotten a long way in a relatively short period of time. To Dacy, that could only mean that Sidra and her magic was fully in control of Abby.

Despite the fear of Sidra's magic that was lingering in the back of her mind, Dacy sped up to a full run. Without turning, she heard the elf's footsteps on the pavement behind her as a reassuring presence for whatever was about to happen.

In a few heart-pounding moments, Dacy had closed the gap. It was them. Dacy could clearly see Abby's face, her eyes closed in the stillness of what otherwise would look like a restful sleep as her body glided along, supported by some unseen force. Sidra walked along behind Abby's body, serene and seemingly untroubled by the possibility of being interrupted. She did not turn and gave no indication that she was aware of the approach of her pursuers.

Sidra's confident, relaxed posture continued until Dacy and the elf were only a few feet behind her. Then, Sidra suddenly spun, thrusting her arms outward toward them, with red-tinged waves of magic flowing outward from her fingers. With a wild and angry expression on her face, she shouted at Dacy a wordless aggressive roar that stretched out over several seconds, "Raaaaaaaah!"

Too late, Dacy realized that she was helpless against the wave of magic that was about to hit her. She tried in mid-run to collapse her legs and drop to the pavement underneath the oncoming burst, but she was only in mid-fall before it struck.

The magic caught Dacy and immediately halted her forward momentum with a concussive jolt. It knocked the wind from her lungs and drove Dacy down onto the pavement. Reanah, too, was caught in the wave, but the blast caught the full front of the elf's body and shoved her harshly in the opposite direction. The two landed in jumbled heaps of arms and legs, bent in directions that they were not meant to go.

Pain surged through Dacy, though she did not pass out. But, still pinned down by Sidra's magic, she could only manage to straighten out her limbs into more normal positions and roll over on her back.

Satisfied that she was the victor, Sidra halted her shout and cut off the magic flowing out of her hands. Looking up, Dacy saw Sidra striding toward her with an expression of expectant glee, her wicked smile made all the more frightening by her extended canine teeth.

Dacy panicked and she gave up any thought of rescuing Abby at that moment. Self-preservation took over. Whatever it was that Sidra might do, Dacy knew she had to get out of there or she would meet the same fate as the two men back at the church. She had no intention of becoming a vampire's next meal.

Despite the lingering pain in her joints, Dacy rolled and quickly got her feet beneath herself. She drove toward the nearest exit from the street, an open doorway in a storefront toward her left.

It was only a few steps, but Dacy had expected to be stopped in mid-stride. To her own shock, she made it easily. Once inside the building's entrance, she turned to see what was going on behind her.

Reanah was lying on her side on the ground, and Sidra's hungry, wild eyes were focused on the elf as she came in for the kill. Reanah's dagger was on the ground a few feet away from her, out of her immediate reach. As Dacy watched, helpless to intervene, she saw the elf withdraw a small object from her belt and extend it toward Sidra.

Sensing a challenge, Sidra's smile broadened and she raised her arms to unleash another burst of red magic. She pulled back her elbows toward her body, and magic blossomed around her hands and outstretched fingers as she built up her power.

When she was within a few steps of the elf, Sidra extended her hands, unleashing the pent-up magic in a wild burst that was accompanied by a thunderous clap of sound that echoed harshly between the surrounding buildings.

It caught the elf and lifted her up from the pavement, throwing her back several yards. The elf tumbled awkwardly down onto the pavement, her head striking the stone surface. Reanah lay still on the ground, stunned, but she still clung tightly to the device in her hands. Sidra strode confidently toward her, her face glowing with her power and the satisfaction of an impending kill over an elf soldier.

For the moment, Sidra seemed to have forgotten about Dacy, who looked on from the nearby doorway with a mixture of disbelief and horror. To the side, Abby was motionless and floating on an unseen magical stretcher, seemingly unconscious and oblivious to what was going on around her. Dacy's dagger was on the pavement between them, well out of easy reach.

About thirty feet to Dacy's right, Sidra approached the elf with an obvious intent to deliver a kill shot. Dacy was unarmed and lacked any magic ability. For a brief instant, she considered fleeing while Sidra's attention was away from her and on the elf.

Instead, Dacy did something which, if she had a moment to consider her options, would have made no sense. She charged at Sidra as fast as she could sprint, quickly crossing the space between them. Dacy raised her forearms to protect herself, and threw her body at Sidra's back. They collided with a dull, heavy thump, and Sidra gasped in surprise as air was driven from her lungs. Both of them tumbled to the ground.

Dacy caught herself in mid-roll and placed her feet beneath her. She was rising to her feet as Sidra, still on the ground, turned her face toward Dacy.

Sidra, embarrassed at being caught unaware, hissed, "You little piece of filth. How dare you!" With her face clenched in rage, she slowly raised herself from the pavement into a standing position. Her magic, temporarily doused after the impact, began to bloom once again as crimson energy around her hands and fingers.

Dacy felt exposed and helpless. She braced herself for whatever was about to come.

In those few precious moments, the elf had recovered herself enough to act. Reanah pushed herself to her hands and knees, and lobbed the object in her hands toward Sidra's head. It looked like a polished, flat, black stone, about the size of the palm of her hand. As it tumbled in the air toward Sidra, Reanah called out, "Ave mater mea! Audite me!"

The stone flared to life with magic of its own. A deep green, almost black, magic poured out of it. The effect in its immediate area was not light but the absence of light, as if the night was suddenly let loose from a hiding place and bursting forth from the stone into the full light of day.

The object's dark void contacted Sidra, engulfing her entire body, and the stone itself was drawn onto Sidra's chest, where it stuck as if applied there by a sticky glue. Sidra shrieked in pain, her face twisting into agony as she tried unsuccessfully to pry the stone off with her fingers. Sidra's magic seemed to vanish almost instantly, like a candle blown out by a sudden puff of wind.

Dacy heard a sound behind her, like a heavy bag of flour falling onto the street. She turned to see Abby on the pavement, no longer floating in the air. Sidra's hold on her had vanished, but Abby did not appear to be conscious. Dacy began to move toward Abby to see if she could help her.

But before Dacy managed to move only slightly in that direction, Reanah reached her and grabbed her by her right hand. The elf began urgently tugging her toward an alleyway to their right. Confused, Dacy spun her head around as the elf shouted in her face, "Come with me! Hurry! This will only last a few seconds."

Dacy hesitated, her eyes darting between Abby's helpless, still body and Sidra's pained face. It seemed like an opportunity lost. But the elf's warning rang in her ears. This might be the only realistic chance she would have at an escape. Reluctantly, Dacy nodded at the elf. She gasped, "Let's go."

The elf returned the nod, and the two bolted for the alleyway, running as fast as their legs could carry them. Reaching the far end, Dacy risked a look back before turning the corner. A dazed Sidra was just lifting herself off the ground. She was returning her focus to Abby, who was still motionless on the ground a few feet away. That image locked into Dacy's memory, as if permanently imprinted there by loss and guilt.

But Dacy and Reanah kept running. As she raced away from the scene, Dacy wondered whether she would ever see Abby again.

NINE: THE CHASE

Propelled by the fear of Sidra and her magic, Dacy and the elf kept running until they were completely clear of Pearl City. It was only after they had cleared the last row of buildings, and had passed through the outer fields and reached the first screen of trees at the edge of the forest surrounding Pearl City, that they finally stopped. Tired and winded, they both spent several minutes hunched over, grabbing their knees and gasping for air.

For both of them, their flight had the feel of a humiliating, panic-stricken retreat. Reanah was a professional, trained soldier who had seen combat in skirmishes with bandits and criminals in her patrol zone. But this creature, Sidra, wielded the crimson magic of the dead, and Dacy had named her as a vampire. Whether that was the case or not, even in broad daylight, trying to battle that possibility was a frightening, overwhelming prospect. It was only her magical well, an elvish device that sucks magic into itself for a brief period, that saved them both.

For Dacy, having seen Sidra kill before her eyes, the fear was justified, but her escape still unsettled her to her core. She was not used to running from anyone or anything, even if all she had to defend herself was her now-lost dagger. She felt as if she had abandoned Abby to a terrible fate. It was only then, in Abby's absence, that she realized that she had grown to view Abby as a friend, more than just a traveling companion. In her imagining of a better future, she would finally have someone to travel the world and share her experiences with. And that person was now ripped from her, like everything else that had ever been good in her life.

When Dacy was finally able to speak, the words burst from her in a torrent of frustration, "Fuck it all, Reanah! Who, or should I say what, was that woman back there? I thought it was a Sister and it turned out to be a fuckin' vampire! Sucked the blood out of two blokes, then killed 'em! I ain't never seen nothin like that me whole life!"

Reanah shook her head at the wonder of it. "Neither have I. Never been up close to a vampire before. Never even thought they actually existed. It's like the world's gone mad!"

"She'd have had the both of us, that's for sure," Dacy answered, regaining her composure in increments. She took a couple of deep breaths as her thoughts turned to Reanah. "But what the hell are you doin' here, anyway? I ain't never seen no actual elf soldier by herself this far west. What the hell are you doin' here, anyway? You say you was lookin' for Abby?"

Reanah answered crisply, "Yup. Tracked her all the way here from Jade City. I was to bring her back with me, once I located her."

Dacy did not like the sound of that. "What for? Was she wanted for somethin?"

Reanah shook her head. "Not wanted, if you mean for a crime. Just for questioning. Our resident Sister in Jade City wanted to talk to her, that's all."

That response did not make Dacy feel any better. She distrusted the Sisterhood, and anyone in it. As far as she was concerned, there was no such thing as a Sister simply wanting to talk to someone. She countered, "But if you found her, you have made her come back with you. Right? That's how them Sisters operate. Least that's been my experience. Ain't no choice in the matter. Abby comes back with you or it's bad for her."

Reanah grew impatient with Dacy's tone. It sounded like an accusation. "No, that's not it at all. I had no intention of bringing her back in irons. I'm not that kind of soldier. I had helped her once, and I would have offered to help her again. She would have wanted to come with me."

Dacy did not believe that. From what little Abby had said about being in Jade City, she seemed relieved to have made it out of the place. Dacy shot back, "But it ain't always up to one lieutenant, is it? Even if you is nice, they's always others that are willing to screw you over." Dacy was starting to get agitated. "Really, I don't trust soldier types any more than I trust them Sisters. Put 'em in charge of a post or gate, or just get 'em drunk at a bar, and they've license to rough you up if they don't like the look of ya. Believe me, I've had more than my share of scrapes and bruises from just trying to go on about my business."

The conversation was taking an ugly turn, and Reanah's frustration boiled over. "Fuck you! I'm not like that! Don't question me, you little bitch! When I say that I was going to bring her back with me, and that I was going to help her, it's all true. You don't know me but you'll just have to take my word for it."

Dacy was startled by the ferocity of the anger coming from the elf. She did not mean to insult Reanah, but once again, she was a little too honest for her own good. And she knew she was going to need the elf's help if she had any hope of saving Abby.

She raised her hands to reassure the elf that she meant no disrespect, and softened her tone when she spoke, "Easy, friend. I didn't mean it like that. O.K., I'll takes your word that you're true to your duty. But my friend is still with that woman. That creature, I should say. God knows what she's goin' to do to Abby. We both want to rescue her. Right? Which means we's got to do somethin' about it."

306

Reanah's face softened as she caught her anger. She replied in her own calmer tone, "Yes, of course. My mission here is not done. Not until I bring Abby back to Jade City. But my horses and my supplies are on the other side of town. And if we're to confront this Sidra creature, we must be ready for her."

Dacy did not like the idea of side-tracking to recover Reanah's possessions, but it reminded her that her backpack and all her accumulated possessions were back at the church in the center of Pearl City. "Well, if we's goin' to get your stuff, we can get mine, too," Dacy answered. "As long as we don't lose Abby, right? You can still track her?"

Reanah nodded. "I'm counting on it. Whatever hold Sidra has on Abby is through magic. My detector will be able to locate her from some distance. And if we have horses, we should close the gap quickly once we begin tracking them."

That sounded promising to Dacy, but she still did not like the idea of rescuing Abby only to have this elf drag her all the way back to Jade City. But she could deal with elves. To her, they were peculiar, but understandable. This Sidra woman (or vampire or whatever she was) posed the real threat to Abby's health.

Dacy stuck out a hand for a bargain-sealing handshake, "O.K., friend. You and me. Abby's my friend and she's your mission. It's seems like there's some common ground there, eh? Let's work together to beat that Sidra bitch down and free Abby."

Being the practical sort of elf, Reanah had been assuming that the two of them would set off together to find Abby. Against this Sidra creature, she knew she needed all the help she could get, even if she had no idea of Dacy's capabilities in a fight. But the formality of Dacy's offer of a handshake caught her off-guard. Reanah seemed skeptical at first, given the way the two were snapping at each other only a few moments before, and she really had no idea of what Dacy intended by the gesture.

But after a moment she returned Dacy's handshake to seal their newfound partnership, whatever it was. "Of course, friend. Surely, we can help each other in this. My only concern is the magic that Sidra wields. How are you going to help me with that? Once I recover my supplies, I'll have a few more defensive baubles and tricks that will surprise Sidra. But I can't be defending myself from magic and protecting you at the same time."

Dacy did not like being thought of as the weaker of the two, but when she spoke she sounded more confident than she actually was. "Leave that to me, miss. I can take care of myself. Always have. You get me in there and I'll have your back. Don't you worry! You'll be glad I'm standing next to you when you're facing that Sidra creature."

Whatever further doubts the elf had, she did not articulate them. "Fine, Dacy," Reanah replied. "Let's get moving. We've got to get started before we lose the daylight."

Looking around their surroundings, Reanah was able to get her bearings. At a light jog that allowed them to keep moving quickly without stopping, the two wound their way through the streets of Pearl City to the church at the center of town.

Once there, Dacy retrieved her backpack from the inside of the church foyer, and brought it out to where Reanah had her horses tied by tether to a hitching post. Dacy stood next to Reanah as she tightened the straps on the saddle of her dark black mare and prepared to ride.

To Dacy, the fact that Reanah had brought two horses was a measure of her confidence in her ability to bring Abby back to Jade City. Now, it would serve as Dacy's mount.

The only problem was that Dacy was not good with horses. As much time as she spent wandering the roads of the Queendom of Distan, she had only done so by foot or, if she was lucky, on the back of someone else's wagon or cart. Horse riding and horse care were skills she never learned as a child, despite the commonality of the need for horses. She was a city girl, and city girls could get along just fine without one. At least, that is what she told herself as she traveled from place to place.

But Dacy knew that if she did not adapt, she would be left behind. Once finished with her own horse, Reanah stepped to the other, a sturdy chestnut with patchy brown and white markings, rearranged the supplies on its back and strapped a blanket and saddle, which had been tied onto the top of the load, into riding position. Reanah then managed to lift Dacy's heavy backpack onto the horse and strap it all tightly down. All it needed now was a rider.

With trepidation in her heart, Dacy slowly approached it, cooing softly, "Come on horse. Be nice to me. We can be friends."

Despite some jittering steps, the weighted-down horse basically stood in place and let Dacy grab its harness. She put one foot in the stirrup and awkwardly lifted herself up into the saddle, initially catching a toe as she lifted one leg over before successfully inserting her boot into the stirrup on the other side. For a moment, she sat in the saddle, relieved at the accomplishment.

The reins had been tied to the pommel, so Dacy freed them and tugged on them, trying as an experiment to get the horse to turn. At first, the horse balked at the stranger's command. But after Dacy spent a few moments tugging on the reins and gently kicking its sides, the horse whinnied and began to move, slowly walking around the front of the church.

By this time, Reanah had mounted her own horse, and watched Dacy's awkwardness with stern, concerned silence. The last thing she needed at this point was an amateur who would slow her down.

With no fanfare and with no additional conversation, Reanah snapped the reins of her horse, gently kicking its sides into a brisk walk away from the church. Dacy fell in behind her, relying on her horse to simply follow the other as opposed to forcing it forward. To her relief, that seemed to work. In the yellow-red light of a late afternoon spring sun, they were on their way.

They headed through the streets of Pearl City, with Reanah leading them south. From time to time, the elf withdrew a small round device from her pocket and stared down at it for several seconds. To Dacy, it looked like a compass, but she had no idea what it actually was. Although elves as a race had their share of ones with magical abilities, most elves, like most humans, had none. Yet even non-magical elves, especially members of the Elven Defense Force, seemed to possess various devices and tricks that allowed them to have some benefit from magic.

Finally, Dacy could not help herself. "Hey, Reanah. What the hell is that thing?"

Reanah's first reaction was a harsh look, as if she intended to give a none-of-your business answer. After a moment, though, she visibly softened. "A magic detector, or 'magicae sensorem' if you want to get technical," she answered. "It will point me in the direction of the most prominent source of magic nearby."

"But how do you know it's Sidra or Abby? Isn't Pearl City itself sitting on magic? How can you tell what you are looking at?"

Reanah nodded, "Yes, but I am looking for a spike that shows a magic user concentrating power for her own use. That is how I found you in the church. On my arrival to Pearl City, my device was pinging off the scale and it led me there."

Dacy was still confused. She did not know much about magic but thought she knew at least a little of the basics. "But what about outside of Pearl City? Won't the device stop working when that Sidra bitch loses contact with the wellspring? Even she has to get her power from some source."

Reanah shook her head. "I don't know. I've been thinking about that as well. All I can tell you is that I'm still getting a reading. She must be well away from the wellspring by now, but something is sustaining her magic. I don't pretend to understand it, but there it is. The better for us to track them."

The thought made Dacy uncomfortable. Despite leaving Pearl City, and the wellspring beneath it, Sidra still possessed the power of her magic. Dacy had hoped that by the time they had caught up with Sidra and Abby, that Sidra would lack the ability to use magic against them. As a vampire, she would still be dangerous, but Sidra would be much less formidable without that red fire flowing from her fingertips. Two on one, with Reanah's elvish tricks to aid them, the odds would be more in their favor.

Throughout her life, magic had always made Dacy uncomfortable. Early on, she realized that she lacked a talent that others took for granted. Even within her family there were the haves and have-nots, but she always dismissed the advantages of the ones that did as being too dependent on being near a source of magic. Whenever the subject of magic and those that could wield it would come up, she would dismissively say, "Just gets them away from a wellspring. Them and me's just the same. Only I's just a little smarter and tougher than they are, 'cause I have to be." Which would end the discussion, as far as Dacy was concerned.

After riding along for a few more minutes, Dacy had to ask, "How is she doing it then? How is she keeping her magic going?"

Reanah shrugged, "Don't know. She must have some sort of a storage device for magic. But those generally don't help very much. There are only a few talismans that can hold much more than a little bit of magic. Unless…"

Reanah's words triggered a memory in Dacy's mind. She replied, "But what if Sidra did have something? A large golden key. That's how she defended herself from Abby at the church. At first, Abby was winning. Then, Sidra pulled out this thing—a key with a red crystal on the big end. It sucked Abby's magic right into it!"

Even from behind, Dacy could see Reanah stiffen and her face blanch. Her voice trailed off as she paused to look again at her magic detector. She shook her head in disbelief. "But I can't imagine she would have one of those. Those devices are guarded jealously, and even if she were to have obtained one, its rightful owner would move heaven and earth to get it back. No, something else must be going on here. None of this makes any sense, and I intend to get some answers from her once I find and defeat her."

"And rescue Abby," Dacy added quickly.

Reanah cocked one of her arching eyebrows at her. "Of course. That goes without saying. She's my ticket home."

Dacy grimaced. To her hearing, Reanah sounded a little less confident than before. Dacy knew she needed Reanah, a professional soldier, to aid her in rescuing Abby. There was no other way, even if the best outcome was that Reanah would become Abby's captor instead of Sidra. She did not like the idea of that, but whatever promises she had made, Dacy had no intention of letting the elf take Abby back to Jade City, or wherever she intended to go with her.

For the moment, though, she was willing to go along with Reanah. That was the reason for Dacy's formal handshake, sealing in Dacy's mind their temporary partnership to defeat Sidra. But Dacy also meant it as an agreement to free Abby, once that was done. Let Abby chose where she wanted to go. And Dacy would let Reanah take the lead, even though that was not something she was used to doing. Once Abby was free, though, Dacy would deal with the elf as best she could.

They rode on the rest of the day, more or less in silence. As dusk came and night descended around them, they were leaving Pearl City behind and winding their way through cultivated fields surrounding it. They moved with a slow but steady pace, letting the horses amble along with an unstressed gate. They had no reason to think that Sidra was quickly moving away from them. She did not seem to be using horses herself, and whatever magic she was using to confine Abby and move her would not allow her any sort of speed. With Reanah tracking Sidra's movement with her magic detector, Dacy expected that they would come upon Sidra soon enough.

Overhead, the stars came out and a quarter moon lighted the scene around them in a dim grey light. As they reached the end of the cultivated fields around Pearl City, the edge of the forest loomed before them as a dark, formless void.

Dacy looked at their path ahead with unease, not wanting the coming confrontation to occur in near total darkness. But as she watched Reanah riding calmly on the horse ahead of her, she realized that Reanah had no intention of stopping. Unless the horses could not go on, Reanah intended to catch her prey sooner rather than later.

They passed beneath the trees at the edge of the forest, and the open, starry sky overhead vanished. The darkness was near total. Now, finally, the horses seemed to have trouble, not with fatigue or thirst or hunger, but with the simple ability to see the trail before them. Dacy could feel the horse beneath her picking its way carefully ahead, with the occasional trip and awkward step disturbing its balance.

Yet Reanah kept moving forward, and the horses were able to make their way along the road, albeit slowly and with more commotion than was prudent in the dead, blanketing stillness of the forest. Dacy had no sense of anything in the surrounding darkness beyond what was directly in front of her horse. She felt suddenly very vulnerable, and kept one hand on the hilt of her sheathed dagger as she listened for anything usual in the sounds in the forest around her.

For the moment, everything was almost totally silent, as if the forest itself were a living being intently listening to the intruders in its midst. There was no rustling of the leaves, chirping or squawking birds, or ground creatures shuffling about—the sounds Dacy would have expected in a normal traverse through the forest. Even the air was perfectly heavy and still.

Dacy lost all track of time as the minutes blended into each other. She was on the verge of asking Reanah to halt so they could light a fire. Or, at least, she was going to ask Reanah if she had anything that could provide light as they moved forward. As much as that would have drawn even more attention to themselves, the darkness was total and claustrophobic, and Dacy's nerves were on edge.

Then, suddenly, Reanah pulled her horse to a stop and breathed a quick, harsh, "Sh!" Dacy, her nerves on full alert, stopped her horse and held her breath in her throat, listening for whatever had drawn Reanah's attention.

Ahead of them, there was the sound of movement along the forest floor—twigs snapping, leaves rustling. Whatever was coming, whether man or beast, there were several of them, moving in their direction at an alarming rate.

Dacy stiffened, unsure of what to do. She had not expected to be rushed at by multiple attackers. Should she stay on the horse? Should she dismount and hide? Her instincts were on full alert, warning her that she was in great danger. Dacy looked to Reanah for a clue as to what to do, but in those last few seconds, Reanah was just a barely visible form in the darkness on the horse ahead of her. The approaching sounds grew closer and more distinct. As fear and terror shot through her, Dacy froze in place.

Suddenly, intense white light bloomed from Reanah's hands, driving away the darkness and illuminating the scene around them in a high-relief clarity. The abrupt brightness was enough to make Dacy wince, and she hid her eyes against the glare.

Ahead of her, Dacy saw Reanah on her horse, framed by the surrounding trees on either side of the dirt road leading away from them. The rushing sounds of whatever was approaching continued to grow as they came toward Reanah's light. Dacy wondered in that instant if the intensity of the brightness would slow whatever was coming, but the sounds never hesitated. To Dacy's rising distress, she began to identify separate attackers in the approaching noises, moving through the leaves and forest debris to their front and left. There were several of them. And whatever was out there, it would be on top of them almost immediately.

Then, to her left, there was a sudden charge, a blur of motion out of the edge of the darkness and into the light. Dacy lifted her left leg to dismount on the right side of her horse, away from the attacker. She dropped to the ground and pulled her dagger from its sheath. For a second, she lost sight of whatever was coming at them.

Dacy peeked around the rump of the horse. A figure about Dacy's size, dressed in tattered, torn clothes, charged at her. To her utter shock, it was a young girl, recognizably human but not so any longer. Her eyes were clouded over and her face was twisted into an expression of savage hate. Launching herself like a wild animal, the girl crossed the last few feet between herself and Dacy, attacking with her arms outstretched and her fingers clawing for Dacy's eyes.

Dacy raised her dagger and tried to hold off the girl with her free hand as their two bodies thudded into each other. The girl had no weapon, but the intensity and force of her attack was enough to shove Dacy back and off her feet. The two tumbled to the ground, with Dacy stabbing at the back of her foe with her dagger while trying to keep from being overwhelmed by the force of the attack.

As they fought, Dacy was face to face with her attacker. It was a girl in her early teens, a slightly more slender version of Dacy herself. But there was no humanity or expression in her face—her eyes were glassy and unfocused, as if she was staring past Dacy even as they struggled only a few inches apart. She was unarmed, using her fists and arms to pummel Dacy and trying to bite Dacy on the exposed areas of her face and neck.

In the desperation of the moment, Dacy gave no thought as to why this young girl was attacking her so viciously. Dacy fought in pure self-defense, desperately jabbing the tip of her dagger into the back and sides of the girl, further shredding the rags of her clothes in the process. The girl seemed unnaturally strong and resistant to any pain from Dacy's knife thrusts. Dacy was doing all that she could to ward off the girl.

Nearby, Dacy could hear Reanah also fighting with an attacker. For the moment, each was defending herself as best she could. With her struggle a fairly even one, Dacy hoped that Reanah would defeat her opponent quickly and could move over to assist her. But each fight seemed close to a draw, and looked to last quite a while with the outcome uncertain.

Then, suddenly, from the south, two figures emerged from the darkness, running into the bloom of Reanah's light. They were a man and a woman, humans dressed in

matching grey uniforms of the Queen's Guard.
They each withdrew an arrow from the quivers
slung on their backs, and notched them in the
longbows that they slipped off their shoulders.

They let arrows fly into Dacy and Reanah's
attackers. The arrows struck them solidly in
their bodies with enough force that they fell off
to the side, rolling away on the forest floor.

Grateful to be temporarily free, Dacy
rolled and set her feet beneath her, raised her
dagger and lunged. She pounced on the girl's
body, pinning her on the ground. Dacy was
ready to finish her attacker. This time, it was
the dead-eyed girl who was raising her arms up
from the ground, trying to defensively hold off
the blow.

As she fought, the woman who had
intervened called out with an air of authority,
"Wait! Hold there, miss!"

To Dacy, full of fight and in the heat of
the moment, stopping her self-defense seemed
to be a ridiculous request. The command did
make her pause for an instant, and she leaned
back.

But Dacy's attacker was not done. The
pause gave a new opportunity to her opponent,
who pushed up from the ground and renewed
her assault. Despite having an arrow sticking
out of her side and having absorbed dozens of
pokes and stabs from Dacy's dagger, the girl
gave Dacy an unnaturally powerful shove with
her arms. She threw Dacy from her with
enough force that Dacy was tossed in the air,
landing a few feet away.

With the two separated, the newcomers stepped in between them. The woman who had called Dacy off tossed a handful of powder at the crazed girl and shouted, "Enough! Demon ego mitto vos!"

The powder ignited in a white flash of magic and chemical reaction. Even against the background of Reanah's bright illumination, the intensity of the sudden, bursting glare made Dacy turn away, temporarily blinding her for several seconds.

When she turned back, the girl's body lay lifeless on the ground. To Dacy, the difference in her appearance was startling. The raging anger and twisted hate was gone from her face, replaced by a placid expression, as if she were merely asleep. She looked almost normal, disturbingly so. Even though she was still winded and her nerves tingled from the stress of her battle, Dacy felt regret. Poor girl, she thought.

The two strangers that had rescued Dacy, though, never hesitated. They moved to Reanah, who was still fighting a few steps away. The woman tossed another handful of powder at Reanah's attacker and ignited it with words of magic. There was a second, intense burst of white light and a concussive pop that again blinded Dacy.

When her sight cleared, Dacy looked over to Reanah. Reanah's attacker was also lifeless body on the ground. It was a young boy, only a little older than the girl, with similar facial features. They looked like they had been brother and sister. The realization only made Dacy feel worse.

Although she knew the answer, Dacy had to ask, "The boy? He's dead, too?"

Reanah was leaning over him. She returned Dacy's gaze with a grim, tight-lipped expression and nodded to answer in the affirmative. Reanah remained silent as she went through his pockets. Dacy and the others watched her for several seconds. Reanah stood up, shaking her head in frustration. There was nothing to identify him or where he was from.

That left only the two strangers who had ridden in and saved them, and Dacy turned her attention to them. It was obvious enough that they were Queen's Guard, soldiers of the national army of the Queendom of Distan. It was not only the uniforms, but their smooth competence that marked them as professional soldiers. They were both in their late thirties, with grim, serious expressions, wearing long robes and hoods which were piled loosely on the back of their shoulders. Although the badges of their ranks were obscured, the woman carried the air of authority between the two. The man stood slightly behind, waiting for the woman to take the lead.

Now, though they had just rescued Dacy and Reanah, the two eyed them coolly and with suspicion. Unsure of what was wrong, Dacy tried to break the tension with a smile, "Thanks for your help, lady."

The woman did not return any pleasantries. Her eyes passed harshly over

Dacy's face before turning and settling on Reanah. "What is going on here, elf?" she demanded. "You're a little ways from where you belong."

Reanah head twitched in surprise. "My business is my own. What concern is it of yours?" Her stern expression demanded a reply.

The woman failed to answer, staring at Reanah with hostility and distrust. For Dacy, having come from the border area around Jade City, where humans and elves mixed freely, it was confusing to see such open hostility between soldiers of two military forces that were supposed to be allied with each other. But, apparently, Reanah was not welcome there.

Not granted a reply, Reanah continued with a little less aggression, "I am helping this girl find her friend. She was kidnapped by a rogue magic user and we were tracking her through this area."

The woman pointed at the tiny device on the ground nearby that Reanah was still using to illuminate the otherwise dark forest around them. "But that is a self-sustaining illuminer, is it not? One of the more clever and rare elven devices, as I understand it. Requires no wellspring or magic user to operate it. My understanding is that only members of the special forces of the Elven Defense Force possess such devices, and even then only those with certain clearances are allowed to possess them. Yet from your uniform you appear to be a mere Scout. So I don't suppose that you are just traveling about on a lark, eh? In an area currently under military quarantine? Tell me, what is your true purpose here, elf?" She ended by emphasizing the last word in a way that emphasized Reanah's race, in a way that made Dacy uncomfortable.

Trying to be gracious and trying to hold her temper, Reanah answered, "Yes, well, allow me to introduce myself. Lieutenant Reanah, of the Fourth Scouts Platoon headquartered in Jade City. Not Special Forces, yet, though I aspire to that, someday. It is a pleasure to meet you."

The human soldiers did not return the courtesy by identifying themselves. To Dacy, they seemed secretive about their very presence. Instead, the woman answered with an obvious hostility, "Then, lieutenant, what is your business here? This is a restricted area by order of the Queen. Only those with special clearances can be here." She stepped toward Reanah and held out her hand. "Let me see your travel papers."

Dacy watched this back and forth as a confused bystander. She could not understand the hostility of the woman toward them and toward Reanah in particular. Trying to diffuse the situation, Dacy interjected, "Hey, now. There's no need for that. We's all friends here, ain't we? My name's Dacy, by the way."

The woman snapped her head around. "Be quiet, little one. I'll deal with you next."

That sparked Dacy's anger. "Now, wait a minute! There ain't no need for that tone with us! I mean, we's grateful that you helped us, but this is a bit much. We ain't done nothin' to trouble you, miss."

Reanah chimed in, in a calmer tone than Dacy was able to manage. "What is your authority here, ma'am? If this is a quarantine area, this is the first I've heard of it. Certainly, there were no signs or postings to warn us to stay away."

The woman snapped back, "Then consider me as a signpost with big red lettering: 'Stay Out!' If you were from this area, you would know all about the restrictions that were put into place by the Queen after the tragedy that befell Pearl City."

Maintaining her composure, Reanah answered, "Then who is governing this area? Are you military, or a Sister? You wear the uniform, but I assume you are a Sister as well. You certainly appear to have your own tricks up your sleeve."

The woman's face betrayed surprise at Reanah's guess, but she answered as if there should have been no need to state the obvious. "Of course, I am a Sister. I am Sister Catherine. This is my colleague Thomas. We were riding to link up with army units east of here when we saw the light. You are lucky that we came upon you when we did. These ghouls were a grave threat to you."

Turning toward Reanah, she continued, "Whether you be military or not, this is magic, and beyond your qualifications, I imagine. You should go back the way you came, and leave such matters to those better able to deal with them."

Reanah seemed as if she finally had enough of this woman's attitude. She protested, "See here, now! There is no need for this! Sister or not, our business is our own, and it is urgent. Ghouls or no, you did hear me say that a magic user, probably rogue, is near here. Our friend is her prisoner. We must find them before they escape."

Sister Catherine answered curtly, "I heard you. We have also sensed the presence of a magic user in this vicinity. But you will agree that this matter is strictly within the jurisdiction of the Sisterhood and the Queen's Army of Distan. Certainly not the concern of an elf well away from where she should be."

Reanah opened her mouth to reply, but Dacy jumped in, "But what about my friend? She's prisoner of some weird magic-using woman. Sidra, I think she said her name was."

The name made Sister Catherine and Thomas visibly start in surprise, and they exchanged a quick glance between themselves. It took a moment for Sister Catherine to regather her calm air of authority before she spoke. "We know all about this woman, this Sidra. She used to be a Sister, but now she has given herself over to the dark arts. If we locate her, we will defeat her and bring her to justice."

Dacy was frustrated by Sister Catherine's inability to understand Sidra's threat. "That's not even the worst of it," Dacy shot back. "She's a vampire, sure as I'm standing here.

You should see what she did to two men back in Pearl City. Drank their blood, then killed them. It'd have curled your toes if you'd seen it! And this is the bitch what's got my friend."

The expression on Sister Catherine's face was a mix of disbelief and shock. Dacy could not tell whether Sister Catherine already knew that Sidra was a vampire or not. Or, whether she simply thought that Dacy was the crazy one.

But Dacy kept up her gambit. She stepped between Reanah and the two human soldiers. "So, if you ain't gonna help any more, me and my elf friend's gonna be on our way. If you don't mind."

The soldier Thomas finally spoke, inserting himself into the conversation with a low, warning grumble, "You're not going anywhere, ladies." Turning to Reanah, he stuck a finger in her chest. "Now, elf. The Sister has already asked you for your papers, once. Do not force me to help you find them."

Reanah's face reddened and her face tightened in anger. Dacy could tell that as much as she wanted to snap back at the impudent human, Reanah was holding her fire for the moment. Reanah mumbled something that Dacy could not hear as she strode to her horse and opened up a leather purse on her saddle. Within a moment, she had pulled out a set of folded parchments, bound loosely with string.

As Dacy waited, she was struck by the incongruence of the two strangers' insistence on seeing Reanah's documentation, while the bodies of a young boy and girl lay forgotten a few feet away from them. Dacy herself seemed a bystander in the push and pull between the professional soldiers. But time was slipping away, and the humans' hostility and distrust seemed focused on not letting Reanah continue on her way. That was not acceptable to Dacy. Her mind was already racing, trying to come up with a way to get away from the soldiers and continue south to find Abby.

Reanah, still red-faced, handed her papers to Sister Catherine and stood impatiently while Sister Catherine and Thomas studied first one sheet then the other, even feeling the raised seal on one document to confirm its presence.

Finally, Reanah could not help herself, "So, you see. It's all in order. Enough of this nonsense! Let me go on my way."

But Sister Catherine shook her head, sighing as if she had no choice in the matter. "No, elf. You and your friend are not free to go. As I said, this area is under the jurisdiction of the Sisterhood and the Queen's Army. The two of you must come with us. We'll let our superiors deal with you."

Reanah rolled her eyes skyward and exhaled a non-verbal, angry gasp of protest.

Before she could speak, Dacy interjected, "But why? This ain't right!"

Sister Catherine pointed to the two bodies on the ground and shot back, "You see why, right before your eyes. Those ghouls were normal children once. There is some malicious, powerful magic that has turned the local residents into mindless, barely living creatures, and controls them from some distant place. There are many more of them between here and Sapphire City. That seems to be the center of all of this."

Both Dacy and Reanah started in surprise at the mention of Sapphire City, as if Sister Catherine's invocation of the name had brought some long-lost ancient city suddenly back into the world as a real place. Dacy replied, "What do you mean? Sapphire City ain't no city. Just a bunch of empty ruins full of grazin' animals, not people. At least, not for a long, long time."

Sister Catherine and Thomas looked at each other, as if Catherine had already said too much. The Sister answered, "Never you mind. Just know it's not safe for anyone between here and there."

With that, Thomas stepped in to end the back and forth. His voice was a growling warning against trying to argue, "You know all you need to know. The point is you're coming with us. Whatever it is you were looking for, leave it to us."

By then, Dacy was completed flustered. "My friend Abby is a 'who', not a 'what', you asshole! She's just a short ways ahead of here. Leave us be to find her! Every second we spend here jawing, the farther away that Sidra bitch is!"

Surprisingly, it was Reanah that raised her hand to calm her. "It's all right, Dacy. I'm sure these fine people will follow through for us. They helped us out, after all."

Dacy's face whipped around to her in disbelief. After all that they had gone through to escape from Pearl City and to reach this point, she could not believe that the elf would give up so easily. Her eyes met Reanah's, pleading for her to keep going.

But Reanah continued in a calm, measured tone, gesturing toward their horses, "Come, Dacy. Let's prepare to go."

Dacy frowned at her, her mouth open in advance of a new protest. But as Reanah turned to go back to her horse, Dacy caught the smallest nod of Reanah's head, coupled with a twitch of her eyebrows. It took Dacy a heartbeat to realize that Reanah was trying to get her away from the two soldiers. She closed her mouth and took two steps toward her horse.

With a quick move of her right hand, Reanah reached beneath her belt to a hidden pocket. She withdrew a small object, and with a casual, smooth toss, lobbed it at the two soldiers.

Too late, Sister Catherine and Thomas realized that they were caught unprepared, managing only to raise their arms in instinctive self-defense. The object, a small round stone, followed its slow, looping trajectory toward them until it burst into life in the air in front of their faces. But instead of light, a cone of electrical bolts shot out from it, surging through their bodies and detonating with enough force that it knocked them off their feet and forced the air from their lungs. They landed heavily on the ground, unconscious, their bodies twitching and involuntarily gasping for air.

Dacy watched with an expression of stunned amazement and shock. She did not know whether to feel relieved or horrified about what Reanah had just done. As much as she wanted to keep going in pursuant of Abby and Sidra, it would never have occurred to her to fight to get away from the two soldiers of the Queen's Army, especially with one a Sister. For her, they represented the law of her land, and for all her time as a teenager spent trouble-making and skirting the law, she had never actively resisted or fought against those in authority.

Dacy quickly moved to the two soldiers to check on them. She bent down and patted Sister Catherine on the cheek, but the woman remained unresponsive and her face impassive. She cried out to Reanah, "What have you done?"

Reanah did not seem flustered or bothered. Instead, she calmly walked toward her horse as she answered, "They should not have been permanently injured. By the time they awaken, we should be far from here."

Dacy first checked Sister Catherine and then Thomas for signs of a pulse, applying her fingertips to their necks and wrists. She could feel their hearts beating, confirming they were alive. There were no obvious cuts or awkwardly bent limbs, and their breathing had evened out despite their unconsciousness. As far as Dacy could tell, they had simply been blown over and knocked out by Reanah's device. She could smell burnt hair, the smell tickling her nose as she stood up. "They're alive, at least. Ain't no telling what else might have happened to 'em."

Reanah was already readying her saddle to continue their journey, and seemed unconcerned. "They'll be fine, I assure you. In fact, it may only be a few minutes before they revive. My suggestion is that you mount up so we can get the hell out of here before they do."

That spurred Dacy into action. She did not want to be there when Sister Catherine woke up. Despite being overwhelmed by all that she had experienced since they had stopped, she nodded and retrieved her dagger from the ground. She returned it to the sheath on her belt, then moved toward her horse and pulled herself up into the saddle.

Reanah quickly moved about the area, recovering both the rock she had used to shock the soldiers, and the larger self-illuminer stone that was still providing the ball of light that pushed back the blackness of the surrounding forest. She also made a point of taking an extra moment to recover her travel papers from the forest floor near Sister Catherine, carefully refolding them and tucking them back into the pocket on her saddle.

"Don't think them papers is going to help you now, Reanah," Dacy observed. "They know who you are. The Sisterhood will be after you for sure for this."

Reanah shrugged. "Let them. I'll worry about that after I complete my mission. And if the ones hunting me are as foolish and clumsy as these here, evading them should be no problem at all."

Returning to her horse, Reanah closed her eyes around the illuminer stone and mumbled something that Dacy could not make out. The light from the rock suddenly stopped, plunging the scene back into almost total darkness. Dacy heard, rather than saw, the creaking of Reanah's leather saddle as Reanah remounted her horse.

It took several seconds for Dacy's eyes to adjust. Finally, in the dim moonlight that managed to make it through the forest canopy overhead, Reanah snapped the reins of her horse, urging it again forward down the barely visible road before them. Dacy gently kicked the sides of her horse, and she followed a short distance behind.

As they did, Dacy turned around to take one last look. But the darkness at the place where they had just been was almost total, and she could not make out the four bodies on the forest floor that she knew were there, two dead children and two unconscious soldiers of the Queen's Army.

She shook her head at the thought. As much as she liked to consider herself as a traveled woman of the world, this was something beyond her experience. For Dacy, it was so much simpler as a lone traveler on the roads, not caring where she had come from or where she was going next. She always enjoyed her lack of responsibilities, needing nothing beyond keeping herself going day to day.

Now, she was heading into a dangerous area, chasing a woman who was probably a vampire, hoping to free someone who had only recently become her friend. And her current companion and protector was an elf far from her homeland, who had just assaulted members of the Queen's Army and would face being hunted for that. Whatever consequences that meant for Dacy in the future, she knew they would not be safe or pleasant.

Dacy replayed Reanah's takedown of the soldiers in her mind. Before that moment, Dacy was just another homeless vagabond, someone who was invisible and forgotten by the rest of the world. Now, though, the authorities would consider her an outlaw, and hold her as accountable as Reanah whenever the law managed to catch up with her. Perhaps there would even be a bounty placed on her name.

Yet, she kept riding down the path behind Reanah. And, the more she considered it, the more Dacy made up her mind that she would keep going until she saw it through. As unsure as she was about what was going to happen, every instinct told her that she was doing the right thing. From her previous life with no set direction, timetable, or goals, Dacy felt as if she had somehow discovered her own fate. And it lay on the path to find and rescue Abby.

She turned around and faced forward. Trying to will her thoughts to wherever Abby was, she whispered, "Stay strong, Abby! I'm on my way!"

TEN: SAPPHIRE CITY

Captured and held by Sidra's magic, Abby spent the days after Pearl City barely conscious, his mind fading in and out of a magic-induced haze. For most of the trip south toward Sapphire City, he was unconscious, floating above the ground with his body rigid and arms and legs pinned, like a patient being pushed along on an unseen gurney.

Day and night, Sidra held Abby with her power, walking along behind Abby's rigid, floating form. The oversized, golden key with its imbedded red crystal, the Crystal Key, had been partially recharged during Sidra's battle with Abby, and it now provided the magical energy that Sidra needed to maintain control over her prisoner.

The Crystal Key rested on Abby's chest, tied to him by the same magic that bound his arms and legs, and Abby could feel its ever-present, sickening foul magic flowing out under

Sidra's control. As they moved, Abby tried to resist. More than once, he was able to call his own magic to life. But the instant it left his body, it was redirected into the red crystal that was imbedded in the Crystal Key, disappearing instantly into its seemingly bottomless depths. And each time, the effort left Abby weakened and despairing of ever being free of his bindings.

Sidra seemed to tolerate, and even enjoy, Abby's efforts to free himself. "Yes, yes, my pet!" she cackled. "Struggle against that which you do not understand. You only aid me and my master's cause." Sidra repeated it over and over with minor variations as some sort of weird mantra.

The power stored in the Crystal Key intoxicated Sidra. They were well away from any fixed wellspring, such as the ones in Pearl City or the newly rejuvenated one in Sapphire City, yet Sidra had all the magical energy she needed for her full range of spells and powers.

Once Sidra realized that Abby also could generate magic without being near a geographical wellspring, she considered her mission complete. Surely, Sidra reasoned, Hadrea could not be too mad at her for not bringing a male magic user back, as Hadrea had demanded, if the one she captured could fulfill the same role. As far as Sidra was concerned, if this Abby girl could act as a portable wellspring once they had consolidated their power in the area around Sapphire City, they would be free to wreak havoc on the rest of the known world.

To Abby, it was a mystery as to why he was still alive. By that point, Abby expected to already have been another victim of Sidra's appetite for blood. Abby had seen first-hand Sidra's treatment of Tulio and Brendan in Pearl City. Sidra first bit them with her fangs, drank their blood, then use her blade to kill each victim. But as they traveled south, Sidra made no attempt to slake her thirst from Abby.

At one point, Abby weakly asked Sidra, "Why are you doing this? What am I to you?"

Sidra answered with a composed smile, "In time, my dear. You will learn what you are to me when I present you to my master. In truth, you are not what I was looking for, or who I expected to find. But when Hadrea sees how much you have done to recharge the Key, I am sure she will be pleased, whether I have performed my task to the letter or not. You will help us, immensely. I am sure of it."

This made no sense to Abby. It was bad enough to be in the body of a teenage girl in a reality that bore little resemblance to his own. Yet the one talent that he apparently had, this magical ability that had already rescued him more than once from a sticky situation, was now impotent against Sidra's magic and the golden key resting on his chest. He was unable to break free, but even worse, unable to understand why all of this was happening to him. The realization contributed to his lingering despair.

Between Abby's occasional impotent efforts to escape, Sidra did try to initiate conversation with him, trying to needle information out of him. Of course, with Sidra being ignorant of Abby's true identity, the questions were framed as ones that an adult would ask a teenage girl: What is your name, dear? Where are you from, sweetheart? Tell me about yourself, honey. Go on, talk to me, girl.

The way Sidra kept talking down to him as she asked the questions made it easier for Abby to resist answering them. Abby was not going to give up his remaining secrets that easily, so he let the questions hang in the air without even acknowledging them. Still, it surprised him that Sidra was only trying verbally to extract answers. From what he had seen from Sidra in Pearl City, she might be capable of anything. To Abby, Sidra seemed capable and ready to do violence, even if her demeanor was calm and collected.

But Sidra did seem to genuinely enjoy Abby's futile attempts to use magic to escape. The more Abby tried to break free, and the more it pleased Sidra that he was trying and failing. Given that, the more Abby wondered if simply waiting her out was a better plan.

Abby wanted so much for a real chance to escape, to feel less helpless, but he knew that he could not do it alone. What bothered Abby the most was the thought that Dacy did not seem to be trying to come to his rescue. If Dacy, or anyone else, could just disrupt Sidra's attention for a few moments, Abby could try to loosen Sidra's magical bindings and throw away the ornamental key that seemed to pull Abby's magic into a bottomless well. Something more than his pitiful, flailing efforts so far.

But that led to another thought that kept nagging at Abby: where the hell was Dacy? Abby thought the two were friends, or at least had gone past the threshold from being strangers. Was Dacy really that much of a loner, that she would abandon Abby when they faced their first real problem? That did not seem like Dacy. If the situation was reversed, Abby was sure he would have pursued and tried to help her. Yet, there was no sign of Dacy, and Sidra gave no clue that she believed anyone was pursuing them. The realization only deepened Abby's despair.

Finally, somewhere on the road to Sapphire City, Abby gave up. He stopped trying to resist Sidra's bindings with his magic. As difficult as it was to Abby to do, he resolved to do nothing more to escape as they kept moving south.

So, on the final approach to their destination, Abby was a passive, mute passenger, held immobile by Sidra's power. It gave Abby time to think about the clues Sidra had offered as to what they would find when they reached Sapphire City. They were on their way to some unknown destination, to meet the unknown woman that Sidra served.

It was an unpleasant thought to realize that this woman was probably far more powerful and dangerous than Sidra. Abby tried to ask Sidra more about the woman that commanded her, but she was tight-lipped about it. The best that Abby managed was that Sidra and she had at one point both been members of the Sisterhood, that Sidra was her apprentice. Nothing more.

As the days passed, Sidra kept moving south unimpeded, without any sign of any other person. Abby found that odd, that they saw no one as they traveled on what must have been a main road. The road itself did seem less traveled, even forgotten, than the road between Jade City and Pearl City, with scattered weeds and grass growing on the surface of the road, and broken tree branches and loose rocks and holes blocking the way.

The few scattered farms and homes along the way were empty of people as well, with some looking as if they had been vandalized simply for destruction's sake. There were no living farm animals or dogs or cats, only the occasional shredded and bloody corpse of what must have been a cow or horse, and mangled piles of feathers indicating what used to be a chicken or domestic duck. Abby could only wonder what sort of creatures or wild animals had rampaged through to erase the living so thoroughly from the area.

It made the silence around them as they traveled unnatural and foreboding. When neither Sidra or Abby was talking, the only sounds were the wind rustling through the tops of the trees on either side of the road, and the occasional caw of crows scavenging about. Even the songbirds seemed muted and fearful.

In his previous life as Tom, in his modern world of science and technology, walking alone in a park or woods was how he could unwind and relax. Taking a walk on the nature trail outside of his apartment complex was as much regular exercise as he could tolerate.

Now, though, in Abby's world, the same sounds betrayed an unnatural lack of life, as if the life that was supposed to be there had been ripped away and replaced with emptiness. All the signs indicated that something terrible had happened not too long ago in this area. Even though Sidra did not explain her connection to the destruction that Abby was seeing all around him, he realized that Sidra, and her master Hadrea, were somehow behind all of it. And with each step, Sidra was taking Abby farther into the heart of the emptiness, and Abby was helpless to do anything about it.

So, day and night, the journey continued. Sidra herself seemed to not need sleep, or food, or water. Occasionally and strangely, she would stop and leave Abby floating in midair in the road and walk off a few feet to the edge of the woods and lapse into some sort of a trance. She closed her eyes and seemed to be meditating, occasionally mumbling something out loud that Abby could hear snippets of.

Actually, these meditation sessions sounded to Abby's ears as if Sidra was talking to someone, like one side of a telephone call. Abby only heard Sidra's side of the conversation, but it sounded as if she was actually speaking to another person. And whomever or whatever she was speaking to was doing most of the talking, and Sidra most of the listening, occasionally replying with "yes" or "no" or "I understand." Abby presumed it was Sidra's master, this Hadrea that Sidra had mentioned. To the extent Sidra did speak, they were mostly short updates about the distance traveled toward their destination, and her timetable to arrive with Abby.

The most interesting portions to Abby, though, were when Sidra was justifying her capture and retrieval of Abby. Sidra had already admitted to Abby that he was not who Sidra was tasked to find. And the person on the other end of Sidra's communications did not seem pleased with Sidra's apparent disobedience.

In one session, Sidra protested, "But it has to be her. She has been refilling the Crystal Key with copious amounts of magic. You will be astounded by the sheer amount the Key now retains!" Then after a pause, Sidra insisted, "No! I searched for some time! There was no man anywhere near Pearl City with any magical abilities whatever. If this girl is not the one you seek, she will help us nonetheless." The session ended abruptly at that point, with Sidra's head snapping back as if the link was abruptly cut off on the other end. Upset and musing over what had just transpired, Sidra returned in a self-absorbed funk to the monotony of pushing Abby's imprisoned body farther down the road.

Despite Sidra's foul mood, Abby decided to test a theory that had formed in his mind.

"Tell me, Sidra," he said, before continuing in a more mocking tone, "Or should I call you Sister Sidra? You were supposed to find a man in Pearl City and you found me instead. Won't your mistress be upset when you present me to her?"

Sidra snarled a reply, "That's none of your business. And I am no Sister, bitch. Not anymore." But after a couple of seconds of angry silence, Sidra could not help herself, "She is already upset. But her directive to find a magic-wielding man was secondary to my real task—to recharge the Crystal Key." Her tone grew defensive. "But, thanks to you and your pathetic attempts to escape, I have done exactly that. The Key has regained a good portion of its power, in a much shorter time than she or I could have imagined. My master can continue her plans. Surely, that is worth more than obeying the letter of her directives!"

Sidra then cut herself off before she betrayed any more, her intense eyes and angry expression wordlessly telling Abby it was the end of their conversation. But it was enough for Abby. Sidra was looking for a man and had found Abby instead.

If only Sidra knew. Whatever body Tom had inhabited in this reality, he still thought of himself as a man, and his soul, his mind, emotions and memories, were still the same as they had always been. Abby was just a name invented on the spur of the moment. When Reanah had discovered him in this unknown girl's body and refused to accept his actual name of Tom, he had first called himself Abstinence as sort of an inside joke. It was a comment on the pathetic, friendless nature of Tom's life in his previous reality. Shortening it to the nickname of Abby rendered it acceptable to Reanah in his new existence, and he had gone by it ever since.

To Tom, Abby was more a construct than a real person—the public face from the merging of the girl's body and the accompanying new identity that Tom was creating for himself. It was just the tool he used to interface with this new world. But in his mind, he was still Tom and would always continue to be Tom.

But if he had not told this to anyone yet, he certainly was not going to tell Sidra, at least voluntarily. He was perfectly content to let the apparent dispute fester between Sidra and whomever was giving her the orders. But he was not sure what would happen when they reached their destination. Surely, Sidra's master, presumably a magic-user even more capable than Sidra, would know how to pry his most intimate secret from him. The thought made him nauseous whenever he thought about it.

As the two moved south, Sidra paid little attention to the physical needs of her captive. Sidra did not seem to need any sleep or water or food or rest, but that was not true of Abby. Sidra's magic forced his body to stay in a rigid horizontal position, with no wiggle room to turn his body onto either side, and Sidra made no allowances or stops for food, water, or urination or defecation. And the rigidity of Sidra's magic made it difficult for Abby to relax or sleep. As the days wore on, Abby felt as if he was caked in a baked-on sweat, and his hair was a tangled, greasy mat.

The sum of all this made Abby extremely uncomfortable as they moved, conscious but trapped in a rigid stasis. During the day, his eyes faced toward the sky, watching the clouds drift overhead and Abby was only vaguely aware of what was going on the ground around him.

It was on their final approach to Sapphire City that other creatures began to flit in and out of Sidra's presence. At first, seeing them only in the periphery of his vision, Abby thought that they were local men and women passing through. But even though at first glance they seemed like ordinary people, Abby soon realized that something was very, very wrong with them. Their faces were blank and uncomprehending, as if their minds were not connected to their bodies. They walked with a quick, shuffling gate, but with limps or hitches in their steps, as if all of them were suffering from some sort of injury. Their clothes, to the extent that they were clothed, were ragged, matted and dirty, as if months had gone by without any attempt to change. Otherwise, their bodies were naked with blotched and bruised, diseased skin open to the elements.

Yet, other than the sounds of their movements, there was a hushed, unnatural silence in their presence. They did not speak, to each other or to Sidra when she interacted with them. Sidra assumed an instant air of authority over them, barking orders for this or that to meet her needs. Their response was to carry out her orders robotically and simply, as if that were the limits of their capabilities. But, all obeyed her.

It was when the face of one of these creatures passed right before Abby's eyes that he finally realized just how much there was wrong with them. It was a man with a wild, feral expression, his eyes glazed over and unfocused, but still able to see. There was no thinking behind the expression, just a reactive, frenetic energy, restrained only by Sidra's will. Despite the humanity of his face, he seemed more like an animal, a bundle of nerves and instinctive reactions bound together in human form.

This difference became emphatic when it was time for Sidra to feed. The creatures, whatever they were, brought Sidra the living victims to satisfy her need for blood, unfortunate souls who had lingered too long or finally flushed from their hiding spots. One day it was an overweight man in his thirties, two days later it was a young girl less than ten years old. Another day it was an elderly woman. Each was dragged before Sidra, kicking and screaming until Sidra knocked them out with her magic. Sidra feasted on their blood until they were near death, then stabbed them in the heart with her dagger in a final, killing blow. Their bodies were then tossed aside and forgotten. Sidra ended their lives betraying no more emotion than if she had slaughtered a pig, cow or chicken as food, their deaths having meaning only in service to her continued existence.

But for Abby, frozen in place as a silent, helpless witness, each death was a terrifying, rendering experience that left him stunned and desperate to help. But if at any point he tried to fire his magic to do something about what was going on around him, the magic was instantly sunk into the bottomless well of the ornamental key bound to him.

There was something, however, that Abby began to notice. Each time that Abby called forth his magic, he noticed that it triggered more easily and quickly with each reach for its power. In small, tentative steps, Abby was bringing his magic within his conscious control. But that was a small comfort compared to the overwhelming helplessness and despair of being Sidra's prisoner. Abby could only hope that he could summon the power when the first real opportunity to escape arose. This was the faith that kept him going.

Even so, after almost two weeks, Abby was ready for this horrendous experience to be over, one way or another. To himself, Abby begged for someone, anyone to end his misery. In his previous life as Tom, he described himself as religious, but not a church-goer. Prayer was something he did on special occasions or as a quick "please forgive me" if he did something he felt guilty about. Now, as Abby, he prayed to God for mercy, even if in his heart he felt abandoned and forgotten by Him, trapped in a reality that was not his own.

So, it was with a mix of relief and dread that Abby received the news from Sidra that they were approaching their final destination. Abby could see in his peripheral vision the wrecked and desolate buildings sliding by, and they were increasing in size and concentration. They were in a ruined state, with missing roofs and empty windows and grass and moss growing on broken timbers and loose stonework, the end product of decades of decay and neglect. Abby could only wonder why anyone would value such a place, even as he began to sense below him the presence of the magic of the blue wellspring beneath the city. It was a tingle at the fringes of his senses, an unfamiliar feeling that he could not yet easily identify. If anyone had asked Abby if he knew what it was, he would have had no idea. But, gradually, he came to realize that there was a third force in the environment around him, besides his own awakened magic, and the Crystal Key which tugged and stole from him whatever power he could muster.

Then, there were also the frenzied, mindless creatures, the former humans that became more numerous and noticeable as they flitted in and out of Sidra's presence. As best as he could, Abby kept trying to see into their faces, looking for evidence of personality or thought, some gesture as small as simply looking back into Abby's eyes for a momentary touching of consciousness. But there was nothing. Whatever power and mind that held their obedience was somewhere else, directing their efforts in a coordinated way. Sidra barked orders at them, and they obeyed.

But as they crowded around Sidra, she seemed disgusted by them. Despite numbering in the dozens as they pressed into the heart of Sapphire City, Sidra made no effort to engage them as equals in conversation. Sidra would only pause for a few moments from time to time, close her eyes and commune silently with her master, seeking guidance on her next step. Abby had no idea what passed between them, and Sidra gave no clue as to what they had discussed after each session was over. Abby knew he was going to find out soon enough.

Finally, at the town's center, a large, blocky, sturdy wooden structure loomed into Abby's field of view. Abby realized that they were at the end of their journey. As Sidra glided his prostrate form toward the main entrance, Abby made an effort to twist his head from side to side to get a better look at what was around him.

Here, the mindless servants of Sidra and her master milled around with a frenetic, aimless energy, but, as Sidra pushed Abby through the throng, the crowd parted without the need for a vocal command. It was a frightening, surreal sight that fed Abby's helplessness and desperation.

Sidra guided Abby's body up the steps and through the open double doors of the hall's entrance. Thick, aged wood beams supported the walls and ceiling, and the well-worn floor clacked with each of Sidra's steps as she continued down the hallway. Beams of sunlight shone through the weathered and broken windows, illuminating the ever-present dust that floated in the air.

On the first floor, there was nothing else but loose piles of debris scattered around, remnants of the furniture and decorations. At the end of the main corridor, there was a wide set of stairs to the second floor. But instead of heading towards them, where Abby had assumed Sidra's master waited, Sidra instead turned left, went through a side room and toward a narrow doorway. There, Sidra maneuvered Abby's body down a set of stairs leading into darkness below.

They passed from the natural light coming through the first floor windows into the closeted stairway. There were no lamps or candles in the mounts in the walls. But as they descended, Abby noticed a blue glow, an artificial, source-less illumination that revealed the walls and steps in a colorless relief. The glow grew in intensity as they reached the basement level, lighting Sidra's calm, composed face in blue tinged with black shadows.

With the growing intensity of the blue light, Abby sensed the imminent presence of the background magic around him as well. The pulsing, alive wellspring beneath him gave

Abby the sensation of floating on the top of a soap bubble welling up underneath him. The power of the magic passing through and around him resonated in his chest in an unfamiliar, but comforting way.

Abby wondered whether the additional magic from the wellspring would be enough to break free of his bonds. He had no idea. It only added to his frustration and desperation that he was almost completely ignorant of magic and how it worked. Even so, he held onto the possibility of making an escape, as Sidra guided him into the center of the main, open room of the basement.

As best he could despite his limited mobility, Abby's eyes quickly scanned the room, looking for Sidra's master. But even in the dim, eerie blue light that filled the room, he saw no one else. For a moment, he wondered whether perhaps Sidra's master did not actually exist, that Hadrea was actually some schizophrenic voice in Sidra's own head, and that all of her communing sessions as they made their way to this place were only conversations she was having with herself.

So, when Sidra announced to the empty room, "I am here, mistress. And I bring to you your prize," there were a few anxious seconds as Abby wondered whether anyone at all would answer.

Yet, there was an answer, in a woman's disembodied voice that came from everywhere and nowhere in the room, and was filled with an intense sarcasm. "My prize, indeed! This young girl does look like the older man that I told you to find, doesn't she? Yes, well done, Sidra!" The voice boomed into the room with an increasing hostility. "You idiot! My sense of the Continuum was that it was being accessed by an entity with a distinctly male energy. Thus, I told you to find a man, an older one, that was his own source for his magic. A human wellspring. That was who you were looking for, not some random, wet-behind-the-ears rogue witch! What a waste of our opportunity, Sidra. We have no time for your failures!"

Abby turned and looked into Sidra's face as the voice spoke. Sidra had feared her master's rebuke, but the entity's harsh words clearly stung her. Her already pale face blanched even more, and she looked as if she wanted to interject and defend herself but was hesitant to do so. For the moment, she seemed too intimidated to interrupt.

So, the voice kept on its harangue. "We do not have time for such an error! I have had all I can do to keep our servants in bondage, and to keep this region free of any that may oppose us. The improved wellspring of this place sustains me, but at best I can only maintain what we have achieved so far. We need more, much more power before I, that is we, will have any sort of secure permanence, and we are in a position to strike out against my enemies. Sidra, this is unacceptable. Unacceptable!"

The voice paused as if it was trying to gather its composure, then concluded with an impatient, mocking tone, "So, Sidra, what do you have to say for yourself? Well?"

As the last echo of the voice reverberated in the room, Sidra finally found her own voice. "I did as you asked, Hadrea, in spirit if not in the details. I have found a human wellspring. This girl is the one you are looking for. She has to be. Her magic needs no connection to a wellspring, and there is a great, raw power within her. I have seen it for myself. If you trust in me at all, you will believe in my judgment in this."

It made an impression on Abby how small Sidra seemed at that moment. When Sidra spoke, Abby did not see the ruthless killer that he had seen since Sidra's first appearance in Pearl City. He saw an insecure, timid woman groveling for her mistresses' approval.

Sidra stepped to Abby's side and reached for the ornamental key resting on Abby's chest. With both hands, she lifted it into the air and held it before her face. "See for yourself, Hadrea. When I departed, the Crystal Key was almost fully drained of its power. Now, it is substantially recharged, and it is due solely to this little girl and her futile struggles to free herself. That is what you wanted. Even if she is not the older male you seek, the result is the same. With her in our service, you will have the power you require, Hadrea. In the end, is that not all that matters?"

Sidra held the Crystal Key in her outstretched hands, waiting for her master to examine it. As Abby watched in startled fascination, the air around Sidra's hands seemed to swirl and curdle as an unseen presence focused on the Key. Did Sidra serve something which had no physical form? If so, what was Hadrea—a ghost or spirit or demon? Clearly, it was not human.

Abby was dumbfounded. Of all the things he had seen in his post-Tom life, this was perhaps the strangest—a being in spirit form. What hope did he have to get out of his current predicament? How could he fight something that was not truly there?

Sidra reacted as if the entity had said something to her. "Yes. So, you see, Hadrea. The Key possesses far more magic than I could have ever stored within it. And it was charged by this girl, for the most part well away the wellspring at Pearl City." She turned toward Abby. "She was the source of this magic, acting as her own wellspring. To be sure, I benefitted from her ignorance of how to use it, using her own power to trap her and hold her during the entire journey to this place. The more she struggled, the more magical power was stored in the Crystal Key, and the more powerful I became. We can, Hadrea, turn this to our continuing advantage."

Turning back to the entity, she concluded, "I do not understand your insistence that I was to find a magic-wielding man. That discernment of yours turned out to be false. Or at least inaccurate. For she is the one you are looking for. I am certain of it."

There was a long pause as Sidra waited for a reaction from the entity. It still swirled silently around the Crystal Key, absorbing whatever power or information it could glean from the contact. Finally, the entity separated itself from the Key and Sidra's hands, and glided over toward Abby.

All Abby could see of Hadrea was a distortion in the artificial blue light of the wellspring's glow, rippling in the air before him. Its lack of features was frightening, with no limbs or face or eyes to identify it as human in any sense. Wide-eyed, Abby watched its approach with horror filling his heart. He squirmed and struggled against the magical bindings keeping in his prone position.

The entity distorted itself to reach for Abby. As it made contact with Abby's head, Abby felt its power reaching out to touch his mind. Fighting the sensation, Abby closed his eyes and tried to shut the spirit out.

Almost as an instinctive reaction, his magic flared within himself. With Sidra still holding the Crystal Key in her hands, Abby thought he had a fleeting opportunity to strike out against his captors. He tried to burst his power out away from him in as powerful and explosive shock as he could manage.

But Sidra was too quick for him. She was already at his side, and pressed the Crystal Key onto his chest. As she had done during the entire journey to Sapphire City, she was able to bend and shape Abby's power, using the Key to harness and directing it yet again into the bottomless well that was the Crystal Key. Other than a brief flare of white illumination in the room, Abby's magical burst came and went with barely a whimper.

Sidra then extracted punishment from Abby by refocusing the magic that was holding Abby in place. Abby felt the bindings around him tighten even more, until the pressure around his chest was so restricting that he could barely move air in or out of his lungs. He grew lightheaded, and thought he would pass out at any moment. Helpless, Abby croaked in desperation, "Please, please. Let me breathe!"

Sidra hissed down to him, "Do not struggle, little one. We are your masters here." For emphasis, she waited as the magical bindings froze Abby in its tight embrace until Abby's face reddened from the intensity of the pressure and the lack of air.

Finally, Sidra was distracted. She cocked her head as if the entity had given her an order. Sidra relented, waving her hand over Abby's body and adjusting the magic to a more comfortable state. Relieved but still held in place, Abby took a few deep breaths to regain his composure as he awaited whatever was going to happen next.

For the moment, the entity had ceased its probe of Abby's mind. It hovered within inches of Abby's head, as if still trying to puzzle out what sort of mystery Abby was.

In the intervening silence, Sidra gestured toward the entity. "In the event you have not already deduced it, this is my mistress and friend, Hadrea. She is my master, and now your master as well. Say hello, little one."

Abby hesitated. Unsure of what the entity was, he did not want to address it directly. Instead, he answered Sidra as if she was some sort of translator for it. "Tell it 'hello', I guess. But if you think that dragging me here and holding me will make me help you, or whatever this thing is, you're delusional. Release me. Then, we can talk. If I've already been such a help to you by recharging your Key, maybe we can work out a deal to let me go."

Hadrea answered angrily, its disembodied voice echoing loudly in the room, "Speak to me directly, bitch. I am in charge here! You are in no position to negotiate your freedom. You will do as I say and your fate henceforth rests with me!" The entity paused to let that sink in with Abby before continuing in a slightly softer tone. "If you prove yourself a worthy follower of my path, then you can accrue privileges and a certain degree of freedom. But only after you have fully committed yourself, and earned such respect from me."

Trying to be feign respect, Abby answered, "Please, Hadrea. Ma'am. I'll not fight you anymore. You're too strong. But after being dragged here and held against my will, unable to even sit or stand up, it is hard for me to think I would ever help either of you."

The entity seemed buoyed by Abby's tone of resignation. "That's right, dear. We are in charge here. The sooner that you realize that cooperation is better than resistance, the easier it will be on you. If Sidra was correct and you have the abilities that she believes that you do, placing your talents in my service will have its benefits. Believe me. Just mind your betters, and this can be a mutually beneficial situation."

As his mind raced, trying to come up with other options, Abby tried to keep the conversation going in a non-confrontational way. "Well, ma'am, it's true that I don't know what I'm doing. I'm new to this world, just trying to figure out things as I go along." Abby stopped and caught himself. Had he just said too much?

Sidra picked up on Abby's mistake immediately, "What do you mean 'new to this world'? Are you not from Distan? Where are you from, girl?"

Abby tried to recover. "New to Distan. You're right. I'm not from around here. That's what I meant."

Sidra bore in on Abby, "Well, that is obvious from your accent. I truly have never heard anything like it. I have met travelers from the other Queendoms, rare as they are, and their speech was nothing like yours. But, tell us the truth, please. This will be a good gesture for you to make to us. Tell us where you are from. And none of your bullshit."

Abby's mind raced, trying to come up with something plausible. But he realized that he had such little knowledge of this world that it would be difficult for him to make up something that they would believe. "Well...O.K. I mean, my travel papers said I was from Quartz City..."

Sidra cut him off immediately, "Bah! Spare us. Your speech is nothing like someone from that region. I know. I've been there. Try again. Are you from anywhere in the Queendom of Distan?"

Abby shook his head. "No. Nowhere in Distan."

Sidra pressed him. "Then where? The Golden Islands? The Queendoms south of the Endless Desert? The so-called 'Lands of Origin'? Where? Even accepting that you found some means to make such a journey, why would you undertake it at all? Someone as young as yourself would have no reason, much less the resources, to journey to Distan. What would you find here that would justify coming at all?"

Abby faltered. "Um...Well, that's right. I guess you could say that my coming here was not voluntary. I found myself here?"

Sidra was incredulous. "Found yourself here? Are you serious? One day, for no reason you woke up in Distan. Is that what you are saying?"

Abby did not answer. He was as close to revealing who he truly was as he had ever been, but revealing his secret to Sidra and this ghostly entity seemed like the worst thing he could do at that moment. But it was on the tip of his tongue.

Hadrea, who had been silent during the exchange, was the one who finally guessed the truth. Her disembodied voice spoke with a smooth confidence, "Don't you see, Sidra? She is saying that she is not of our world entirely. Our little friend here is a traveler from another universe or dimension. Another reality. For all we know, she is not even human. She has just assumed the form of one in our world."

The pressure of the conversation was beginning to panic Abby. He protested, "No, I'm human! Just like everyone else here. I mean, the other humans. A few things are different, of course."

"Like what, specifically?" Hadrea pressed. As if she already knew the answer, Hadrea asked directly, "Were you in fact a man in your previous incarnation?"

Abby felt boxed in. He felt he already gave away his secret through his careless choice of words. Although he could not believe he was revealing it in front of his present company, Abby blurted out quickly, "Yes. I was a fifty year old man. In a different reality, one without magic. My name was Tom." Part of him actually felt relief at finally being able to say it.

"Ha!" Hadrea exclaimed as Sidra gasped in surprise. Hadrea continued triumphantly, "I told you, Sidra! The disturbance in the Continuum felt as a male presence, even though it is firmly established that men cannot wield magic. This girl is the solution to that dilemma. A male soul was put into a female body. Given the standard physics of magic, this is the only way it was possible."

There was a pause as both Hadrea and Sidra absorbed the truth. Hadrea then continued as if she were narrating her thoughts aloud, "And, even more remarkably, the soul used was not even from our reality. One without magic? How strange and random that must be. No wonder this girl is at once so powerful and yet untrained in even the most basic uses of her power. Even a teenaged rogue witch would have acquired some knowledge of how to wield it by this point in her life. But for this one, it is brand new to her. Is that not right, little lady?" She put an extra note of derision into her voice for the last two words.

But Abby ignored the jibe and answered truthfully, "Yes, that's right. I've only been in your world for a few weeks now. From one minute to the next, I went from the world I was born into, and lived to fifty years old, to your world in this girl's body. It was in the elven kingdom, high in the mountains. I was found by a scouting patrol a short time after. I've been like this since."

Sidra interjected quickly, "Then, what of your powers? Were you a magic wielder in your world?"

Abby shook his head. In a defeated tone, he said, "No, Hadrea is right. My world has no magic at all. Only science. The magical powers you take for granted in your world are all new to me."

Sidra shook her head in disbelief, "Remarkable! I transported you this entire time, and I had no idea of your true nature. It would explain so much, Hadrea. Why the Sisterhood did not already have her. Why her magical abilities, while powerful, are so haphazard and inexperienced. All of this is new to her. But why? This girl, or whatever she is, is no random event. Too many natural laws were broken for her to be formed as such a person, from two different realities. What is going on here?"

Hadrea's voice took on a note of concern, "Yes, the fact of her existence is its own mystery. Certainly, she is not here of her own agency. Someone, or more likely, some greater entity brought her here, for its own purposes. That is a concern to us going forward."

Addressing Abby, Hadrea concluded, "That is true of you, too, my dear. You are a pawn in someone's else's game. As a result, a little less hubris in you would be in order. Perhaps you would do well to cooperate with us, for your own selfish reasons. We will certainly teach you how to harness and project your power out into this world. That may be your only true course. Certainly, you fell into our lap easily enough, when we were not even searching for someone such as you."

Oddly enough, Abby agreed with Hadrea. He was here for a reason. Being in this world, in this body, could not have been some sort of freak occurrence. It felt much more real, more tangible, than some fever dream or heart attack-induced hallucination. He did not even believe in his heart that this was some sort of purgatory or hell. This reality was too big, with too many other people in it, for it to be solely constructed by God to punish him.

Yet, at the same time, his instincts recoiled from any thought at helping Hadrea or Sidra. Yes, they probably could teach Abby much about his power and how to use it. But Hadrea the disembodied, power-hungry entity and Sidra the cold-blooded, killer vampire did not inspire any empathy, or trigger any desire on Abby's part to follow where they might lead. They were to be resisted, and fought, whenever and however Abby could manage to do so.

For her part, Sidra picked up on the negative implications of Hadrea's intuition. With concern in her voice, she said, "But, Hadrea, this girl does not exist for our purposes, surely. For all we have had to overcome to reach this point, including the death of your natural body, I cannot believe that this girl was sent to assist us in recharging the Key and furthering our plans. Unless we ourselves are pawns in some greater unseen game. Can that be, Hadrea?"

Hadrea answered cooly, "Do not despair, Sidra. Fate can be guided, my dear, but it is never absolutely preordained. Thus far, we have bent our destiny to our will, and can continue to do so as long as we have power of wellsprings and the Crystal Key supporting our efforts. To the contrary, you might even say that circumstances fell into place for us rather conveniently. Based on my perceptions of the Continuum, I send you to Pearl City looking for a magic-wielding man. You go there and this girl drops into your lap. Rather than continue looking for the man of my description, you bring this girl here and present her to me as the fulfilment of your mission. Along the way, you recharged the Crystal Key with her magic, despite no apparent connection to any proximate wellspring. And, in the end, by her own confession it turns out that she was the man that I intended you to find all along. How can that be anything else than the beneficence of Fate's hand? We are certainly ascendant, are we not?"

Sidra answered with despair in her voice, "It cannot be that easy, Hadrea. I hope you are correct, that this girl was dropped into our lap to further our cause." Risking first a quick glance at Abby, she continued bluntly, "But what if she was planted here to undo us? For all we know, we have introduced a wild tiger in to our midst, secured only by the thinnest of leashes. If you cannot convince her to join us, what will we do?"

Hadrea answered immediately, "Then she will die. Her only course is to aid us. Otherwise, her life in this reality ends here and now."

Hadrea's words sent a quick shiver of terror through Abby. This was about to be Abby's moment of truth, as Hadrea clearly intended to coerce cooperation from Abby or punish him for disobeying. Still pinned in place by Sidra's magic, he readied himself as best he could for whatever pressure or pain or torture was about to be applied to him.

Strangely, it was Sidra's comment about a 'tiger on a leash' that bolstered Abby in that moment. Was Sidra actually afraid of Abby? It did not seem possible, as easily as Sidra had bested Abby whenever Abby had tried to break free. But Sidra had seen Abby's magic over an extended period. Apparently, she had come to respect it, and even worry about its potential. It bolstered Abby's determination to resist whatever Hadrea was about to do, at all costs.

Silence, heavy and expectant, came over them as the three faced each other. And it was at that exact moment, when Hadrea was about to demand that Abby choose to obey or die, that Fate decided to intervene.

Suddenly, there was a commotion at the entrance of the room, where the stairs exited from the floor above. Abby turned his head in time to see a group of five ghouls stumble into the room, shrieking in agitated high-pitched wails as if they were being pursued from behind. Sidra's first reaction was annoyance at the intrusion. "Do not interrupt! We are..." She stopped herself when she saw the cause of the ghouls' distress.

Then, to Abby's shock, the elf Reanah, her face intense and full of purpose, charged down the basement stairs after them. She cocked an arrow in a large bow, drew it back and released it into the chest of the closest ghoul. Then, standing her ground, she pulled one arrow then another from the quiver on her back, letting each loose into the chest or head of each ghoul in the cluster before her. The thudding sound of each arrow's impact silenced each ghoul in turn.

Behind her, and to Abby's utter amazement, Dacy followed. As Reanah worked her bow, Dacy came bounding down the stairs with her dagger drawn. She charged past Reanah, slashing and stabbing at any ghoul that tried to come at the pair. Seeing the diminutive Dacy next to the tall, athletic elf was a startling enough sight, but Abby's mind could not comprehend how the two of them had fallen in together, fighting side to side at that moment.

Within a minute, Reanah had felled the last of the ghouls, leaving her and Dacy only a few paces from Abby. Reanah and Abby's eyes met. It had been many weeks since they had last seen each other, the night before Abby's escape from Jade City, seemingly a lifetime ago given all that had happened to Abby since. It had never occurred to Abby that the elves might pursue him once he had left the elven kingdom.

Yet, incredibly, here Reanah was. Abby saw the determination in her eyes. This was the same steely soldier that had found Abby in the elven mountains, after Abby had managed to drag himself out of a cold, rushing river in his first moments in this new reality.

But even though Reanah and Dacy had dispatched the ghouls with quick efficiency, Abby knew that they were in great danger. Sidra alone was a fearsome creature, and Abby realized that his two rescuers might not even be aware of Hadrea's disembodied presence. How could they defend themselves with bow and arrow and dagger, from the powerful magic that would be unleashed on them?

Abby tried to warn them, calling out, "Look out! There are two of them!"

Reanah, though, was already making her next move. Reaching into a pocket in her pants, she withdrew a small circular object ringed in white and blue gems that glittered in the blue light of the wellspring magic that permeated the room. With a gentle toss, she lobbed it into the center of the room, right next to Sidra. As it landed, she cried out, "Excitant!"

The object sprang to life, sending out a pulse of white light that for an instant lighted everything in the room in stark relief. Sidra's instinctive reaction was to call forth her own magic and strike at the object. She raised her hands toward it, with her magic tinged blue from the power of the wellspring underneath them, already pulsing around her fingers.

Hadrea, though, tried to intervene, crying out in warning, "Sidra! No!"

But Sidra was already unleashing a pent-up burst of magic. It exploded from her fingers, shooting out thin streamers of blue lightning toward Reanah's object. But instead of touching and destroying the device, the object acted as a mirror to Sidra's power, reflecting it back instantaneously towards her.

With a load bang, Sidra's own magic concussed against the front of her body, flinging her backwards through the air across the room. She landed in a heap against the stone foundation of the building, striking the back of her head, leaving her unconscious and her body crumpled on the floor.

As Sidra fell, her hold over Abby vanished. The magical bindings securing him in place vanished, and his body fell to the ground with a thud. Abby instinctively caught himself with the points of his elbows and the back of his legs, managing to do it without striking his own head on the stone floor. But the contact sent sudden shoots of pain coursing through his body. "Ow!" he cried out.

But after weeks under Sidra's control, held in a fixed horizontal position with his arms and legs pinned, Abby was finally and gratefully free. As the blood rushed back into his limbs, he rolled over, flexing his stiff muscles and gauging his ability to try to stand.

Dacy and Reanah rushed to him, gently helping him up to a seated position. Dacy whispered quickly, "Are you alright, Abby? What did she do to you?"

Despite the lingering pain, Abby shook his head. "I'm not hurt badly. Actually, it feels good to finally be able to move." He quickly glanced around the room. He lowered his voice and whispered quickly, "Where is the other one?"

Dacy glanced quickly around the edges of the room. "What other one? There was only you and the pale bitch down here when we came in."

Abby shook his head. "No, you don't understand. There was a spirit, an entity. Even looking right at it, you could barely see it. It called itself Hadrea. For all I know, it's still here right now."

Reanah started in surprise. "Sister Hadrea? It cannot be. She was executed in Pearl City some weeks ago for witchcraft and treason."

"Let me guess," Abby countered. "That was right about the time that Pearl City was cleaned out and there were a whole bunch of ghouls where the people used to be."

Reanah stared wide-eyed at him. "Yes, that is true, but. . .all I know officially is that she was executed. The rest is just rumor and speculation. But yes, the two events seem to be tied together."

As she spoke, Abby glanced around the room, trying to sense Hadrea's presence. After a few tense seconds, he said, "She's not here, for the moment at least."

Dacy grabbed at Abby's forearms to lift him to his feet. "Then, we need to get the fuck out of here. Come on. Let's go!"

Abby nodded. With Dacy pulling his arms and Reanah helping raise him from the back, he rose unsteadily to his feet.

As Dacy held Abby to help him regain his balance on his feet, she looked him in the eyes. "Can you walk, at least?"

Abby tested his stiff and sore limbs, shaking and stretching them out. "I think so. I should be able to walk. I just won't be able to go so fast."

Dacy began to hustle him toward the stairs. "Too bad. 'Cause you'll need to run once we hit the ground floor. Them ghouls is swarming up there."

Abby's heart sank. He was not sure he was up to it. But he knew there was no other choice. He nodded and let himself be pushed along.

As they moved toward the stairs, Abby risked a glance over toward Sidra's still unconscious body. Awkwardly crumpled up against the far wall, Sidra seemed so vulnerable at that moment. Abby considered asking the others to finish her. But could they actually kill a vampire? In Tom's world, the lore of vampires held that driving a wooden stake through the heart would kill one. But that was the lore for a fictional character. In Abby's world, vampires were apparently very real, and he had no idea what it would take to actually kill a vampire. And if Sidra woke up, or Hadrea suddenly returned, their opportunity to flee might be gone for good. So, Abby kept silent as Dacy shuffled him toward the stairs leading upwards.

Reanah took a quick detour to retrieve her gemmed device from the floor. She tucked it into her pants side pocket, before hustling to bring up the rear.

The three hurried up the stairs. At the landing at the top of the stairs, they paused. Ahead of them, several ghouls of varying sizes milled about in the open area of the main floor. For the moment, the ghouls took no notice, but Abby realized that trying to escape by rushing past the creatures would likely prove suicidal. For the moment, the creatures seemed relatively calm, their movements unfocused. But once the ghouls' swarming behavior was triggered, there would be no way that the three would make it out alive.

After an instant's hesitation, Dacy led the way into an empty side room. Abby followed quickly, and as Reanah entered she gently closed and latched the door behind her. They were alone and out of the sight of the ghouls. For a few seconds, the three listened breathlessly for any sign that their presence was noticed, before finally exhaling in relief at the lack of any agitation on the other side of the door.

Abby looked at the other two and whispered, "Now what? How do we get out?"

Reanah nodded as if she had the answer. She withdrew the same gemmed, round object that she had tossed at Sidra. "With this," she said quietly, turning it over in her hands so that the light coming in through the window glinted off the blue and white gems that ringed its edge. "It is called a 'speculum magica'. It works by reflecting magic back to its source.

The vampiress found that out when she attempted to strike out with her power, only to be felled by it.

"On our way to this place, I used it to create a safe space around myself and Dacy. The creatures outside are bound and controlled by a magic. It keeps them obedient, and prevents them from attacking and shredding each other. Once activated, the device will mirror the ambient magic surrounding the ghouls. As long as we stay quiet and move slowly, the creatures will think we are part of their collective."

Dacy harrumphed. In a low voice, she said, "Coming in, it scared the piss out of me. Having to walk with them things all around and hope they doesn't see you."

Abby countered with hope in his voice, "But it worked, right?"

Dacy nodded, but the expression on her face showed she was not looking forward to trying it again.

Abby, though, whispered, "Then let's do it! We've got to get as far away from this place as we can before Sidra and Hadrea start looking for us."

Reanah having watched the exchange between them, shook her head. She said quietly, "For the moment, we cannot. At least, not until we can recharge the device with magic."

She handed the device over to Abby. "Dacy tells me that you have the talent, Abby. I suspected as much when you were able to escape from headquarters in Jade City." Reanah used a fingertip to tap at a large white crystal at the center. "You need to direct your power into this gem. Once there is a sufficient amount in there, we can leave."

Abby grimaced. While he did not expect that Dacy could have spent days tracking Abby to this place without telling Reanah about his magical ability along the way, he was still disappointed that there was now another person who knew he was a rogue witch. But that was a problem for later. At that moment, he just wanted to escape.

"Fine," Abby said, "Let's give this a try."

With all the times he had accessed his magic during his captivity, Abby now had the confidence that he could call on his magic when he wanted to do so. Focusing on the storage crystal, Abby closed his eyes and tried to connect the power within him to it. Within a few seconds, he felt the familiar surge of power within him. Trying to regulate it as best he could, he released it through his fingertips into the device.

Abby heard both Dacy and Reanah gasp beside him. He could feel the magic pouring out of him, but was afraid to open his eyes to see what was happening.

After a moment, he risked a peek at what was happening around him. The room was filled with a brilliant white light, so intense that it was all Dacy and Reanah could do to shield their eyes from it in self-defense.

With no Crystal Key sucking his power into an almost bottomless well, Abby's magic was bright and unrestrained. The intense white light penetrated through the outer walls of the building, rendering them transparent. Several ghouls in the space outside of the building were caught in the intensity of the glow, and they shrieked in pain from the contact. As quickly as they could, they recoiled and scrambled and shuffled out of reach of Abby's light.

The ghouls in the building certainly were aware of the presence of Abby and Dacy and Reanah now. The walls of the side room in which they were hiding no longer concealed them. The ghouls began to skitter and chatter in their agitation. But Abby's power was warding them off.

Sensing an opportunity, Abby shouted, "Let's go!" He used his free hand to tug at Dacy, then Reanah, urging them to follow him through the opening created by his magic. As Dacy and Reanah kept their eyes tightly closed, the three held onto each other and Abby led the way out through the doorway. They shuffled down the hallway, with the ghouls in the interior shrieking in pain from Abby's magic and retreating and scrambling out of contact with the intense light.

After a moment, the three emerged through the front entrance, crossed the outer porch and passed down the steps into the open area outside of the town hall. Though it was a sunny, bright afternoon, the light of Abby's power was like a star emerging into the open air.

Here, dozens of ghouls had been milling about, waiting for their masters' directions. Suddenly, though, there was chaos. Contact with Abby's magic drew wails and shrieks and cries of pained distress from the creatures, and there was a disorganized, tumbling rush as the ghouls scrambled away into the side alleys and streets. Within moments, Abby and Dacy and Reanah were alone.

The area was now free of ghouls, but Abby guessed that it would only be a matter of moments before Hadrea or Sidra returned to rally them. With Dacy and Reanah holding him around his waist, and with one hand still clutching Reanah's device, Abby led them slowly across the square into an empty nearby building. The outer door was damaged and would not latch shut, but Abby swung it closed behind them to provide some barrier between them and any pursuers.

Abby's magic was still a torrent of power, blinding in its intensity. But Abby felt helpless to stop it, as if he had turned on a fire hose but could not shut it off. The walls surrounding them began to grow transparent as the magic coursed through it.

In desperation, Reanah grasped Abby by the shoulders and looked into his face. Her voice was almost a shout as she tried to get Abby to focus on her, "Fight this! Get hold of yourself!"

Abby nodded and concentrated on the waves of magic flowing outward from himself. He closed his eyes and used his mind to isolate the sensation of the magic and its flow through his body. After several moments, his effort began to pay off, and he was able to restrict his magic. It gradually and steadily lessened until it stopped flowing out from him.

Abby opened his eyes. Dacy and Reanah were staring at him with a mixture of wonderment and fear. "Sorry about that," he whispered to the others. "I know it's too much. I can't help myself."

Dacy unleashed a wide smile. "Damn! That was fine work there, Abby." She chortled and clapped Abby on the back.

Reanah, though, was less impressed. She said gruffly, "We are only safe here momentarily." She turned to Abby and indicated that she wanted him to hand over the gemmed magical device. "Let's see what you managed to accomplish with all of that. After all, recharging my speculum magica was the intent in the first place."

Abby handed over the device. Reanah turned it over in her hands, frowning. Then, she said with disappointment and frustration in her voice, "No, no, no! Despite all of that, not nearly enough of your power went into the storage gem itself. There is only a small charge here."

Reanah sighed and cast her eyes toward the ceiling. She rubbed her forehead, mulling over their options. Finally, she looked at Abby and said, "At least we know now that you can cast a transparency, Abby. Let me guess. You've done that before. That's most likely how you escaped from headquarters in Jade City, isn't it?"

Abby's face reddened. He nodded and answered, "Yes, it was almost by accident, really. I touched an illuminer and I lit up like a beacon. The walls vanished and I just walked out of there, like we did right now."

Reanah replied, "I suspected as much. But we are in a far more dangerous situation now. If you cannot focus your power and do what you intend with it, you will not be much use to us."

Abby protested, "But I did something, right? I drove away those creatures. We're safe for the moment because of me." He was starting to get angry. "But your device received some of my magic. Tell me there is enough in there to get us out of here."

Reanah sighed. "Perhaps. It is too much of a risk for us to have you make another attempt at this moment to further recharge the device. To make it safely out of Sapphire City, we will have to go by stealth. We can't have you lighted up like a beacon to anyone who can track magic. We'll have to just go as far as we can for now before we stop and have you try again."

Dacy's expression soured. She blurted out, "Crap on a cracker! I thought with all of that we'd be scot free."

"Me, too," Abby replied quietly. "Again, sorry I couldn't do better. This is all new to me, you know."

Reanah patted Abby on the shoulder. "It's alright. Keep your composure. We'll need you to make it all the way out of Sapphire City. It'll be about a four hour walk to an abandoned barn, west of here, where Dacy and I left the horses. Just get us there, Abby."

Abby nodded. "O.K. I'll do my best."

Dacy interjected, "But, Reanah. What about your device? Is there enough in that toy of yours to get us out of here?"

"Enough for now," Reanah replied grimly, "And not enough to get us safely away. But the challenge will be greater this time. The ghouls and their masters will be actively searching for us." Gesturing toward Abby, she continued, "They will not just let their mobile wellspring walk out of here without contesting it."

Abby nodded that he understood, but all of this was too much to take. He could feel the tears welling in his eyes, and was on the verge of sobbing. But the others looked to him as the means for their escape. He could not falter now, and there was no time for crying. He wiped his face to sober himself up.

Instead, Abby tried to focus on the task immediately before them. He asked Reanah, "So, how far can we get with what you've got in your device?"

Reanah shook her head. "Not far. But if we can get some distance from here, perhaps we can find a safe location and give ourselves an opportunity to try again to recharge my device."

The others nodded in reply. Minutes were passing, and they could feel time working against them. Their window of safety was surely closing quickly. For better or worse, they knew they had to leave.

Reanah gestured for Dacy and Abby to gather themselves next to her body. Dacy pressed up against Reanah's torso, wrapping her arms around the elf. As Reanah raised the gemmed device over her head, Dacy whispered to Abby, "Come on, Abby. We've got to all fit underneath that thing."

Abby nodded and moved next to Reanah, using his arms to wedge himself against her much taller body. With the three of them huddled together, Reanah held the gemmed device over her head. Lifting her eyes toward it, she repeated the same word she had yelled out in the basement of the town hall, this time as a whispered incantation, "Excitant...excitant… excitant."

In reply, the device gave an audible pop, and the air surrounding the three wavered as a barely visible field stretched down from it toward the floor. Reanah whispered to the others, "Let's depart. It's now or never."

Hugging each other, they shuffled awkwardly toward the door. Abby realized that it must have been difficult enough to have Dacy hugging Reanah all the way into the center of Sapphire City on their way in. Now, there would be three bodies rather than two within the area affected by Reanah's device. That was going to slow them down significantly. But this was the only hope they had to escape.

First to the reach the outer door, Dacy swung it open and the three moved out into the brightly sun lighted street, pressing tight against each other. Abby flinched at the sight before them in the open courtyard. Ghouls of various sizes were moving about quickly but haphazardly, searching for their prey in a state of agitation. Abby pressed his lips tightly together, fighting the urge to cry out.

Reanah led them forward, heading toward a street exiting the square. Despite the forced slowness of their movements, they were fortunate in their initial escape. No ghoul accidentally bumped into them, and even though ghouls at times passed at times within a few feet of the three, the ghouls did not seem to notice their presence. However Reanah's device worked, Abby knew it was protecting them, at least for the moment.

Slowly and steadily, Reanah directed them forward, tacking from side to side to avoid contact with the ghouls around them. Dacy and Abby tried to move with Reanah as best they could, but they jostled and bumped each other, and their feet and legs occasionally tangled and tripped over each other. But they kept themselves huddled under Reanah's device, and the ghouls still took no notice of them. Soon, Abby was bathed in sweat from the effort.

They moved from one street to the next, gradually moving west in their slow progress. Abby was surprised at the direction, just assuming that Reanah and Dacy had come in straight from the north. Apparently, though, they had taken a path around the outside of Sapphire City before making their way into the center. He hoped the misdirection also fooled their pursuers.

Minutes passed in slow agony. The movement of the ghouls around them was frenetic but unfocused, as if they were tripwires waiting to be triggered, rather than being specifically directed by a superior consciousness. By that point, Abby assumed that Hadrea and Sidra had recovered from the attack on them in the basement of the town hall. But for now, they were nowhere to be seen. As long as Reanah's device cloaked them, Reanah and Dacy and Abby could keep up their escape.

After moving for a time that to Abby seemed interminable, but was in actuality less than an hour, Reanah found a promising-looking, relatively intact house on one of the side streets. She steered them toward the open doorway, and guided the others inside. She closed the door behind them, slid the latch shut. Taking a quick look in the barren interior around them, they could see that they were alone.

With a short verbal command in elvish, Reanah turned off her device. As it popped off in reply, all three let out gasps of relief.

"Finally!" Dacy exclaimed in a tempered tone. "Thank the Maker!"

"Indeed," Reanah replied in a cautious whisper. "We've made a good start. But most of the way is yet to go."

Abby, too, was relieved, but one question tugged at him. He asked with some trepidation, "How much more power do you have in your thing there? Can we make it the rest of the way?"

Reanah wrinkled her nose in reply. She spent a moment turning over her device in her hands, and examined the central storage gem with the tips of her fingers. She answered with disappointment in her voice, "It is almost spent, I'm afraid. You will need to try again to put more magic in the storage gem, or we will never make it out of here. But once you engage your magic, I'm afraid that will give away our location to any magic user within a dozen miles of this place."

Abby knew what that meant. As much as they needed Abby's magic to complete their escape, it would be another attempt by Abby to use his magic without letting it loose in a wild, attention-getting burst. And this time, he needed to properly guide his power into the storage gem on Reanah's speculum magica. So far, he had not managed that very well at all.

With a bit of frustration in his voice, Abby answered, "So, it all falls on me, again. Tell me, though, what the hell were you doing coming into Sapphire City in the first place? If you had enough power in your mirror of magic to make it in but not out again, what was the point of that? All you did was endanger yourselves. Didn't you have a plan to get back out again?"

Dacy cut in, "Abby, really! There wasn't no time to think things through. We were haulin' ass to find you! And we did get you out of there, didn't we? A little gratitude might be appreciated at this point."

Reanah shook her head and answered more soberly, "To be honest, I did not expect the numbers of those creatures. It is one thing to confront one or several, but not dozens or perhaps hundreds. At first, we tried evasion or, for one or two of them, a quick kill. But there were too many, and this device became the only way to progress toward the center of the city. I suppose we were not thinking much beyond that, I'm afraid. Nevertheless, as Dacy says, here were are."

Dacy chuckled, "But you should see this girl in action!" She made a gesture as if shooting an invisible arrow. "She is one bad ass with a bow and arrow, let me tell you."

Reanah seemed a little embarrassed. "Only a product of good training, I assure you. And as I say there is only so much one can do with a bow and arrow against such an enemy." She put one hand on Abby's shoulder in reassurance. "That is why we need you to try again, my dear. You must call forth your magic again. But this time, please attempt to control yourself. The more you are able to focus and direct the power into the storage crystal, the less likely it will be that we will be located. It is our only viable option at this point."

Abby nodded, "Sure. I think I can do better this time. Really." He did not know where that confidence was coming from, or whether he even believed it in his heart. But he knew he had to try.

He accepted the magic mirror from Reanah. Dacy and Reanah lapsed into silence as Abby turned the device over in his hands, clearing his mind and preparing to access his magic.

As the others looked on intently, Abby closed his eyes and focused on the storage gem. This time, when he felt the magic rise within him, he did his best to concentrate and limit exactly how much power he was releasing.

From deep within Abby, the flow of white magic began. In his calmer state, Abby found he was able to regulate it much better than he had done before, and he was able to better control where the magic was flowing. The familiar white glow began to envelop Abby's body, but most of the power began to flow through Abby's hands into Reanah's device in a more controlled, efficient manner. For the first time, Abby felt as if he was in control of his magic, instead of it behaving in wild and unpredictable ways.

Even so, Abby knew that this use of his magic would attract attention. Surely, he assumed, Sidra would surely be called in this direction. With a sinking feeling, he knew it was only a matter of time before he would see her again. He shuddered at the thought. If only they could reach Reanah's horses in time, they might have a chance for a clean escape.

Abby held his concentration for several minutes, until Reanah softly tapped him on the shoulder and whispered, "Enough, Abby. That should be sufficient."

Despite his success up to that point, the effort to halt the stream of magic was a bit more than Abby anticipated. Several frustrating seconds passed as Abby tried to stem the flow. Finally, his mind connected with the source of his power, and the flow of magic cut off abruptly.

Abby opened his eyes and looked down at his body. The bare skin showing on his arms still shone white with the afterglow of his power. He looked up at the others. Despite any doubts about his control over his magic, their smiles showed their approval at his effort. He smiled back at them. It felt good to finally do something with his power that he intended to do, without losing control of it. In that moment, Abby hoped that would be the start of something new with his ability, that he would control his magic instead of being a victim of it.

Reanah accepted her device from Abby and turned it over in her hands. There was hope in her voice when she spoke, "Yes, it is fully recharged. Well done, Abby. This should take us the rest of the way."

Dacy exclaimed, "Yes! There you have it, ladies. Our way out!" Reanah frowned at Dacy's overconfidence, but did not correct her.

Reanah and Abby's eyes met and they shared a quick moment of silent understanding. He knew they were thinking the same thing. There was still a significant risk of being found and caught. But, perhaps, they really could make it safely out of Sapphire City.

With that, it was time to move again. The three gathered themselves in their familiar huddle around Reanah, and moved toward the door. Dacy and Abby waited for Reanah to turn on her device.

But before Reanah opened the door to leave, she quickly looked down at Abby. "Tell me just one thing, Abby. Or Abstinence, or Leanna, or whatever your real name is. When you escaped from our headquarters, it appeared as if you had left a piece of paper behind with some markings on it. You tried to say something, but we could not make any sense of it. What was it that you were trying to say? Tell me. It's been under my skin ever since."

Abby started. He had almost forgotten that he did that. "What? The note? I don't know why you couldn't read it. It was in English, just like we're speaking now. I don't remember what I said, exactly. I was just trying to thank you. But you didn't get that from what I wrote?"

Reanah shook her head. "No, the lettering was incomprehensible to us."

Abby could not make sense of that. "But what are we speaking now? I'm talking to you in English, aren't I?"

Both Dacy and Reanah chimed in. "No." Reanah went on, "We are speaking Common, the language of humans and the second language of the other races. Our written language is based on the ancient Alphabetum, which is the basis of all the living languages."

Dacy interrupted impatiently, "So, what is English? Is that the land where you're from?"

"Not exactly," Abby answered. "The language English is from England, but that's not where I'm from…" He stopped himself. The others were looking at him, waiting for him to continue. It would take too long for the rest of the explanation, and he was not sure he wanted to repeat his confession to Hadrea and Sidra that he was from another, separate reality. "But it's a long story that we don't have time for right now. Let's just get going."

Reanah said, "So, your message was to thank me. For what?"

Abby shrugged. "I felt bad for leaving, and I knew you were going to catch shit for it. But I had an opportunity to escape and I used it. Sister Dana was creeping me out and I did not want to wait around for whatever other magical tricks she wanted to try out on me."

Reanah sighed in exasperation. "Sister Dana drove you away. I guessed as much. Truly, I wish I had been able to shield you a little better from her." She nodded to herself.

"I'll do better next time. Trust me. But we've no time to go over all of that now."

Reanah's remark sent a chill through Abby. He hoped there would never be a next time with Sister Dana. Or, any other member of the Sisterhood, for that matter.

Dacy's impatience ended the conversation. She said with insistence, "Right, friends. This ain't the time or place for gab'n. Let's get to the barn where we's got the horses. We can braid each other's hair later."

Abby and Reanah chuckled despite the tension. With that, all three knew it was time to leave the safety of their hideaway. Abby and Dacy huddled close to Reanah and nodded that they were ready. Reanah lifted her magic mirror over her head and repeatedly whispered "excitant" until Abby heard an audible pop, signaling that it was working.

With her free hand, Reanah swung the door open and the three shuffled out into the street. Abby quickly glanced up and down the street. The area was mostly silent and deserted. A few ghouls scurried about, agitated but not seeming to focus on anything specific. For the moment, they were safe to move.

Reanah resumed their journey, and the three began their slow, shuffling motion, heading westerly down the debris and grass covered side street. Here, the decaying remnants of Sapphire City looked less menacing in the full light of a bright spring afternoon, despite the unending repetition of collapsed roofs, broken windows, rotting wood, and foundations with loose and missing stonework.

Reanah did her best to guide them safely around the hazards around them, maintaining as much separation from the ghouls in the area as she could. They made slow but steady progress, to the point where Abby began to relax his guard, just the slightest bit.

As time passed, the early afternoon sun warmed the pavement and the air around them, beyond the point where Abby was still comfortable. With Dacy and Abby still pressed closely against Reanah's body, perspiration glistened on their exposed skin, and Abby felt sticky and sweaty underneath his clothes. Given that he had not changed since before his capture in Pearl City, Abby could only imagine how badly he smelled to the others. His labored breathing was a drained, hushed rasp.

The others, too, were taxed by their awkward, slow movement and the heat in the air. But they kept moving, too afraid to stop again unless they absolutely had to. Each dealt with the heat as best they could, but no one suggested stopping to cool off in the shade.

The hours passed. Around them, the structures became less dense as they moved into the outer environs of Sapphire City. Abby was encouraged by the declining number of ghouls around them. Instead of being a constant, buzzing presence around them, they became occasional hazards. Often, the group moved without any threat in their immediate vicinity. Abby was too afraid to ask out loud how much longer they had to go, trusting that at some point he would see the destination in sight. Just keep going, he told himself. It will be alright.

But there was a dread tugging at him, and it felt more than just a mere intuition. He could feel a presence, Sidra's presence, looming behind them. He did not know if this was a general worry about being caught, or whether he had some actual, intuitive connection with her.

For the moment, he distrusted his sense of her, as if it were more a product of a stressed, anxious mind rather than anything real. He knew Sidra would be looking for them, for him. The thought of being caught and held again by his kidnapper was a horrifying one, and shredded any confidence Abby had accumulated that they had already actually escaped. The question was whether she would actually know where to look to find them. If they could reach the horses hidden ahead, the difference in speed might be all they would need to break free of Sidra's pursuit.

Abby kept silent about his sense of Sidra's presence, not trusting it enough to tell the others. But as the three shuffled along slowly under the protection of Reanah's device, dodging ghouls that were fewer and farther between, Abby's sense of Sidra kept pressing on him, becoming more distinct and close.

Finally, the sensation was pressing on him too much for him to bear alone. Abby tugged at the fabric on Reanah's free hand, and whispered in a hush, panicked voice, "Reanah. It's Sidra! She's almost on top of us!"

Reanah whispered back in surprise and disbelief, "What? You're having me on. What do you mean?"

She stopped and the three quickly looked around. It was late afternoon, and the sun was now a looming ball of red fire in the western sky in front of them. They were stopped in an open area among a cluster of abandoned houses on either side of the street. The buildings were rotting and decrepit, receding into the earth around them, with beams sticking up like broken bones through the collapsed roofs, and the broken and missing windows looking like empty eyes staring back at them. There was an eerie, still silence.

No ghouls were in sight. By the standard of what they had just come from, the scene was as empty of threats as they had seen that day. But Abby's instincts were ringing like alarm bells. It felt as if Sidra was almost on top of them. His eyes darted around, looking for any movement. He opened his mouth to warn Reanah.

In that moment, there was a humming sound as an object flew toward them. Before Abby could articulate any warning, a long thin iron rod, several feet long, landed with a sickening thud, into and through Reanah's chest.

Reanah let out a surprised, pained grunt and dropped to one knee. Blood spurted from the wound in her chest. Her magic mirror clattered as it tumbled to the pavement.

Dacy and Abby reacted to the shock of the attack by instinctively by wrapping their arms tightly around Reanah and trying to hold her up. One end of the rod that had pierced her body smacked the ground, and Reanah let out a pained, startled cry as the length of it bent from her weight. With the others unable to keep her standing, Reanah dropped to her knees.

Abby looked into Reanah's eyes, wild with pain and shock. As he leaned in to try to help her, Dacy tugged urgently at his elbow.

"There!" Dacy shouted, pointing at an opening between the buildings.

Abby's eyes followed the line of Dacy's arm until he saw Sidra gazing back at him. She was striding toward them and grinning at her prey, evidently satisfied with her first strike. She was about one hundred feet away, and closing at an unhurried walking pace. Behind her, a cluster of ghouls maintained a short gap between them and their master, but they would be ready to pounce if Sidra gave the command. The sight sent a sharp rush of fear through him. Sidra looked pleased and expectant, as if she had already won the battle.

Abby returned his focus to Reanah. The rod had pierced her right side, right through a lung. Blood continued to flow from the wound, drenching the fabric of her tunic. Reanah's breathing came in short rasps, gurgling from fluid in her throat. Abby knew she was gravely wounded, perhaps mortally.

That was terrifying enough by itself, but he could not imagine how they would beat Sidra and her minions without her.

Dacy, too, was beginning to panic. But of the three, she was first to put herself into motion, yelling into Abby's face, "Come on! Help me to pull this out of her." She put one hand on the free end of the rod that was sticking up into the air. She gestured for Abby to follow suit.

In that instant, a sharp crack of unleashed magic flew toward them, striking a low stone wall behind them and splintering stone and plaster into the air. Abby flinched and instinctively ducked. Abby heard a quick cackle from Sidra. If she had wanted to strike them directly with her magic, she could have done so easily. But he knew that was just a warning shot. Sidra was toying with them.

The thought spurred Abby to grab the rod alongside Dacy. He shot a quick glance at Reanah's face. Her eyes were wide and scared, dreading what was about to happen.

With no countdown or warning, Dacy barked, "Go! Pull!"

Abby and Dacy gave one, hard yank on the rod with all their strength. The rod moved, slowly at first, then gained speed as it passed through Reanah's chest. The tip of the rod came free, and Abby and Dacy released it in mid-air. Its momentum carried it a few feet away from them, the metal clanging harshly against the street as it landed.

Despite the blood in her throat, Reanah let out a quick, horrified shriek that echoed between the buildings. Her pained cry sent an electrical jolt rippling down Abby's spine.

Free of it, Reanah fell flat on the pavement stones, curling into a ball of pain and helplessness. She covered the wound on the front of her chest with her hands, unable to help herself beyond applying pressure against the wound.

Abby turned. Sidra was now within a few feet, and Abby counted seven ghouls hanging behind her. Dacy faced her, and raised her dagger toward Sidra's face.

Sidra laughed at the gesture. "Really, now," she smirked. "Put that down. The only thing preventing my guards here from tearing you to shreds is my command. That tiny blade will make no difference, believe me."

Dacy, though, kept the tip of her dagger pointed at Sidra's face. "Have at it, bitch. You'll not take me without a fight!"

Sidra growled, "I have no intention of taking you anywhere, whelp." Gesturing toward Abby, she continued, "Your companion here is all I and my master need. You and your elf friend here are no consequence to us. Once I have fed upon your lifeblood, I will dispatch you quickly."

Abby quickly glanced back at Reanah. She was on her side on the pavement, gasping for air with a stream of bubbled spit and blood coming from her mouth. Her limbs were still beyond a few feeble, involuntary twitches. She was fighting for her life. Abby could not tell whether she was even aware of the others around her.

Turning back to Sidra, Abby said, "Then let them go. If I'm all that matters to you and Hadrea, let my friends leave. I'll stay here and go with you voluntarily." As bravely as he could, he concluded, "You do not wish to fight me, Sidra. You may have beaten me before, but I know you are afraid of me. I can feel it."

Dacy was the one who objected first. "Bollocks to that, Abby! I ain't leaving you behind. No way, no how!"

Sidra laughed at them. "Oh, Abby, you are mistaken. This is not a negotiation. I have no intention of letting your friends depart from this place. It's true that they have no importance to me, but they are not free to leave." She stepped toward Abby, her voice low with menace, "The only thing you can decide for them is the manner of their death. With or without pain as they are shredded to death. Come with me, and I will promise them a quick, merciful death. Otherwise, the ghouls will have at them, and you will have the privilege to watch."

Abby shook his head, but did not answer. This was all too much. He could feel his uncertainties and self-doubts pressing in on him. But he instinctively recoiled at the idea of giving in to Sidra, despite her obvious mastery of magic and the threat of the jittering ghouls behind her. He had to fight, if only for the sake of fighting. If he did indeed have a unique access to magic, now seemed like the best time to unleash whatever forces he could muster in self-defense.

Dacy was apparently thinking the same thing. "Come on, Abby. You've got the magic too. If we's gonna go down, let's die on our feet. Give 'em everything you've got."

Abby nodded. Even if he could not yet control his magic as much as he needed to, he knew he could light the spark within himself and fling his power outwards at Sidra. And he would let loose as much magic as he possibly could, however wild and uncontrolled that might be, and let her defend herself from it. Whatever might happen, he thought, it was worth a try.

But before Abby could make the attempt, Sidra had one last card to play. As Dacy was talking, Sidra reached into a large leather pouch attached to a cord around her waist. After loosening the leather tie at the top, she slowly withdrew an object and lifted it with both hands so that Abby could view the length of it only a few inches from his face.

It was the Crystal Key, the oversized, golden ornamental key with a red storage crystal in its large end, the same one that Abby's magic had recharged as he had struggled to resist his capture on the long road to Sapphire City. The sight of it sent a wave of anxiety and insecurity through Abby, a visible reminder of the impotence and helplessness he felt when he was unable to use his magic to free himself. To Abby, the Crystal Key was an almost bottomless well into which his magic vanished as soon as it contacted with the Key. It was a disheartening sight, and it made Abby pause his attack.

As he stared at it, he noticed a distortion and swirling in the air above the Key's storage crystal. Though barely visible in the afternoon sunlight, Abby recognized it as Hadrea. Her disembodied voice spoke in a mocking tone, "So, you see, there is no point in trying to resist us. We are your masters here."

Sidra's wicked smile widened at the sound of her master's words. Whatever Abby and Dacy tried to do, they would have to overcome both of them, and the ghouls which backed them up. The realization made Abby freeze in place, unsure of what to do. Sensing Abby's hesitation, Dacy stared at him, waiting for Abby to do something, anything.

Abby glanced anxiously back at Reanah, hoping that somehow she could intervene. But she lay on the pavement with her eyes closed and her face contorted in pain. Blood still oozed from the wounds on each side of her torso, her gasping, forced breaths the only signs that she still lived. As much as Abby wanted to help her, he was desperate that Reanah might have some defense or device to help them fight back.

Inserting herself into the pause from Abby's inaction, Hadrea's voice continued smoothly, "The elf can no longer help you. Not that she cared for you any more than we do, surely. Don't you realize that?"

Abby viewed that as an insult to Reanah. It made him spin his head around and address the swirling presence angrily. "What do you mean? She found me and helped me when I was new to this world. She was kind to me when I had no idea what the hell was going on."

Hadrea scoffed, "But to whose benefit? Do you not wonder why she came looking for you after you left the elves? Surely not of her own volition, or on her own time. Whether she has told you or not, she is most certainly here on orders of the Elven Defense Force to bring you back to the elves. You are their prize to claim as well. And because of your previous contact with her, she was the most suitable candidate to do so. You might even trust her enough to return with her on your own volition."

Frowning, Abby exchanged a glance with Dacy. Was that true, he wondered? But Dacy only stared back helplessly, as if she had no idea what Hadrea was talking about.

Hadrea continued with a sureness that disturbed Abby, "Whether you stay with us here, or go with the elf from this place, either way you will be a prisoner. You and your abilities will end up as a tool of the elves, or the Sisterhood, or the dwarves or some other power. You have been given abilities that no one in our known world possesses. But that does not mean that you have free will here. Whomever possesses you possesses your power. It is only a matter of who your master will be."

Abby shook his head in confusion. The thought of remaining with Hadrea and Sidra and their slavering army of ghouls made him physically nauseous. But he had not given any thought as to why Reanah had tracked him all the way from Jade City. Was Hadrea right? If they somehow escaped and he went with Reanah, could he refuse to go back with her to Jade City? Would Abby be Reanah's prisoner if he refused to do so?

Sensing Abby's wavering, Hadrea pressed on, "My only consolation is that the elves probably only have a hint of your capabilities. Otherwise, they would have sent more than a single Scout to retrieve you. For now, you are only a curiosity to them, a shiny object that they can study until they understand your capabilities. But I assure you, little one, that when they fully realize who and what you are, you will be as much a prisoner of them as you fear you will be with myself and Sidra here. The only difference is that I will always be honest with you in these matters. Believe me, they will attempt to trick you and lure you with kindness and fake offerings of friendship. But in the end you will be as beholden to them as if you were bound by chains or locked in a cell. And they will use you for their purposes, not your own."

As Hadrea went on, Dacy did not like the way Abby was listening to the disembodied entity. She interjected, "You ain't listening to this, Abby? After all they's put you through, you're goin' to stand there and let them work on you like that. Really?"

But Abby wasn't being persuaded, not with Reanah dying on the ground behind him. Whatever her superiors' intentions, Abby knew Reanah was a good, honorable soldier. Abby was simply lost, unsure of what to do. He glanced anxiously at Dacy, looking for something from her to help him. She looked back at him, wild-eyed and with a fierce expression on her face, but not betraying any hint that would help him in that moment.

Hadrea, though, seemed to think that she was winning Abby over. "Let me be the one to open up your potential to the world. Let me show you how to truly use your gifts, and you and Sidra will be my right and left hands as we remake his world!" The entity swirled excitedly above the Crystal Key in Sidra's hands.

Abby felt frozen and helpless. As much as he wanted to fight back, in that moment of high stress, he was again having trouble reaching for the source of his magic. He lacked a quick trigger, some magical object that would ignite his power. Without something, anything, that he could use, he was just standing there with nothing to fight back.

Abby quickly looked around for anything that could help him. After his eyes quickly glanced up the length of Reanah's body on the ground, his sight continued on a short distance further away on the pavement. A glint of light from one of the gems on Reanah's magic

mirror caught his sight. It was his only chance.
Even if he did not know how to use the device,
the storage gem imbedded in its center would
be the catalyst he needed.

Trying to catch Sidra and Hadrea off
guard, Abby took two steps towards it, then
jumped to close the remaining distance, his
arms and fingers outstretched to touch the
gemmed object.

Sidra suddenly realized the danger. But
she could not cast her magic while holding the
Crystal Key in her hands. Without hesitation,
she lobbed the Key, with Hadrea's spirit
hovering around it, a short distance from her.
The Key clattered as it turned over, before
finally coming to rest among the broken stones
of the street. Hadrea's spirit flickered, almost
disappearing, before it recovered and swirled
angrily over the Key's storage crystal.

As Sidra raised her arms to attack, Abby's
body landed on the pavement with a painful
thud. His fingertips touched the center gem on
the magic mirror. In that instant, his mind
triggered whatever was inside of him that
opened up his power.

Brilliant white light flared from the length
of his body. Abby rolled over on the ground,
then quickly rose to his feet to face his
attackers.
Sidra had already summoned her magic, the
length of her arms and hands glowing blue as
she accessed the power of the wellspring
beneath Sapphire City. She smiled a weird,

wide grin at Abby, relishing whatever was about to happen.

Hadrea, too, had given up the pretense of persuasion. Her spirit began to call forth magic from the storage crystal on the Crystal Key, and a red fire infused her swirling presence as it gathered itself to attack.

And in that moment, as the three magic users prepared to unleash their powers, Dacy stepped in front of Abby with her dagger raised, ready to thrust at Sidra. But she was exposed and vulnerable to the forces that were about to be released in that small space.

Seeing Dacy move in front of him, Abby shouted, "No, Dacy! Get out of there!"

But Dacy, her face clenched tightly with aggression and her eyes focused on Sidra, kept moving forward until she was almost centered in between the blooming balls of magic around her—white from Abby, blue from Sidra and red from Hadrea.

At that moment, Hadrea's voice called out, a wordless yell urging attack. Both her red magic and Sidra's blue magic flared forward, heading toward Dacy and Abby. Abby instinctively and without any sort of trained focus, unleashed her white magic outward with as much fury as he could muster.

The three magical bursts met at Dacy with a loud concussive bang. The blue and red and white magic engulfed Dacy in a ball of intertwined, swirling power. The intertwining magic produced a sound resembling a continuous rumble of thunder. Dacy let out a surprised, pained whelp, and disappeared from Abby's sight. Abby heard Dacy's dagger clatter to the ground.

Dacy was nowhere to be seen. Terrified and not understanding what had just happened, Abby called out above the din, "Dacy! Dacy!" But there was no reply and no sign of her.

A sudden wave of frustration and anger went through Abby. He cried out a shout of rage, as loud and as long as his lungs could manage. In reply, the outflow of his white magic increased noticeably, a sudden torrent of power accompanied by a loud, earth-shaking thunderclap. Abby's magic overwhelmed the blue and red streams of his attackers, pushing them back on their casters.

The blowback crashed like a wave into Hadrea's spirit, extinguishing it like a candle. She disappeared. With no mind to command it, the Crystal Key failed to draw any of Abby's magic into itself. It lay on the street, inert and lifeless.

Sidra resisted a little better, aided by her physical presence. She raised her arms to ward off the incoming magic, her blue magic forming a shield that protected her as Abby's white magical wave blew around and over her. Still, the force of the attack staggered her rearward. After a few retreating steps, she tumbled backwards onto the pavement, the back of her head striking the stones awkwardly. Sidra's blue fire vanished as she lost consciousness.

With no other power to resist him, Abby cast his sight behind her body, toward the ghouls waiting behind. He sent a wave of white fire toward them. Although Abby did it without understanding the effect of it, his magic unbound the ghouls from Sidra's control. The souls that animated the creatures, trapped by Hadrea's spell that converted them from human to ghoul, were finally free to leave the near-dead, rotting bodies for their next plane of existence. Only their corpses remained behind.

The suddenness of his victory surprised even Abby. Seeing Sidra helpless on the ground snapped Abby back into trying to regain his self-control. Remembering the way Reanah had urged him earlier in day to rein himself in, Abby managed to pull back his power. His magical output fell away, until he cut it off with a final effort of will. There was an immediate, unnerving silence.

Abby took a few hesitant steps toward Sidra as she lay unmoving on the ground. It was the second time she had been knocked out that day. Vampire or not, it had to be taking a toll on her. Abby hoped it would be some time before Sidra would regain her consciousness again.

There was no sign of Dacy. As he moved forward, Abby bent down and picked up Dacy's dagger. He took a quick glance at where Dacy had stood. Strangely, her clothes and shoes lay in a heap on the street. It was as if her body, alone, had suddenly disappeared from existence.

Abby took a quick look to his right. Reanah lay unmoving, curled into a protective ball. He could not tell if she was alive or not.

For the moment though, there was only Sidra. Abby closed the distance to her, standing over Sidra with his right hand clenched on the dagger's handle. She was alive but unmoving, her eyes closed and her breathing shallow and wheezing from whatever injury she had sustained when Abby's magic had crashed into her shield and driven her against the ground.

The days that Sidra had tormented Abby were still fresh in his mind. He wanted to stab and stab Sidra, thrusting the dagger into her arms and chest, until she felt his anger and fury before she died in agony.

But as Abby stood over her for several seconds, breathing heavily and feeling his emotions surging and his nerves trembling, he could not do it. Even though he knew that Sidra would attack him without hesitation once she recovered, Abby could not strike her when she was helpless at his feet. He had no experience in this life or his previous life with that kind of naked violence. And to do that seemed completely wrong to him at that moment.

Abby decided he would be better served by trying to help Reanah. So, he quickly turned and jogged back to Reanah to see if there was anything that he could do for her. He knelt down beside her. Abby gently grabbed Reanah on her shoulder and side, pulling down until she lay flat on the street.

Reanah groaned weakly in a pained protest. The sides of her face were coated in mix of blood and spit and dirt, and her breathing was shallow and raspy. She was holding a hand over the open wound in her chest. Her clothes and the ground beneath her were covered in blood.

Abby looked into her half-shut eyes. "What can I do to help?" he asked desperately. "Do you have anything with you that can fix this?"

Reanah weakly shook her head, and only managed a weak whisper in reply. "No, it's only first aid. I am too badly hurt for that, I fear. A true healer is needed."

Abby felt helpless. He knew nothing that could help her. In his world, Tom would have called an ambulance and let someone who knew what he or she was doing provide the medical attention and a trip to a hospital. Now, in that moment and in that desolate place, he could only watch as Reanah's life slipped away from her.

Abby wanted to ask Reanah if it was correct what Hadrea had said, that Reanah had been ordered to search for and return him to the elves and Sister Dana in Jade City. He assumed it was true. Otherwise, why had she come for him?

But he kept those questions to himself. Instead, he felt pity at the depths of Reanah's pain and injury. Tears began to well in his eyes.

He asked again, "What can I do? Please. There has to be something."

Reanah answered, "Unless you can harness your power to heal, nothing." She swallowed hard, and gasped for a couple of seconds. "Time grows short for me. There is only one thing I have to tell you." She tugged weakly at Abby's sleeve.

Abby nodded and waited, holding Reanah as best he could to make her comfortable.

Reanah continued in a halting whisper, "Hadrea, or whatever she is now, will come for you again. But never believe her. Your power will be coveted, truly. But there are good people in this world—elves, humans and dwarves—that will be worth your talents. Seek them out. Serve the greater good. Not her selfish, twisted aims."

Abby whispered in reply, "Of course. I knew she was bullshitting me. On the way here, Sidra kept me trussed up the whole time with her magic. And then I'm supposed to turn right around and help them? Never! I have better sense than that."

Reanah nodded slowly. She closed her eyes for several seconds, gathering herself. Finally, she breathed, "Promise me."

"What?" Abby answered. He reached up and caressed the side of Reanah's face, and leaned over to better hear her reply.

"Go back to Jade City. Find Sister Dana. The Sisterhood will help you."

Abby wrinkled his face. Sister Dana? That was the last person he wanted to see again. She had been ready to force Abby with magic to reveal his true identity. She was the reason Abby left Jade City in the first place.

But at that moment, staring into Reanah's face and fearing her imminent death, there was only one answer Abby could give. "Sure, Reanah. I promise. I'll go back and find her."

Reanah nodded, accepting Abby's word. By then, the blood was drained from Reanah's face, and her breathing was becoming more weak and shallow as the moments passed.

Tears were streaming down Abby's face. He bit his lips together to keep from fully sobbing. He felt completely helpless. If only there was some way that his magic could help her. But if there was, he had no idea how to do it. He assumed that a "true healer" used magic to repair injury. But for Abby, it was another example of something he did not know how to do.

So in those last moments, as he watched Reanah die in his arms, Abby made himself another promise. If magic could heal, he would become a healer. The best damn one in this world. He vowed silently to himself that he would never be helpless in the face of death again.

ELEVEN: TRANSFORMATION

Abby held Reanah through death, keeping her close and reassuring her with his presence until he could no longer feel her pulse. He wept openly, overwhelmed with all that had happened to him, from his first moment in this world to this last day. Emotion flowed out from him in a torrent, and he was helpless until it slowed. He cried and cried as he never had before, not as Abby, and not during the fifty years before as Tom.

Finally, after some time, he began to recover himself. Sidra. It was the thought of her that finally returned him to the present moment. She should still be there, behind him. As the last of Abby's sobs faded, it was time for him to decide what to do with her.

Abby stood up, exhausted and worn, and moved slowly across the street to where he had left Sidra. On the way, he paused next to the pile of Dacy's clothes, left where Dacy had stood during the exchange of magic between Abby and Sidra and Hadrea. Abby stopped and stared, unable to fathom what had happened to her. How could she have disappeared so completely, while leaving her clothes and shoes behind?

As he stared down, trying to puzzle it out, Abby noticed a movement beneath the loose folds of Dacy's tunic. He knelt down to study it. His first instinct was to take his palm and strike down on it, killing whatever lay underneath. Whether it was a mouse or spider or snake, he did not want to have to deal with vermin at that moment. Just kill it and move on to Sidra.

Curiosity, though, stayed his hand. Abby reached out and gently unfolded the fabric on top of the creature, ready to leap back if it jumped out at him. After a few seconds, Abby had pulled back enough material to see what it was.

But nothing would have prepared him for what he saw. Lying within the folds of Dacy's tunic was a blue, glowing form about six inches long. Thin and delicate, with the body and arms and legs of a human woman and the wings of a dragonfly, it crawled, dazed, over the folds of fabric. Surrounding the creature was a ball of blue magic, the same blue glow as the Sapphire City wellspring.

Abby stared in wide-eyed wonderment at the tiny face of the creature. It was Dacy. Almost as an involuntary reaction, Abby cried out, "Dacy! Oh my God!"

The creature, confused and wobbly, looked up in disbelief at the giant form staring down at it.   A tiny, barely audible squeak of a voice answered, "Abby? What the fuck?"

Abby could not believe what he was seeing. As his mind raced, he asked, more to himself than to Dacy, "What? How?" After a pause, he could not help stating the obvious. "Dacy, you're so tiny!"

Dacy answered in her high, barely audible voice, "And you're fucking huge! What is going on?"

"No idea," Abby replied, shaking his head to try to make sense of the thoughts dashing through his mind. "You were smack in the middle of the three magic streams, then suddenly you were gone. Whoosh! I had no idea what happened to you!"

By then, Dacy, had begun to recover from the transformation. She straightened her body and rolled into a kneeling position, gathering herself. Her new wings now fully unfurled themselves from her back. Like a dragonfly, the top two wings, slightly longer than Dacy's body and translucent with blue and purple highlights, extended out perpendicular to her torso. The bottom two wings were a little shorter, and angled slightly down. Now freed from being pinned beneath her, they started to move and flap slowly, almost involuntarily, like new parts of Dacy's body over which she had no control.

Out of the corners of her vision, Dacy seemed to notice her new appendages for the first time. With an expression of utter shock on her face, she turned her head from side to side, watching the wings move as if they belonged to someone else. Finally, Dacy's mind grasped the connection to them, and she began to twitch first the left pair, then the right pair, as she experimented with controlling their movements. Abby stared down in stunned silence as Dacy flicked and flapped her newborn wings.

Finally, Dacy could not resist trying to speed up the motion of her wings as much as she could. They suddenly blurred into motion, and there was enough thrust to lift Dacy up and off the surface beneath her. She went up several inches in the air, twisting and rolling awkwardly and almost tumbling over. At the highest point, her feet were over her head, and she was looking back down at the gap to the ground.

Dacy panicked, and abruptly stopped the movement of her wings. She squealed, expecting a quick fall and painful landing back toward the clothes on the pavement. Instead, like a down feather, she fell slowly and lightly down toward the ground. She even had enough time to right herself and land squarely on her tiny feet, like a gymnast sticking a landing. The ease of it seemed to surprise Dacy herself.

Now standing, she turned and faced Abby once again, her wings outstretched and trembling, ready to move again. To Abby, the sight was surreal. Dacy was a naked, moving female figurine with colorful dragonfly wings, glowing with blue magic, with Dacy's face and expression animating it.

Their eyes met. Dacy blurted out, "My fuckin' god, Abby. I'm a fairy!"

Although Abby had been thinking the same thing, he replied, "Are you sure? I thought there weren't any fairies."

Dacy shook her head. "No one knows, for sure. They disappeared centuries ago. Ain't no one seen one since. At least, when they's sober. Plenty of stories, yeah, but I never believed 'em myself."

Abby had no idea. It was just another feature of this strange reality in which he found himself. But whatever Dacy was now, she did not appear to be human anymore.

Even so, Abby tried to be encouraging. "That's probably not right, Dacy. Magic did this to you, but it was completely unintentional. You were just in the wrong place at the wrong time. I can't believe you were accidentally turned into a creature that's been extinct for hundreds of years. That doesn't just happen. Maybe this is just temporary. Or, there's some way to change you back."

Dacy's mood was starting to transition from shock to anger. "You don't know that! Ain't nobody that knows where fairies came from or where they went to." She stomped one foot toward Abby. "But whatever's happened here, you've got to turn me back, right now. I ain't puttin' up with this crap no more, whatever it is I am. Not one second more."

Abby felt helpless. "I don't know, Dacy. I don't think I can do anything. Not that I know what I'm going with my magic anyway. You know that. Besides, it was my magic and Sidra's and Hadrea's all combined together that did this to you. And unless you want to get them back here to fire it all up again, I don't think I can help you, at least, right now."

The thought shook Abby back out of his complacency. What about Sidra? He had almost forgotten to check on her.

Dacy was about to speak again but Abby held up the palm of his hand to hold her off. "Just a second," he said quietly.

Abby rose quickly from his crouch and strode quickly toward the spot on the street where Sidra had stood, then fallen, during their confrontation. His heart sank.

There was nothing but bare pavement. He looked farther back, into the spaces between the adjacent derelict buildings. The corpses of the ghouls were where they had died, but there was no sign of Sidra.

But what about the Crystal Key? Abby looked to his left and made several quick strides in that direction, his eyes scanning the ground quickly as he went. Again, nothing. It was gone from the spot where it had lain unattended only a short time before.

Somehow, Abby realized, Sidra had recovered herself enough to rise and flee with the Crystal Key. To do that with Abby and Dacy so close by, and not have them notice her departure, probably meant that she had used her magic to do so. But, however she had done it, Sidra was again on the loose, with the Crystal Key to bolster her power.

Abby exhaled a sigh of frustration. He could not sense Sidra in the immediate vicinity, so Abby assumed she, and probably Hadrea too, had retreated to a safe distance. As much as he was relieved that the immediate fight was over, Abby knew that he and Dacy were not out of danger. Abby had no idea whether Hadrea and Sidra would send more ghouls to fight in their stead. They probably would. The familiar, unpleasant fear of being hunted returned to him.

Abby quickly returned to Dacy and announced the bad news. "They're gone, but we need to keep going. It's not safe here."

Dacy, perched on the pile of her old clothes, chirped up in her new, barely audible voice. "But we need to find them. Beat 'em again and make them help you change me back! Right now!"

Abby sympathized with the feeling. It was no fun being stuck as something you were not. But he answered grimly, "Look, Dacy, we've got to get to the horses." He flicked his head in the direction of Reanah's body. "Reanah's dead. We're not going to be able to use her magic mirror to shield ourselves again. We've got to get out while we have the chance. If we go marching back into the center of town, we'll have a magic-wielding spirit, a vampire, and god knows how many of those ghouls ready to tear us to shreds. It'd be suicide. The only thing we can do is get the hell out of Sapphire City. And I think deep down you know it, too."

Through the blue haze of the glow around Dacy, Abby saw that she was about to cry. "No, no," she wailed. "This can't be! How am I supposed to live like this?" Her wings twitched in agitation.

Rather than answer, Abby quickly returned to Reanah's body. Although he felt uncomfortable in doing so, Abby grabbed the magic mirror from the pavement, and gently unbuckled Reanah's waist belt with its series of pouches and loops stuffed with items. Perhaps, at some point, they would be able to use some of her elvish magic devices and baubles to help themselves.

Abby used his fingertips to test the various attachments to Reanah's belt. There was one that did not have any sort of hard object in it. Abby gently untied the top of a small, thin leather pouch. In it, there were a couple of folded slips of paper. He carefully opened one. Written with a quill pen, the writing was the same indecipherable script that Abby could not read. A couple of red circular stamps at the bottom gave them the appearance of an official document. He guessed that the paper was Reanah's identification. He quickly refolded it and returned it to the papers to their place. If he did in fact return to Jade City, he would make sure that Reanah's superiors would receive these. It would be the right thing to do.

That just left Abby's and Dacy's departure. It made Abby nauseous to just leave Reanah's body there, but he did not feel he had any other choice. With Dacy in her newly transformed state, he would be the only one to bury Reanah's body. As much as he wanted to do it, to give Reanah that last bit of respect, the fear tugging at him was too immediate and real. If he and Dacy wanted to escape, they would have to do it right then.

Abby quickly buckled Reanah's belt around his own waist. It fit much more loosely on him, but the outward curve of his hips was able to keep it from sliding from his waist. That would be good enough until he could get out of Sapphire City.

Abby returned to Dacy. "Come on," he said soberly, "we've got to go. You've got to lead us to wherever you stashed your horses."

An argument was on the tip of Dacy's lips, but she did not give voice to it. Instead, Dacy simply nodded, resigned to her current fate.

It would be straightforward enough for Abby to walk the rest of the way. But, Abby wondered, how does one transport a fairy? His imagination contemplated one buzzing around his head like one from a cartoon animated movie. But Dacy seemed unable to do that. At least, not yet.

"Come on, Dacy," Abby said quietly. "Let me carry you." Abby gently reached down and lay the back of his hand on the pavement next to Dacy. After a moment's hesitation, Dacy stepped into Abby's palm, and Abby gently lifted her up until he was able to cradle Dacy loosely against his stomach. He could feel

Dacy's tiny hands grabbing the edges of his fingers to steady herself.

In a low tone, Abby asked, "O.K., Dacy, where to?"

In a resigned voice, Dacy answered, "Keep going down this road. It's really not far. We were almost there."

After taking one last, sad, lingering look at Reanah's body, Abby turned and headed west, down the street leading out of Sapphire City. He walked quickly, too afraid to look behind him. He would have to trust whatever extra intuition was given to him by his magic to warn him of danger. For the moment, though, there did not seem to be any immediate threat around them.

As they made their final escape from the remnants of Sapphire City, Abby and Dacy remained silent, lost in their own jumbled thoughts. Before them, the sun was beginning to set as the last of the broken and rotting buildings passed behind them. Soon, the area around them was scrub and weed-filled former farmland, interrupted by the occasional remnant of a farm. Shadows lengthened around them.

Dacy finally interrupted the silence. From her perch by Abby's chest, she called up, "So, what happens now? Where do we go?"

Abby shook his head. "I don't know. Reanah asked me to go back to Jade City and find the Sister there. I said I would, but I don't know if I really want to. That lady spooked me pretty good. She's why I got out of there when I had the chance."

In a plaintive tone, Dacy asked, "But what about me? You have to find someone that can help me. If not the elves, or the Sisterhood, who can help to turn me back?"

In his heart, Abby felt that Dacy was likely going to stay just as she was. Just like he had to stay as he was. But he did not want to tell her that. Instead, he answered, "Who knows? If fairies haven't been around for hundreds of years, I doubt we can find anyone who would be an expert about such things. Don't worry, though, we'll certainly try to figure it out."

Dacy did not answer immediately, letting the implication of that sink in. Finally, she replied, "There's got to be someone. Anyone. I can't be stuck like this."

Abby answered, "Well, if it helps, I know how you feel. A little more than you think."

Dacy looked up into Abby's face. "What do you mean?"

Abby knew it was finally time to tell her. About his real identity, as Tom. About the world, the different reality, that he came from. "Well, Dacy," Abby said. "Let me tell you who and what I really am."

The End of
The Wellspring

Book One of the
Crystal Key Trilogy

ABOUT THE AUTHOR

The author is a real estate attorney living in a small town in Western New York State. His hobby is growing grapes and making fermented beverages therefrom.